RECIPE FOR]

Desire, Oklahoma 11

Leah Brooke

MENAGE EVERLASTING

Siren Publishing, Inc.
www.SirenPublishing.com

A SIREN PUBLISHING BOOK
IMPRINT: Ménage Everlasting

RECIPE FOR DESIRE
Copyright © 2016 by Leah Brooke

ISBN: 978-1-68295-652-6

First Printing: October 2016

Cover design by Les Byerley
All art and logo copyright © 2016 by Siren Publishing, Inc.

Printed in the U.S.A.

PUBLISHER
Siren Publishing, Inc.
www.SirenPublishing.com

RECIPE FOR DESIRE

Desire, Oklahoma 11

LEAH BROOKE
Copyright © 2016

Chapter One

According to the calendar, spring had arrived, but the nip in the air made Emma Smith shiver as she drove down the long main road into Desire, Oklahoma.

Dark clouds got even darker and more ominous with every mile, the low rumble of thunder in the distance promising that an early spring thunderstorm would release its fury at any moment.

She shivered again, her overheated body feeling the cold more intensely.

Wiping her damp forehead, she pressed her foot harder to the accelerator, desperate to be in town before the thunderstorm hit.

Within seconds, a sharp gust of wind blew her small car halfway onto the shoulder, forcing her to slow again. Wrestling with the wheel, she whimpered at the stab of pain in her lower side, breathing a sigh of relief when she finally managed to get her car back into her lane.

Pressing a hand to her side, she gulped back nausea and slowed her car to a crawl, alarmed that the pain didn't seem to be easing.

She'd never felt such pain, a pain that had steadily increased since she'd started out that morning, becoming so overwhelming that she had trouble concentrating on her driving.

Fighting the urge to drive faster to beat the storm, she gripped the wheel tighter and focused on staying in her lane.

She had to get to town for some help.

Trying to ease the nausea that had begun about an hour earlier, she'd opened her car window several inches for fresh air but had been forced to turn the heater on when the interior of the car got too cold.

When she got too hot, she turned the heater down but, almost immediately, got too cold and began to shiver again.

She hoped to find a doctor, or at least a hotel room where she could lie down until the pain and nausea passed.

According to the sign she'd just passed, she had only a few miles to go, but several deep breaths later, she realized she wouldn't make it that far.

The nausea wouldn't be kept at bay any longer.

Whipping her small car to the shoulder, she took several more deep breaths, breaking out in a cold sweat.

With hands that shook, she hurriedly shifted the car to park, struggling to open the car door.

A whimper escaped and then another as she pulled at it, expending more energy than she could afford to push it open.

Another whimper escaped when it slammed shut again.

Gripping the steering wheel for leverage, she turned in her seat, bracing a foot against the door to keep the wind from slamming it closed again.

Finally managing to turn enough to get out, she shoved the door with her foot, a sob escaping at the pain to her lower side. Pressing a hand to the door to keep it from closing on her, she held her side and finally managed to get to her feet, the fierce wind whipping her hair around her face and making it impossible to see.

Stumbling out, she stayed hunched with a hand pressed to her lower side, and holding on to her car for support, clumsily made her way to the side of the road.

She couldn't hold the nausea back any longer.

Dropping to her knees in the grass, she doubled over in pain and became violently ill, the intensity of the pain and nausea leaving her breathless and alarmingly weak.

She dragged herself several feet before collapsing again, knowing she could go no farther.

The nausea subsided somewhat, but the pain just kept getting worse. She wiped her mouth with the wad of tissues she'd stuck up her sleeve, hoping like hell she didn't get sick again.

She didn't have the energy for it.

The rain she'd hoped to beat started to fall in buckets, drenching her almost immediately.

Most of the nausea had passed, but the pain kept her from getting to her feet again.

Lying close to the car kept most of the wind from reaching her, and the cool rain felt good on her overheated body.

Curling into a ball, she got as comfortable as the pain would allow, knowing that even getting into the car again would be impossible.

If she was going to die, this was as good a place as any.

She was going to die on the side of the road—alone—as she spent most of her life.

With her knees to her chest, she tucked her arm under her head to pillow it, closing her eyes against the rain stinging them.

If she could just rest a few minutes, maybe she'd have the energy to get back into her car again.

Maybe.

A crack of thunder made her jolt, and crying out at the sharp pain caused by her involuntary movement, she opened her eyes, realizing that it might be too dangerous to lie outside.

Staring up at the line of trees bordering the road, she whimpered in horror and knew she'd run out of time.

If lightning hit one of the trees, or her car, she could be in trouble.

She tried to remember everything she'd ever heard about what to do in a thunderstorm but drew a blank.

Panicked, she knew she had to get up and get back into her car.

Hot tears caused by pain and weakness ran down her face to mingle with the cool drops of rain, making everything a blur.

"Come on, Emma. You can do this. It's not very far."

Her pep talk to herself had little effect.

From her position, it felt like *miles*.

It seemed to take forever, but somehow she managed to get to her hands and knees, the pain almost more than she could bear.

She not only trembled now but shivered, the cold rain and strong wind penetrating her soaked clothing and going all the way to her bones.

Biting her lip, she reached for her rear bumper just as the wind picked up, plastering her long, wet hair against her face.

A sob escaped, and then another, each small movement causing excruciating pain that made it impossible to straighten.

Just as she managed to get to her feet, her left foot slipped on the slick, wet grass, sending her sprawling, crying out in agony.

The pain was excruciating.

Lying there on the side of the road, she curled into a ball and cried, waiting for the pain to ease enough to allow her to get up.

Waited to die.

She jolted again at another crack of thunder, one that was followed almost immediately by a bolt of lightning that was far too close for comfort.

She prayed that some white knight would appear and help her.

She hadn't seen a single car since she'd turned onto the road to Desire and doubted if she would.

No one would be out in the middle of a storm like this—not even a knight in shining armor.

She was on her own.

Alone.

As usual.

* * * *

Hunter Ross cursed as another bolt of lightning lit the darkening sky, raising his voice to be heard over the thunder that followed. "Damn, it's really coming down, isn't it?"

He and his brother, Remington, had gone into Tulsa that morning to order a new lawnmower and had planned to be back before the storm hit.

Glancing at his brother, he frowned. "I guess we shouldn't have stopped for lunch in Tulsa."

He hadn't been in any hurry to get back home. Now that he and Remington had finished remodeling the house they'd grown up in, there wasn't much left to do.

He was bored.

He was bitter.

Even surrounded by friends, he and his brother were alone.

Remington frowned back. "To hell with that. I was starving, and I sure as hell didn't want to wait 'til we got back to town to eat." After a companionable silence, broken only by flashes of lightning and cracks of thunder, Remington turned to him again. "If we rent the house, it's gonna be a pain in the ass to have someone around."

Hunter gripped the wheel tighter, struggling to keep their truck on the road against the strong wind. "Yeah. I like the privacy. Having a tenant isn't exactly my idea of fun. A whole lot of bitchin' and complainin'. Loud noise and someone always knocking on our door for something."

Remington shrugged. "If we're not moving into the house, we should really rent it."

Hunter nodded. "I agree. Keeping it sitting there vacant is just a waste. But if we're gonna move away, it would be better just to sell the whole damned property." Feeling his brother's sharp scrutiny, Hunter glanced at him again, waiting for the next crack of thunder to die away before speaking.

"Don't look at me like that. We've talked about it. Mom's not here to see what we did for her, and the house just has too many bad memories. My stomach knots every time I go inside." He slowed even more and turned the wipers on high, the rain coming down so hard he could barely see. "I certainly have no intention of living there and reliving all those memories."

"I wish Mom could have seen it. We did everything in that house she would have wanted." Remington stared out the window, his hands fisted on his thighs. "It's a shame we weren't older. I would have loved to put that man through a wall."

Hunter snorted angrily, the subject a sore one. "You would have had to beat me to it. Dying in prison was too good for that son of a bitch."

"Hunter! Slow down." Remington shot up, rolling his window down and sticking his head out, his hair immediately plastered to his head. Raising his voice to be heard over the rain and wind, he ducked back inside, pointing out the windshield. "Do you see that?"

Alarmed to see a car pulled off to the side of the road haphazardly, Hunter slowed to a crawl, pulling in behind it and putting his flashers on. "What the hell? Do you see anybody?" He threw it into park and jumped out, immediately soaked to the skin.

Remington cursed and jumped out the other side. "Hunter, look! Someone's lying in the grass."

The wind carried most of Remington's voice away, but Hunter heard it—and read the panic in his eyes.

Hunter's heart pounded as he raced toward the person lying curled in a ball on the side of the road, hoping like hell the prone figure was still alive. "Call Ace." As he got closer, he could hear sobs, prompting to hurry. Skidding to his knees beside the small soaked form, he froze, looking up at Remington. "It's a woman!"

Her weak sobs tore at him, but when he touched her arm and she turned to him, the look of pain and hopelessness in her eyes turned his insides to jelly.

"Please. Help me. It hurts so much."

He barely heard her over the wind and rain and leaned over to protect her from the worst of it the best he could.

His first instinct was to pick her up and rush back to the truck, but her claim to be in pain made him hesitate.

He didn't know what had happened to her and couldn't take the chance of hurting her worse. Looking for blood, he ran his hands over her. "We're going to help you. Don't you worry about a thing. Tell me what's wrong. Where do you hurt?"

"Here." Her small hand shook as she laid it over the right side of her abdomen, another sob escaping. "Please. Can you take me to a doctor? I couldn't make it to town. I got so sick."

Hunter stopped running his hands over her to lift her face to his, alarmed when he felt her hot skin. "Sick? You weren't in an accident or anything like that?"

"No. Sick. Something's wrong. I think I'm dying. I never knew anything could hurt so much."

With Remington hovering over her talking to Ace, Hunter slid his arms under her and lifted her slight weight. "Easy, baby doll. You're not gonna die."

God, he hoped not.

Remington lifted his gaze from her to meet Hunter's. "Ace said Doc Hansen's making rounds at the hospital today." He touched her arm, his eyes dark with concern. "We'll get you there. Just relax and let us take care of everything." Remington disconnected and shoved his phone into his pocket. "Ace is calling the doc to tell him to expect us. He said he'll catch up with us and we can follow him. He'll use his lights and siren."

"My purse. Please. Oh God, it hurts."

Remington reached for her. "Give her to me."

"I've got her." Hunter tried to convince himself that he didn't want to jostle her unnecessarily by passing her to his brother but knew that he held on to her because he couldn't stand the thought of letting her go.

The combination of fear and pain in her eyes knotted his stomach as much as the trust in them.

She trusted him to take care of her.

It was a heady feeling—and he sure as hell wouldn't let her down.

Remington's glance spoke volumes—holding a yearning that Hunter didn't want to see—as he held the passenger door open.

Ignoring it, Hunter eased into the seat as gently as he could, trying not to jar her any more than necessary. "Don't worry, honey. We'll get you to the hospital in no time. Ace is on his way with sirens blaring. He's the sheriff. Rem will get your purse."

Settling her on his lap, Hunter pushed her hair back from her pale face. "We'll have you there in no time. Tell me what I can do to make you more comfortable."

* * * *

Emma pressed a hand over her mouth. "Please. It's too hot. It's making me sick again."

The man holding her leaned forward to turn down the heater that he'd just turned up. "Hell. You're shivering and soaking wet."

Whimpering in pain as they sped toward the hospital, she kept her eyes closed and focused on breathing, fighting to hold her nausea at bay. "My car! Everything I own is in there. My papers!" Months of work would be lost if something happened to her car.

Distantly aware that the man holding her spoke, it took her a while to realize that he was speaking into a cell phone, his voice raised to be heard over the siren of the sheriff's SUV directly in front of them.

He spoke to a man named Ryder about her car, his voice filled with tension. "Thanks, Ryder. It's on the shoulder on the road heading into town. Can you get it towed to our house and make sure it's locked up? It's locked now. The keys are in front of the right front tire. Thanks. Yeah, we're rushing her to the hospital now. Yeah, we'll let you know. Talk to you later."

After disconnecting, he tossed his phone aside and gathered her closer. "There. Your car will be taken care of. Nothing's going to happen to it, or anything inside. Ryder will make sure it's locked up good and tight. Hell, it'll probably even run better by the time you get back to it."

She leaned heavily against him, no longer possessing the energy to lift her head. Opening her eyes, she looked straight into the hard, cold eyes of the other man, who kept glancing at her as he drove. "Thank you for helping me."

The man driving nodded once, reaching out to her, but pulling her hand back at the last second. "You're welcome. What's your name?"

"Emma." She gasped at another stab of pain, curling into a tighter ball against the man holding her. Surprised at the firmness of muscle surrounding her, she shifted carefully, struggling to get into the most comfortable position she could manage.

A muscle worked in his jaw, his eyes gentling. "Hold on, Emma. We're almost there. I'm Remington Ross, and my brother, Hunter, is holding you."

She whimpered again, the pain unbearable. "It hurts. I never knew anything could hurt this much. I don't know what's wrong with me."

"Easy, honey." Hunter pushed her damp hair back from her face, his touch gentle. "Just a few minutes more. We're almost there. Hang on, honey. How long have you been in pain?"

"On and off a little since this morning, but the real pain started a little over an hour ago. Thought it was just a stomach ache. Thought I could make it to Desire."

Hunter stiffened, sharing a look with his brother before staring down at her again. "Do you know someone in Desire, someone we should call?"

She didn't know why he seemed so tense and was in too much pain to care. "No. I liked the name of the town and decided to make it my next stop. Oh God!"

Hunter rubbed her back, helping her into a more comfortable position.

He'd never felt so helpless. "Is there someone you need me to call? Any family you need me to contact?"

The possibility of a man in Desire waiting for her tightened his gut.

Shaking her head, she moaned again and gripped him tighter. "No. I'm on my own. I'm sorry to be such a burden to you. I can't tell you how happy I am that you stopped."

"You're no trouble at all. I'm just glad we went by when we did."

"Oh God." She paled even more, something he hadn't thought possible. "How much farther?"

"Easy, honey." Remington made a sharp turn, pushing her deeper into Hunter's embrace. "We're here." He slammed on the brakes, bringing the car to a squealing stop outside the emergency room doors. "Take her inside. I'll park the truck and be right there."

Holding her tightly against him, Hunter leapt from the truck and rushed through the hospital doors, his expression fierce. "I've got you. Hang in there, Emma. You're doing so good."

Through the whirlwind of activity that followed, she was constantly aware of their presence.

Focusing on them—strangers she'd met only moments earlier—helped her deal with the fear and the pain that just kept growing.

Although neither man raised their voice, the steel in their tone was unmistakable.

Holding her in his arms, Hunter glared at the nurse. "Does she look like she can fill out forms? I told you everything I know. Get the rest of it later."

Despite their obvious impatience, at least one of them was constantly by her side, talking to her in low, soothing tones.

Half the time she didn't know what they said, but just their strong presence gave her a sense of security she desperately appreciated.

Their no-nonsense attitudes as they barked out orders and demands to see Dr. Hansen distracted her and eased some of her anxiety.

Secure in the knowledge that they would take care of everything, she blocked out everything except them.

Through the fog of pain surrounding her, she focused on Remington, who kept her hand in his as she rode on a gurney down a long hallway.

When she was pushed into a room, a brief battle ensued between Hunter and the nurses.

The relief of having someone on her side brought tears to her eyes.

Finally, the Dr. Hansen they'd been asking for arrived and said something to them under his breath, somehow convincing them to leave the room.

The kindly older doctor poked and prodded her while a nurse gave her sympathetic smiles and asked what seemed liked hundreds of questions.

She found herself wheeled down another hallway for tests, had blood drawn, and before she knew it, was being told that she had to have immediate surgery.

Her hand shook as she signed the consent form on the clipboard the nurse held for her, and scared and in pain, she gripped the nurse's hand before she could move away.

"Are those two men who brought me in still here?"

The nurse smiled. "Honey, it's taking everything we can do to keep them from beating down the door. They haven't been more than twenty feet away from you since they brought you in. Only Dr. Hansen's able to keep them at bay because he's keeping them informed. They know you're going to have an emergency appendectomy."

"Okay." She wished she could see them before she went into surgery.

Reminding herself they were strangers, she nodded. "In case I don't see them again, would you please thank them for bringing me here and staying with me?"

Patting her hand, the nurse grinned. "Oh, honey, something tells me you haven't seen the last of those two."

Chapter Two

Aware of Ace's steady stare, Remington continued to pace. "What the hell's taking them so long?"

It had been hours since they'd been forced to turn Emma over to the hospital staff, and he couldn't stand that she might think they'd abandoned her.

She was in a place full of strangers, and she had to be scared and feeling alone.

He couldn't stand it any longer.

Stopping abruptly, he eyed the waiting room doors, his decision made. "I'm going back there." He started forward, intent on finding her.

Getting to his feet, Ace moved surprisingly fast and cut him off, shaking his head. "Doc Hansen will be out as soon as he knows something. He's with the surgeon and knows we're waiting. You've never seen this woman before?"

Remington glanced at Ace, watching Hunter pace out of the corner of his eye. "No."

"Did she say what she was doing in town? Is there someone waiting for her?"

"She said there wasn't." Remington glanced at the doors again, scrubbing a hand over his face. "Jesus, Ace, she was in so much pain. I hate that she's alone. I know that we're not the best choice, but we're the only people she knows."

Shaking his head, Ace made a notation on the pad he held. "If you and your hard-headed brother ever get those chips knocked off your shoulders, you might actually see the truth." Ace's expression hardened. "Poor thing.

Her car's at your house like you wanted, but if you don't want responsibility for it, Dillon and Tanner said they'd be happy to keep it in the garage."

"No." Hunter appeared at Remington's side. With a sigh, he dropped into a chair and picked up one of the cups of coffee Ace had brought them. "Leave her car where it is. We'll take care of it. We told her we would, and I'm not about to go back on my word."

Ignoring Ace's speculative look, Remington looked toward the doorway again, impatient for the doctor to make an appearance.

Dropping into a seat, he shared a look with his brother, struck by the bitterness glittering in Hunter's eyes.

They'd both made up their minds long ago not to put any woman through the horror of having them in her life, and being around Emma was a sharp reminder of what they couldn't have.

But Remington couldn't just walk away and leave her here alone.

He tried to convince himself that as soon as he saw that she was all right, he would be able to put her out of his mind, but he had a feeling that walking away from her wouldn't be so easy.

The sound of the waiting room door opening had him jumping up and spinning toward it, his heart in his throat when he saw Doc Hansen.

Hunter beat him to the doctor. "Well? How'd it go? How is she?"

Dr. Hansen, still wearing scrubs, smiled, moving farther into the room to drop into a seat next to Ace. "She's out of danger now. I stayed in the operating room the entire time. Dr. Reed said that she had only minutes before her appendix would have burst."

His gaze settled on Hunter's. "She was damned lucky the two of you came along when you did. You probably saved her life."

Hunter nodded, a muscle working in his jaw.

"Can we see her?"

Doc Hansen shook his head. "I'm afraid not. She's going to be in recovery for a while. Why don't you go on home? You can visit her tomorrow."

"We're staying."

Remington and Hunter answered simultaneously, sharing a look that had them both shifting their feet.

Dr. Hansen nodded, a faint smile playing at his lips. "Somehow I knew you would say that. She yours?"

A muscle worked in Hunter's jaw. "No."

Dr. Hansen raised a brow. "Why are you looking at me like that? I know how the men of Desire operate, and seeing you so worried…"

Remington touched his brother's arm, inwardly wincing when Hunter cursed and walked away. Facing Dr. Hansen, he glanced at Ace.

"You both know damned well that neither one of us will take the chance of having a woman in our lives. Our father's blood flows through our veins."

Dr. Hansen clenched his jaw as he always did when the subject of their mother's abuse came up. "You're nothing like your father. You're both gentle men, and because of what you've seen, more tender than most."

Glancing at Hunter, who stood at the window looking out at the darkness, Remington sighed. "We can't let ourselves get too close to her. But Emma doesn't know anyone around here, and we feel responsible for her."

Just the thought of her, alone and defenseless in a hospital bed, made his stomach clench.

Hunter turned back to them. "Rem, there's no sense sitting here all night when we can't see her." He turned to Dr. Hansen. "You have our number. Call us if anything happens."

Dr. Hansen shared a look with Ace before meeting Remington's gaze again. "I'm leaving. Miss Smith is going to sleep all night, but if anything comes up, Dr. Reed will let me know, and I'll call you. She can have visitors tomorrow."

Remington nodded once, knowing that any objections would only invite more conversation about the subject of their father. "Fine."

Hunter appeared beside him. "Let's go. We haven't had dinner yet."

* * * *

Dr. Hansen waited for them to go, smiling at the speculative look on Sheriff Ace Tyler's face. "They seem really concerned about her."

Ace blinked, and his expression went blank. "Hunter and Remington have always been protective of women. That's why they do their best to avoid them."

"It's a pity they're alone. They're good men."

Ace inclined his head. "They are."

"I wish they could believe that they're nothing like their father. Everyone keeps hoping that some woman would come along and knock them on their asses." He stared after them. "Makes me wonder if that day has finally arrived."

Ace's lips twitched. "Hunter and Remington would never allow that."

"Seems to me that you thought the same way not too long ago."

"Hunter and Remington won't let anyone in."

"I don't know. Miss Smith seems to have gotten to them already—just like Hope got to you."

Ace shrugged. "Emma was sick and needed them. It won't be long before they put as much distance between her and them as they can." Turning, he smiled. "I'm surprised at you, Doc. Matchmaking?"

Getting to his feet, Dr. Hansen frowned. "I'm not matchmaking. I'm just encouraged to see their interest in Miss Smith."

Ace chuckled softly. "I'm married to Hope, Doc. I know matchmaking when I see it."

* * * *

Hunter slid behind the wheel of their SUV, glancing back at the hospital and trying to judge which room belonged to Emma.

"I hate leaving. I don't like the idea of her waking scared and alone."

"She looked so damned lost." Remington scrubbed a hand over his face. "I think I saw her suitcase in the back of her car. We'll bring that to her tomorrow so that she has her own things. Maybe that'll make her feel a little better."

Hunter said nothing as they pulled out of the parking lot, his thoughts centered on Emma.

He cared about her because she'd been sick and weak.

She'd needed them.

He'd feel responsible for anyone under those circumstances.

"What if we hadn't found her?" Remington's voice held a hint of anger and fear that Hunter understood very well.

"We *did* find her." It was something Hunter kept reminding himself.

"What if we'd spent longer picking out a new lawnmower, or if we hadn't stopped for lunch?"

"It didn't work out that way."

Thank God.

Remington straightened and turned toward Hunter. "If she belonged to us, she wouldn't have been driving around like that alone. That's for damned sure."

"She doesn't belong to us—and never will."

After a pregnant pause, Remington glanced at him. "I know that." Turning to look out the windshield again, he blew out a breath. "I'm just glad we found her in time."

Hunter couldn't forget the way her eyes looked, clouded with pain.

With trust.

"I wonder why she was headed for Desire. She said she doesn't know anyone there."

Tapping his thigh, Remington glanced at him. "She said she liked the name of the town. I wonder if she plans to stay."

Hunter hoped not.

Emma was already a danger to him. He already felt a hint of possessiveness toward her that he had no right to feel.

Caring for her was a luxury he couldn't afford.

Ever.

Chapter Three

Emma woke to a strange sound and the feel of something squeezing her upper arm.

Irritated, she reached to push away whatever had wakened her, but a hand covered hers, and a female voice came from just to her left.

"It's okay. It's just the blood pressure cuff."

Opening her eyes, Emma first became aware that it must have either been very early in the morning or very late at night.

"Am I all right?" Her sore, dry throat made her voice husky and raw, but the nurse apparently understood her.

With a smile, she efficiently took her blood pressure and temperature, jotting down the information before checking her IV. "You're going to be just fine. Now all you need to do is rest and heal. The doctor will be in soon, and he'll be able to answer all your questions, but everything went fine."

Emma had to swallow several times before she could speak again, grimacing each time she swallowed. "How long will I have to be in here?"

She vaguely remembered seeing another nurse several times throughout the night, a kindly nurse who spoke softly and gave her an extra blanket when she got cold.

The nurse poured a glass of water and stuck a straw in it, lifting it to Emma's lips. "That's one of the questions you'll have to ask the doctor. I'll be right back with the things for your bath."

The small sips of water the nurse allowed helped ease her dry throat. "Thank you."

"No trouble. Let's get you cleaned up. You'll feel much better, and your breakfast should be here soon."

By the time Emma had been bathed and forced down some of the scrambled eggs and fruit cup—ignoring the gray oatmeal—she was exhausted but felt much better.

When the nurse gave her a dose of pain medication, she felt even better.

She'd just started to drift off again when she heard a commotion in the hallway.

Drowsy, she turned toward the door, just in time to see it open and two doctors come into the room.

The first, a younger man with a friendly smile, a man she recognized from the operating room, came straight toward her. "Hello. How are you feeling?"

She struggled to remember the doctor's name, relieved when it finally came to her. "Fine, Dr. Reed. Tired. That pain medication really works. Keep it coming."

Chuckling, he lifted the edge of her gown, pulled back the bandage, and nodded in satisfaction. "Good. You'll be on them around the clock for today and tomorrow. I want you to get some rest and not move around a lot. Since you're keeping food down, we'll take your IV out later today. After that, you'll be on pain pills, but after tomorrow, I only want you take them when you need them. Do you have any questions for me?"

The other doctor stayed back, holding the door partially open while speaking in low tones with someone in the hallway. "I'll ask her." He closed the door and approached, an older man with a friendly smile that she recognized immediately. "How are you, Miss Smith?"

"I thought we agreed that you'd call me Emma."

Nodding, he patted her hand. "Of course. I'm glad to see you looking better. Dr. Reed is taking good care of you."

Dr. Reed smiled and checked her chart. "Those two in the hallway are determined to make sure I'm doing my job." His eyes gentled. "They seem to care about you very much."

Since she didn't know anyone else around, she assumed he referred to the men who'd brought her in. It took her just a second or two to remember their names. Hunter and Remington.

Despite her grogginess, her heart beat faster. "They're here?"

Dr. Reed chuckled. "They sure are."

Emma's face burned. "We don't even know each other. They found me, so they're probably just checking on me. That's really nice of them." Emma smiled, getting into a comfortable position again. "How long do I have to stay here?"

Setting her chart aside, the young doctor grinned. "Don't you like our hospitality?"

"Everyone is so nice, but the food's horrible."

Nodding, he moved to her side, his lips twitching. "Yeah, we hear that now and then." Laying a hand on hers, he smiled gently. "I'll be back tomorrow morning to check on you. I want you to stay in bed today except for using the rest room, and later on, I'm going to have the nurse let you sit in the chair for a while. If everything goes well today, tomorrow we'll get you up and walking around. We'll see how it goes from there."

Emma forced a smile, finding it increasingly difficult to keep her eyes open. "Okay. Thank you."

"You're welcome. Get some rest." He lifted his gaze to meet Dr. Hansen's. "Make it clear to them that she needs her rest."

"I will."

Emma waited until Dr. Reed left before lifting her gaze to Dr. Hansen's. "I can't believe they came back to check on me."

Dr. Hansen smiled. "Hunter and Remington are very anxious to see you."

Emma struggled to focus and blinked several times in an effort to wake up. "I'd like to see them. To thank them." She sighed and looked at the ceiling. "It's strange. They're perfect strangers, but I trusted them right away." Grinning, she waved a hand in a clumsy movement. "I was afraid I was dying anyway, so I guess that isn't too hard to believe."

The kindly doctor smiled. "You're too new here to realize just how unusual their interest in you is. Let me rephrase that. They're protective of all women, but they usually don't show it the way they have with you. They've been very concerned about you. They tried to distance themselves and went home last night, but after they ate, and checked that your car was safe at their house, they grabbed your suitcase and came back. They've been sitting in the waiting room drinking coffee since about four this morning."

"They have?" Shifting restlessly, she lowered her head and toyed with the edge of the blanket, inexplicably nervous to see them again.

Dr. Hansen smiled, a grandfatherly smile that made her feel a little better. "They wanted me to ask you if they could visit you. They want to make sure you're all right and that we're all doing our jobs."

Emma glanced at the closed door. "You're kidding."

"No. I'm not—something you'd understand if you knew them better." He smiled again. "Would it be okay if they came in? I'm telling you that they won't leave until they see you." His smile widened. "They'll camp out in the hallway, which is causing quite a commotion at the nurses' station."

Smiling at the memory of how amazingly masculine both men were, Emma nodded. "I can imagine." Struggling to keep her eyes open, Emma gestured toward the door. "If they want to come in, it's fine with me. They'd better hurry, though. I'm falling asleep again. That pain medicine is wonderful."

Making his way to the door, Dr. Hansen turned with his hand on the handle. "Good. You need your rest."

Her breath caught when Dr. Hansen opened the door and Hunter and Remington rushed in, their long strides as they crossed the room bringing them to her side in seconds.

Even though she was drowsy and uncomfortable, their impact on her senses made her heart beat faster.

Hunter frowned, making him appear even more intimidating. His dark hair looked as if he'd run his fingers through it repeatedly, his dark chocolate-colored eyes raking over her from head to toe. "Are you all right?"

Emma blinked. "Hi."

"Hi yourself. Are you all right? You still look too pale. Too weak." He stepped closer, reaching out for her hand but pulling back at the last second.

"I'm fine." She smiled at Remington, her breath catching at the intense look in his lighter brown eyes. "Thanks to both of you. I can't thank you enough for bringing me here. The doctor said that you saved my life."

"Yeah." Hunter went to stand at the foot of her bed, his gaze sharpening as he looked her over and then turned his attention to the IV and machine she'd been hooked to that measured her heart rate and pulse.

Both had probably gone way up in the last minute.

Remington set her suitcase aside and paused next to her bed, his hands fisted on the bedrail as he stared down at her. "Why are you talking like that? Are you sure you're okay?"

"Hmm. The pain medicine. I'm having trouble staying awake, but I wanted to thank both of you for helping me."

Remington's hair, slightly longer than Hunter's, curled around his face, so thick and silky looking that her fingers itched to touch it.

The last time she'd seen him, it had been plastered to his head and dripping wet.

It, too, appeared disheveled, as if he'd run his fingers through it several times, and his eyes held the same concern as Hunter's.

Both men stood several inches over six feet tall—Remington an inch or two taller than Hunter—and were dressed in well-worn jeans and T-shirts, much like the day before. Their wide shoulders and height made the small room seem even smaller.

They were both gorgeous in a ruggedly masculine way, and she hoped like hell she got to see more of them once she'd recovered.

Frowning, Remington followed Hunter's gaze. "You're welcome. Are you still in pain?"

"No." Smiling, she settled back against the pillows to enjoy the view. "The pain medicine they gave me is wonderful! God, you two are gorgeous."

Dr. Hansen chuckled from somewhere behind Remington. "I've got to get back to town. Make sure she gets her rest."

Hunter nodded, not taking his eyes from her. His hard features softened, the tenderness and amusement in his eyes a sharp contrast to the stiff way he held himself.

When the door closed behind the doctor, Remington's brows went up. "Do you usually blurt out whatever you're thinking?"

She automatically glanced at their ring fingers, inordinately pleased to find both bare. "Yeah. It usually gets me in trouble, but for now, I prefer to blame it on the pain medicine."

Wondering if they were the type of men who didn't wear rings, she decided to be sure. "Dr. Hansen said that the two of you were here early. Didn't your wives mind?"

Hunter's jaw clenched. "We're not married." He gestured toward her tray. "You hardly touched your breakfast. You have to eat to get your strength back."

Emma smiled. "I ate most of the eggs and the fruit cup. I left the oatmeal. It's awful. You're welcome to it."

From beside her, Remington chuckled, surprising her by reaching for her fork and scooping up some of the remaining eggs. Tasting them, he grimaced and tossed her fork back onto the tray. "Not exactly Gracie's cooking."

"Gracie?" Averting her gaze to hide the surge of jealousy she had no right to feel, she adjusted her covers, her clumsy movements making a mess of them. "Is she a girlfriend?"

Hunter moved closer and straightened her covers, the brush of his hand against her shoulder like an electric spark.

Jerking his hand away, he stepped back, his expression one of panic before going blank. He cleared his throat, crossing his arms over his chest again as if to keep from touching her again. "She and her husbands own the diner in Desire. That's where we eat all of our meals."

Emma blinked, struggling to appear unaffected, but his touch had left a lingering heat behind that ignited her senses. Fisting one hand over the other, she attempted a smile. "You eat *all* of your meals there? Don't you cook at all?"

Remington looked at her as if she'd lost her mind. "No. Of course not."

Something else he'd said came back to her, making her wonder if the pain medicine had affected her hearing. "Wait a minute. I think I must have heard you wrong. Did you say Gracie and her *husbands*? Plural?"

Remington nodded, his eyes cool and watchful. "Yes. Husbands. Do you have a problem with a woman having more than one husband?"

Emma blinked, fighting the effects of the pain medicine. "I don't know anyone who has more than one husband. I've heard of ménages, of course, but I thought it was only for sex."

Hunter smiled, but he eyed her steadily. "There are many ménage marriages in Desire."

Emma blinked and tried to sit up, surprised at her weakness. "Really? That must be fascinating. How does it work? Is it legal? How do they decide who sleeps together? Don't they get jealous?"

Smiling, Remington eased her back, jerking his hands away when she jolted at another surge of heat, his smile falling. "Sorry. Yes, it can be interesting at times." With a glance at Hunter, he stepped away from the bed. "Do you need anything?"

Disappointed that they seemed eager to leave, she shrugged. "You brought my suitcase. I'll just need my car keys and my car so that when—"

Hunter stepped forward, stopping abruptly. "You won't be in any condition to drive when you leave here. We'll take you where you want to go. Meanwhile, your car's safe at our ranch."

Now that the adrenaline rush at seeing them again had started to fade, Emma found she had trouble keeping her eyes open. Lifting a hand to smother a yawn, she blinked several times, finding it harder to focus. "You have a ranch?"

Hunter smiled indulgently and tucked her hand under the covers again. "A small one. It's really just a large yard now that we got rid of the horses. Why?"

Finding it increasingly difficult to stay awake, Emma let her eyes close, imagining what the two of them would look like on horseback. "So romantic. Do you really eat in the diner every day?"

"Yes. Why?" Smiling at the suspicion in his voice, Emma shifted slightly into a more comfortable position. "Is the food good?"

"Of course." Remington's voice lowered. Gentled. "If not, we wouldn't eat there. Why don't you go to sleep?"

"Hmm." Emma let herself drift, promising herself that as soon as she got out of the hospital, she'd visit the diner they spoke about.

She could talk to Gracie and get recipes while seeing how a woman would handle having more than one husband.

Remington stepped closer, his voice coming from right next to her bed. "Would you like us to bring you some lunch from the diner?"

Forcing her eyes open, she turned her head to smile at him, thrilled to have the chance to see them again. "Would you? I'd love to try Gracie's cooking. But not if it's too much trouble."

He smiled faintly, his entire demeanor wary and hesitant as he glanced at Hunter. "Uh, sure. I mean, not at all. What would you like?"

Stifling a yawn, Emma took a deep breath and let it out slowly. "Whatever you're having."

"Okay." Remington sounded slightly amused. "You go to sleep. We'll watch over you."

"Hmm." She heard one of them lower themselves to the chair in her room, but other than that, a peaceful silence followed.

Sleepy, she couldn't stop thinking about Gracie and how she could go through life with more than one husband. Forcing her eyes open, she found Hunter staring at her from the foot of the bed. "How do Gracie's husbands feel about sharing a wife?"

Lowering himself to the deep windowsill, Hunter shrugged and looked out the window. "They all love her. They're brothers. Several brothers share a wife in Desire. They all seem happy."

Intrigued, Emma fought to stay awake. "You're brothers. Do you plan to share a wife?"

Hunter's jaw clenched. "We share women for sex but don't ever plan to get married. Go to sleep."

The combination of anger and sadness in his voice struck her, but the resignation in his tone had her forcing her eyes open again. "Really? You don't ever plan to get married? Why not?"

Hunter rose, coming closer to straighten her covers again. "It's just not in the cards for us. The doctor said you're supposed to rest, and it's obvious that it's not gonna happen while we're here. We'll be back later with your lunch."

Emma's eyes closed and wouldn't open again. "'kay. Thanks."

"You're welcome. Get some sleep."

Chapter Four

They only made it as far as the truck before the clenching of Remington's stomach made it clear that he couldn't leave her alone.

With his hand on the door handle, Remington paused and turned back, staring at the hospital window, the image of Emma lying pale and vulnerable imprinted in his mind.

"I can't leave her there. Damn it, Hunter. She's all alone."

"She's sleeping—and surrounded by nurses." Hunter scraped a hand through his hair. "Damn it, Rem! We can't let ourselves get sucked in. You know that as well as I do. We got her the help she needed. We'll watch out for her, but we've got to keep as much distance between us at possible."

Remington gritted his teeth. "As you said, she's sleeping. She won't even know I'm there." Releasing the door handle, he rounded the truck, pausing to glance at his brother. "But I will. She doesn't have anyone here, and I can't just leave her there alone."

"Damn it." Clearly irritated, Hunter yanked the door of the truck open. "Fine. Stay if you want. I'm getting the hell out of here before I get any more attached to her. I'll be back later with lunch."

Remington nodded once and turned, striding back toward the hospital, the knots in his stomach loosening with each step. "Fine. I'll see you later." He stopped abruptly when his brother called out to him.

Hunter leaned against the truck, his expression grim. "Don't get attached to her, Rem. She's not for us. No one is. Remember that."

Remington turned and met his brother's gaze, bile born of bitterness rising in his throat. "How the hell could I forget something like that?"

He turned away again, anxious to get to Emma and spend as much time with her as he could while she needed him.

They'd never had the opportunity to take care of someone before, and probably never would again, and he was determined to make the most of it.

When he got back to the room and found her sound asleep, Remington quietly moved the recliner in her room to a position where he'd be able to watch her.

Settling back, he stared at her, taking in her delicate beauty.

Her hair, now washed and dried instead of plastered to her head, curled around her face in soft, silky looking waves that framed her face and made her look like an angel.

It appeared to be slightly longer than shoulder length and lighter than he'd expected. The streaks of blonde than ran through it seemed to catch the light pouring in from the window next to her, making it shine.

He wanted to see her eyes again.

They'd been dark brown on the drive to the hospital, but when she'd looked up at him earlier, he could see they were a combination of a light brown, gold, and an amazing emerald green.

He couldn't help but wonder what color they would be when she was in the throes of passion.

Cursing himself for even thinking about such a thing while she lay in a hospital bed, he stiffened when she moaned in her sleep.

A small whimper had him surging to his feet and rushing to her side. "Easy, darlin'. You're okay."

Another whimper had him reaching for her, running a finger over her cheek. "You're all right. I'm here to watch over you. Go back to sleep, honey."

She reached out a hand toward him, smiling faintly when he caught it in his before she sighed and settled again.

Shaken at her apparent response to his voice, Remington stared down at her for several long seconds, imagining having her as his own.

A woman who would belong to him and Hunter.

A woman they could cherish.

A woman who would be there for them in good times and bad.

A woman they could spoil.

They would be responsible for her safety and well-being.

Her happiness.

Until they inevitably ruined it.

Her ready smile that caused flutters in his stomach would disappear.

The light would go out of her eyes, and she'd end up walking on eggshells around them, scared of displeasing them in some way.

With shaking hands, he pulled up the blanket she'd dislodged, releasing her hand to tuck it under the covers.

A minute later, he stood at the nurses' station, attracting the attention of the closest nurse. "She's moaning and whimpering in her sleep. I think she needs more pain medicine."

The nurse smiled, the appreciation and interest in her eyes irritating him. "Sir, she was given pain medicine about an hour ago. She can't have any more for a few more hours. When you left, I checked on her, and she was sleeping. She's fine. I promise. She just needs to rest."

Remington fisted his hands on the counter. "If she was fine, she wouldn't be moaning and whimpering in her sleep." Frustrated, he turned away, pulled out his cell phone, and called Dr. Hansen, who answered on the third ring.

"Dr. Hansen."

"Doc, something's wrong with Emma. She's moaning and whimpering in her sleep."

"She's fine, Remington. I promise. She may be a little uncomfortable when she moves in her sleep, but if she was in pain, she wouldn't be sleeping."

Remington frowned and peered into the room again, not wanting his conversation to wake her. Finding her settled and sleeping again, he let the door close and moved away. "Then why is she moaning?"

"I understand you're concerned, but I promise you, she's fine. Let her sleep. She's had surgery and needs to recover. If there's anything to report, I'll call you."

Remington strolled to the end of the hallway and looked out the window, his eyes going to the empty space where their truck had been parked. "I'm staying here."

"That's good. Just don't bother the nurses, and let Miss Smith get her rest."

Frowning at the amusement in the doctor's voice, Remington scowled. "It's just because she's alone."

"It's real nice that you're willing to put your fears of hurting a woman aside to stay with her. The nurses will be coming in to check on her, so you don't have to worry about being alone with her."

Remington stiffened, his stomach knotting. "What the hell kind of monster do you think I am?"

"I don't think you're a monster at all. You do. Miss Smith is going to go through times when she's uncomfortable and in pain. She might snap at whoever's closest. If you're going to spend any time with her, that's going to be you."

"She just had surgery! Do you really think I'm going to hurt a woman who's lying in a hospital bed?"

"Not for a minute. If I did, I wouldn't let you anywhere near her. Just wanted to make sure you realized that you wouldn't."

Shifting restlessly, Remington felt the knot in his stomach loosen. "I've got to get back to her, Doc. She seems to settle when I talk to her."

After a pregnant pause, Dr. Hansen spoke again. "I'll stop by later."

"Good. I don't know this Dr. Reed, and I want to make sure that you're looking out for her." Remington disconnected and went back to the room, wanting to be there for Emma if she started whimpering again.

He cared because she was alone.

He felt responsible because he and Hunter had found her.

It was nothing more than that.

* * * *

Two hours later, Remington stared into his coffee, catching a movement out of the corner of his eye.

Emma sighed in her sleep, a soft sigh that tugged at his heart. Shifting her legs, she started to roll to her side and whimpered before rolling to her back again.

Seeing that she'd inadvertently kicked the covers from one leg, Remington rose and went to her, tucking the covers back around her. He lifted his gaze to hers, surprised to find her watching him.

"You stayed." She reached out a hand, smiling when he took it in his.

Smiling faintly, he nodded and, without thinking, lifted it to his lips. "I don't want you to be alone."

She smiled wearily. "Thank you." She tried to move again and grimaced. "Could I ask you a favor?"

"Anything."

When she looked at him with such trust in her eyes, he'd kill for her.

"Could you help me turn to my side? I need another pillow, I think."

"Sure." Glad to be able to do something for her, he smiled and released her hand. "Don't move. I'm going to go get some more pillows."

He found two in the closet they'd given to her to use and went back to the bed, tossing one near her feet. Holding the other pillow in one hand, Remington started to reach for her with the other and paused, gulping when she lifted her arms and reached up for him.

A surge of adrenaline went through him, the need to hold her in his arms—just to hold her—overwhelming him.

Frowning up at him, she dropped her arms, obviously weak. "Is something wrong?"

Feeling ridiculous, Remington shook his head. "No. Of course not. Just trying to figure out the best way to do this without hurting you. Let's see if we can get you into a more comfortable position."

Looking into her eyes, he eased his arm around her, slowly lifting her against him. "Slow. Nice and slow. Let me do all the work."

She felt so soft against him. So pliant. So trusting.

She depended on *him* to help her.

"Okay, darlin'. Let me wedge the pillow in behind you." Hoping the pain medicine still in her system kept her from feeling any discomfort, he gently pushed the pillow slightly under Emma and between her and the bedrail at her back.

The trust in her eyes nearly undid him.

"I got another pillow in case you need it." He eased her down, helping her turn slightly to the position she sought. "Is that more comfortable?"

"Hmm. Wonderful." The pleasure in her sigh made his chest swell. "Would you put the other one in front of me to hold on to?"

"Of course."

She settled, hugging the pillow and closing her eyes again with a sigh. "Oh, that feels so good."

Proud of himself, he smiled and smoothed the blankets over her again. "Good. Let me make sure you're covered up."

Emma moaned, a pleasure-filled moan that made his cock stir. "I don't think I've ever been so comfortable."

Swallowing heavily, he released her, desperate to put space between them. "Good. I'm glad you're comfortable. Go back to sleep. You need your rest."

After straightening her covers again, Remington stood next to the hospital bed, listening to Emma's breathing, watching her long after her breathing evened out again.

She looked so calm. So peaceful.

So defenseless.

She had no one to look out for her. No one to take care of her—except him.

He'd thought he'd accepted his curse years earlier, but meeting Emma had brought all the emptiness and pain back to the surface.

Facing a lifetime of loneliness, Remington glanced at Emma again and slowly made his way back to the recliner.

Quietly lowering himself into it, he leaned forward and stared at his hands.

Big hands.

Work-roughened hands.

Hands that could do a lot of damage to a woman, especially one as small and delicate as Emma.

Hands like his father's.

Hands that could kill a woman with very little effort.

* * * *

Standing at the counter at the diner, Hunter couldn't stop thinking about Emma or Remington's reaction to her.

He understood his brother's preoccupation with her, but he couldn't let Remington get too attached.

Seeing the life their mother had had with their father, both of them understood just how vulnerable and defenseless a woman could be.

They wanted desperately to have a woman of their own to protect, but losing their mother to their father's temper at such an impressionable age had made them leery of even attempting it.

Gracie came up to the counter, interrupting his thoughts and grinning up at him. Even though she had two grown daughters, she had the look of a much younger woman. "Hey, Hunter. Heard you had a little excitement yesterday." She glanced around. "Where's Remington?"

Aware that the sound level in the diner had decreased dramatically, and that several of his friends watched and listened, Hunter sighed. "He's at the hospital with her. I need three specials to go."

Gracie smiled and turned away. "I assume one of them is for her. Good. Nobody can get better eating hospital food. My food will help her get her strength back. I heard she was in bad shape when you found her. How's she doin'?"

"She's still groggy and in some pain, but the surgery was successful. She was going to sleep when I left a couple of hours ago."

Clay and Rio Erickson, sitting at the counter sipping coffee, both nodded. Clay set his cup down and turned slightly. "Best thing for her.

Heard you got her to the hospital just in time to keep her appendix from bursting. What's her name?"

"Emma. Emma Smith." Hunter smiled in gratitude when Gracie set a hot cup of coffee on the counter in front of him. After a sleepless night, he needed the kick of caffeine.

Rio frowned. "Can't say I remember that name. Does she know anyone here, or is she just visiting?"

Lowering himself to the stool, Hunter wrapped his hand around the cup. "No. We asked if there was anyone we could call, and she told us no." Frowning into his cup, he shrugged. "We don't know why she's here, other than she liked the name of the town."

Clay blinked. "Because she likes the name of the town?"

Hunter shrugged. "That's what she said. We really haven't had the chance to talk to her much." Staring into his coffee, Hunter couldn't help but wonder why a woman would be driving around alone and stop at a town just because she liked the name.

Rio turned on his stool to face him fully. "So are you and Remington gonna claim her?"

Hunter stiffened and turned away. "No. Jesus. Is that all you people ever think about?"

Clay sighed heavily. "Hunter, I know that you and Remington don't want to get involved with anyone, and I know it's gotta be hard for you to look after a woman. I'll take Jesse to the hospital, and we'll sit with her."

"No." Getting to his feet as Gracie approached with the bag of food, Hunter reached into his pocket for his wallet. "We'll take care of her. Thanks, Gracie."

Gracie slid a glance at Clay and Rio, one that Hunter pretended to ignore. "How long will she be in the hospital?"

"Few days. I don't know yet. Depends on how she does. Thanks again." With a nod in Clay and Rio's direction, Hunter turned and walked away, aware of their curious stares.

He hated being the subject of gossip, but he knew that the town of Desire would have a lot to say about his and Remington's casual involvement with Emma.

They'd make more of it than the situation warranted, but he couldn't do anything about it.

Once Emma recovered, they'd see that there was nothing between them and the talk would stop—at least talk about them.

He had no doubt in his mind that Emma would be the topic of conversation for some time.

After securing the food in his truck, he climbed in and glanced back at the crowded diner, grimacing at the thought of standing by while one of his friends claimed her.

* * * *

Clay stared thoughtfully after Hunter before glancing at Rio and Gracie. "It's a shame Hunter and Remington are so damned stuck on the belief that they're just like their father. He was a damned monster, while they're protective and tender with every woman they meet. The only time they lose their temper is when someone mistreats or talks bad about a woman. I just don't understand how the hell they don't see that."

Shaking his head, Rio lifted his cup again, a small smile playing at his lips. "Yeah, well my money's on Emma Smith. They usually avoid single women like the plague, but they can't seem to stay away from her. For some reason, they think that because they like to dominate a woman during sex, they're like their father." Setting his cup aside, he looked at several other residents of Desire—men who'd been their friends for years.

One of them, Lucas Hart, strolled closer and dropped onto the stool Hunter had just vacated. Smiling, he set his cup down for a refill. "Yes, I noticed Hunter had a look of panic on his face that I've never seen on him before. Interesting. Not much ruffles that man."

Refilling their cups, Gracie looked up with an impish smile. "Hunter and Remington are gonna need a nudge. Those two are *not* gonna give in gracefully."

Lucas lifted his cup. "Sounds like a conspiracy in the making."

Michael Keegan, one of the owners of the bar in Desire, grinned from the end of the counter. "I'm in. Maybe if those two have a woman, they'll stop starting bar fights."

Clay held up a hand. "Wait. We haven't met this woman yet. We don't even know what she's like. The last thing either one of them needs is a woman who isn't right for them." He glanced at his brother. "Rio and I will go in with Jesse later on and check on them."

Gracie grinned. "Take one of my pies."

Amused, Clay shook his head and shared a smile with Lucas. "It seems that, in Desire, a full-blown conspiracy takes only a few minutes."

Gracie nodded. "It's the only way to get those two to see reason. They deserve to be happy. We all know what's best for them better than they do. Their mother would have wanted them to have a family."

Clay rose. "Let's wait until we see them together before we decide."

Lucas nodded, his smile falling. "I wouldn't want to see them mixed up with the wrong kind of woman. They need someone special."

Michael tossed bills onto the counter and stood, his smile not reaching his eyes. "Don't we all?"

Chapter Five

Hunter strode past the nurses' station and to Emma's room, ignoring the looks of interest from the two nurses on duty.

If they knew what was inside him, they'd run away screaming.

Not sure if Emma still slept, he pushed the door open as quietly as possible with his shoulder and peered around the corner, disappointment and relief warring inside him to find her still asleep.

He eased into the room, disturbed to find Remington sitting forward in the recliner, staring down at his hands. "How is she?"

Remington jumped up, the brief glimpse of misery in his eyes disappearing almost immediately. "She's been sleeping." He hurried to Emma's side, hovering protectively over her with an ease that told Hunter that his brother had done it many times. "I helped her get into a more comfortable position. She likes to sleep on her side. She seems to settle when I talk to her."

Smiling, he pushed her hair back from her face, using his thumb to stroke the curl that wrapped around his finger. "There she is. I'll bet you're hungry, aren't you, darlin'?"

Emma's drowsy smile tugged at Hunter's heart while setting off a barrage of alarm bells. "Hmm. Something smells delicious, but I'm too comfortable to move. Thanks for helping me get into this position."

"You're welcome." Remington leaned on the bedrail, bent over her with an intimacy that had grown alarmingly in the last several hours. "The nurse said that you can sit in the chair for lunch and dinner. As a matter of fact, they really want you to. When you're done eating, we'll get you back into this position again. By that time, you'll have another pain pill and can go back to sleep, this time with your belly full of good food."

She smiled again and closed her eyes. "Sounds wonderful." Shifting her gaze, she smiled. "Thank you, Hunter, for bringing it."

Her voice, husky with sleep, tightened the fist around his heart.

Remington chuckled, obviously already under her spell. "Come on, baby doll. Wake up. You can't eat your lunch from there. Open your eyes, darlin', and I'll help you sit up so I can carry you to the chair." Lifting his gaze to Hunter's, he grinned like a fool. "They took her IV out earlier."

Hunter set out the food, trying not to watch the way his brother helped Emma into a sitting position.

He tried not to notice how comfortable they looked together or how gently Remington spoke to her.

He failed.

He couldn't take his eyes off of them.

He pretended not to notice how Remington's hands lingered on her arms and back as he sat her up in the bed and tucked pillows around her, but his own arms itched to hold her.

Hunter turned away and went back out to the nurses' station, startling the nurse sitting at the computer. "Is she really allowed to get out of bed?"

The nurse recovered quickly and smiled. "Of course, Mr. Ross. I'll come in now."

Hunter could do nothing but watch, feeling useless as the nurse placed a soft blanket on the recliner, stepping forward when she went to the bed and lowered the side.

"I'll help you to the chair."

Remington rushed forward, nudging Hunter out of the way. "I've got her."

With a hand at her back, Remington slid the other under her thighs, his eyes dark and narrowed as he lifted her against him.

Realizing that the hospital gown would be open in the back and that her bare thighs would be supported by his brother's arm, Hunter bit back a groan, wondering what kind of man would be thinking about feeling the thighs of a still recovering woman.

A man like his father.

Remington carried her as gently as he would a newborn baby and slowly lowered her to the recliner, the tenderness in his eyes striking. "Are you comfortable, baby doll?"

With a grateful smile, Emma reached up to touch his arm. "It feels wonderful to be able to sit up. Thank you." She eyed Hunter expectantly. "I'm dying to try Gracie's food. What did you bring?"

There was nothing even remotely sexual about the look she gave him— a look of anticipation and happiness that hit him hard.

Used to women who wanted nothing from him except sex or money— women who knew the score and embraced it—Hunter found himself mesmerized by her naiveté and sweet demeanor.

And the sparkle of challenge in her eyes.

Meeting it, he got an insight into her personality that intrigued him, despite his best effort at indifference.

"Hunter?"

The amusement in his brother's tone brought Hunter back to the present. Lifting his gaze to Remington's, he resumed setting out their lunch.

"Uh. It's chicken and dumplings day."

Meeting his brother's knowing smile with a glare, Hunter watched Emma eat, pleased to see that her color was better than it had been that morning.

Her eyes were clearer, with a mischievous sparkle that he desperately tried to ignore.

Every once in a while, though, he could see a glimmer of pain in her beautiful eyes.

She ate slowly, closing her eyes occasionally as if savoring every bite.

"This is really good. I love chicken and dumplings. Thanks for bringing it. It sure beats the food they serve here."

"You're welcome." Hunter dug into his own lunch, which he'd balanced across his legs. "I opened the trunk of your car to see if you had any other luggage. I saw a few more suitcases that I can bring if you need them."

"No." Shaking her head, Emma scooped up another bite. "I have plenty of clothes for now."

Pleased to see her enjoying her lunch, Hunter eased back to watch her. "I was a little surprised to find boxes of pots and pans in the trunk."

Along with pots and pans, there'd been all sorts of dishes in every color he could think of, cooking utensils and boxes of index cards.

Her soft laugh ended in a wince of pain. "I do *a lot* of cooking."

Hunter watched her eat, unable to stop sneaking glances at her.

The glances became looks.

The looks lengthened, and soon he found himself staring at her, fascinated by everything about her.

The tilt of her head when she listened to Remington speak.

Her smile.

The way her eyes lit up when she laughed.

Even the way she ate, savoring every bite.

Wearing a hospital gown, her hair disheveled and her cheeks flushed from her nap, she looked absolutely adorable.

He and his brother avoided adorable at all costs.

But he'd already become addicted to the way her face lit up when she saw him.

Remington couldn't seem to take his eyes from her. "So, you like cooking?"

Emma grinned, showing dimples that made her appear even more adorable. "I write cookbooks. I've been travelling around the south, collecting recipes. I test them out and compare them before I decide which ones I put into my cookbooks. I planned to stay in Desire a couple of months before I move on. I'd hoped to get some more recipes while I was here and finish putting my next cookbook together."

Hunter and Remington exchanged a look, and stabbing his fork into a piece of chicken, Remington turned his attention back to Emma. "Why Desire?"

"You know, I think this needs a little more black pepper." Scooping another forkful, she shrugged. "I told you. I liked the name. I was nearby, so…Hey, do you know of anyone who has a house or apartment that I could rent for a few months?"

Amused at the rapid change of subject, Hunter glanced at his brother, uneasy that Remington appeared captivated.

Remington turned his head, meeting Hunter's gaze squarely as he spoke to her. "You know that when you leave here, Emma, you won't be able to stay alone."

Hunter broke out in a cold sweat, knowing damned well what his brother planned to do.

He gave his brother a warning glare, which Remington met with a raised brow, clearly ignoring Hunter's warning.

Emma sipped her water. "Of course I can. I've been on my own for years. Besides, there doesn't seem to be any choice." Pausing, she tapped the straw against her lips and stared thoughtfully at the door. "Isn't there a hotel or motel or something in Desire? I could stay there while I look for something else. I don't need anything very big, but I do have to have a kitchen."

Hunter clenched his jaw at the thought of her being alone at the hotel, and at the thought of Ethan Sullivan and Brandon Weston, the unattached owners of the hotel, fussing over her.

Remington closed his take-out container and stood, making Hunter more nervous by the minute. "No. You need to have someone with you when you're discharged. The doctor insists. He won't let you leave unless someone is with you."

"What he doesn't know won't hurt him." Emma waved her hand negligently in the air before scooping another bite. "I'll be fine."

"No. You'll stay at our house." Hunter froze, stunned that he'd made the offer himself.

What the fuck was wrong with him?

Damn it!

Remington looked just as surprised, a slow smile tugging at his lips. "What a great idea."

Clenching his jaw, Hunter got to his feet and went to the garbage can to throw away his empty container.

Crossing his arms over his chest, he scowled at Remington before giving his attention to Emma.

"You won't be living with us. We have a house that we just finished remodeling. We don't live there. We live in the guest house out back. We can be close enough if you need something and can check on you, but we won't be in each other's way. You'll have the house to yourself."

He injected a hint of coolness into his tone to make it clear that his offer wasn't a play for her.

Emma seemed just as surprised by his offer as his coldness. She played with her food in silence for several long seconds, eyeing him cautiously. Her eyes had lost some of their sparkle, and he knew he was the one to blame for it. "Why don't you live there?"

"We just don't." Annoyed at himself, something that seemed to happen often around Emma, Hunter gave her his most intimidating look.

It didn't help his mood any that she didn't appear to be the least bit intimidated.

Instead, she looked sad. Resigned.

And determined not to show it.

He felt like a heel.

Closing her container, she set it aside and reached for the small, plastic glass of water again and turned her attention to Remington. "I don't understand. Why don't you live in the house you've just remodeled?"

Remington gave Hunter a dirty look before turning to her, taking her free hand in his. "We remodeled it for our dead mother. It has everything she wanted. It was the house we grew up in, but neither one of us will ever live there again. Too many bad memories."

The conversation ended when the nurse came in with another pain pill.

Hunter gathered the remnants of her meal, frowning to see that she hadn't eaten even half of it. Seeing that she had trouble keeping her eyes open again, he decided not to address it, promising himself that he'd make sure she ate more at dinner.

The realization that he'd already planned to be there for dinner stunned him and irritated him even more.

The nurse pushed the tray aside. "Let's get you back into bed. You can sit up again later."

Stepping forward, Remington smiled. "Ready, darlin'?"

Nodding, Emma blushed. "Ready."

Remington gently slid a hand behind her back and one beneath her thighs, lifting her against him. "Nice and easy, honey."

Hunter's hands ached to hold her, the intimacy between Emma and his brother unnerving him.

He was jealous as hell, wishing he could be as comfortable with her as Remington was.

After the nurse left, Emma settled back against the pillows with a sigh as though sitting up and eating her lunch had drained all of her energy. "Are you sure about the house?"

Remington moved in next to her. "We're sure. Do you want me to put the pillow the way it was before?"

"Please." Emma sighed gratefully, a soft moan escaping at the feel of Remington's arms coming around her. "That feels so good."

Remington paused, leaning back to look down at her. "What does, darlin'?"

Smiling up at him, she could feel Hunter's sharp attention. "My back aches, and your hands are warm on my sore muscles. I'm probably just stiff from being in one position for so long. I'm usually always moving."

Remington grinned, seeming pleased that he'd done something to make her feel better. "How about a nice, gentle back rub?"

Emma sighed again when his hands began to move, the firm gentleness and warmth melting the stiffness with each slow caress.

Hunter stepped forward, his eyes warm. "Remington, why don't you go? I'll stay with her a while."

"No." Remington continued to rub her back, the heat from his large hands easing the ache. "I'm staying."

Lying on her side, with the pillow wedged against her, she looked down toward the foot of the bed, meeting Hunter's gaze head-on. "You regret offering me the house. Don't worry. I'll find another place to stay. The hotel will be fine until I find something with a kitchen."

A muscle worked in his jaw as Hunter stepped forward. "No. You can stay at the house."

"I don't want to impose."

"You won't." Hunter turned away to stare out the window. "I told you we live in the guest house."

"If you're sure." Emma let her eyes close as the pain medicine and Remington's slow massage worked their magic. "How much is the rent?"

Remington eased his fingertips over a particularly tight spot. "No rent. You said you like to cook. You can cook for us—after you've recovered. Yeah, right there. Damn, your muscles are tight. We're going to have to do this more often."

"I don't want to bother you. It's a deal about the rent. I have a lot of recipes I haven't had the chance to try out yet and staying in the hotel wouldn't give me the chance. You can be my guinea pigs and give me your opinions."

"See?" Remington smoothed both hands up and down her back. "It works out for everyone. Now, why don't you go back to sleep? I'll be right here when you wake up."

Emma sighed, nearly asleep. "Promise?"

She had to admit that it made her feel better to know that someone was close by.

Remington bent close, chuckling next to her ear. "Promise."

* * * *

Rubbing her back, Remington slowed his strokes, pleased with himself. Smiling when her breathing evened out, he ran a hand over her hair before straightening to look at his brother.

Hunter stared down at her, his jaw clenched. "You're playing with fire, you know that, right? You're already too attached to her."

Pushing aside his unease at the knowledge that his brother was right, Remington shrugged. "You know we can't leave her alone in the hotel. That's why you jumped to offer the house to her.'

Hunter's eyes remained hard and cold. "Ethan and Brandon would take care of her."

Tensing, Remington fought jealousy. "I'm sure they would, but you can't let that happen any more than I can. We'd both be afraid they'd want her for themselves."

"Something wrong with them wanting her for themselves?" Hunter crushed his paper cup and tossed it in the direction of the trash can. "At least they have something to offer her. Hell, you and I know everything there is about pleasing a woman when it comes to sex, but neither one of us has a clue about how to make love to one."

The reminder set Remington's teeth on edge. "They're too busy to take care of her. Now that the house is finished, we have nothing but time on our hands."

"You're getting attached."

"So you've said." Remington knew his brother was right, but walking away from Emma, or turning her over to someone else to take care of, didn't sit well with him. "It's nothing I can't handle. We'll take care of her until she's back on her feet. She'll be leaving in a few months anyway. Why not enjoy her company while we can?"

Hunter straightened and glanced at her again, a muscle working in his jaw. "It's a mistake, one we're both going to regret."

Chapter Six

Fascinated, Emma watched Jesse Erickson interact with her *two* husbands, Clay and Rio.

Surprised that Hunter and Remington's friends had come to visit her, Emma was even more surprised to learn that Jesse was one of the women in Desire who had more than one husband.

Fascinated to see how such a relationship could work, she watched them closely.

Jesse's extremely tall, muscular husbands stood on either side of her, their love for her evident in every look. Every casual touch.

It seemed that neither one of them could keep their hands off of her.

Jesse seemed to glow, her happiness blatantly obvious.

She looked entirely comfortable with both men and giving them both adoring looks.

Leaning against Rio, she held Clay's hand as they were introduced before taking the large basket Clay carried and quickly making her way to Emma's bedside. "You poor thing. How are you feeling?"

Liking her immediately, Emma smiled and tried to sit up. "Much better thank you. It's so nice to meet you."

Remington rushed forward, wrapping his arms around her and slowly easing her to a sitting position. "Hey! Easy, honey." He tucked the pillows behind her back. "Don't try to do it on your own. I'm here to help you."

Jesse seemed amused by Remington's fussing, staring up at him wide-eyed for several seconds before turning her attention back to Emma again, obviously struggling to hold back a smile. "Go away, Remington. I want to talk to Emma without all of you men hovering over us."

Surprised that Jesse's eyes glimmered with tears, Emma smiled at Remington. "Thank you."

Remington patted Jesse's back. "Thanks for coming."

Jesse nodded, elbowing him in the stomach. "We women have to stick together. I know how intimidating you men can be. Now go away and talk to Clay and Rio while Emma and I get acquainted."

The firmness in her voice contrasted sharply with the tears brimming in her eyes.

Remington nodded, his smile falling. "Of course." He started to turn away, turning back abruptly. "Emma, do Hunter and I intimidate you?"

Something in his tone and in his eyes created a flutter in Emma's stomach. "Of course you intimidate me—in a good way. When I get out of here, I'm going to show you just how much you intimidate me. Wait until you see me intimidate you back."

Clearing his throat, he took a step back. "Let's just get you out of here and settled so you can recover. I'm sure you'll feel differently once you get better."

When he turned away, Emma opened her mouth to object, hurt that he could dismiss her so easily.

Jesse stopped her with a look and a hand on her arm. Lowering her voice, she leaned close and fussed with the covers. "Don't. He and Hunter don't think they can ever have a woman in their life. We'll talk more later. God, it makes me so happy to see the way they are with you. You're the answer to our prayers."

Glancing at the men, Emma sighed. "You don't even know me."

"I know enough, and I know Hunter and Remington. They wouldn't be taken in by just a pretty face. They hated to see you so helpless and alone, and they started to feel responsible for you. If you knew them, you'd understand that they take that very seriously. It's forced them to spend time with you, and the more time they spend with you, the more they're falling for you. The fact that they're fighting so hard not to pay attention to you while neither one of them can look away from you more than a second or two speaks volumes."

Emma frowned, glancing at both men to find them watching her. "I don't want them to spend time with me because they feel obligated."

"It started out that way, but now they can't seem to stay away from you. Clay told them that he and I could stay with you, and Hunter shot that down without any hesitation at all." Jesse glanced behind her, keeping her voice low.

"They've never trusted themselves to be in a relationship. They're too scared of screwing it up because they think they're like their father. We'll talk later, but in the meantime, I have a present for you that I hope will make you feel better."

Straightening, she smiled and handed Emma the huge basket, balancing it on Emma's thighs. "My sister, Nat, my best friend, Kelly, and I own a store in Desire called Indulgences. We make and sell soaps, lotions, shampoo, and all sorts of things. I know that the stuff in the hospital isn't all that great."

Glancing back at the men, who stood on the other side of the room, Jesse leaned closer, whispering again. "I don't know how you feel about Hunter and Remington, but I thought you might want something to make you soft and smell delicious."

Peering around Jesse to watch Hunter and Remington interact with Clay and Rio, Emma couldn't help but smile at the obvious closeness they shared.

Emma sighed. "They've both been very kind to me. Hunter seems wary sometimes, but they've both been so sweet."

"They're both sweet and very protective of women. They're not as hard and cold as they think they are, and it's so damned nice to see them so flustered over you."

Emma blinked. "I haven't done anything."

Jesse shrugged. "They like you. For men determined not to let a woman into their lives, it's a hard pill to swallow." Glancing behind her, she spoke in a normal tone again. "So, how long do you have to stay in here?"

Shifting her attention back to Jesse, Emma sighed, her thoughts centered on Remington's comment. "A few more days. When I leave, I'll be renting

Hunter and Remington's house from them—the house they remodeled. I think they regret their offer."

Jesse snorted, glancing back at them. "I'm sure they do, but not for reasons that you might think. You'll be living on their property so they'll see you every day. If they're already showing this kind of interest, I can imagine what it'll be like when you've recovered."

Emma giggled, patting Jesse's hand. "I think you've been watching too many soap operas. We hardly know each other!"

Jesse smiled. "Yeah, but there's something there." She turned to look over her shoulder and sighed. "Sometimes it happens in a heartbeat. It did with us."

Clay and Rio both turned to Jesse as though they'd felt her gaze, both men searching her features.

Smiling, Jesse shook her head and turned back to Emma. "Some men are just too compelling to ignore." Shaking her head again, she blew out a breath. "Enough about them for now." She touched one of the bottles in the basket. "We didn't know what fragrance you like so we included several, along with some unscented things."

Letting her attention be drawn to the basket, Emma blinked back tears when she saw the amount of things Jesse had brought her. "Oh my! This is amazing." Incredibly touched, she shook her head, blinking back tears. "I can't accept that. It's too much. You don't even know me."

Jesse giggled, a sound that had both of her husbands' heads whipping around, their smiles indulgent. "I have a feeling you and I are going to be good friends."

Using the edge of the blanket to wipe away a tear, Emma smiled. "It was so nice of you to come and visit me and to bring this. I can't wait to try them. Thank you."

"It was my pleasure." Jesse's eyes sparkled. "Everyone in town is talking about you and is dying to meet you. I'm just glad you're feeling better."

Even though the two women had just met, Jesse's eyes darkened with concern. "I heard it was pretty scary."

"And painful." Emma glanced at Remington. "I don't know what would have happened to me if Hunter and Remington hadn't come along. They were so confident and knew just what to do. They talked to me the whole time. It made it a lot less scary."

"Thank God they did come along." Jesse leaned close again. "They're special. You're a lucky woman."

"It doesn't hurt that they're gorgeous in a masculine sort of way and so damned sweet that I just want to take a bite out of them. Nice butts, too." Emma frowned and glanced at Hunter, surprised to find him watching her. "I've never met men like them before."

Jesse smiled and glanced back at the men. "I know it's something you're probably not used to—I know I wasn't—but they wouldn't be happy unless they share a woman."

Keeping her voice at a whisper, Emma leaned forward, gasping in pain. "I don't think that's something I have to worry about."

Hunter rushed forward, gripping Emma's shoulders and easing her back. "You moved too fast and it hurt, didn't it? Lie still. I mean it. I'm gonna go ask the nurse if you can have another pain pill."

Emma could only stare up at him, stunned that he'd been paying that much attention to her.

Jesse touched her arm. "I'm sorry." Once Hunter moved away, she leaned forward, keeping her voice at a whisper. "Not something you have to worry about, huh?"

Emma forced a smile despite the pain. "As much as I'd like to believe I could have them in my life, we barely know each other. I'd probably drive them nuts." She took several deep breaths, grateful when the pain began to ease. "I'd only planned to be in Desire a few months anyway."

Remington moved to her side and took her hand in his, preventing her from saying anything else. Although he smiled, his eyes remained dark with concern. "Once you take your pain pill, we'll get you into a more comfortable position. Okay?"

"Okay." Touching his hand, she forced another smile. "I'm fine, Remington. It's just a twinge."

"Liar."

Jesse patted her arm. "We'd better get going. You need to rest. My home phone number and the number to the store are on a card in the basket. Call me if you need anything."

"You've already done so much."

"It's nothing. Call me if you just want to talk."

Remington took Jesse's hand. "Thank you. It was very nice of you to bring those things for her."

Clay and Rio exchanged a glance before Rio came forward, wrapping an arm around Jesse's waist. Smiling at Emma, he pulled his wife closer, his love for her evident. "It was nice to meet you, Emma, and I hope you get out of here soon. I understand you're going to be staying with Hunter and Remington."

Remington stiffened. "Not with us. In the main house. We'll be close enough to help her, but not crowd her."

Hunter strode into the room, looking none too pleased. "Damned nurse. Said you're not due for more pain medicine for two hours. *Two hours*! What the hell good is pain medicine if you can't take it when you're in pain?"

Remington frowned. "It'll be okay. We can fix the pillows the way we did before."

Emma smiled. "That would be nice."

Hunter went around to the other side of the bed, looking slightly panicked. "Easy, Rem. I'll help you, and then I can rub her back until she goes to sleep."

His unease with her made her uncomfortable. "You don't have to do that."

"Afraid I'll hurt you? I won't."

Emma blinked. "I never thought you would. You're both the gentlest men I've ever met."

Hunter stilled, glancing at his brother. "I wish we were, honey. I wish we were."

* * * *

Smiling, Jesse took her husbands' hands and left the room. She walked between them down the hall, waiting until they got to the elevator before speaking. "They've got it bad."

Holding her against his side, Clay bent and touched his lips to hers. "Yeah. They have that stunned look on their faces, the kind of look Rio and I had when we met you."

Jesse snorted inelegantly and started forward when the elevator door opened. "That's bull. You didn't look stunned at all. You were both bulldozers."

Rio slid a hand over her ass as they made their way into the elevator. "We had to make sure you didn't get away."

"Behave." Jesse knew she'd ruined her reprimand by leaning into him, but she couldn't resist. "What are we going to do? I like her, and it's obvious Hunter and Remington like her, but she said she's only in Desire for a few months." Straightening, she eyed both of her husbands. "Damn it! It's not fair. They deserve to be happy. They deserve to have a wife and family. Why do they have to be so hardheaded? Men! Well, we're just going to have to do what we can to show them what they're missing."

"Speaking of bulldozers." Clay shared a look with Rio. "Don't worry, baby. We'll do what we can, but Hunter and Remington are going to have to see the truth for themselves."

Rio pulled out his phone and began dialing. "I'll have to let Gracie know that Emma's a sweetheart and Hunter and Remington are already hooked."

Leaning back against the back of the elevator, Clay pulled Jesse close. "I hope your new friend is the one to do it. We're just going to have to wait and see what happens when they get to know each other better."

"You and Rio didn't seem to need all that much time figuring out that you wanted me." Grinning, Jesse reached up, wrapping her arms around his neck to pull him down for a kiss. "I can't wait. It's going to be worth it to see Hunter and Remington happy."

Clay frowned. "Don't get your hopes up, Jesse. Hunter and Remington are set in their ways. They're not like we were when we met you. I have a feeling that the closer Emma gets to them, the more they're going to push her away."

Gripping his hand, Jesse shook her head. "We can't let that happen."

"It's not our choice, love. You're going to have to accept that."

* * * *

Hunter continued to rub Emma's back long after her breathing evened out, enjoying the opportunity to touch her. Leaning over her, he frowned and lifted the corner of the blanket, making sure that the pillow they'd wedged against her didn't press against her wound. "At least she's not in pain anymore."

"Thank God. It makes me feel damned helpless." Remington tucked the blanket around her shoulders again and reached out to touch a silky-looking curl.

Lifting his gaze, he looked pointedly at where Hunter continued to rub her back. "You seem to care about her more than you want to admit."

Jerking his hand away, Hunter glared at his brother. "She's a woman, and she's been hurt. Like you said, there's no one to look out for her except us. Don't read anything more into it. We don't even really know her."

He looked up when the door opened again, surprised to see Rachel, Boone, and Chase tiptoe into the room.

Rachel glanced at Emma and smiled, keeping her voice at a whisper. "We just passed the others and they said she was going to sleep. We won't bother her. She really is pretty, isn't she?"

"Yes. She is." Pausing when she moaned, Hunter rubbed her back again, a fist clenching around his heart when she smiled and settled once again.

Moving away from Emma's sleeping form before anyone got the wrong idea, Hunter went to greet their visitors, beginning to get a strange feeling in his gut.

Rachel came forward, standing on her toes to kiss his cheek while peering around him to see Emma. "Hi, Hunter. How's she doing?"

Hunter resisted the urge to look back at Emma and shook hands with Boone and Chase. "She's still in pain off and on, especially when she moves, but at least we can get her comfortable enough to go to sleep. We just have to get her into the right position and rub her back." He looked at his watch. "She's due for more pain medicine in about an hour and forty-five minutes."

Boone and Chase exchanged a look before shaking hands with Remington.

Boone shook his head. "We passed where you found her right before you did and nobody was there. I'm just glad you went by. I heard she was in bad shape."

Hunter didn't want to imagine anyone else finding Emma, and he didn't want to acknowledge the jealousy that tightened his stomach at the thought of anyone else taking care of her.

Rachel smiled and set the bag she'd brought and her purse aside. "I hear that when she's released from the hospital she's going to be staying with you and Remington."

Remington glanced at Hunter. "Not with us. In the main house. She can't be on her own, and we'll be close enough to help her if she needs us."

Uncomfortable with the subject, Hunter started for the door. "I'm gonna go get some coffee from the cafeteria for everyone. When Emma wakes up, she's gonna have to eat something. I'll get her something to eat while I'm there." He met Rachel's look of surprise. "She doesn't like the food here. Does anyone want anything?"

Boone shook his head. "Thanks, but we're having dinner with the Prestons. Erin wants to go out for dinner."

Rachel grinned. "My sister's feeling a little cooped up. She's due soon and is getting very uncomfortable." She gestured toward Emma. "I can't blame her for not liking the food. When I had Theresa, Boone and Chase brought me food all the time. We'll have to do the same when Erin's in here."

Chase dropped into one of the hard chairs the nurse had brought in. "You don't have to worry about dinner, though. Nat's coming in with Jake and Hoyt, and they're bringing dinner for all three of you."

Remington grinned. "Where's the little angel?"

Hunter smiled at the thought of Boone, Chase, and Rachel's daughter, an adorable little girl named Theresa.

Chase smiled, the pride in his eyes unmistakable. "She's with her aunt and uncles. Erin wanted to come, but Jared, Duncan, and Reece are keeping a sharp eye on her and getting her to rest as much as possible. Theresa gets her to sit and watch a movie or play dolls, and Jared, Duncan, and Reese spoil both of them rotten."

"I can imagine." Hunter pursed his lips, knowing his friends well. "It's nice of all of you to come and check on Emma. I just hope that's all you're doing."

Rachel blinked, her look of innocence not fooling him for a minute. "What else would we be doing? We just figured you'd need a break. As a matter of fact, I can stay here with her and you two can go home."

"No." Hunter and Remington both answered simultaneously.

Rachel grinned. "I see."

Remington shrugged, averting his gaze. "I was thinking about running home, taking a shower, and getting a change of clothes."

Hunter nodded. "They're in the car. I'll bring them in with the coffee. There's no reason you can't use the shower in here. I'll be back in a bit."

Boone stepped forward. "I'll come with you to help you carry the coffee. Baby, do you want coffee or something else?"

Rachel grinned. "Coffee sounds great. Thanks."

Once they left the room and started down the hall, Boone glanced at him.

"I'm sure it's irritating to be under the microscope, but everyone's just concerned for you, and delighted to see your interest in Emma."

Jabbing the button for the elevator, Hunter blew out a breath, deciding to confide in his longtime friend—a man who'd been through his own sort of hell regarding a woman.

"She's alone. She needed us. The only other woman who's ever needed us was our mother, and we let her down."

Boone frowned. "You didn't let her down. You were too young to know everything that was going on. It was a hell of a position to be in."

When the elevator opened, Hunter paused, waiting for the occupants to exit before he and Boone stepped inside. He waited until the doors closed before turning back to Boone.

"You know damned well that Rem and I like to dominate women—just like out father. If we share that with our father, who's to say we don't share the rest? We can't risk hurting her."

Boone frowned, his eyes flashing. "Don't be ridiculous. You've never hurt a woman in your life. Neither has Remington."

Shaking his head, Hunter watched the numbers overhead. "We've never put ourselves in a position to hurt one. We've never been alone with a woman. The only times we've ever had sex, it's been in the club."

He met Boone's gaze again. "A woman like Emma would need tenderness. Lovemaking—not fucking. Rem and I have no experience with something like that. We could hurt her so easily, Boone. Emotionally. Physically. How the hell can we take a chance like that?"

Boone touched his arm as the elevator stopped. "You couldn't hurt a woman, but you should know that caring about her will make you more gentle than you even thought possible."

Hunter stepped out of the elevator, his stomach in knots. "I wish I could believe that. I just can't take the chance. She's so sweet. So damned adorable. If I hurt her, I'd never forgive myself. We'll take her home with us and watch over her, but we've got to keep our distance. We don't even know how to love, Boone. We're not the men for her, but she needs us and we won't let her down."

After confiding in Boone, Hunter was more relaxed when he walked back into the room.

They'd talked about Emma's condition and the Preston brothers' impending fatherhood, the casual conversation so normal that Hunter began to settle.

His heart beat faster, though, when he walked back into the room and saw that Emma was now awake and holding court.

Turning, she grinned, her eyes alight with pleasure. "Hunter! They said you'd be right back, but I didn't believe them. I thought you went home. That back rub felt great."

Aware that Chase and Rachel eyed him curiously, he avoided looking at them as he carried the tray of coffee to the table. Struggling to hide his own pleasure at her welcome, he straightened, frowning at her. "Do you feel any better?"

"Yes. Thank you." Her blush, and the sparkle in her eyes made him feel ten feel tall, and embarrassed the hell out of him.

"You're in pain." He could see it in her eyes and in the way she moved, and the fact that she'd just lied to him about it pissed him off. He tossed the duffel bag he'd retrieved to Remington on his way to Emma's bedside.

Hunter leaned close, keeping his voice at a whisper so as not to be heard above the other's conversation. "You don't need to lie. I can see it in your eyes."

Emma smiled faintly, her eyes dark with pain. "I've already been enough trouble. I'm not about to be any more. Did you see what Rachel brought? It's from her and her sister, Erin. I told her she shouldn't have done it."

Hunter reached out to touch the light purple nightgown and robe, trying hard not to picture Emma wearing it.

Made of the softest cotton, it would cover Emma from her neck to her knees. It would be comfortable and look beautiful on her.

Turning, he looked at Rachel, smiling in appreciation of her thoughtfulness. "Thank you. It looks like it'll be comfortable to wear while she's recovering. If you have any more like this at your shop, put them aside and one of us will come in and pick them up once we get her home."

He'd love having Emma wear something he'd bought, especially something that would make her comfortable while she recovered.

Leaning back against Boone, Rachel smiled. "Sure. I'll put some things aside tomorrow. Come in whenever you're ready."

After getting Emma some ginger ale, Hunter moved away, letting the conversation flow around him while he sipped his coffee.

He knew that his friends came by because they were curious about Emma, and how he and Remington responded to her, but the way Emma fit in with the others surprised him.

Not long after Rachel, Boone, and Chase left, Nat came through the door with her husbands, Jake Langley and Hoyt Campbell.

Nat greeted Hunter and Remington and made a beeline for Emma. "Hi. I'm Nat. We brought meatloaf and mashed potatoes for dinner. Apple pie for dessert." She glanced at Hunter and Remington, clearly displeased. "The nurses have their panties in a bunch about all the visitors you're getting today. You'd think they'd know us by now. When someone from Desire's here, we're *all* here."

She looked over her shoulder as the nurse came in, not bothering to lower her voice. "They don't realize we have to save you from their food. Besides, we're all dying of curiosity to meet you."

Jake shook his head and handed one of the bags he carried to Hunter. "Easy, Nat. She just had surgery and is probably on pain medication. Let's get this food sorted out. I'm starving."

Emma smiled tiredly. "You're going to eat with us? That's wonderful. Everyone's been so nice."

"We're all wonderful people. The best." Nat grinned. "And very modest. You'll love us. I promise."

Emma's laugh ended with a gasp and had Hunter setting the bag down and rushing to her side, feeling helpless that she was in pain.

Nat slapped a hand to her mouth, instantly contrite. "I'm so sorry. I wasn't thinking."

"No. It's fine." Emma's grip on Hunter's hand told him it wasn't. "I needed a good laugh. You're all so friendly."

Jake smiled gently as he began to unpack the bags, filling the room with the delicious smells of Gracie's husbands' cooking. "It must have been very scary to be in that position, and to be in the hospital surrounded by strangers. We just want you to know that you have people around who you can call on."

Hoyt stepped forward and introduced himself. "I'd be willing to bet that you've got a bunch of phone numbers since you got here."

"I have." Emma leaned against Hunter, letting him take her weight.

Hunter loved being able to support her and would have gladly spent the night holding her.

The nurse eyed each of them in disapproval. "Miss Smith needs to rest."

Hunter turned to glare at her. "Which she will as soon as she has her dinner and one of those pain pills that you're so stingy with."

Remington slid Emma's bed tray into place, glancing up at the nurse as he arranged her dinner on it. "We'll be staying the night."

"No. You won't."

Remington's slow smile was one that Hunter knew well, a smile so cold and icy that the nurse immediately backed down. "We'll just see about that. Call Dr. Hansen."

The nurse left in a huff.

As soon as the door closed behind her, Hoyt chuckled. "The people who live in Desire never fail to surprise me."

Nat snuck a glance at him. "You live there now, too. Get used to it."

Jake lifted his hand, and Nat immediately moved to his side and put her hand in his. "He will. We still have a lot to get used to."

Hunter watched Emma eat, noticing the way she surreptitiously watched Nat interact with Jake and Hoyt.

She seemed intrigued, as she had with Clay, Rio, and Jesse, as well as with Boone, Chase, and Rachel.

He watched the way Jake and Hoyt hovered over Nat as they ate.

The same way Chase and Boone had stayed close to Rachel, and the way Clay and Rio surrounded Jesse and watched her possessively.

Chilled at the reminder of what he couldn't have, he watched Emma eat, determined that she make up for not finishing her lunch.

Realizing that he and Remington stood on either side of Emma, each keeping an eye on her in case she needed them, Hunter stiffened and started to move away, stopping abruptly when he realized that it would only be natural to stay close to her.

She might need something and would only come to either him or Remington for it.

They'd been the only ones she'd allowed to see her weakness and her pain.

His chest swelled at the thought.

He knew it would only last temporarily, but it felt good to have a woman to care for.

It might be the only chance they ever got, and he planned to savor every minute of it.

Chapter Seven

Surrounded by pillows, Emma got her first look at Desire from the backseat of Hunter and Remington's truck.

It was a warm day, and with the window open, she could smell the riot of flowers already blooming in flower boxes on both sides of the street.

It appeared that every business in town had flowers planted outside and that the residents took great pride in their town.

Everything appeared bright and clean—without even the smallest piece of trash to litter the sidewalk, despite the heavy foot traffic.

"It's beautiful here! Busy, too. You know, I didn't think it would be so busy."

People bustled along the sidewalks on Main Street, most carrying shopping bags.

What surprised her the most was that almost everyone she saw had smiles on their faces.

Remington turned in the passenger seat. "It's Saturday. We've had a lot of new businesses open here, and the weekends are usually busy. It slows down a lot during the week."

Aware of Hunter's sharp glance in the rearview mirror, Emma focused her attention on Remington. "Everyone looks so happy. They look like they're on vacation."

Hunter spoke for the first time since leaving the hospital. "People come to Desire to live out fantasies. Living out fantasies makes people happy. Buying clothing, perfumes, and sex toys to live out those fantasies makes people happy, too."

"I can imagine." She watched his eyes in the mirror. "You live here. Why are you so damned grumpy? What fantasy do you have that you're not living out?"

Hunter's eyes narrowed as they met hers in the mirror again. "None of your business."

Remington shot a glance at his brother as he turned back to face forward again. "Some fantasies are just that—fantasies."

Intrigued, she wanted to question him, the flash of pain she'd seen in his eyes and her own attraction to him tempting her to help him fulfill his wildest desires.

A twinge of pain had her adjusting the seatbelt, and she decided to shelve the subject for another time. "Are there any places to eat, other than the diner and hotel restaurant?"

"No." Hunter glanced at her as he stopped for a light. "We won't let any chains come here, and the two restaurants are all we need. We used to have a bakery and an ice cream store, but they're gone now."

Emma smiled at the arrogance in his tone. "You can't really keep chains out."

Hunter glanced at her again, lifting a brow. "Of course we can. The longtime residents of Desire own every inch of this town. There were a few properties that ended up in other people's hands, but we're gradually getting them back. That's how the founding fathers wanted it. Only the people who live here can own any of the property, and no one opens a business here without our approval."

Emma's jaw dropped. "You're kidding. What do you do, get together at the town hall and vote?"

Remington turned in his seat to grin at her. "The sheriff's office, actually." His gaze lowered to her breasts, settling there long enough to make her nipples bead, before it slid lower to wear she held the seat belt away from her body. "You okay?"

"I'm fine. Thank you. How much farther?" She really wanted to get out and stretch her legs, and she was anxious to see her new, albeit temporary home.

"We're almost there." Remington reached out to touch her knee, drawing his hand back with a curse. "Sorry."

"Don't be. I like when you touch me." She didn't know why they'd avoided touching her for the last two days, but it hurt.

Remington stilled, glancing at Hunter before turning to look out the windshield again. "Don't say things like that."

Emma shrugged, fascinated by her first look at Desire. "I don't see the need to play coy. You and Hunter fascinate me, and I'm very attracted to both of you. It's been giving me some very erotic dreams. You both stopped touching me, though, and it's irritating. I thought you liked me."

Hunter's eyes narrowed as they met hers in the mirror. "Do you *always* blurt out what you're thinking?"

"Not always." Smiling, she wrinkled her nose at him. "Just most of the time."

Once they got to the end of the long street, they made a left turn, and about a quarter-mile later, a right, pulling into a driveway.

Frowning, Emma looked around. "Where's my car?"

Remington turned to her, pointing to the attached two-car garage. "It's in the garage. We knew you wouldn't be able to drive it for a while. We'll get your stuff out of it later."

Nodding, she stared up at the large, two-story house, finding only the large front porch appealing.

The grayish brick house had a cold, dark feeling about it, one that made her shiver.

She'd expected something different. Something warmer. Rustic.

Something with personality.

Although everything looked new and of the best quality, it looked stark and cold.

No landscaping. No flowers. No color at all.

The lack of personality and warmth made her sad.

Hunter got out without a word and began to gather her luggage and the bags of gifts Jesse and Rachel had brought her.

Remington got out and reached for her. "So, what do you think?"

Holding on to his forearms, she held herself stiffly as he eased her from the truck. "It's beautiful, but I don't understand why you don't live here."

"We prefer our house."

She looked around, but saw only a large shed in the back and off to the right. "Where's that?"

Remington bent to lift her, frowning when she shook her head and pushed at him. "On the other side in the back. What's wrong? I won't hurt you. I just want to carry you inside."

Surprised when he picked her up anyway, she gasped and automatically pressed a hand protectively over her incision. Thankful that he'd caught the soft cotton dress behind her thighs when he lifted her, she breathed a sigh of relief that nothing showed.

"I want to walk." Holding on to his shoulder, Emma lifted her face to the sun. "It feels great to be outside. It's hot today. Don't look at me that way. You heard the doctor say that he wants me to walk."

Gathering her things, Hunter started for the house. "Carry her anyway. She's gotta be tired and in pain from the ride. I'll go get some lunch and pick up the nightgowns Rachel put aside for her. When I get back, she can eat and take another pain pill, and then it's straight to bed."

Emma gritted her teeth. "I want to walk. I don't feel like going to bed, and I'll take a damned pain pill when I need one. You're my landlords, not my doctor, and certainly not my keepers."

Remington smiled. "You're probably restless and bored, but we can't let you do something that's gonna delay your recovery. You're upset. You're probably tired. The house is fully furnished so you've got plenty of places to sit and rest."

"Goody."

Remington shot her a look, raising a brow at her sarcasm. "You must be *really* tired and in pain." He went through the front door and made a right to the living room.

"No, I'm just being bitchy." Even though it felt wonderful to be in his arms, she couldn't let them treat her like an invalid. "Remington, please. Put me down."

With a smile, he placed her gently on the sofa. "There you go, darlin'. Now just stay put and I'll be right back."

As soon as he disappeared into the next room, one she assumed to be the kitchen, Emma sat up. She'd go crazy if she didn't move.

Getting up proved more difficult than she'd expected, but she knew that the more she moved, the better.

Sitting and lying around for days had made her stiff and sore.

Following the direction Remington had gone, Emma passed a staircase and went through a wide doorway, and as she'd expected, found herself in a large kitchen.

The sun coming through the large windows over the kitchen table made the white cabinets and stainless steel appliances gleam.

The warm feel of the large kitchen made her smile, and she knew she could gladly spend hours cooking in it.

Walking farther into the room, she ran her hand over the large granite island, taking in the enormous amount of countertop. Immediately picturing herself using the six-burner stove and double ovens, she moved across the room and opened the refrigerator, surprised to find it stocked with milk and juices.

"What the hell are you doing up?"

Turning at the sound of Hunter's deep voice, Emma smiled. "Admiring your gorgeous kitchen—temporarily *my* gorgeous kitchen. Thanks for stocking the refrigerator with juices. I need to get to the grocery store, though. I'd better start a grocery list. Hunter, did you bring my purse?"

"Yes. Sit down and I'll get it for you." Hunter disappeared into the living room and reappeared within seconds. Placing her purse on the counter, he stared into her eyes. "I put your pain medicine over there by the sink."

She patted his hand, trying not to show any signs of hurt when he pulled his hand away. "I don't need my pain medicine, Hunter. I'm fine. I want paper and pen to make a grocery list. That reminds me. I have to go to the bank. The doctor doesn't want me to drive, and I hate to put you to any more trouble, but can one of you take me to the bank and to the grocery store?"

Remington sighed and led her to one of the stools. "I don't think that's a good idea. You just got out of the hospital. You shouldn't be out walking around."

Digging through her large purse for the pad of paper she kept there, she glanced up at both of them. "Don't give me those *I'm putting my foot down* looks. They won't work with me."

Finding the pad of paper and a pen, she laid both on the large counter. "Look, I appreciate all that you've done for me, but I have things I need to do."

"All you have to do right now is rest and recover."

"Hunter, I need money to live." Noticing the way he stiffened, she smiled sadly and shook her head. "No. Don't look at me like that. I'm not asking you for money. I have my own, but I need to go to the bank to cash a check. Jeez, what kind of women do you hang around with?"

Crossing his arms over his chest, Hunter eyed her in frustration. "Ones who are a hell of a lot less trouble than you are. Don't blame me for looking suspicious. More than one woman has made a play for our money. Write a check to me and I'll cash it. Make out a list of the things you need and I'll pick them up for you."

"You're rich?"

Hunter glared at her. "Like you didn't know."

Insulted, Emma shot to her feet but, with sudden insight, understood the hurt behind his anger.

She was also beginning to understand that they used anger and coldness to keep others at a distance.

If they didn't let anyone close, no one could hurt them.

She had an overwhelming desire to get closer.

Remington cursed and rushed forward, gripping her arms and settling her back onto the stool. "Damn it, Emma. Don't move like that."

Hunter dropped his hands, the pain in his eyes ripping her heart to shreds. "You okay?"

Emma nodded, her anger melting away. "I'm fine, rich man. I really want to go out."

"Not gonna happen." Hunter's eyes narrowed, the dare in them as unmistakable as the pure male interest. "Make your list and I'll cash a check for you. Hurry up. I have things to do, including getting you something to eat."

Seeing through the anger, Emma hid a smile. "I want to go."

Hunter's brow went up. "No."

"Fine." Emma suspected that she'd have to choose her battles, and decided to concede this one.

She didn't feel like walking through a supermarket anyway but had no intention of letting him know that.

"Fine. I'll make a list and write you a check." She tapped her pen on the pad of paper. "Just don't plan on winning all the time."

Hunter's eyes narrowed again, a small smile playing at his lips. "We'll see."

Emma gulped, stunned at the answering desire that tightened her stomach and made her incision sting. "It'll take a few minutes for me to get everything together."

A flash of amusement glittered in Hunter's eyes. "Take your time. I'll go get lunch and do the rest while you're lying down after you finish eating."

"Fine." Emma stood, immediately tripping on one of the legs of the stool.

With a cry, she threw her hands out to break her fall, terrified that she'd rip her stitches open when she landed.

She didn't know how he did it, but Remington moved like lightning and caught her.

Cursing, he lifted her against him with a gentleness that was in direct contrast to his cold expression and carried her past a scowling Hunter and straight back into the living room to the sofa. "Easy. Damn it, Emma. I hope like hell you didn't rip your stitches out."

Shaking in reaction, Emma gripped his shirt, pressing her other hand to her bandage. "Thank God you caught me. Thank you." The pull to her stitches hurt like hell, bringing tears to her eyes.

Standing over her, Remington scowled. "What the hell were you thinking—moving like that?"

Emma considered her words, thankful that the pain had started to ease. "Hunter's always scowling at me. I don't know what the hell I ever did to piss him off, but I have no idea why he thinks I'm after his money. It's insulting."

She wanted to bring everything out in the open. She needed to challenge their opinion of her and make them see her for who she was before she could even begin to get close to them. "I'm not going to be judged by what other women have done."

A muscle worked in Hunter's jaw. "You didn't do a damned thing."

Remington knelt next to the sofa, with his brother hovering over him. "Darlin', let me see if you ripped your stitches."

"No!" Shaking a hand, Emma pressed her dress to her thigh. "I can do it."

"No. You can't. You won't be able to see as well as we can." Remington's glare, just as sharp as Hunter's, surprised her. "Hell, Emma, do you think we're going to attack a woman we just brought home from the hospital?"

Cringing at the anger in his tone, Emma shook her head. "Of course not. I'm just not in the habit of baring myself to strangers."

Remington nodded once. "Good policy. But we're not exactly strangers." He reached for the hem of her dress again, sighing when she held it against her thigh. "Emma, I need to see if you ripped your stitches. If you don't let me see, I've got no choice but to take you back to the hospital and let them check."

Embarrassed to be making a big thing about nothing, she shot him a dirty look, lowered her hand, and dropped her head to the armrest. "How would you like it if you had to pull down your jeans so I could look at you?"

Remington smiled, but his eyes remained dark with concern. "Darlin', you can see my cock anytime you want to."

Emma couldn't help but smile. "I want to see what you do if I hold you to that."

Remington's eyes narrowed. "You're awfully brave for a little kitten in a lion's den. Now, behave yourself and let me check you out."

He grimaced when she jolted at the touch of his hand on her thigh. "Please be still."

Hunter hovered, peering over Remington's shoulder. "Easy, Rem. Damn it. Be careful."

Remington lifted the hem of her loose sundress, baring her panties. His breathing hitched as he slid a warm hand over her belly. "I *am* being careful. There's no blood on the gauze. Let me just lift the corner. Damn, baby. You're black and blue." His gaze went to hers. "I didn't realize you'd be so bruised. You're gonna have to really take it easy for a couple of days." He peeled the tape back, wincing at her gasp. "The doctor said that we can take this off tomorrow. If you behave yourself for a couple of days and take it easy, I promise I'll take you to town this week."

He inspected her incision and pushed the tape back into place. "It won't be as busy then, so hopefully you won't get jostled."

Remington's hand slid over her thigh, his gaze on her panties. "Pink panties. One of my weaknesses. Son of a bitch. You're so damned beautiful." With a curse, he rose and turned away, storming out the front door and slamming it behind him.

Blowing out a breath, Hunter covered her again, his eyes unreadable. "Let me get you that paper and pen so you can give me that list."

Before she thought better of it, she gripped his hand. "Hunter, have I done something to upset you and Remington?"

"No, Emma." He pulled her hand from his grasp. "You're just a temptation neither one of us can afford."

* * * *

Hunter was still thinking about that temptation much later that night, hours after she'd turned off her bedroom light.

Leaning back against a post on the small front porch of the guest house he shared with his brother, he stared up at the window of the room where Emma slept.

They'd settled her in the master bedroom hours earlier, and had wanted to stay, but Emma had kicked them out.

They'd reluctantly left to come to their own house in order to give her privacy, but it didn't sit well with him, and he couldn't sleep.

Emma's appearance into their lives sharpened the hunger for a wife like never before.

The screen door to his right opened, and his brother stepped outside, a bottle of beer in each hand.

"Her bed's comfortable. She should get a good night's sleep. Once I figure she's asleep, I'm going over there and crash on the sofa. Someone should be there in case she wakes up."

Hunter accepted one of the bottles from his brother, wishing for something stronger. "I just wish she'd taken a pain pill. I know she's trying not to take them, but she was still sore after tripping over that damned stool leg."

Moving to stand beside him, Remington followed his gaze. "And she insisted on putting the groceries away by herself. God forbid we put something in the wrong place. How the hell was I supposed to know she didn't want the tomatoes in the refrigerator?"

After a long silence, Remington spoke again. "She seems to like the house, especially the kitchen."

Hunter sighed and sipped his beer. "We imagined what we would have done for Mom if she'd been alive. Even if Dad had been able to afford it, he never would have done it for her. Since they found all that oil, we've got plenty of money. Now that the house is done, we don't have a damned thing to spend it on and an empty house that neither one of us will ever live in. Hell, we even got rid of the horses. Something's gotta change, Rem. I don't like not having something to do."

Or having too much time to wish for things they couldn't have.

Light from the bedroom window had him jumping to attention. "She's up. Something's wrong."

Tossing his beer aside, Hunter took off toward the back door of the main house at a dead run, digging into his pocket for the key just as he reached it.

His hand shook so badly he had trouble getting the key into the lock. "Fuck."

"Hurry up. Something could be wrong."

"Don't you think I'm trying? Stop breathing down my fucking neck."

He breathed a sigh of relief when he finally managed to open the door and rush inside.

Without pausing to turn on the lights, he raced to the stairway with Remington close behind. Not wanting to run into Emma, he hit the light switch as he ran past it. "Emma!"

He took the stairs two at a time, reaching the top just as Emma screamed.

With his heart in his throat, he raced into the master bedroom, the sight that greeted him ripping his heart to shreds.

Emma stood pale and shaking beside the closet door, her eyes glimmering with tears. Wrapping her arms around herself, she took a shuddering breath on a sob. "Christ, you scared the hell out of me!"

Hunter swallowed heavily, the terror and tears in her eyes like an image straight out of his nightmares.

His gaze lowered to her bare legs, inwardly wincing when he noticed that they trembled.

Moving slowly toward her, he reached out a hand with the intention of helping her back to the bed. "I'm sorry, honey. I saw your light go on and thought you might need some help. We were in a hurry to get to you. What happened?"

Remington scrubbed a hand through his hair and went to the bed to straighten the covers. "When you screamed, you scared the hell out of me. Come on. Let's get you back to bed. It's freezing in here, and you're only dressed in a nightgown."

Hunter felt like a pervert for noticing that her beaded nipples poked at the front of her soft nightgown, but he couldn't help it.

Shaking her head, she moved away from him, her slow, cautious movements proof that she was in pain. "I got up to go to the bathroom. I didn't know it was going to cause such a fuss."

Hunter dropped his hand, fighting not to show his hurt at the rejection. "We were just worried about you. You're in pain. Did you take a pain pill before you went to bed?"

Shaking her head, she went into the bathroom, closing the door behind her. "No. I didn't need it."

Hunter bit back a curse, raising his voice to be heard through the door. "Well you sure as hell do now."

Remington's jaw clenched. "I'll go get her pills."

Hunter turned to lean back against the wall, rubbing his burning eyes. "We didn't mean to scare you."

From the other side of the door, he heard nothing. "Emma? You okay?"

"I'm fine, Hunter. Go away."

Hunter realized suddenly that there would be no way he could leave her alone again. Tilting his head back, he stared at the ceiling. "I'm afraid I can't do that."

After several minutes, he heard the sound of water running and then nothing. Straightening when the doorknob turned, he automatically reached out a hand to help her.

To his stunned amazement, she not only took his hand but came close, pressing her face against his chest. "It hurts. When I heard the back door crash open and heard your footsteps, I jumped up and pulled my stitches again."

"I'm sorry, honey." Even without meaning to, he'd managed to hurt her.

"No. It's not your fault." Lifting her face to his, she clung to him. "I was having trouble getting comfortable even before then." Her gaze shifted to Remington's as he came back into the room. "I can't get the pillows in the right position the way Remington did at the hospital."

She took the pain pill Remington offered without an argument, telling Hunter just how much she had to be hurting. Handing the glass of water back to Remington, she turned and started back toward the bed.

Hunter caught her arm, wrapping an arm around her to support her and helped her lie back, trying not to notice how smooth and soft her skin was as he caught her legs behind her knees and carefully eased them into the bed. Staring down at her while Remington arranged the covers around her, Hunter made a decision that he knew would mean a sleepless night. "I'll stay with her."

Remington surprised him by sitting at the edge of the bed and removing his boots. "We both will. Come on, baby doll. Let's get you propped up the way you'll be comfortable, and I'll rub your back until the pain pill kicks in. We've got this down pat. You'll be asleep in no time."

Hunter went around to the other side of the bed and removed his own boots. "At least *you'll* be able to sleep."

Chapter Eight

Humming to the song on the radio, Emma stirred first one pot of chicken and dumplings and then the other, checking the index cards again to make sure she'd followed both recipes exactly.

She swung her hips as far as she could without pulling her stitches, the freedom to move and the anticipation of seeing Hunter and Remington again putting her in a great mood.

She couldn't remember a time she'd looked forward to each day the way she had since she'd met them.

She just hoped they liked her cooking.

Gracie's chicken and dumplings had been excellent, but she suspected that two of the recipes she had were better.

Both were as good as she'd remembered, but she'd already decided which one would go into her new cookbook.

She just wanted Hunter and Remington's opinion to make sure.

The sound of the back door opening had her spinning in that direction, wincing at the pull to her stitches.

She hadn't seen either man since the night before. After falling into a deep sleep snug between them, she'd overslept and they'd been gone when she woke.

Seeing them, looking so masculine in their usual T-shirts and well-worn jeans, made her heart race and brought back the memory of how their bodies felt pressed against hers.

Something told her that making love with either one of them would change her life forever.

"What the hell do you think you're doing?" Hunter crossed to her in three strides, yanking the spoon out of her hand and jerking her back to the present.

Blinking, Emma pressed her hands to his chest, smiling at the flash of surprise in his eyes and his sharp intake of breath. "Cooking. Are you hungry? I could sure use your opinion." She reached for the spoon he held, frowning when he pulled it out of her reach.

Remington went to the stove, sliding a hand over her shoulder as he passed her. "This smells good, but why are you cooking? You knew we'd be back with lunch." Smiling, he reached out to touch her hair, which she'd pulled back into a ponytail, but yanked his hand back at the last instant. "You overslept and missed breakfast, but you had to know that we'd be back with your lunch."

"I didn't miss breakfast. I had some yogurt and fruit."

Lifting her chin, Hunter studied her features. "You still look tired."

"Gee, thanks." Holding out her hand for the large spoon, she raised a brow until he narrowed his eyes and handed it back to her. "I got enough sleep. I overslept, remember? I'm bored, and I have a lot to do to get this book ready. I've finally got the time to try out recipes, compare them, and decide which ones should go in my book. This kitchen is a dream."

Remington leaned back against the counter, looking right at home. "How many cookbooks have you written?"

"Three." After stirring the contents of both pots, Emma set the spoon aside and moved around Remington to a cabinet for some bowls. "Can you try these for me? I really want your honest opinions."

The sound that Hunter made sounded suspiciously like a growl. "I'll get the damned bowls. Sit down before you fall down!"

Emma couldn't help but notice that his gaze kept lowering to her breasts, making them swell and her nipples tingle.

She'd worn a turquoise, short-sleeved button-down shirt and had impulsively left the top three buttons unbuttoned.

The long gray cotton skirt she wore with it had softened with repeated washings, the T-shirt-like material soft against her skin and comfortable against her healing incision.

She moved around the kitchen barefoot, the tiles cool despite the warm day.

Waiting until Hunter lifted his gaze again, she smiled to let him know she realized what he was doing. Sliding a hand up his chest to his shoulders, she leaned closer, breathing in his clean, masculine scent. "You don't have to be embarrassed that you're looking at me. I like it."

His eyes flashed and narrowed, a look that made her regret that she hadn't fully recovered yet. "Damn it, Emma! You're almost spilling out of that top."

Fluttering her lashes, she ran her fingertips over the upper curve of her breast. "You should be so lucky."

Smiling, she turned back to the cabinet to retrieve the bowls, acutely aware of Remington's interest in her exchange with Hunter. "Sit down. You're both hovering."

Bracing a hand on the countertop, Hunter bent until his face was level with hers, his eyes flashing with anger and something else—something that made her heart beat faster. "I said I would get the fucking bowls. Now, either go sit down, or I'll carry you to bed and make you stay there."

Delighted that he wasn't as immune to her as he pretended to be, Emma leaned closer until his warm breath caressed her lips. "Yeah? And just how would you keep me there?"

A dead silence followed, one filled with sexual tension.

A flash of hunger and challenge came and went in Hunter's eyes, the heat in it breathtaking.

He looked as if he wanted to say something, but it lasted only a heartbeat before his eyes went flat and cold again and he straightened. "Sit down."

Irritated that he'd closed her out so easily, Emma smiled politely, inwardly pleased when his jaw clenched. "I appreciate all that you've done for me, but I'm *not* your responsibility."

Remington's eyes went just as cold, and with a muffled curse, he yanked the cupboard door open. "The hell you're not." He glared at her as he took bowls from the cupboard. "You don't have anyone else to take care of you. We're the ones who found you."

"Finders keepers, huh?"

"For now at least." Remington frowned when she took the bowls from him. "How are you feeling?"

"Better. The bed was very comfortable, and I slept like a log between the two of you. I don't think I've ever felt so warm and safe before, especially sleeping in a new place. Thanks for staying with me. It helped to be propped against you." Filling two bowls from one of the pots, she gestured toward the refrigerator. "Get yourself something to drink and sit down. I made some sweet tea this morning, and I saw beer in there."

Hunter's eyes narrowed again. "Been a busy little thing this morning, haven't you?" He yanked the cupboard open with far more force than necessary and slammed the glasses on the counter.

"Yep." She set both bowls on the island and went back to fill two more from the other pot. "Sorry you have to sit at the island. I'm organizing recipes on the kitchen table."

Turning with the bowls, she placed one in front of each of them, along with spoons and napkins.

"I don't remember if I thanked you for bringing in all of my pots and pans and all the dishes."

"You're not supposed to be lifting anything. Hey! You didn't pick up those pots when they were full, did you?"

"Nope. I had to add water a little at a time. I'm not stupid, and I want to recover as soon as possible. Eat. I'm dying to know what you think."

With a grunt, Remington dug into the first bowl. "Why do you travel with a box full of dishes and silverware?"

Hunter pushed the first bowl aside and dug into the other. "And how the hell did you get into writing cookbooks?"

Emma shrugged. "When I got divorced—"

Both men lifted their heads at the same time, their eyes wide.

Remington dropped his spoon into his bowl. "You were married?"

"Yes."

"For how long?"

"I left him after three days. I got an annulment."

"What?" Remington glanced at Hunter, who just stared.

Emma sighed, reluctant to talk about it, but not wanting to hide anything from them. "I married him on Friday, and by Monday, I was at a lawyer's office. After our wedding night, he left, supposedly for a bachelor party that his friends had organized since we got married on a whim. He cheated on me twice over the weekend—not with strippers—with his ex-girlfriends. I must have been a hell of a shitty lay."

She couldn't forget the humiliation, nor would she ever forget the sense of failure. "His excuse for cheating on me was that he was just saying good-bye to them. He spent Saturday night with one of them and Sunday night with the other. When I got back from the lawyer's office, he'd emptied the apartment and moved in with one of them."

Hunter's jaw clenched. "How long ago was this?"

Emma shrugged and turned back to stir the contents of both pots, no longer hungry. She took her time with it and turned off the burners, caught up in memories she wanted to forget.

"About five years ago. I'd just turned twenty-one when I married him. Anyway, I'd met him because he was my boss's son. I worked as a secretary for an accounting firm. Naturally, after we split up, he went to his father and talked him into firing me. So, since he'd given up the apartment, and I'd already moved out of mine, I ended up with no job and no place to live. I only had a bag of clothes and my car. I lived in my car for months, taking jobs wherever I could get them, usually working in a kitchen washing dishes or waiting tables."

"And that's how you started collecting recipes?" Although Remington kept his voice low and even, the underlying cold steel in it and the hard glint in his eyes made his anger clear.

Emma nodded. "I used to watch the cooks and learned how to cook from them. When I saved enough money, I started driving south to a warmer climate. Living in my car in the middle of winter in Missouri was no fun. I worked for a while and then quit. Drove a little farther south and then worked again. I bought dishes in second-hand stores, but I had to save a long time for the good cookware. It was cheaper to make a meal than to buy one. I experimented with recipes and made them my own."

Remington shared a look with Hunter. "Don't you have any family?"

She smiled at his comforting tone. "No. I've been on my own since I was sixteen. My mom had remarried, and her new husband…made a pass at me. She was too high to care, so I left and never looked back. Donny and I lived together for several months before we got married."

Hunter looked ready to spit nails. "Where did you live before then—when you first left home?"

Emma smiled at the memory. "At the high school. The janitor used to let me sneak back in after school and I stayed in the girl's locker room. There were showers, and the food was cheap. I worked in restaurants when I could, and by the time I graduated, I'd saved up enough for a used car. When I got the job in the law office right after graduating, I stayed in a low-rent apartment. That's when I started experimenting with cooking and with the recipes I'd gathered. When Donny and I got serious—well, when *I* got serious, he never was—I moved in with him. I wanted…" Irritated that a sob escaped, she swallowed heavily before continuing. "I wanted to be part of a family—a *real* family. We lived together for about six months before we got married."

Her sob knotted Remington's stomach.

He wanted to throw something, but instead, he listened, struggling to keep his voice low and soothing. "So what happened then?" He breathed a sigh of relief when she turned to face them again—until he saw the tears in her eyes.

Her smile looked forced. "By then I'd bought a nicer car. I lived in it until I got another job. Cheap motel rooms. Another move farther south. Another job. Another motel room."

Hunter rose to his feet as if too restless to sit still. "So how did you get into writing cookbooks?"

Emma turned, her smile genuine. "I started giving recipes in exchange for other recipes. One of my bosses urged me to put them in a book. I went to the library and did some research on writing cookbooks and saw how they were written. Bought a cheap camera. I started collecting colorful platters, plates, and bowls from second-hand stores. It took me over a year to put my first book together, and to my surprise, it sold. *Really* sold."

Shrugging, she picked up the glass of sweet tea that Hunter had poured for her. "I had enough recipes for the next, so I put that one together. To my shock, it sold even more." Her impish grin settled something inside Remington, showing him clearly exactly the kind of woman he wanted in his life.

"I bought a better car."

Remington studied her features, pleased to see that, despite what she'd been through, she didn't seem bitter. "Why haven't you settled somewhere?"

She shrugged again. "I've been moving around collecting recipes, and it's been fun. I guess I never found a place I wanted to stay. A few months is about it for me. Don't worry. I won't be a permanent tenant. Now, tell me which one of those you liked the best and why. Do you want any more?"

Remington shared another look with Hunter, amused at another of Emma's quick subject changes, but his heart ached for her.

Sitting back, he rubbed his stomach and smiled, going along with her obvious effort to lighten the mood. "Both are better than Gracie's. If you tell her that, though, I'll deny it. You were right about the pepper." He pointed to the bowl on his right. "I like this one. As a matter of fact, I'm going to have another bowl."

He watched her jot down notes on the recipe cards, smiling at Hunter's curt answer.

"That one." Hunter pointed to the same one.

With a heartfelt sigh, Emma looked up from her note cards. "Why?"

"Because it's better."

"That's not much of an opinion."

"It's the only one I've got. It tastes better. I sure as hell don't know why."

Enjoying watching them together, Remington dug into his food and had just bit into a large bite of chicken when she finished with her cards and straightened.

"I know that you said that the two of you would never marry, but if you did, would marry the same woman?"

Remington covered his mouth to keep chicken from spewing everywhere while Hunter just stared at her as if she spoke a foreign language. Swallowing heavily, Remington reached for his tea and took a healthy swallow. "What?"

Emma helped herself to a bowlful from the pot on the left, the one that he and Hunter had chosen as the best tasting. "I mean, what if one of you fall for a woman the other doesn't like? How do you know if you want to share a woman? How the hell do you handle something like that?"

Hunter sipped his tea, hesitating before answering. "We share women, but neither one of us will ever marry."

Setting the bowl on the counter across from them, she moved carefully to slide onto the stool. "You said that before. Why not?"

After a long pause, Hunter sighed and turned away again. "We're not the type."

Watching Emma, Remington wished for the hundredth time that things could have been different.

He could spend hours nibbling at her full lips, the nights of staring at them while she slept in the hospital conjuring erotic dreams he could have lived without.

Scooping up a spoonful, she frowned. "You're not? I would say my ex-husband wasn't the type, but you seem so different. He cheats. I can't imagine either one of you doing something like that, but I'm obviously not a good judge of character. Tell me, why don't you think you're the type?"

Fisting his hands at his sides, Hunter gathered his bowls and took them to the sink, his movements slow and careful—too careful. "Remington and I were raised in a violent home and carry that inside us. Leave it at that."

Stunned, Emma gaped at him. "What kind of violence? How bad was it?"

"The worst. Our father beat our mother on a regular basis."

Emma frowned, secure in the knowledge that she couldn't have misjudged them *that* much. "Are you trying to convince me that you and Remington beat women?"

With a hand fisted on the counter on either side of the sink, Hunter bowed his head, the muscles in his back tight. "Of course not, because we avoid situations where it might become an issue."

Intrigued, she scooped up the last dumpling and watched him. "How do you do that?"

Glancing over his shoulder at her, he surprised her by starting to wash the dishes. "We don't allow ourselves to be alone with a woman."

Smiling, Emma dropped her spoon into her bowl and reached for her iced tea. "You're alone with me now."

Hunter's eyes narrowed. "Not for long. We've got work to do. We just came to check on you since you were still sleeping when we brought breakfast."

"You checked on me?"

Hunter's slow smile stole her breath, mostly because it was a genuine smile, filled with affection. "Covered you up. You know, you have a habit of kicking off the covers. I like sleeping in a cold room, too, but you get cold because you have a bad habit of kicking off your covers."

Emma grinned and leaned forward. "*You* could keep me warm."

Remington cursed and grabbed his own dishes. "You're playing with fire, Emma. I understand that you want to flirt, but we're not the type of lovers you need."

Watching his butt as he began to dry the dishes, Emma raised the glass to her mouth again. "Seems you two aren't the type for much at all."

"Careful." Hunter's voice had deepened even more.

Ignoring the threat in his tone, Emma got down from her stool and picked up her bowl and spoon, her appetite gone. "So the two of you are celibate?"

As she approached the sink, Hunter turned, taking her bowl and spoon from her. "Not hardly. Just because I can't have a woman in my life doesn't mean I'm willing to give up sex."

Glancing from Hunter to Remington and back again, she lowered her voice to a husky whisper. "So how do you take a woman?"

"Together." Remington's gaze raked over her, his voice just as low and intimate. "We fuck women *together*. A cock in her pussy and a cock in her ass. Hands everywhere. She never knows where the next caress will be."

He eyed her nipples pointedly, making them tingle and bead so tightly that she had to fight the urge to cover them. "The next pinch."

Hunter turned and leaned back against the counter, the erotic threat in his eyes drawing her in. "A nice firm smack on the ass." His eyes narrowed. "The inner thigh."

Emma's bottom clenched in response, the mental image of being naked between them almost more than she could stand. She hadn't had sex in years. She hadn't wanted to.

It seemed now that it was all she could think about.

Raising a brow, she looked at each of them, smiling at the thought of having their undivided attention in such a primitive way. She had no doubt that they would be intensely sexual lovers, a far cry from anything she'd experienced. "So you *do* hit them, but not to hurt them?"

Remington sighed and dried his hands. "A nice smack on the ass is a good way to teach a woman to behave and remind her who's in charge."

Emma blinked at that, hardly believing that a man would say such a thing. "Excuse me. Did you say *teach a woman to behave*?"

Remington glanced at his brother. "Women are too soft and weak to protect themselves. They're too fucking fragile and need to know what's expected of them so their men can protect them."

Emma sensed a story there, but guessed that in their present moods, neither wanted to discuss it. "If you're not celibate, and you don't allow yourself to be alone with a woman, how can you have sex—and don't tell me together."

Remington turned, his big body barely touching hers as he braced a hand on either side of the counter, forcing her back against it. Bending slightly to stare into her eyes, he smiled, a smile of pure sexual intent. "We fuck them in the club with other people watching to make sure we don't go too far."

His voice lowered, filled with self-disgust. "We give them more pleasure than an innocent like you could imagine. Nothing is off-limits. We take their mouths. Their pussies. Their asses." Leaning closer, he lowered his voice to a near whisper, his attempt to scare her off only drawing her in even more.

"Their breasts are bare. Smooth. Soft, but firm. Vulnerable for whatever we decide to do. Not an inch of a woman's body escapes our attention."

Emma sucked in a breath, and then another, every erogenous zone in her body screaming for attention. She had to swallow heavily before speaking, her mouth dry. "And what would you do?" Inwardly wincing at the breathlessness in her voice, Emma stiffened and leaned back.

The breathlessness in her voice seemed to both arouse and anger Remington. He didn't let her put any distance between them, leaning closer until only a breath separated them, his eyes hard and cold with a hunger that made her heart beat faster.

"Tease them. Caress them. Your nipples bead all the time so I assume they're very sensitive. I would touch you everywhere except your nipples until you go wild with frustration."

He leaned back slightly, just far enough to stare down at her breasts before holding her gaze with his hooded one while he reached out to unbutton another button. "Until your nipples ached and tingled so badly that you'd do anything to get my attention there."

Placing his hand back on the countertop, he leaned over her again. "I'd use my mouth on them. First one." He lowered his gaze to her breasts again. "And then the other. I'd lick them. Suck them. Pinch them."

Emma gulped, wondering if he realized that he no longer spoke about some other woman and had started talking about *her*. "P-pinch them?"

She took a steadying breath that did nothing to steady her. "W-wouldn't that hurt?"

She ached to find out.

Remington lifted a hand, smiling at her gasp, but instead of touching her breast the way she'd anticipated, he toyed with the loose tendrils of hair that had escaped from her ponytail. "Yes. But it would also give pleasure. A *lot* of pleasure."

Struggling to concentrate on their conversation, she pushed at him before she gave in and threw herself at him.

Surprised when he smiled faintly and lifted his hands as if to show her he wouldn't touch her without her permission, she paused. "And you only do this at a club?"

Hunter's gaze sharpened. "A club for men who have a need to dominate a woman."

Emma swallowed again, desperate to understand them, and to understand her own response to them. "So you like to dominate women?"

Remington crossed his arms over his chest and leaned back against the counter, the hunger and challenge in his eyes weakening her knees. "Yes. *Together.*"

His devilish smile, obviously intended to intimidate her, made her even more determined to show only confidence.

"So by dominating them, you mean that you beat them? Hurt them? Ever send anyone to the hospital? Do you cut them? Burn them? Break bones?"

Hunter's mouth dropped. "Christ, you're morbid. Of course not!" Anger flared in his eyes, his entire body tightening with fury. "Hell, what you must think of us. It's just a little erotic pain. Spankings. Nipple clips. We like to be in control, and we fuck them in front of other people so we don't lose that fucking control. God forbid we get carried away."

The misery in his tone had her stepping closer to him.

"Have you ever gotten carried away?" She would bet anything that neither one of them had ever hurt a woman in their lives.

With a sigh, Hunter turned away. "No. We make sure we're never in that kind of situation."

Shaking her head, she thought about their tenderness while taking care of her. "What the hell makes you think that either one of you would hurt a woman?"

Remington's body tensed, a muscle working in his jaw. "Violence is in our blood."

"That's ridiculous. Why would you think that?"

"Because our father was the same way. He liked to be in charge, and once he took a woman of his own, our mother, he used his fists to enforce his authority—until the day he killed her."

Emma gasped, frozen in place.

"Dear God."

She couldn't even begin to understand what they'd gone through.

Determined to confront their opinions of themselves, Emma nodded. "I get it. You think because your father liked to dominate women, and that he was violent, and *you* like to dominate, that you must be violent, too."

Remington nodded once. "Exactly."

Nodding again, Emma glanced at them as she wiped the counter. "So I can understand why you want to avoid me. My mother was a drug addict, so you assume I must have that need inside me as well. Funny that you think that and keep pushing the pain pills."

Remington slapped a hand on the counter. "Damn it! That's not true. We think no such thing."

Blowing out a breath, Hunter scrubbed a hand over his face. "Emma, that's only part of it." He glanced at Remington. "We believed that so strongly that we avoided situations where we might be alone with women—except the women who went to the club. Neither one of us has ever even been on a date. We wouldn't know how to treat you the way you need to be treated, or how to establish the intimacy a relationship requires."

Remington ran a hand through his hair, his eyes hooded. "In short, neither one of us knows the first thing about love. We'd just end up hurting you."

Hunter straightened. "So now that you're feeling better, we'll check on you from time to time, but we won't be around much anymore. You know how to reach us if you need us. You've been through enough. You certainly don't need men like us in your life."

Emma rushed forward, biting back a wince as they started for the door to grip Remington's sleeve. "I'm so sorry for what happened, but you can't actually think you're like him, do you? People are what they choose to be. You're the gentlest men I've ever met."

"You're recovering. Gentleness doesn't last, especially when passion's involved." Turning, Remington covered her hand with his and pulled it away. "We're not about to take any chances."

He pulled away and followed Hunter out the door.

Emma caught the screen before it slammed closed. "Neither one of you is capable of hurting a woman."

Without turning, Remington shook his head. "You don't know us well enough to know that. Stay away from us, Emma, for your own good—and for ours. After what you've been through, you need someone who'll know how to give you what you need."

Chapter Nine

With a heavy heart, Emma sank into one of the seats at the kitchen table, pushing her cards and notebooks aside to drop her head in her hands.

Tears stung her eyes, her heart breaking at Hunter and Remington's opinions of themselves.

They were the most incredible men she'd ever met, and after all they'd done for her, she owed it to them to prove to them just how wonderful they were.

She owed it to herself to show them that she was the woman they needed in their lives—and that they had already given her more than any man ever had.

Too restless to sit, she got up to put the leftovers away, learning a long time ago not to waste food, and finished cleaning the kitchen. By the time she'd wiped the sink, she was exhausted, a sharp reminder that she hadn't yet fully recovered.

She glanced toward the doorway with a smile.

If Hunter and Remington weren't reason enough to try to rush her recovery, she didn't know what would be.

Deciding that the rest of her unpacking could wait until later, she started up the stairs with the intention of lying down for a while, stopping abruptly at the sound of the house phone ringing.

Wondering who could be calling, especially since Hunter and Remington didn't live in the main house, she turned and went back to the kitchen to answer it.

"Hello?"

"Hi, Emma. It's Nat. How are you feeling?"

Grinning, Emma wandered back into the living room, happy to have made some new friends. "Fine, thank you. How did you get this number? I didn't even know the phone was hooked up."

Nat laughed. "I asked Hunter what the phone number was to the house, and when he said the phone hadn't been connected, Jake asked him if he was really going to let you stay there without a phone. Within an hour, Hunter had the phone connected and called to give me the number."

"Oh. Well, it's great to hear from you. It was so nice of you to come visit me in the hospital. I haven't tried all the stuff you and Jesse gave me yet, but I love what I've tried."

"Great. You'll have to come to the store sometime."

Making her way to the stairs, Emma smiled. "I'm looking forward to it. The doctor won't let me drive for a couple of weeks, though. Remington did say that he'd take me to town one day next week."

"Well, lots of people want to meet you, but everyone's aware of what you've been through so they're leaving you alone for a while. Hunter and Remington made it *very* clear to everyone that they want you to rest."

Inwardly wincing, Emma started up the stairs again. "Sorry about that. I'm fine. I promise."

"You sound tired."

"Just a little. I was trying out a recipe and just finished cleaning up. I might have overdone it a little, but don't tell Hunter and Remington. They want me to lie in bed all day. They don't realize that I need to move." She entered her bedroom and crossed her room to the bed, wishing that Hunter and Remington were with her.

Nat giggled. "Your secret's safe with me. You'll learn fast that the women in Desire stick together. We have to because the men do, and they outnumber us."

Frowning again, Emma lowered herself the bed. "Sounds like a war."

Nat laughed softly. "Not quite, but you'll understand when you've been here a while. I don't want to keep you, but the reason I called is because I wanted to know if you needed anything and wondered if it would be all right if I stopped by tomorrow morning to visit. I want to talk to you without Hunter or Remington around. Woman to woman."

Easing back, she tucked one of the pillows under her head. "Sounds ominous."

"Not at all. Believe me, honey, the entire town wants to see them happy, and seeing them with you has given all of us hope."

Frowning again, Emma rolled to her side. "I hope that means that you all approve of me going after them, because that's exactly what I intend to do."

"If you can make them happy, we're all for it." Nat sighed. "We want Hunter and Remington to realize that they're not the men they think they are. I'll explain it all to you when I see you."

"They told me about their father."

After a pregnant pause, Nat blew out a breath. "They did? Well, that's a start at least."

"It was a warning to stay away from them. They said they'd check on me but think it's better if they keep their distance—for my own good."

"And you're going to do what they said?" Nat's disappointment came through loud and clear, her tone incredulous.

Emma smiled to herself, a plan already forming. "Of course. I'm going to give them *exactly* what they asked for. I'm just going to make sure that they realize that's not what they really want."

She only hoped that it didn't backfire on her.

Nat giggled. "Good girl. I can see that you and I are going to get along just fine. We'll talk more tomorrow. If there's anything I can do to help on your mission, just let me know. The men in Desire are more than a handful."

* * * *

Hours later, Emma woke, disoriented, her first thought of Hunter and Remington.

Feeling more rested, she sat up, her fingers closing over the soft throw that had been folded at the foot of her bed when she'd fallen asleep but that now covered her.

Smiling, she rose and folded the throw again.

They'd checked on her and had covered her.

A little thing, but one that solidified her decision to make them see themselves for what kind of men they were.

Two caring men who needed love in their lives as much as she did.

The three of them could be so good together. She just had to show them.

* * * *

When her back door eased open about an hour later, she turned from the oven, smiling at the look of shock on Remington's face. "Hello. Would you like a cookie?"

"Damn, it smells good in here." Remington came forward. "Why the hell are you making cookies?"

Emma shrugged. "Nat's coming tomorrow morning for coffee. I thought it would be nice to have some cookies in the house." Gesturing toward the shiny ovens, she glanced at Hunter as he closed the door behind him, his jaw clenched. "Those double ovens are great. I don't even have to bend to use them. Dinner will be ready in a few minutes."

She stirred the tomato sauce bubbling on the stove before adding pasta to the pot of boiling water. Turning to look at each of them over her shoulder, she smiled again, her heart pounding furiously to find both men watching her. "I hope you're hungry."

A muscle worked in Remington's jaw, and with a glance at Hunter, he shook his head. "We just came to check on you. We just wanted to know if you feel better after your nap, and to see if you want something from the diner. If you already have dinner, we'll just eat there."

"Oh." Emma stirred the pasta and went to the refrigerator to retrieve the salad. "Are you sure? I've got plenty of food. I thought we had an agreement. Meals for use of the house."

Hunter moved closer to the tray of cookies, eyeing them hungrily. "We changed it. We don't need the money, so don't even go there. It's not good for the house to be empty. You're doing us a favor by staying here."

Hiding a smile, Emma set the salad on the island and picked up the spatula, eyeing both of them as she began to transfer the cookies to a cooling rack. "That doesn't sound like a fair arrangement."

Remington took one of the cookies, blowing on it before shoving the entire thing into his mouth. "It's fair. Hey, these are good. We bought milk, didn't we?"

"Forget the damned milk." With a glare at Emma, Hunter grabbed a cookie and turned away. "Come on. Let's go."

Leaning against the island, Emma stared after them.

They'd wanted to stay. She'd seen it in their eyes.

But they hadn't wanted it enough.

It was up to her to show them just what they were missing.

* * * *

Remington took a sip of his beer, looking around the crowded bar before glancing at Hunter. "We're doing the right thing in staying away from her."

Sitting at the table across from him, Hunter nodding, clenching his jaw. "I know that. She's so damned innocent. I shudder to think about what damage we could do to her. She's already been through enough thanks to her family and that asshole she married."

"I can't believe she was married before." Remington realized that he had no right to feel the jealousy that turned his insides, but it was there, and he had to find a way to get rid of it. "The kitchen smelled incredible. I'll bet that dinner she fixed was delicious."

"It was."

Remington looked up at Ace as the sheriff lowered himself into one of the vacant seats at their table. "How the hell do you know that?"

Setting his cup of coffee in front of him, Ace smiled, his eyes dancing with amusement. "I went out there to check on her."

Remington's stomach knotted. "Afraid we'd hurt her?"

A muscle worked in Ace's jaw. "Nope. She's a stranger in town, and I wanted to know a little more about her. I also wanted to give her my number in case she needed to go to the hospital again and you weren't around."

Hunter slid a cold glare in Ace's direction. "If she has to go back to the hospital, we'll take her. What the hell makes you think we won't be around?"

Ace shrugged. "Because you avoid women like Emma like the plague. I stopped at your house, but you weren't there. Heard you stopped here."

Remington inwardly winced. "Do you know everything?"

"Yep." Ace calmly sipped his coffee. "I saw the lights on in the main house and heard a crash so I ran over there. I was afraid Emma had fallen."

"A crash?" Remington jumped to his feet a second before Hunter did, whipping out his cell phone. "What happened? Is she all right?"

Waving them back to their seats, Ace nodded. "She's fine. She was trying to stand on one of the stools to put a serving bowl away and dropped it."

Scrubbing a hand over his face, Remington met Hunter's furious glare, knowing that they were both thinking the same thing.

If she'd belonged to them, she'd have a red ass for pulling such a stunt.

On the heels of that came another thought.

They should have been there.

Feeling as if he'd let her down, Remington dropped to his seat again. "Why the hell was she standing on a stool?"

"Said she didn't want to reach and pull her stitches."

Hunter sipped his beer and slammed the mug on the table. "Damn fool woman."

Ace shrugged. "I cleaned up the glass. She was walking around in bare feet and I was afraid she was going to cut herself. She asked if I'd eaten, and I hadn't. The kitchen smelled incredible, and when she offered me that pasta dish she was making, I couldn't resist. Then I ate all the cookies."

Lifting a brow, Ace eyed each of them in turn. "She said that she'd made enough dinner for the three of you, but you didn't want it. You missed a great meal. The garlic bread—hell, even the salad was delicious. Did you know that she makes her own dressing?"

The fact that he didn't pissed Remington off. "Does Hope know you ate with Emma?"

Ace's lips twitched at the dig. "Of course. She called while I was there and actually talked to Emma. They made plans for next week."

Reaching for his beer again, Remington shook his head. "Emma shouldn't be running around. She's still recovering."

Ace finished his coffee and stood, reaching for his hat. "We're aware of that. Hope won't let her hurt or tire herself. Emma wants to shop for some things but doesn't know her way around. Hope wants to meet her, and my wife is always looking for a reason to shop."

Remington got to his feet, unsurprised that his brother did the same. "Well, I'm glad you checked on her."

Ace smiled slowly. "So am I. The spaghetti and homemade meatballs were delicious. Too bad there's no leftovers. You could have had some and found out for yourself."

Sparing a glance at his brother, Remington nodded and tossed bills on the table. "We should go check on her."

Setting his cup aside, Ace headed for the door. "She went to bed already."

Hunter's eyes hardened. "How do you know that?"

"She was going up when I left her." Pausing at the door, Ace turned. "I have a feeling your tenant is going to cause an uproar."

Remington got an odd feeling in the pit of his stomach. "What kind of uproar?"

Ace shrugged. "She's the talk of the town. Every single man in town in dying to meet her. The only thing holding them back from coming out to the house is your warning to stay away until she's recovered. Once she is, I have a strong suspicion that your driveway is going to look like a parking lot."

Remington didn't want to think about Emma with another man, especially his friends. "You can tell them that it's no use. She's only staying a few months."

Ace lifted a brow, his eyes dancing with amusement. "You know as well as I do that the men in Desire can be pretty persuasive. I have a feeling that whoever claims her will do whatever it takes to get her to stay."

* * * *

Hunter couldn't sleep.

Again.

Standing on the small front porch of the house he shared with his brother, he leaned back against a post and stared at the window of the master bedroom where Emma slept.

He couldn't stop thinking about how good she felt in his arms.

Once he'd gotten into bed with her, he hadn't expected to be able to sleep, but with her warm softness pressed against him, he'd slept better than he had in years.

Ace's words kept playing over and over in his head.

The possibility of having to watch Emma with someone else for the rest of his life made a cold knot form in his stomach, one that wouldn't go away.

He and Remington would have to move away, a choice that became more unappealing by the day.

Finding himself stuck between a rock and a hard place made him even more restless.

He'd worked hard to maintain every aspect of control over his life since his father had killed his mother, but with Emma's arrival, he felt that control slipping away.

He couldn't allow that to happen.

For his own peace of mind, he had no choice.

He had to harden his heart against her and avoid her as much as possible.

Chapter Ten

By the time the sun started to come up over the horizon, Remington had come to the conclusion that staying away from Emma wasn't an option for him.

He'd been awake for hours, and sipping his third cup of coffee, he stared out the window at the main house, picturing Emma curled up in bed, soft and flushed with sleep.

Hunter had been quiet all night, unusually quiet, and hadn't gone to bed until the early morning hours.

Remington suspected it was because his brother couldn't stop thinking about what Ace had said earlier.

The recent marriages in Desire had just made the single men hungry for what made their friends and neighbors so happy.

Hunter and Remington were no different in that, but their hunger to have a woman in their lives, and the chance to have a family—a real family—had been brought to the surface in a way neither one of them could ignore any longer.

The more time Remington spent with Emma, the more he craved what he couldn't have but wanted more every day.

He knew he shouldn't go see her, but the need to check on her outweighed his own need for self-preservation.

He heard his brother moving around and heard the shower start.

Unwilling to explain himself to Hunter, he set his coffee aside and rose, shoving his feet into his boots and heading out the door.

Crossing the yard, he thought he heard male laughter and hurried his steps, jealousy clawing at him.

If someone had spent the night with her, he'd take a great deal of pleasure in knocking him on his ass.

He didn't bother to knock, pushing the door open with enough force to send it slamming back against the wall, his jaw clenched at the thought of catching one of his friends with her.

He stopped abruptly, feeling like a fool as he took in the scene in front of him.

"Oh!" Emma jolted, spilling the coffee she'd been pouring all over her hand.

Jake and Hoyt both cursed and jumped up from their seats at the island and rushed to Emma.

While Hoyt held Emma's hand under cold water, Jake reached for a towel, shooting a glare in Remington's direction.

"Nice entrance, Rem."

Nat hovered over her on the other side of Hoyt. "Are you okay, honey?"

Feeling like a fool, and furious at himself for causing Emma to hurt herself, Remington strode to the sink and tried to push Hoyt aside.

The retired Navy SEAL, however, didn't budge. Raising a brow, Hoyt looked down at Emma, who nodded.

"Thanks, Hoyt. It's feeling better. Go drink your coffee and have another cinnamon roll."

Remington knew his smile was strained as he stared down into Emma's beautiful eyes. "So that's what smells so good. I'm sorry. I didn't mean to startle you. Let me see." He edged closer as Hoyt made way for him.

Nat nodded and smiled at Remington. "Hi, Remington. How are you?"

Remington leaned over Emma, studying the red mark on her hand, still holding it under the cold water. "I was fine until I caused this. How are you?"

"Good."

He looked back at Jake, gritting his teeth at the smug smile on Jake's face, narrowing his gaze when his longtime friend bit into the thick cinnamon roll he held. "What's going on?"

Nat wiped a smear of icing from the corner of Jake's mouth, the act appearing more intimate than the casual gesture warranted. "I came to visit Emma. Jake and Hoyt decided to bring me and come visit you and Hunter while they waited for Emma and me to finish talking."

Hoyt grinned. "We came in to say hello and got sidetracked. This is my third." He lifted his own cinnamon roll and bit into it.

Nat sighed, smiling playfully. "I can't bring them here with me anymore. They're gonna get fat."

Jake's eyes narrowed, raking over his wife in a way that left the usually unflappable Nat red-faced and flustered. "I'll work it off."

Emma turned off the water and wrapped her hand in a towel, watching Nat and Jake, her eyes glimmering with envy. Averting her gaze, she glanced at Remington briefly and smiled. "Have a cinnamon roll, Remington. There's fresh coffee if you'd like some."

Although she looked happy to see him, her tone had a distance to it that set off warning bells.

He needed distance between them, but for her to put it there pissed him off.

Nat pinched off a piece of the cinnamon roll and popped it into her mouth with a moan. "God, this is good. I have to stay away from you. If I get fat, these two will leave me."

"Never." Jake took her hand in his and licked the icing from her fingers. "We'll just have to make sure you work it off, too."

Surprised at how comfortable Emma looked with the others, Remington poured himself a cup of coffee and went to stand next to her at the island. He reached for one of the cinnamon rolls, content to listen to their conversation.

Lowering herself onto a stool, Emma smiled and broke off another piece of the cinnamon roll on her plate. "I'm glad you like them. It's one of the recipes going into my new cookbook."

"It deserves to." Hoyt pushed his plate aside and picked up his coffee. "You're not only beautiful and adorable as hell, but you can cook like a dream. You're going to have a line of suitors out the door."

Nat's eyes narrowed. "Is that a dig?"

Hoyt laughed and wrapped an arm around her, dropping a hard kiss on her lips. "Not at all, baby. You're beautiful and adorable, too, and just contrary enough to keep me on my toes."

Jake rose. "And I don't mind the fact that you only cook when you're upset. I'm more interested in some of your other talents." He glanced at Remington, running his hand over Nat's shoulder. "Hunter home?"

"Yes." Although Remington had seen Jake, Hoyt, and Nat together hundreds of times, he found himself fascinated by Nat's blush and the love and happiness for her two husbands glimmering in her eyes.

Hoyt nodded and finished off his cinnamon roll. "We'll go pop in and see him. You coming?"

"In a minute." Turning his head, he looked down at Emma, who stood stiffly against him, her smile not reaching her eyes.

She looked tired and, to his chagrin, sad.

Touching her elbow, he bent to stare into her eyes as the back door closed behind Jake and Hoyt. "Are you all right?"

Giving him another of those fake smiles that made him want to turn her over his lap, Emma turned away. "I'm fine."

Retrieving the coffee pot, she poured Nat and herself each a fresh cup of coffee. "Jake and Hoyt are probably waiting for you."

He hadn't had any intention of staying, but he bristled at her attempt to get rid of him. Raising a brow, he lowered his voice, giving her his most intimidating look. "You tryin' to get rid of me, baby doll?"

After setting the pot back in place, Emma turned, frowning. "I thought you and Hunter were trying to stay away from me."

Remington went to the coffee pot and poured himself another cup for an excuse to stay a few minutes longer. "We will, but you're still healing. You look tired. Have you been sleeping?"

"Like a log." She sat back at the island, turning her back to him. "Nat, I can't tell you how much your visit means to me."

Nat, who'd been silently watching them, slid a glance at Remington. "I wanted the chance to talk to you some more. You were kind of groggy in the hospital, and I wanted to get to know you better. Everyone wants to meet you, but Hunter and Remington told everyone to leave you alone until you felt better."

"I feel fine." Turning, she sent Remington a dark look.

He met it squarely. "You're not fine. You look exhausted, and I can tell by the way you're moving that you're in pain." He gestured toward the table, covered with pieces of paper, index cards, and notebooks. "You've been working."

"I'm bored." She broke off another piece of her cinnamon roll. "The worst that could happen is that I get a paper cut."

Nat glanced toward the table. "You must have met a lot of interesting people in your travels. You really go around collecting recipes and writing cookbooks?"

Emma smiled and nodded, her eyes sparkling. "Basically. My recipes are for everyday people who don't have a lot of time to cook. Some people will just gladly turn over a recipe, and others require a little persuasion. Once I get a recipe, I have to try it out to make sure it's easy enough that someone can make it without getting frustrated or that it takes too much time. It also has to taste good. I'm trying to find the best-tasting southern favorites."

Nat pinched off another bite of her cinnamon roll. "How do you figure out which recipes you want?"

Emma shrugged. "I go to a lot of diners and smaller restaurants and try different things. I've found some amazing recipes that way."

Nat frowned. "You travel alone?"

Remington stiffened, for the first time realizing how much danger a woman alone could face. "I don't like that."

Emma waved a hand. "It's none of your business." Smiling at Nat, she broke off another piece of her cinnamon roll. "Yes, alone. I meet a lot of interesting people, though, especially the people who run the small diners. I get some of my best recipes from them."

Sipping his coffee, Remington patted her hand. "Honey, I don't think Gracie's gonna give you any recipes. She's very protective of them."

Emma's impish grin stirred his cock. "She will."

Nat shook her head. "I don't know. Gracie's pretty tight-lipped about her recipes, and her husbands won't give up her secrets *or* theirs." Grinning, she glanced at Remington. "You know that Garrett, Drew, and Finn do most of the cooking now."

Sipping her coffee, she turned to Emma. "They're Gracie's husbands. The four of them have been running that diner forever, and they pride themselves on having the best food around."

Emma frowned. "How about the hotel restaurant in town?"

Nat rose and strolled to the window. "That's for when you want to go to a fancier place, and it's much more expensive. They serve meals that you can't get in the diner, and the diner never serves the more elaborate meals you can get at the restaurant." Looking out, she smiled, apparently watching her husbands. "The two co-exist because neither one of them steps on the other's toes."

Emma sipped her coffee, eyeing Nat thoughtfully. "Interesting. I'm going to have to try both of them. Several times."

Remington tried not to think about Emma having dinner in the restaurant with someone else, someone who would eventually want to take her to one of the privacy booths.

Once in the booth, with the curtains closed, they could seduce her. Strip her. Touch her. Make love to her.

Waiters wouldn't intrude, and in fact, wouldn't come into the small enclosure until a button on the table was pressed.

He'd often envisioned taking a woman into one of the booths, but he and Hunter never had.

He could easily imagine taking Emma there, and once the idea took hold, it wouldn't let go.

He found himself more enthralled with everything about her and drawn to her more each day.

He wanted a woman they could spoil rotten. Protect. Love.

He wanted Emma.

It was dangerous—too dangerous—to even contemplate.

But he found he could think of little else.

Emma snuck glances at Remington, wondering what had put such a strange look on his face. She touched his arm, inwardly wincing when he snatched it away as if burned.

His expression closed again, his eyes hard as chips of ice. "I've got to go. If you need something, call my cell."

When the back door slammed behind him, Emma smiled and turned to Nat. "I think I'm getting to him."

Nodding, Nat turned back to look out the window. "They're good men, and they've been unhappy for so long. They really believe they're like their father."

Emma nodded. "I know, and it's bullshit. They're so sweet. So gentle. I hate to see them so unhappy."

Nodding, Nat sighed. "They care too much sometimes. If anyone in Desire is in trouble, they're the first to help."

Pushing her plate aside, Emma lowered herself to one of the stools. "Why can't they see that?"

With a sigh, Nat turned toward the back window. "I don't know. We've all tried to talk to them." Nat waved a hand, looking around the kitchen. "They gutted this house as soon as they got enough money and have spent years redoing it the way their mother would have wanted. It's like a shrine to her. They've never spent the night in this house. No one has. Except you. They blame themselves for not being here when she needed them. Hell, they were barely teenagers and it happened while they were at school, but they blame themselves for her death."

Not wanting to tell her new friend something so personal, Emma didn't mention that they'd spent the night with her. Staring down at her plate, she took a deep breath and let it out slowly. "I'm afraid that I'm falling in love with them."

Nat gasped, spinning and rushing to Emma's side. "That's wonderful!"

Emma took another deep breath, trembling with nerves. "Not so wonderful. Hunter and Remington have both decided to stay away from me. Hell, Hunter's barely speaking to me."

Nat frowned and dropped back onto her stool. "Damn it. Men can be so hardheaded."

Frowning, Emma slowly moved to the window. "Every day that goes by, they get more and more distant. Every day, the hunger in their eyes is a little sharper."

Her breath caught when Hunter looked in her direction, his gaze holding hers for several long seconds before he frowned and turned away.

"Son of a bitch!" Slapping a hand on the counter, Nat jumped up again. "They feel threatened by how much they want you. That's what it is. When you were in the hospital, they were all over you. Because you were hurt, they couldn't do a thing about it, but it's obvious that you're getting better every day."

"Exactly. But I'm not about to pretend to be hurt to get them closer." Grinning, she turned away from her window, went back to the counter, and reached for her coffee cup. "I've never been shy about going for what I want, and if nothing else comes out of this than they realize they can have a woman in their lives, I'll leave happy. They saved my life."

Nat smiled tremulously. "I really want to see them happy, but I don't want to see anyone get hurt."

Neither did Emma. "We're just going to have to see where this goes."

"I can hardly wait to see you married to those two."

Emma's heart lurched when Hunter turned just then, their eyes meeting across the distance. "Don't count your chickens."

Nat looked toward the window again. "I know hunger when I see it."

"I'm sure you do." Emma grinned and stared at her new friend. "Now, I want to know how the hell you handle having two husbands."

Nat sighed and smiled. "I suppose you're going to need some advice to figure out how to handle two men at once. My situation is a little different. It's a long story."

Emma rose again. "I'll put on another pot of coffee."

* * * *

Sitting on the porch of the house he shared with his brother, Hunter glanced at Jake. "Can we get past the small talk to the point of your visit?"

Grinning, Jake leaned back. "Nat wanted to come see Emma, and we thought we'd come along for the ride. We haven't had the chance to talk to you in a while."

"Bullshit." Hunter fought the urge to look toward the house again. "We sat at the club and talked just last week." Irritated at Jake's smug smile, Hunter glanced at Hoyt. "What the hell's going on?"

Hoyt shrugged, his eyes always sharp and moving. "A lot of people—men—in town are asking about Emma. They want to know if you've claimed her. Nobody wants to tangle with either one of you, especially if there's a chance—"

"No." Hunter rose and purposely turned his back to the main house. "We haven't claimed her, and there's not a chance of that happening. We're just watching over her until the doctor releases her. She won't be in Desire more than a few months. We're letting her stay in the main house because she needs a kitchen while she's here to work on her recipes."

Jake brushed a piece of lint from his trousers. "I can find a place in town for her to stay."

"No need." Hunter turned to glance at the house, surprised to see Emma standing at the window.

"There's no reason she can't stay here. The house is just sitting empty."

She just stood there, staring at him as if willing him to come inside.

With her arms wrapped around herself, she looked so sad. So lonely.

Hoyt rose and looked toward the house. "Everyone just wants to make sure you don't have any claim on her. A lot of people want to meet her."

Inwardly cursing for allowing himself to be drawn to her, Hunter turned away again. "She needs rest."

Chuckling, Jake rose to his feet. "Everyone knows what she's been through, Hunter. They're not going to attack her. I'll tell everyone that Emma's available. It'll be up to her to decide whom she wants to see."

Hunter gritted his teeth. "Do whatever the hell you want, but if anybody bothers her, I'm gonna kick their ass."

Chapter Eleven

Hunter walked through the back door of the main house, bracing himself for the sight of Emma.

He'd checked on her each morning and each evening for the past week, his hunger for her growing with each passing day.

She looked better and moved with more fluid grace each time he saw her, the sparkle in her eyes taking his breath away.

The more she recovered, the more he avoided her and the more she consumed his thoughts.

Finding her sitting at the kitchen table surrounding by all the little cards that always seemed to keep her so busy, he sucked in a breath when she lifted her gaze to his.

Her eyes lit up when she saw him, something that never failed to stir him.

"Good morning." Resting her chin on her fist, she raked her gaze over him. "Damn. I love the way you fill out jeans and a T-shirt."

Despite his best effort, Hunter couldn't hold back a smile.

"You know, one of these days that habit of blurting out whatever you're thinking is gonna bite you in the ass."

Getting to her feet, she sauntered closer, her mischievous smile making his cock stir.

"Or I might just bite you in yours."

Raising a brow, he gave her his most intimidating look.

"You like playing with fire, don't you?"

Emma smiled and ran a hand over his chest. "I like a little fire. Don't you?"

Hunter bit back a retort and gestured toward her feet. "Put your shoes on so we can go."

Ignoring her bright smile, he waited for her to slip on her sandals, irritated that the sight of her peach-colored nails aroused him.

He had to take her to the doctor and bring her back home again so he could get the hell away from her.

"Hurry up. We're gonna be late."

* * * *

Understanding him more each day, Emma hid a smile at his gruff tone and hurried toward the truck.

She assumed he wanted her to believe that he avoided her because he wasn't interested, but his eyes told a different story.

He avoided her because he didn't trust himself not to act on his need, and each time she saw him, the tension in the air grew stronger.

One day soon it would erupt.

She couldn't wait.

"Don't run, damn it! You could fall and hurt yourself."

Grinning, Emma turned to him. "You just told me to hurry up."

Gripping her arm, he led her to his truck and jerked the door open. "You really need a keeper."

Holding on to his shoulders as he lifted her into his truck, she raised a brow.

"You volunteering for the job?"

"No." Despite his rough tone, his hands were gentle as he fastened her seat belt.

"Pity." Setting her purse on her lap, she smiled again, pleased that he couldn't seem to take his eyes from her legs. She'd worn shorts because it was a hot day and she'd known they would be going out.

Her decision seemed to be paying off.

"Then it's really none of your business. Is it?"

Hunter straightened, his expression cool.

"No. I guess it isn't."

Emma winced when he slammed the truck door, inwardly smiling again when he got in on the driver's side and glanced at her legs again.

If she had her way, he wouldn't be able to hold out much longer.

* * * *

Hunter paced the waiting room at Dr. Hansen's office, so intently watching the door to the examination rooms that he jolted when his cell phone rang.

Without looking at the display, he moved toward the window and answered.

"Ross."

"Hunter, it's Rem. What did the doctor say?"

Hunter began pacing again. "I don't know. She's still in there."

"What the hell's taking so long?"

"How the hell should I know?" He came to an abrupt halt when the door finally opened and Emma came through, smiling as she headed for the desk. "She just came back. We'll be home shortly."

He pulled out his wallet and started toward the desk, glancing at the receptionist. "How much?"

Emma smiled up at him as she handed over several bills. "You're not my keeper. Remember?"

Biting back a curse, he tucked his wallet away. "What took so long? Is everything okay?"

Accepting the receipt, Emma smiled at the receptionist and turned away. "Everything's fine. On the way home, can you show me where the drugstore is?"

Hunter led her outside, grimacing at the blast of hot air after the cool air-conditioning in the doctor's office. "If you need to go to the drugstore, I'll take you to the drugstore. There's no point in going out again."

Once they were both in the truck, he started the engine and turned the air-conditioner on high before turning to her.

"What did the doctor say? Did he take out your stitches? He didn't. Did he? I knew you weren't ready. I *knew* you were doing too much."

"Hunter."

"That's *it*! You're not doing any more damned cooking until you've healed."

"Hunter!"

"You have to go to the drugstore for an antibiotic because you ripped the damned thing open and got an infection. Didn't you?" He'd damn well tie her to the bed if he had to.

"No. *Hunter*!"

"What?" Whipping his head around, he narrowed his eyes at the amusement dancing in hers. "What's so damned funny?"

"You are." Grinning, Emma kicked her sandals off. "I got my stitches out. Dr. Hansen said that I'm good to go."

"So what took so fucking long?"

Emma shrugged, turning to look out the side window. "We talked."

Irritated that she'd turned away from him, he threw the truck in gear. "What do you need from the drugstore? I'll stop and get it for you."

Turning back to face him, she gave him an enigmatic smile. "Just a prescription."

Suspicious, he glanced at her as he made his way toward the drugstore. "For what?"

"None of your business."

Gritting his teeth, Hunter pulled into the small parking lot and hit the automatic lock button for the doors. "You're not getting out of this truck until you tell me."

Worried that it was for pain or for an infection, he pulled out his phone. "I'll call Dr. Hansen and ask him."

"He won't tell you." Leaning back, she dropped her head against the headrest and turned to smile at him. "This is fine with me. I haven't seen too much of you this past week."

She pursed her lips, turning back to stare out the windshield. "You've been avoiding me."

"I'm not interested." His stomach rolled at the lie, regretting the flash of hurt in her eyes.

Turning back to him again, she smiled sadly. "If I thought that was true, I'd move out of that house and into the hotel."

Unbuckling her seat belt, she turned to face him fully. "Hunter, I've never felt as close to anyone as I do with you and Rem. We could have something special, but I'm not going to beg you or try to convince you. I've made it clear that I'm willing to try."

Reaching out, she touched the hand he'd rested on the center console, sending heat up his arm, which seemed to spread everywhere.

"I'm not afraid of you. I never was. I never will be. I trust you. I trust Rem. Completely."

The knots in Hunter's stomach tightened painfully. Turning his hand, he closed it around hers, staring down at their hands and fighting the urge to yank her onto his lap. "I couldn't live with myself if I hurt you."

"You can't live with yourself now."

Hunter sighed, the knots getting tighter. "I've learned to live with who I am and what I'm capable of."

"Everyone's capable of hurting someone they're supposed to be close to. Abuse comes in many forms." Taking his hand in both of hers, she squeezed lightly. "Did your father ever hit you or Remington?"

"No." Hunter tried to pull away, but she held firm. "He saved his fists for our mother, and always did it while we were at school."

"And yet he hurt you—filled you with a pain that you've carried for years." Lifting his hand to her lips, she smiled, her eyes brimming with tears. "Please don't let him win. Please don't throw away happiness because of what he did to all of you."

Hunter yanked his hand away, furious at himself for almost believing. "I don't want to talk about it."

Emma nodded and turned away. "All right. Open the door so I can get my prescription."

Relieved that she'd changed the subject, Hunter folded his arms across his chest and leaned back, mimicking her posture.

"What's the prescription for, Emma?"

"Birth control pills."

Jealousy and rage swirled inside him, boiling over in a heartbeat.

"Not a fucking chance in hell."

Jerking upright, he threw the truck into drive and took off.

"They have side effects. Besides, you're not fucking anyone so you don't need them."

Emma smiled and shook her head. "It's only a matter of time before this chemistry between us takes over."

"No. I won't let that happen."

"And if it does?"

Hunter's control snapped.

He slammed on the brakes and turned to her, pulling her close enough to see the gold flecks flashing in her eyes.

"When I take you, it's sure as hell not going to be a one-night stand, and I won't give a flying fuck if you get pregnant!"

Her eyes widened, the wonder in them stunning him to his core. "Hunter!"

Hunter's chest tightened, his heart beating nearly out of his chest. "Don't. Don't look at me that way." He dropped his forehead to hers, struggling to catch his breath. "You're too much for me. I want you too damned much. I want to see you pregnant with our child more than I've ever wanted anything in my life."

Releasing her with a curse, he hit the gas again, furious with himself for losing control. "For my own sanity, I've got to stay the hell away from you."

Chapter Twelve

Wearing more comfortable shorts and a tank top, Emma leaned back in her chair on the front porch and propped her feet on the railing, prepared to sit back and enjoy the view.

She and Hunter hadn't spoken since his outburst, and as soon as they'd gotten home, he'd disappeared.

The look of fury on his face hadn't invited conversation.

She hadn't seen him since.

She'd wanted to run after him, but she hadn't known what else to stay.

Deciding that it would be better to give him time to think about their conversation, she'd gone into the house and raced to the kitchen in time to see him storm into his own house, slamming the door shut behind him.

She hadn't been able to think about anything except carrying their child since then, finding it impossible to even focus on her work.

She'd watched him come out again, dressed in shorts and boots, his chest bare as he began chopping wood.

When she heard their new lawnmower start, she'd decided to sit on the front porch, finding it too stuffy to stay indoors on such a beautiful day.

Still unsettled after her conversation with Hunter, she desperately wanted to see Remington, hoping that he could help her settle again.

Settling back, she waited for him to come around to the front of the house.

The sun warmed her bare feet and legs, the rest of her body slightly cooler in the shade, and soon she started getting drowsy.

Warm and comfortable, and with the sound of the lawnmower droning in the background, she started to doze, dreaming of what it would be like if Hunter and Remington loved her.

When the sound of the lawnmower got louder, she came wide awake, turning toward the sound.

Wearing jeans, boots, and a cowboy hat, Remington came into view, making her heart beat faster.

His chest, back, and wide shoulders glistened with sweat, every muscle clearly defined.

He looked good enough to eat.

He'd noticed her as soon as he came around the corner—the brief flash in his eyes gave him away— but he pretended not to, keeping his gaze averted as he navigated the corner.

Amused, she ogled him, imagining what it would be like if he belonged to her.

If they belonged to each other.

Her nipples tightened almost painfully as she watched him ride the mower in her direction, her pulse tripping when he stopped right in front of the large porch.

Scowling, he turned off the motor, avoiding her gaze.

Removing his hat, he wiped his forehead. "What did the doctor say?"

With a slow smile, she let her gaze rake over him. "He said that I'm a fast healer. I can drive again and resume *all* normal activities."

He whipped his head around to stare at her and stiffened, swallowed heavily.

She fluttered her lashes, laughing softly when he cursed and started the mower again, glaring at her as he rode away.

From behind her, the front door opened and closed, and with a smile, she tilted her head back, catching Hunter looking down at her breasts. "You like what you see?"

Hunter's eyes narrowed, and with a gruff sound, he thrust a bottle of water at her. "What are you doing out here? It's too hot. You should be inside resting."

Emma accepted the water and twisted off the cap, which he'd already loosened. "When you called Dr. Hansen a little while ago, he told you the same thing he told me. I'm fine. Pretending I'm still recovering is your way of keeping me at a distance."

Hunter stepped away from her, leaning against the side of the porch. "How did you know I called?"

Emma grinned. "Because he called me and told me. When I was in his office, he told me that you and Remington would probably hunt him down and ask about me, so I signed a paper stating that he had my permission to tell you. That's part of what took me so long."

With a grunt, Hunter turned away again and downed his bottle of water.

"Did you tell him that you're not getting that fucking prescription filled?"

"Nope."

"Good thing that I did then. So what the hell are you doing sitting out here?"

She met his scowl with a grin. "There's a better view out here." She gestured toward Remington. "Watching your brother mow the lawn without a shirt is inspiring all sorts of fantasies."

After a stunned silence, Hunter moved to the steps and shoved his hat on his head. "That's all they'll ever be. Fantasies. I already told you—"

"You told me that if you took me, you wouldn't mind making me pregnant."

She gestured with her bottle of water to the two-seated swing on the other end of the porch, changing the subject before he had the chance to argue with her. "That's a great swing. I tried it out the other day. I'm surprised you thought of such a thing when you were redoing the house."

A muscle worked in Hunter's jaw. "Our mother always wanted one."

Watching him closely, Emma set her water aside. "You must have been very young when she died."

"We were."

"Probably too young to do anything about it."

"No." Hunter stiffened and looked out at the large yard. "We should have done something."

Listening to the sound of the lawnmower getting louder, Emma glanced at Remington as he came around the corner again. "So you fixed the house the way your mother would have liked it to make it up to her?"

"You know nothing about it."

Unperturbed at Hunter's harsh tone, Emma nodded. "Thanks for getting me those new nightgowns. They're really comfortable to sleep in."

Hunter whipped his head around, his gaze moving over her legs before meeting hers. "Christ, you change subjects so fast it's hard to keep up with you. You're welcome." His eyes narrowed. "Why are you bringing that up now?"

With a shrug, Emma grinned, raising her voice to be heard over the lawnmower. "Because I was thinking about running some errands tomorrow and looking around the town. I talked to Rachel, and she told me she also had some sexier ones. I think I'm going to buy a few of those. I also need some new panties and some groceries."

A muscle worked in his jaw. "I told you that I would take you to town. I tried to the other day, but you wouldn't go."

"I didn't want to take the chance that you'd be overcome by lust for me and attack me right there in the truck. You'd regret it and blame me for it."

Hunter's eyes narrowed, a small smile playing at his lips. "Not likely. I'm used to a different kind of woman."

Intrigued, Emma braced an elbow on the arm of her chair and propped her chin on her fist. "Really? What kind of woman would interest a man like you?"

Hunter turned to face her fully just as the lawnmower went silent, his gaze lingering on her breasts. "I'm only interested in having the kind of woman who knows the score. I want a woman interested in getting and giving pleasure—incredible pleasure—with no strings attached. A nice submissive woman who'll do what I say without questioning me or being a smartass."

Glancing at Remington, who sat several feet away watching the scene play out before him, Emma smiled and met Hunter's gaze again.

"Sounds boring."

Running her fingertips down her neck to her cleavage, she shivered with excitement when Hunter's gaze followed the trail of her fingers. "If you ever get lonely, you can come over and sleep with me again. This time, it'll be more than sleep."

Hunter's eyes narrowed, his jaw clenching. "Honey, you've got strings written all over you."

"You're the one who talked about getting me pregnant."

Remington stilled, his gaze going to Hunter's. "Excuse me? If she's getting pregnant, I want in."

Hunter jumped to his feet, sending another glare in her direction. "Nobody's getting anybody pregnant." He turned to Remington, gesturing angrily at her with a wave of his arm.

"She got a prescription for *birth control pills!*"

Remington blinked. "Did you tell her that we use condoms?" Smiling, he rested an arm over the leg he'd propped against the top of the mower. "We're safe, by the way."

Hunter snarled and whipped around to her again. "We're not fucking you!"

Sliding a glance in Remington's direction, she caught him staring at her legs. "Well, the two of you don't have to be frightened. I'm not going to attack you, and I'll do my best to stay out of your way."

Recapping her water bottle, she got to her feet. "As a matter of fact, I think I can start some of my errands now."

Aware that both men gaped at her, she hid a smile and went inside, closing the door behind her.

She had their attention but knew it would take much more convincing before either one of them would act on it.

Going to them just made them back off.

She had to find a way to get them to come to her.

With that in mind, she went to get dressed for her trip to town.

* * * *

About twenty minutes had gone by since Emma went into the house, and Remington had finally finished cutting the front lawn.

He'd wanted to go in after her to find out what had happened between her and Hunter while they'd been gone but figured he'd better finish and clean up first.

Using his shirt to wipe the sweat from his chest, he heard the door open and the screen slam shut.

Lifting his face, he tossed his shirt onto the hood of the lawnmower, his cock jumping to attention at the sight of Emma coming down the porch stairs in a short red sundress.

The flirty skirt moved enticingly around her thighs as she walked, accentuating her well-rounded ass.

Her ass twitched with every movement, the skirt flaring around her creamy thighs with each step teasing him with the possibility of a glimpse of her panties.

It had been a long time since the possibility of glimpsing another woman's panties excited him so much.

She turned to give him a saucy grin, making his cock ache. "Hi, Remington. I'm going to town. Do you need anything?"

I need to have you bent over so I can rip those panties off of you.

"No." Irritated at the huskiness in his voice, he cleared his throat. "No. Thanks."

She grinned, and he could have sworn she turned fast on purpose to give him a glimpse of creamy thigh—and pink lace panties. "Okay. Have a good night."

He still stood there like an idiot, watching her pull away.

Hunter came around the corner, also watching her. "Did you see that dress?"

Remington adjusted his jeans, willing his cock to behave. "I'm gonna see that dress in my fucking dreams. She's wearing pink lace panties. *Pink fucking lace*! Where do you think she's going?"

"My guess would be the diner."

"Hell. Tonight's special is fried chicken. The place is gonna be packed. I don't know about you, but I'm gonna go get a shower and go to town."

"Damned right we're going." Hunter took off his cowboy hat and ran a hand through his hair. "Damned woman is gonna flash those panties at everyone just to piss me off."

Chapter Thirteen

Emma was enjoying herself immensely.

The diner had begun filling up right after she walked in, but so far, she'd spoken only to the owners.

Seated in one of the booths in the diner, she introduced herself to Gracie, unsurprised that the older woman already knew about her.

She'd spent years living in small towns and knew how quickly gossip spread.

"Your food is delicious."

Gracie grinned. "I know. I also know that you're going to try to get my recipes."

One of her husbands, Finn, brought Emma a glass of sweet tea. "We're real honored, but my darlin' wife wouldn't like that. Just do me a favor and don't ask me anything." His eyes twinkled with love for his wife as he bent to kiss her cheek. "I get in enough trouble as it is."

Gracie slapped his arm. "That's because you're always up to no good. I don't know why I put up with you."

Finn winked and ran a hand down her back. "Yes, you do."

Fascinated, Emma watched Gracie shoo her husband away, the older woman's face flushed and her eyes gleaming with love for him.

Waiting until Finn went back behind the counter, Emma leaned forward, not wanting to be overheard. "*Three* husbands! I don't know how you do it."

"Patience." Gracie grinned. "Although mine are nothing like Hunter and Remington. You've sure got an uphill battle ahead of you."

Emma sighed and sipped her tea. "They're wonderful men."

"Yes. They are. No one wants to see them get hurt."

Understanding the warning, Emma nodded. "I know. If I hurt them, I'm going to have a lot to answer for. Believe me, the last thing I want to do is hurt them. They're avoiding me anyway. It breaks my heart that they're so convinced that they're violent. Nothing could be further from the truth."

A young woman walked up behind Gracie and bent to kiss her cheek. "Until you got here, they got into bar fights almost every weekend." Grinning, she offered her hand. "Hi. I'm Hope. It's good to finally meet you in person. Can't wait for our shopping trip this week." She stepped to the side as another woman joined them. "And this is my sister, Charity. We're Gracie's daughters. Garrett, Drew, and Finn are our fathers."

"How does it feel to have three fathers?"

Hope grinned. "We're spoiled rotten. Do you mind if we join you? I've been dying to get a chance to talk to you away from your watchdogs."

"Please." Laughing, Emma started to slide in, but Charity stopped her with a hand on her shoulder. "No. You're fine. We know you just had surgery. Stay put. We've got plenty of room."

"I wish everyone would stop treating me like I've just rolled into the recovery room. I'm healed. I promise. Stitches are out. Got the release from the doctor and everything."

"Hunter and Remington keep telling everyone how weak and sore you are." Sitting across from her, Hope smiled. "Everyone's been dying to meet the woman who finally got to Hunter and Remington. God, they're dreamy."

Charity slapped her sister's arm. "Like you're not married to a hunk."

Hope smiled, winking at Emma as she poked her sister's arm. "And you're not?"

Charity smiled and shook her head. "My breath still catches every time I see him."

Emma sighed. "I know the feeling. Scary."

Leaning forward, Hope touched her hand, her eyes gleaming. "Scary as hell, but it's worth it."

"We'll see. I may never know." Emma shrugged and sipped her tea. "I'm afraid I'm falling for both of them and I don't think either one of them is going to let me in. I'll be happy if I can just get them to realize what wonderful men they are. If they do, maybe they can let another woman get close to them."

She tried to hide the hurt at that prospect, but her voice broke.

Hope slapped the table. "Don't you dare give up on them!"

"Oh, I won't." If there was even the slightest chance that she could have such wonderful men in her life, she would take it. Looking up at Hope and Charity, she smiled. "I'm a firm believer in fighting for what I want. I've had to in order to survive."

She was saved from saying any more when the bell over the door chimed and two men walked in, one familiar to her.

He stood slightly taller than both Hunter and Remington, but he was massive.

His sheriff's uniform couldn't hide the bulging muscles, which appeared to shift with the slightest movement.

His dark eyes narrowed as he scanned the room, his lips curling slightly into a semblance of a smile when he nodded at Gracie. Too masculine to be considered truly handsome, he reminded her very much of Hunter.

Watchful. Serious.

And he loved her spaghetti and meatballs.

Turning to say something to the grinning man who walked in behind him, he zeroed in on the booth where Emma sat with Hope and Charity.

The man who walked through into the diner behind him epitomized drop-dead gorgeous.

He looked like a movie star.

Tall, lean, and with eyes that twinkled with mischief and a ready smile, he moved with a grace and confidence that reminded her of Remington.

Hope turned in her seat, grinning impishly at the sheriff. "Well, here's my darling husband now. Ace, it's our turn to buy Emma dinner."

Ace's expression gentled, his smile tender. His arm went around his wife's waist as she rose, and with a look of male possessiveness, he pulled her against his side. "I owe her at least two dinners. I wiped out her spaghetti."

Chuckling, he kissed his wife's hair. "Then I went to find Hunter and Remington to tell them all about it."

Stunned at that bit of news, Emma smiled. "You never did tell me why you stopped by that night."

"I wanted to make sure you were all right." Still smiling, he raised a brow. "I'd already run a background check on you, but I wanted to get to know you a little, especially since you're going to spend time in Desire."

Hope giggled and lifted her face for her husband's kiss. "My husband prides himself on knowing everything that goes on in this town."

Fascinated by the looks that passed between them, Emma watched the other man slide into the booth next to Charity. "I hope I didn't cause you too much trouble."

"None at all. I'm just glad Hunter and Remington found you when they did." Gesturing toward the other man, Ace stepped back to drop onto one of the stools at the counter while Hope scooted into the booth next to Emma. "This is Beau, Charity's husband."

Beau's smile was contagious. "Hello. You *are* a beauty. Everyone in town has been talking about you. Hunter and Remington sure seem taken with you. I can see why."

Charity poked his side. "If I didn't know better, I'd swear you were flirting."

Nuzzling her hair, Beau chuckled. "It's a good thing that you know better. I only have eyes for you, and you know it."

Sitting back, he greeted Gracie as she brought coffee to both of her sons-in-law. "I just can't believe Hunter and Remington are actually letting a woman stay with them."

"I'm not staying *with* them." Emma looked down at the menu to hide her burning face. "I'm staying in the main house."

Ace touched his mother-in-law's shoulder as she passed. "Thanks, Gracie. We'll figure out what we want in a minute. I'm sure Emma's hungry."

"Starving." She fidgeting under Ace's scrutiny and smiled at Gracie. "I want to try something I haven't already had. I'm going to have to come in one day when it's not so busy and talk you into giving me some of your recipes, but I want to know which ones to ask for. I know one of them is your meatloaf."

Smiling, Gracie shook her head. "I'm sorry, honey, but it's my secret recipe, and I won't give it to anyone."

Hope reached out to touch her mother's arm. "Not even to us."

Charity frowned at her sister. "What the hell would you do with a recipe? You can't boil water."

Ace chuckled at that, earning a dark look from his wife, a look he met with a raised brow. "Don't look at me like that. You know your sister's right."

Gracie shook her head. "That's enough, girls." She started back behind the counter, pausing next to Ace. "If I gave away my secret recipes, I'd never see my handsome sons-in-law."

Frowning, Ace straightened. "I'm in here several times a day."

Beau stood and went to Gracie's side. "You know that I only married your daughter to get to you."

Garrett's voice came from the kitchen. "I heard that, Beau."

Gracie blushed and poked Beau's flat stomach. "You always were a rascal."

Raising his voice to be heard in the kitchen, Beau grinned. "Yeah, but you love me."

"Leave my woman alone!" The disgruntled voice from the kitchen had them all laughing.

Fascinated, Emma watched them together, trying to imagine that kind of intimacy with Hunter and Remington and found that she couldn't.

Dear God. I'm really in love with them—and they'll never let me in.

Suddenly feeling more alone and vulnerable than she had in years, Emma blinked back tears. "You're all so lucky. I wonder if you realize how lucky you are to have a family—a real family." Fighting not to cry in front of them, she rose. "Excuse me."

Hope rose at once, touching her arm. "Emma?"

"Hell." Ace's soft curse came from behind Emma as she hurried toward the bathroom.

Once inside, she locked the door behind her, calling herself all kinds of a fool for her outburst.

She studied her reflection in the mirror, grimacing at what she saw.

Her hazel eyes looked dull and red. Because of the heat, she'd pulled her long hair into a ponytail, which served only to emphasize her paleness.

She looked fragile.

Straightening, she thought of Hunter's loss of control in the truck.

She was a fighter—something Hunter and Remington would soon find out.

Seeing Hope and Charity with their husbands, she knew what she wanted and wouldn't settle for anything less.

She took a deep breath and blew it out slowly.

She couldn't give up without a fight. If she did, she knew she'd always regret it.

Seeing what she wanted made her only more determined to have it. With renewed purpose, she unlocked the door and walked out, straight into a very concerned-looking Hope.

"Are you all right?" Taking her arm, Hope led her to the kitchen.

"I'm fine. Just feeling sorry for myself. I'm over it."

Hope hugged her, eyeing her sympathetically. "I'm sorry."

Emma blinked. "For what? You've all been so nice to me. I see what I want for myself, and I'm determined to get it."

Nodding, Hope glanced at her fathers and tugged Emma farther away from them. "We all like you so much, but I guess we haven't been thinking about you and what it's like to fall in love with Hunter and Remington. They're pretty intimidating, aren't they?"

"Yeah. They are."

Intimidating. Breathtaking. Amazing.

Aware of the attention she was getting from Hope's fathers, Emma smiled and walked toward them. "So when are you going to let me in on your secrets?"

Finn grinned. "Sorry, honey. We can't tell you anything."

"I'll get it out of you, you know."

Crossing his arms over his chest, he smiled, his eyes dancing. "Oh, yeah? How do you propose to do that?"

She winked, giving him a slow smile. "I have my ways."

Garrett smiled kindly. "You just worry about setting Hunter and Remington straight. We're all rooting for you, honey. None of us want to see you hurt. Dealing with those two is like banging your head against the wall." He gestured toward the front. "In the meantime, you've got a couple of young men out front waiting to meet you."

Hope smiled and nodded. "John and Michael heard you were here and want to talk to you." Taking her hand, Hope led her from the kitchen. "My dad's very perceptive. He sees things before any of us do. He's right. None of us wants to see you get hurt. Love hurts like hell sometimes. I guess we're all so happy that we forget what it was like before we landed these Neanderthals."

Ace suddenly appeared at their side. "I heard that."

Hope jumped. "Damn it, Ace. How can someone as big as you are manage to sneak up on people? I thought you were out front with the others."

"I was. I had a call to make." His gaze shifted to Emma, his eyes narrowing. "We're a very close-knit town, but we protect our women."

He slid an arm around his wife's waist. "My wife and the others don't mean any harm. They're just all focused on matchmaking. The men in town, however, have been looking out for you." He smiled, his eyes tender. "We're all on your side and will do whatever we can to help you, even if you change your mind about Hunter and Remington. Okay?"

"We all will." Leaning against her husband, Hope touched her arm.

"Thank you. I appreciate the offer, but this is something I think I'm going to have to do on my own."

Ace gathered his wife closer. "John and Michael own the bar in town, and they want to meet you. They're good men, and no one wants to knock some sense into Hunter and Remington more than they do. They want to have dinner with you, and don't try to pick at your food. Everyone knows you need to build your strength."

Feeling much better, Emma turned to Hope. "Do *all* the men in town think every woman's helpless?"

Hope grinned. "Yep. Until we do something to remind them that *we're* the ones in charge."

* * * *

John and Michael were gorgeous, charming, and very friendly—the kind of men any woman with an ounce of brains would fall head over heels in love with.

It just proved that her heart and her brain weren't connected at all.

She liked them, but they didn't affect her the way Hunter and Remington did.

John Dalton had piercing brown eyes, almost as dark as Hunter's—watchful eyes that held a hint of sadness. "We have orders to make sure you eat good. I hope you're not one of those women who only order a salad."

Emma giggled. "Tonight a salad just isn't going to do it. I'm starving."

Michael Keegan, on the other hand, exuded sex appeal and charm. He appeared slightly younger than John, and with jet-black hair, mesmerizing blue eyes, and a ready smile, he drew attention like a magnet.

He insisted on seating her in the booth close to the window and lowered himself to the seat next to her. "So how are you feeling?"

Smiling, she reached for her water. "I'm fine. Fully recovered. You know, having an appendectomy isn't such a big deal anymore."

John handed her a menu. "I understand it was pretty damned scary. I'm just glad Hunter and Remington found you when they did."

Emma nodded, wishing she could be so at ease with Hunter and Remington. "So am I."

She smiled her thanks when Gracie brought her a fresh glass of tea. "Especially when that thunderstorm hit."

John and Michael insisted on buying her dinner, and they ate in the booth she'd chosen earlier while Hope and Charity sat eating with their husbands in a booth across the aisle from them.

Michael waited until Gracie set their plates in front of them before asking about Hunter and Remington. "So, I understand that you're making Hunter and Remington...uncomfortable." Turning to her, he grinned. "Best thing that ever happened to them."

Aware of the attention from the other table, Emma shrugged. "They don't feel that way. I'm afraid they're doing their best to stay upset with me for one reason or another."

John had a calmness about him that she found she needed right now. "Oh? Trying to put a little distance between you and them, are they?"

Emma stirred the mashed potatoes on her plate. "With a vengeance. They check on me to see if I'm all right and are in such a hurry to get away from me that they leave skid marks on the floor."

Michael gave her a captivating smile and leaned forward. "You gonna let them get away with that?"

"Yep." Emma reached for her tea. "I'm going to give them the space they want and just go about my business."

John looked up from his plate with a frown. "So you're going to give up?"

"Not at all." Feeling better and calmer since she'd come out of the bathroom, she smiled. "But I'm not going to chase them. That only makes them more determined to stay away from me. I think they feel threatened. If they want me, they're going to have to come to me."

John glanced out the window, did a double-take, and stiffened. "It doesn't appear that's gonna be a problem. They're here now."

Emma's stomach did a nosedive. "What?" Whipping her head around, she looked out the window in time to see Hunter and Remington get out of their truck, which they'd parked just a few doors down from the diner.

A tense silence fell over the diner, and from the corner of her eye, she watched Ace and Beau turn slightly in their seats as if ready to jump up at a moment's notice.

Michael chuckled from beside her, turning in his seat to rest his arm on the top edge of the booth, his fingers brushing over the back of her neck. "This should be interesting."

Glancing toward the other table, Emma was struck by the expectant looks on the other women's faces.

Hope winked at Emma and propped her head on her hand. "This should be *very* interesting."

With a sigh, Ace got to his feet, glancing at his father-in-law, Drew, who strolled out from the kitchen. "My in-laws aren't gonna be happy if the four of you tear up the diner."

Wiping his hands on a towel, Drew shrugged and looked around. "I don't know. We could use a remodel. Besides, if those boys have to get angry to get their heads on straight, it'll be well worth it. When the first fist flies, I want you girls in the back."

Emma gasped. "You're not serious! Hunter and Remington wouldn't start a fight, would they?"

Lowering himself to one of the stools at the counter, Ace crossed his arms over his chest. "Hunter and Remington live to fight. It's rare for me to go a week without having to break one up."

Emma gaped. "You're kidding."

John sighed. "I wish he was. They've destroyed the bar more times than I can tell you. They pay to remodel it every couple of months."

Emma got an uneasy feeling in the pit of her stomach. "If what you're saying is true, maybe they really are as violent as they think they are."

All heads turned in her direction, the nearly identical looks of shock on their faces making her feel as if she'd missed something.

Michael smiled and patted her shoulder. "They aren't. They just want everyone to believe they are."

"Why would you think that?"

"Because we know them. They've never started a fight with anyone for any reason other than to defend women. They protect women at all costs. It'll be interesting to see how they react at seeing you with us. I've never seen them jealous before."

Emma frowned. "What makes you think they're going to be jealous?"

"Because they want you for themselves. *They* found you, and *they're* the ones who have been taking care of you. You live in *their* house. They're going to be possessive of you, and that's something neither one of them has any experience with. Hell, they've already warned all of us off, telling us not to come over because you're still weak and healing."

"Do I look weak to you?" Emma sighed and shook her head. "They've already made it clear that they don't want anything to do with me. Sometimes I think I'm getting to them, but then they just back off again."

Charity smiled reassuringly. "That's because being around you is making them uncomfortable. I heard from Jesse and Nat how they look at you. I can't wait to see it."

Beau frowned at his wife while taking her hand in his. "Don't try to push Hunter and Remington into anything."

Hope snorted. "They need to be pushed."

Ace spared a glance at his wife. "Stay out of it, or I'll put you over my knee."

Emma gasped again, stunned when Hope pouted and ogled her husband's butt.

"Promises. Promises."

The others all laughed, their laughter cut off when the bell over the door sounded.

The tension in the air was thick enough to cut with a knife as Hunter pushed open the door and strode into the diner.

Turning back, she scooped up a forkful of mashed potatoes, hoping she didn't choke on them as she waited to see what Hunter and Remington would do.

Suddenly, Remington appeared, pausing next to the table, his gaze settling on Emma's.

"You okay?"

Smiling at the frustration in his eyes, Emma swallowed the buttery potatoes. "I'm great." She gestured toward her plate of fried chicken. "I wanted to try out another one of Gracie's recipes. How are you?"

"Fine." He shot a glare at both John and Michael. "Don't you have a bar to run?"

John sat back, sipping his coffee. "We hired a new bartender. He's doing well, and it's Tuesday, Remington. I think he's capable of handling the bar for a few hours. Besides, I'm not willing to give up a chance to have dinner with a beautiful woman." He smiled at Emma. "I was hoping to talk her into having dinner with us at the hotel restaurant tomorrow night."

"We're still trying to hire two more bartenders." Michael grinned and nodded toward Ace and Beau. "We realized that there was no way we could have what they have and be in the bar as many hours as we are."

A muscle worked in Remington's jaw. "Good for you. Emma, you haven't eaten. What's wrong with your eyes? You look tired. You should be at home resting."

"I'm fine."

Hope stood to lean against her husband. "She was upset earlier and started crying."

"Crying?" Remington appeared slightly panicked, his eyes going wide. "Why?"

Emma glared at Hope, unable to believe her new friend would rat her out. "Just tired."

Instead of appearing sheepish, Hope looked smug as hell. "Poor thing's probably exhausted, and she still has shopping to do."

Hunter pushed forward, his jaw tightening when Ace took a step closer. "I knew you should have been relaxing. Come on, Emma. We'll take you home. You need to be resting."

"No, thank you." Emma looked away from him. "Hope and Charity offered to take me shopping. I need some things, and I'd like to get them while I'm in town. Especially groceries."

She could shop for the other things another time.

Remington shook his head and reached past Michael to hold out a hand for her. "Come on. We'll take you."

Shaking her head, and aware of the attention from the others, Emma smiled. "You've already done so much. Besides, you want to stay away from me, remember?"

Michael leaned back and grinned, pushing Remington's hand away. "I'll take her. I certainly don't have a problem with spending more time with her. Besides, she shouldn't be carrying groceries."

Seeing what the others were up to, Emma gritted her teeth. "That's not necessary." The last thing she wanted to do was cause trouble between friends.

Beau ran a hand over his mouth, unsuccessfully hiding a smile. "I'll take them. Charity and I need some things anyway. I'll make sure she doesn't lift anything."

Hunter shook his head. "We need some things, too. We'll take her." He glared at each of the men as if daring one of them to argue. "Move, Michael. Let Emma out."

Michael stood with a smile. "I can be patient. The two of you have already started pushing her away. When you finally manage to do it for good, I'll be waiting." Holding out a hand for Emma, Michael helped her from the seat. "I'll call you tomorrow, Emma. We'll go out to dinner. John and I want to talk to you about some ideas we've had for the bar. We could use your advice."

Remington's eyes narrowed. "What ideas?"

Michael's slow smile had an edge to it. "None of your business."

Delighted, and nervous at the chance to have Hunter and Remington to herself, Emma eased from the booth. Smiling at Hope and Charity, she took Remington's outstretched hand. "Are we still on for shopping this week?"

Hope grinned. "My calendar's clear. Call me."

Turning, she smiled up at Michael, including John in her smile. "Thanks for dinner."

John frowned and gestured toward her plate. "Which you didn't get to eat."

Hunter touched her arm. "Are you hungry?"

"Not really." Her stomach fluttered with excitement, and she doubted she could eat if she wanted to. "I'll get something later."

Remington wrapped an arm around her waist and turned her toward the door while Hunter threw some bills on the table.

"I'll pay for her dinner." Hunter took Emma's other hand. "Let's go so we can get you home."

"But you haven't eaten yet."

"Neither have you. We'll grab something later." He paused at the counter to order three fried chicken dinners and three peach cobblers, telling Gracie that he'd pick them up in about thirty minutes.

They made their way down the sidewalk and past a store that had a variety of bottles and jars in the window.

Pausing, Emma pulled out of their grasp. "Hey, isn't this the store Jesse, Kelly, and Nat own?"

"Yes." Hunter gripped her arm again. "You have enough of that stuff already. Besides, I like the way you smell without all that."

"That's nice. I still want to go in one day. They've both been very nice to me."

"It seems you have that kind of effect on people." Hunter's gruff tone made her smile.

"You sound angry about it."

"Why the hell would I be angry?"

Good question.

"You sound jealous, which is ridiculous. I don't play games, Hunter. I like both you and Remington. A lot. I want you. A lot. I'd love to get to know you even better, but you've made it clear that that's something you're not interested in. I'm certainly not looking for anyone else."

Hunter glanced at her, a muscle working in his jaw as he opened the door to the grocery store. "You're awfully blunt. It's gonna get you in trouble one day."

"So you keep telling me, but it doesn't seem to be working with you." Taking a cart from the front of the store, she started down the first aisle, amused that both men moved in beside her.

"You can't get what you want out of life by being shy about getting it."

Picking out fresh fruit and vegetables, Emma smiled when an older woman approached and greeted both men. "Hi, Hunter. Hi, Remington. This must be Emma. I'm Isabel Preston. My husbands and I own this store. It's nice to finally meet you."

Emma grinned and took the offered her hand, mesmerized that the other woman seemed to glow with happiness. "Hi. Wow. Does everyone know me?"

Isabel laughed, a musical tinkling sound. "It's a small town, and Hunter and Remington with a woman is big news. My phone will be ringing off the hook all night."

Hunter's jaw clenched. "She needs groceries and didn't know where the store was."

Picking out tomatoes, Emma frowned. "Hope and Charity offered to bring me. If I'm inconveniencing you, you can go home. I drove myself to town. I can drive back."

Hunter clenched his jaw again, something she noticed he did often when he was with her. "I told you we need some things."

Emma looked pointedly at his hands. "You're not shopping."

Hunter glared at her and picked up two tomatoes and tossed them into her cart. "There."

"They're going to be bruised."

Hunter's eyes narrowed, a muscle working in his jaw. "I like bruised tomatoes."

Pushing the cart to the side, Hunter turned his attention to Isabel. "How's Erin?"

Isabel's eyes lit up. "She's a trooper. Due to give birth to my grandchild in just a few weeks. Of course, my sons are spoiling her."

"As they should." An older, ridiculously handsome man approached, wrapping an arm around Isabel's waist. "Carrying a child can't be easy."

Leaning against the man with an intimate smile, Isabel shook her head. "It's not, but it's worth it."

Remington touched Emma's arm. "Emma, this is Wade Preston, one of Emma's husbands. The other two are Ben and Conal. They have three sons, Jared, Duncan, and Reese. They're married to Erin, Rachel's sister."

Emma smiled and shook her head as she bagged several tomatoes. "I'll never be able to keep everyone straight."

She didn't want to mention it, but she was surprised at how many women in town had more than one husband.

It also surprised her that they all seemed so happy.

She's expected jealousy and snide comments and couldn't help but wonder what happened behind closed doors.

Wade nuzzled his wife's hair. "Jared's on the phone. He wanted to tell you how Erin's doctor's appointment went."

Isabel grinned and straightened. "I've got to go. I hope to see more of you soon, Emma."

"Oh, you will."

Picking out more tomatoes, Emma stilled at the feel of Remington's body pressing against her back.

His hands closed over her waist, his lips warm against her ear. "Your legs are incredible."

Emma gulped, leaning back against him. "I'm glad you think so."

"Did you wear that dress to drive me crazy?"

Emma giggled at that and reached for another tomato, glancing at him over her shoulder. "Is it working?"

The feel of his cock pressing against her lower back while his warm lips moved over her ear had her trembling so hard that she dropped the tomatoes.

"I saw a glimpse of those pink lace panties. You wanted me to see them, didn't you?"

His hands clenched, pulling her back more firmly against him. "Do you know how long it's been since the brief flash of a woman's panties turned me on?"

His teeth scraped over the side of her neck. "Hunter and I have become jaded. Edgy. Hard and cold. It takes a lot to excite us, but you arouse me just by walking into the room. Just the flash of pink panties made me hard."

Watching Hunter out of the corner of her eye, she gasped at the feel of his tongue sliding down her neck "W-what are you d-doing?"

Remington nipped her earlobe, the slight sting sending sharp jolts of heat to her nipples and clit. "Isn't this what you said you wanted? You wanted my attention, and you've got it."

His hands slid to her hips, pulling her closer. "You're so damned adorable. Sweet. It drives me nuts. I don't like what you're doing to me."

Emma took a shuddering breath, her gaze meeting Hunter's unreadable one. "Too bad. I want you and Hunter."

Releasing her abruptly, Remington stepped back, his eyes narrowed to cold slits. "Be careful what you wish for. You couldn't even come close to handling me as a lover, and you may not like what you get. I like it rough, baby, and you're too fucking innocent."

"Is that so?" She slid another glance at Hunter, who stood with his arms folded across his chest and watched her intently. "I know you're underestimating yourselves, and I think maybe you're underestimating me."

Shrugging, she picked up the tomatoes she'd dropped back amongst the others and began to put them in a plastic bag. "I guess we'll see."

Tying the bag, she turned to face both of them. "I know I've got the courage to try. Do you?"

Remington's eyes lit with challenge. Stepping forward, he crowded her against the display, sending the same hot thrill through her. "If we weren't being watched, I'd slide my hands under that dress and rip your panties off of you. I'd love to see how you respond to being forced to finish your shopping knowing that Hunter and I can slip our hands under your dress whenever we want and encounter bare skin."

Hunter watched from across the small aisle. "The way that skirt moves when you walk just invites attention. Wear it in front of me again, and I'm going to accept the invitation."

Remembering Hope's words, Emma smiled. "Promises. Promises."

She gently placed the tomatoes into the cart and began moving down the aisle again, struggling to remember what she needed for the recipes she'd planned to try for the week.

Her mind went blank, so she found herself grabbing things at random.

"Do you really need all that garlic?"

Her face burned at the amusement in Remington's question, and looking down at the bag she'd been filling, she realized it would take weeks for her to use so much of it.

Still, she couldn't put it back and let them see that they'd distracted her.

"I'm making spaghetti and garlic bread. I need garlic for a lot of my recipes."

She hadn't planned to make spaghetti again, but since she'd mentioned it, she felt compelled to get the rest of the ingredients.

Maybe she could get Hunter and Remington to eat it the next time she made it.

Remington's threat had her imagining what it would have been like if he'd actually torn her panties from her.

Amazed at how even the thought of it aroused her, she found herself glancing at both of them repeatedly, trying to figure out if they would actually do something like that to her or if Remington had attempted to scare her off.

She didn't scare easily, and his threat hadn't scared her.

It aroused her.

Without giving herself time to think about the consequences, Emma reached under her dress and yanked her panties down to her knees.

Aware that Hunter and Remington stood watching her in disbelief, she grabbed Remington's arm for support and lifted one leg and then the other, removing her panties and stuffing them in her purse.

She didn't look at either of them as she continued down the aisle, but the stunned silence that followed her had her biting back a smile.

She hadn't counted on how walking around without panties would affect *her*, though, and found herself shifting restlessly as moisture coated her inner thighs.

Spotting the brand of cereal she liked, she looked around to make sure no one else was looking and stood on tiptoe to reach it from the top shelf.

Hunter cursed, flattening his hand at the small of her back as he leaned over her and retrieved one of the boxes. "What the hell are you doing? Trying to show your ass to everyone?"

Taking the box from him, she smiled and gestured around them. "There's no one else around. Besides, Remington's the one who made the suggestion. He was just too chicken to do it."

"Chicken?" Remington started toward her, pausing when Hunter held out a hand.

Hunter gulped heavily. "You're trembling." He released her, stepping away. "Don't worry. We'll keep our distance. You have nothing to fear from us."

"I'm not afraid of you. Asshole." Turning abruptly, she ran her cart into a display of cans, sending them rolling across the floor.

Frustration, anger, arousal, and embarrassment had her bursting into tears. Shoving the cart aside, she rushed to pick them up, mortified that they kept rolling away.

Hunter caught her arm. "Emma, please don't cry. Jesus, anything but that." His voice deepened into a furious whisper. "Go stand by the cart—and for God's sake—don't bend over!"

Standing behind the cart, Emma watched Hunter and Remington pick up and begin restacking the cans. "I'm not crying."

"Of course you're not." Wade appeared at her side, wrapping an arm around her shoulders and glaring at Hunter and Remington. "If you were crying, it would be their fault, and I'd have to do something about it."

Shaking her head, Emma forced a smile. "They didn't do anything wrong. It's me. I guess there's just something about me that has men running for the hills." She gestured toward the last of the cans on the floor. "I'm sorry. I made a mess."

He smiled, his eyes filled with a combination of amusement and concern. "There's no reason to cry over spilled cans. Hunter and Remington have most of them picked up already."

"I'm such a klutz."

Pulling her aside, he whispered close to her ear. "You love them, don't you?"

Emma winced, glancing at Hunter and Remington to make sure neither of them had heard. "It shows?"

Wade smiled tenderly. "If you're looking for it. I was. I'll tell you a little secret. If they don't love you already, they're well on their way there."

Emma sighed, swallowing a lump in her throat. "I wish I could believe that."

"Believe it. I understand you write cookbooks and are trying out recipes for your newest book."

"Good God. Does everyone know about me?"

Wade's slow smile gave Emma a hint of what Isabel had fallen in love with. "Yep. You're new in town and beautiful. Because of you, we all have hope that Hunter and Remington will find what they need." Looking up, he peered over her shoulder to where Hunter and Remington finished stacking the cans. "I just hope they're smart enough to realize it."

"I may not be what they need."

Her fearful admission tumbled out on a breathless whisper before she could stop it.

If she couldn't satisfy a man like Donny, she didn't know what hope she had of pleasing Hunter and Remington.

Glancing up at Wade, she shook her head. "I didn't mean to say that. Forget I said it."

Wade's lips twitched. "I've known those two since they were nothing more than a twinkle in their daddy's eye. I've never seen them look at a woman the way they look at you. Just be yourself. Now, wipe your eyes." His tone returned to normal, telling her that Hunter and Remington approached. "If you need something for your recipes that you can't find, just let me know. I'll get it for you."

"Thank you. I'll let you know. I'm sorry again about the mess."

Hunter started to reach for her arm, pulling his hand back at the last second. "Don't worry about it." He lifted his gaze to Wade's. "Only a couple were dented. We'll pay for them."

Searching her features, Hunter frowned again. "Let's get going. You're tired, and we need to finish your shopping so you can go home and rest."

"I'm fine. I don't need to rest, and if you keep frowning like that, you're going to get wrinkles." Turning, she once again faced the handsome older man. "It was nice meeting you, Wade. I'm sure I'll be seeing you around."

"I certainly hope so." He met Hunter's and Remington's gazes. "You take care of her."

* * * *

"We won't hurt her." Watching Emma hurry down the aisle, Remington gritted his teeth. "We managed to piss her off again, though."

Wade raised a brow. "I've known you for a long time. I've watched you with other women in the club. You claim to be too rough, but you treat women as if they're made of glass. I know better than you do that you'd never hurt Emma physically, but if you're not interested in claiming her, you're going to hurt her in other ways. Only a blind man would miss that she's already more than half in love with you."

A surge of something warm and intense made his chest swell and his heart pound furiously. "No." Whipping his head around, he met Wade's amused gaze. "She can't be." He looked at Hunter, panicked at the thought of having Emma's love and scared to death at the euphoria that made his head swim.

Hunter shook his head. "No. She doesn't know what she'd be in for. Let's go. Nice seeing you, Wade."

Nodding in Wade's direction, Remington caught up to her, grinding his teeth when she shrugged off his hand.

"Hey!" Gripping the edge of the cart, he jerked it to a stop. "You don't have to be afraid of us."

She gave him a dirty look that made him feel as if he'd missed something. "I'm not afraid of you. Jerk."

She reached for several boxes of pasta, dropping all of them when Hunter's hand touched her back. "Then why are you trembling?"

Spinning, she faced both of them. "Because I'm aroused. I'm mad. One touch and I can't think while you stand there looking smug and completely unaffected."

Remington gripped her upper arms, pulling her against him and sliding his hands to her lower back while pushing his cock against her belly. "Does this feel like I'm unaffected?"

Alarmed at her sob, he released her when she pushed away from him. "Emma—"

"I should have known better. How can I be so attracted to not one but two men who seem to take great joy in making me feel like a fool?" Shaking her head, she took a deep breath and seemed to gather herself. Smiling humorlessly, she eyed both of them, the sadness in her eyes like a kick to Remington's gut. "I seem to have a knack for being attracted to men who don't want me."

When she bent to pick up the pasta, Remington stopped her and picked it up himself.

"Emma—"

"Shut up." She tossed the pasta into the cart before turning and poking him in the chest. "Don't talk to me. Don't touch me. You're teases—both of you. You want to keep your distance. Good."

She shoved at him, the combination of anger and need darkening her eyes knotting his stomach. "Stay the hell away from me. I'll make my own way home."

Remington's cock throbbed when she turned away and stormed down the aisle, the need to take her and turn her into a purring kitten clawing at him.

Crossing his arms across his chest, Remington watched her until she turned the corner and disappeared from view before turning to look at his brother.

Amused at the frustration and hunger on Hunter's face as he stared after Emma, Remington chuckled softly. "There's a lot of pent-up passion in that woman."

Hunter's gaze swung to his, his eyes narrowed. "Do you think I don't know that? Let's get this fucking shopping done so we can get her home. I'm going to the club. Hopefully I can get rid of this fucking tension before I deal with her again."

Chapter Fourteen

Sitting at the table, Emma saw a movement out of the corner of her eye and smiled.

Ever since the incident at the grocery store, both men seemed determined to put as much distance between them as possible.

They did, however, take turns checking on her each morning and each evening.

Tucking the recipe cards she'd chosen into her purse, she rose to her feet just as Remington came through the back door.

"Good morning, Rem. Isn't it a beautiful day?"

Remington's greeting came in the form of a grunt. "You got back awfully late from your dinner with Michael and John."

"Yes. I did." She slipped on her sandals and pulled her purse onto her shoulder. "We had a wonderful time. Thank you for asking."

Frowning, Remington made his way farther into the kitchen, looking around as if he expected someone to pop out at any moment. "You going out again?"

She took her cell phone from the charger and tucked it into her purse. "Obviously. Have a nice day." She grabbed her keys and started for the hallway that led to the door to the garage.

"Wait!"

Hiding a smile, she turned back to find Remington directly behind her. "Yes?"

Remington studied her features, not saying anything for several long seconds. "Uh, did you have a good time with Michael and John?"

Emma grinned, delighted that he seemed a little flustered. "I already told you that I had a great time. They introduced me to Ethan and Brandon, who said to tell you hi. I'm going over there now to meet their chef."

Remington stiffened. "So you're going to be with Brandon and Ethan?"

"I guess. I don't know if they'll hang around after introducing me to Pete."

"Oh." Remington reached out a hand toward her, pulling it back almost immediately. "So then you'll be back?"

"Not for a little while. I have some things to do. Did you need something?"

"No." Frowning, he opened the door to the garage and walked out with her. "I just like to know where you are. You're a stranger here, and I don't want anything to happen to you."

He opened her car door for her and reached into his pocket. "Here's the remote for the garage." He pushed the center button, which raised the garage door.

"Thanks." Accepting it from him, she started the engine. "I guess I'll see you later."

She left him staring after her, a position she held until the garage door closed again.

Pleased with her progress, she turned in the wide driveway and headed into town.

* * * *

Remington stood in the garage for several minutes, staring at the closed garage door and cursing himself for the situation between himself and Emma.

A situation of his and Hunter's own making.

She was giving them the distance they'd demanded, and it pissed him off.

It didn't help to remember that their trip to the club had been in vain.

No a single woman there excited them the way Emma did, and the thought of touching any of them made him feel as if he was somehow cheating on Emma.

He knew it would hurt her—a hurt that she might never forgive.

It didn't matter that they'd told her that nothing could happen between them.

He felt as if he belonged to her as much as he felt she belonged to them.

When he heard footsteps coming down the hall, he turned, pleased to have someone to vent his anger on.

Hunter paused in the doorway, frowning. "She went out again?"

"Yes, she went out again. She's going to the hotel."

Hunter's eyes narrowed. "Why?"

Gritting his teeth, Remington went up the steps, brushing past his brother to go back inside. "Because John and Michael took her to the hotel restaurant for dinner and introduced her to Brandon and Ethan."

Hunter followed him in, closing the door behind him. "Hell."

"Yeah." With the intention of getting himself a glass of the sweet tea she always kept, Remington yanked the refrigerator door open, stunned to find it packed full of food.

"They're gonna introduce her to the chef. That's where she went. Hey, did you see all this? Is Emma planning to feed an army sometime soon?"

Hunter came up behind him, looking over his shoulder. "How the hell am I supposed to know who she's feeding? Damned woman is always with somebody."

He reached past Remington for the iced tea. "Did she say she'd be back right afterward?"

Remington poked into a couple of containers in the refrigerator while Hunter got the glasses. "No. She said she had some things to do. She made potato salad. Macaroni salad. She's even got cold fried chicken in here."

Handing him a glass of iced tea, Hunter frowned. "Didn't you just eat breakfast?"

"Yeah, but this stuff looks good. I'm gonna stop to check on her when she gets back. Maybe she'll offer me some. I have to wash the lawnmower. I'll put it out front with the hose so I can catch her when she gets home."

* * * *

Emma felt welcome the moment she stepped into the lingerie shop, Rachel's warm greeting making her feel right at home.

Grinning, Rachel made her way around a very pregnant woman behind the counter and hugged her. "It's so great to see you again. I have to tell you, you look a lot better."

"This is Emma?" The glowing pregnant woman came around the counter, her advanced pregnancy making it a slow journey. "I've heard so much about you. It's good to finally meet you. I'm Erin."

Emma liked her immediately. "Rachel's sister. I see the resemblance. I've heard so much about you, too. Your mother-in-law is over the moon about the baby."

Wrapping an arm around Erin's shoulder, Rachel pulled her close. "Aren't we all? Did you come in for something or just for a friendly chat? Would you like some herbal tea?"

Erin grimaced. "No coffee. I'd kill for coffee. Would you like some tea? It's not that bad—or I'm just getting used to it. Really not sure."

"No thanks. I had a gallon of coffee with Pete at the hotel. I've got more errands to run, but I wanted to stop by." Emma hid a smile when Erin slapped away Rachel's attempt to lead her back to her chair again. "Thank you so much for the nightgown you sent to the hospital. It's beautiful and so comfortable."

"Glad you like it. I'm going to take several with me when I go in. I hate those hospital gowns." Erin sighed when the phone rang and glanced at her sister. "You answer it. Maybe you can convince my husbands that I'm fine."

Rachel laughed and disappeared behind a curtain into what Emma assumed to be a back room. "They adore you. Don't you remember how Boone and Chase fussed over me—something *you* encouraged?"

Smiling, Erin shook her head. "Shut up and answer the phone." Turning back to Emma, she sighed. "I love them, but I needed to get away from them for a few hours. You'd think I was the first person in history to ever carry a child."

In an impulsive gesture, Emma reached out to touch Erin's arm. "You're very lucky."

"I know." Erin's eyes welled with tears. "I never thought I'd find this kind of love."

Shaking her head, she sniffed. "Damned hormones. Now tell me what I can do for you."

In an effort to lighten the mood, Emma leaned close.

"Can I tell you a secret?"

Erin's eyes it up. "God, yes! I *love* secrets."

Emma giggled. "Remington has a weakness for pink lace."

Erin giggled. "Then let's see what we can find."

* * * *

After she finished her shopping at the lingerie store, Emma stopped at the grocery store for some of the things she would need later and started home.

Home.

It seemed ironic that she'd finally found a place she could make her home, a place she knew she could really be happy.

Patting the bag on the seat next to her, she grinned.

She'd bought several more pair of pink panties—some satin and some lace—and bras to match, but it was the soft pink nightgown she was most excited about.

The baby doll nightgown had cutouts over her breasts, the sides held closed by pink satin bows.

One tug of each ribbon would allow the material to fall and expose her breasts.

Her nipples beaded at the thought.

The panties she'd bought to wear with it were sheer and had the same matching bows on either side.

She could imagine Hunter and Remington tugging at the bows, their eyes dark with hunger as her panties fell away.

She would be left standing in nothing but sheer fabric that hung freely, their hands moving over her with a firmness that sent her senses soaring.

Still imagining their hands on her, she slowed and turned into the driveway, her breath catching at the sight of Remington, wearing nothing but a pair of jean shorts and sneakers, standing next to the riding mower, drinking from the hose he held.

When he straightened at her approach, she let her gaze move lower to his chest, her fingers itching to trace the lines of clearly delineated muscle.

Suddenly, he dropped the hose and jumped to the side.

A split second later, she recognized the sound of metal crumpling and came to an abrupt stop.

It had happened so fast that it took her several seconds to figure out what had happened.

When she did, she wanted to crawl into a hole.

"Way to go, Emma. That'll make him want you."

Embarrassed that she'd crashed into his new lawnmower, Emma avoided Remington's gaze, gripped the wheel tighter, and shifted the car to reverse.

Easing back, she winced at the sound of metal against metal.

Not until she'd turned the car off did she dare sneak a glance at Remington.

His incredulous look probably would have made her laugh in other circumstances, but she thought better of it, unsure of his reaction.

He moved closer, eyeing the front of her car, then his lawnmower, and the front of her car again before lifting his gaze to meet hers through the windshield.

"Are you all right?" He strode to her door and yanked it open. "Emma, are you hurt?"

Mortified and shaken, Emma shook her head. "No. I'm fine." Grateful that she wore sunglasses, she looked up at him. "I'm really sorry about your lawnmower. My insurance will cover it."

He eyed her steadily. "You're damned lucky you didn't get hurt." He held out his hand, raising a brow when she hesitated.

Emma eased from the car, throwing her purse over her shoulder. "I wasn't going fast. My foot was on the brake." She couldn't tear her gaze away from his chest, fisting her hands at her sides to keep from reaching out to touch him.

Remington followed her as she made her way to the front of the car. "Did ya ever think of pressing it down before you ran over my lawnmower?"

Emma winced at the damage to the side of the lawnmower, the bent medal making it obvious that it couldn't be used. "I didn't *run over* your lawnmower. I just ran into it a little."

Remington's eyes went wide. "A *little*?"

"I said I'm sorry!"

Looking at the front of her car, he shook his head. "At least your car's not damaged." He lifted his gaze to hers. "You're just an accident waiting to happen, aren't you?"

Hurt, Emma let anger take over. "It's not my fault! You distracted me."

With his hands on his hips, Remington glared at her. "You're gonna try to blame this on *me*? What the hell did I do to distract you? I was just standing there!"

Feeling foolish, she went on the offense.

"Yeah. Standing there half-naked and looking sexy as hell. How the hell can you expect me to concentrate on my driving if you're going to be standing there with no shirt, muscles rippling all over the place, and your cock pressing against the front of your shorts?"

Hiding a smile at his stunned expression, she turned away. "My ice cream's melting."

* * * *

Remington blinked at the sudden change of subject and, with a curse, went after her.

"Are you actually trying to blame me for this?"

Opening the trunk, Emma grinned. "I look at it this way. If you pulled up and I was naked from the waist up, I'd be very offended if you didn't get distracted."

He smothered a groan at the sight of her bent over to retrieve her purchases, damned sick and tired of being hard every time she was around.

Nudging her aside, he grabbed bags of groceries, his cock throbbing when he noticed that the bags she held with her purse came from Indulgences and the lingerie store.

Straightening with his arms full of groceries, he gestured toward the bags she held. "What did you buy?"

Inwardly cursing himself for asking a question that he didn't want answered, he glared at her and slammed the trunk closed.

Instead of being intimidated by his glare as he'd hoped, she smiled impishly. "Lavender bath oil. I just love the way it makes my skin feel. I also got the sexiest baby doll nightgown with matching panties. It's a beautiful soft pink. Sheer in some places, lace in others. Oh, and it's got these ribbons that come undone with one little tug—"

"I don't want to hear it."

Each word was like a stroke to his cock, the thought of her soft and perfumed from her bath and wearing the nightgown she'd described making him so damned hard his cock ached.

Christ, he had it bad.

Gritting his teeth, he followed her into the house, letting the screen door slam closed behind him.

Her smug smile set his teeth on edge.

Grinning, she placed her bags on the counter and began to go through them. "I've never had a thong in my life." She slid a hand down her rounded bottom. "It feels strange, but I guess I'll get used to it. I bought several, and I couldn't wait to put one on."

Biting back a groan, Remington set the groceries on the island, trying not to think about how badly he wanted to turn her over his knee, pull her jean shorts down, and get a nice, long look at her new thong.

Going to the refrigerator, he retrieved the pitcher of sweet tea, not daring to look at the things she unpacked. "I wanted to wash the lawnmower, and it's hot as hell outside, so I took my shirt off. That's not being half-naked."

Setting her other purchases aside, Emma started putting groceries away. "So if I went out and mowed the lawn topless, you wouldn't say I was doing it half-naked?"

Stunned at the effect the mental image had on him, Remington cursed and hurriedly slammed the refrigerator door closed.

To his consternation—and fascination—Emma turned from the freezer, her nipples beaded tightly against her cotton shirt.

She slowly approached him, reaching out to lay a cold hand on his chest. "Half-naked is half-naked."

Remington bit back a groan at the feel of her cool, soft hand moving tentatively over his chest. "You're playing with fire, baby."

His cock pushed relentlessly against his zipper, throbbing with the need to take her.

Looking up at him through her lashes, she gave him a shy, mischievous smile that had the Dominant inside him clamoring to be released. "Am I?"

His hands went to her waist of their own volition, his fingers clenching with the effort it took to keep them from sliding upward to her breasts.

Her low tank top afforded him a tantalizing view of the upper curve of her breasts, a view he couldn't ignore.

Without meaning to, he reached out to trace the edge of her top, his cock jumping at her soft gasp. "You know damned well that I can't take you."

"You mean you *won't*." Bending to touch her lips to his chest, she smiled when he jolted at the surge of electricity that shot through him. "You say you can't take me because you'll hurt me. That's ridiculous. You've never been anything but gentle with me."

His shock turned to stunned disbelief when she gripped the hem of her bright purple shirt and whipped it over her head.

Fisting his hands at his sides, he watched her toss it onto the island, his cock jumping when she ran the tips of her fingers over the edge of her pink lace bra. "I bought this because you seem to like pink so much. Do you like it?"

Gritting his teeth, he forced his gaze from the swell of her breasts, which nearly spilled from her bra and barely hid her nipples.

For his own sanity, he took a step back, the soft, sweet scent of her driving him crazy.

"You think I'm gentle because I've never fucked you, Emma. I'm not a gentle lover. I'm a Dominant, but baby doll, you're sure as hell not a submissive."

She moved closer, lifting her gaze to his as she laid a hand on his chest again.

"Maybe I could be. I've never been with a man who liked to dominate in bed. My ex was a lazy lover. Something tells me you won't be and will be as eager to give pleasure as you are to receive it. You'd make an exciting lover. I want to feel your hands on me. I dream about it."

Smiling, she smoothed her hands up to his shoulder.

"It's what I was thinking about when I pulled into the driveway."

Stunned, he stared down at her, his hands clenching on her waist pulling her inexorably closer until his cock pressed against her belly and her nipples poked at his chest.

Her incredibly soft skin invited his touch, urging him to explore.

Bending closer, he stared into her eyes, fascinated that the emerald green became more prominent as he slid the tips of his fingers up her back.

Delighting at her shiver, he traced his fingertips over the back closure of her bra, his cock twitching at the feel of her hands tightening on his shoulders.

The anticipation and lust swirling in her eyes hit him hard.

Need slammed into him with the force of a sledgehammer, the need to touch her more intimately not to be denied.

Barely breathing, he slid a fingertip under the clasp of her bra, and with a flick of his fingers, unfastened it.

Her sharp intake of breath and the hunger in her eyes satisfied the Dominant inside him.

Just a little more.

Slipping his hands to her sides, he lifted her bra out of the way, baring her breasts to his gaze.

"Yes." Emma's eyes fluttered closed as she arched in invitation.

It was an invitation Remington didn't have the willpower to refuse.

Cupping her full, firm breasts, he bit back a groan at the smoothness of her skin. Sliding his thumbs over her nipples, he stiffened at her soft cry, his cock pounding to be freed.

He wanted her more than he'd ever wanted anything in his life, need for her like a fire in his veins that threatened to consume him.

Once he took her, there would be no going back.

"No!"

Releasing her, he took a step back, catching her bra when it slid down her arms and tossed it onto the island.

Her eyes dimmed with pain, her bottom lip trembling as she dropped her hands, crossing them over her chest to hide her breasts.

"You really don't want me?"

"Fuck!" Instinctively reaching for her, Remington took her wrists and lifted her hands to his shoulders again. "I want you, damn it!"

Releasing her wrists, he cupped her breasts, biting back a groan at the sharp need that brought his need to dominate to the surface.

Feeling his control slipping through his fingers, he knew he had to get the upper hand—and he had to do it fast.

"You think you have it in you to be submissive?" The steel in his voice came automatically, but the huskiness was something new.

Emma arched, pushing her breasts more firmly into his hands. "I want to try. I love the way it feels when you touch me. Tell me how to please you. I never knew I could want so much. I'm so aroused that it hurts."

The breathless hunger in her voice made him impossibly harder, but it was the sadness and fear of rejection in her eyes that made the decision for him.

Struggling for the control that usually came easy for him, he stroked her nipples, his cock jumping at her soft cry.

"You wanna play, baby? Let's play. Keep those hands where they are."

Biting her lip, Emma nodded, her eyes dark with desire.

And trust.

He was in trouble, but he couldn't stop.

Biting back a groan, Remington tightened his fingers on her nipples, searching her eyes for any sign of fear.

Instead, her eyes darkened even more, a cry of shock and delight making his chest swell.

Her eyes fluttered and closed. "Oh, Rem."

"Open those fucking eyes and keep them open."

The helpless delight softening her features gave him a firmer grip in his control. "You're trying to tempt me into fucking you, totally ignoring the risk."

Trembling against him, she lifted her arms higher, sliding her fingers into his hair. "There's no risk, Rem. You'd never hurt me."

She sucked in a breath when he tightened his fingers on her nipples, her sharp cry of pleasure like a fist around his cock. "Please, Rem. Please take me."

Staring down at her flushed face, he brushed his lips over hers.

He could have her.

Right here.

Right now.

He could strip her out of her shorts and have her bent over the table in seconds.

He could rip her new pink, thong panties from her before freeing his cock.

One thrust and he'd be deep inside her.

He'd fuck more cries of pleasure from her until she knew nothing but him.

He'd make her mindless with pleasure and earn her submission, a submission that would grow with each day.

He could have her for life.

His cock leaked moisture, orgasm only a stroke away.

"No! Fuck!" Releasing her, he took a step back, his heart pounding furiously. "Damn it, Emma!"

He kept his arms extended to steady her if needed, yanking them back when she braced a hand on the island and steadied herself.

Running a hand through his hair, he took another step away from her, furious at himself for letting it go so far.

For wanting her too damned much.

His lack of control terrified him and convinced him that taking her would be a big mistake.

Blaming himself for the confusion and hurt in her eyes, he inwardly winced when she reached for her top and held it in front of her breasts to cover herself.

The Dominant wanted to rip it away from her and reprimand her for trying to cover herself from him while the son of his father took another step back, his stomach clenching when she moaned his name and reached for him.

Shaking his head, he turned away, struggling to control his breathing. "I can't, Emma. I'm sorry. I'd hurt you. I want you too badly, and I'm very much afraid of losing control with you. I'm too damned rough."

Turning back, he fisted his hands at his sides to keep from reaching for her to comfort her, not trusting himself to touch her again.

"I just can't. If I hurt you, I'd never forgive myself."

To his surprise and relief, she smiled and nodded. "I know."

She slipped her shirt back on before turning to deal with the rest of the groceries, but she couldn't hide the fact that she shook.

"You're wrong. Worse than that, you're stupid."

Because he found himself transfixed by her nipples beaded tight and poking at the front of her shirt, and fighting the urge to lift her shirt out of the way to take them into his mouth, it took several seconds before her words sank in.

When they did, he stiffened, his simmering anger rumbling to a boil once again. "Stupid?"

"Yes. Stupid." With her hands on her hips and her gold-flecked eyes shooting sparks at him, she had to be the most beautiful and arousing woman he'd ever seen.

Closing the distance between them in three long strides, he gripped her upper arms and lifted her to her toes, shocked at the satisfaction gleaming in her eyes instead of the fear he'd expected.

"You're the one who's being stupid. Don't fucking provoke me!" Releasing her with a curse, he moved away from her. "Neither one of us could handle the consequences."

"Speak for yourself."

"Damn it, Emma!"

"If you weren't so caught up in the idea of not hurting me, you'd see that all you and Hunter do is protect me. Even angry. Even aroused, for God's sake! Right now you're angry *and* aroused, and you're putting aside your own needs out of fear of hurting me. You're wrong about yourself, and I don't know what else I can do—or say—to make you see that."

Turning back, he sighed. "I'm right about myself, and I don't know what to do or say to make you see *that*! Look, Emma—"

"Forget it." She waved a hand. "Go mow the lawn or something. I have to make dinner."

Irritated at her attempt to brush him off, Remington snarled. "I can't mow the fucking lawn! Someone ran over my lawnmower. Remember?"

"I didn't run over the damned thing. I ran *into* it. Dinner will be ready in half an hour."

Knowing that spending any more time with her while they were both aroused and angry would be dangerous, Remington shook his head. "I'll eat at the diner."

"That wasn't our agreement. Remember?"

"Fuck our agreement!" He turned away, more furious with himself by the minute. "I've got to get the hell out of here." He yanked the back door open and started through it.

"You do that."

The underlying hurt in her tone tightened his stomach.

Frustrated at himself—and her—he paused at the doorway, blowing out a breath as he turned back to her.

"We've told you why we can't be your lovers. Why do you have to keep pushing it?"

Turning from the pantry, Emma reached for one of the grocery bags from the island and slowly, almost absently began to fold it.

The silence stretched, and assuming she had no intention of answering him, he turned to walk away.

Pausing when she said his name, he turned back and waited, watching her smooth the wrinkles out of the paper bag with slow precision.

Fisting her hands on top of the bag she'd just folded, she sighed, her eyes shimmering with tears.

"I've never met men like you and Hunter before. I want both of you in my life very much. I want the kind of relationship with you that can exist in this town. Love. Family."

Straightening, she smiled, a forced smile that didn't erase the misery in her eyes.

"You're gentle. Caring. Patient."

Her lips twitched.

"You're also the most exciting men I've ever met. You're stubborn and headstrong, which can be a pain in the ass sometimes, especially when you've made up your mind about something." Meeting his gaze, she smiled again, her smile wobbly.

"You're also strong. You have the kind of strength a woman can rely on. You probably have no idea how rare that is."

She folded her arms around herself in a protective gesture that tore at his heart. "I'm afraid I've fallen in love with both of you."

Remington sucked in a breath, stunned at the effect her softly spoken words had on him. Shaking his head, he hurriedly stepped back.

Shaken at the thought of having Emma's love, he had to swallow several times before speaking.

"No. You can't." He tried to look away from the misery in her eyes but couldn't tear his gaze from hers.

"You're too damned sweet. I'm the wrong kind of man for you. There's too much violence inside me. Don't love me, Emma."

She smiled sadly, ripping his heart to shreds. "I'm afraid it's too late for that."

She took a step toward him, her eyes flashing with hurt when he stepped back again.

Instantly regretting it, he stepped toward her, but she'd already turned away. Closing the distance between them, he closed his hands over her shoulders, biting back a curse when she stiffened and tried to pull away.

"I'm sorry, Emma. I'm sorry for hurting you, but I can't be what you need."

Knowing that anything else he said would only make the situation worse, Remington sighed and released her, fighting the urge to press a kiss to her hair.

He'd almost reached the back door when the sound of her voice, coming from directly behind him, stopped him in his tracks.

Laying a hand on his back, she sighed.

"You're wrong about that. So wrong. You're exactly what I need, and I'm what you need. You're just too blinded by the ridiculous belief that you're like your father."

Without turning, he stared unseeingly out the screen door, wondering how the feel of one small hand on his shoulder could affect him so deeply.

"You're wrong about that. It won't do any good to want something you can't have—for either of us."

Shrugging off her hand, he pushed the screen door open and strode outside, rounding the house until he got to the lawnmower out front, his anger growing with every step.

She loved him.

Emma loved him, and there wasn't a damned thing he could do about it.

"Fuck!" He kicked the lawnmower, giving it one more dent, but it did nothing to alleviate his fury.

He had to get the hell out of there before he did something he was sure to regret—like going back into the house and giving in to the most incredible hunger he'd ever experienced.

Chapter Fifteen

Hunter had hoped that expending energy chopping firewood would help him stop thinking about Emma, but so far, it hadn't worked.

He couldn't stop thinking, and his thoughts centered on Emma.

Ever since their trip to the grocery store, he hadn't been able to get the image of her stepping out of her panties out of his mind.

He didn't think he'd ever forget the defiance and challenge that had flashed in her eyes, nor would he ever forget what it had felt like to watch her ass while she finished her shopping, knowing damned well that her bottom was bare under her dress.

He paused, looking up as Remington stormed past him, raising a brow at the string of curses pouring from his clearly furious brother. Tossing a log aside, Hunter wiped his brow with the back of his forearm.

"Problem?"

His brother didn't even slow down. "Yeah, a stubborn woman—and she's driving me nuts! I'm gonna get showered and go to the club. There's an auction there tonight. Remember?"

Hunter frowned and watched Remington storm into the house, slamming the door behind him. "I remember."

Neither one of them could even look at another woman, a hard fact they'd had to face when they'd gone to the club after taking Emma to the grocery store.

He didn't know why Remington would think it would be any better at the auction, but for his own peace of mind, he was willing to try.

Turning toward the direction his brother had come, Hunter stared at Emma's house.

He didn't know what the hell had happened to put his brother in such a mood, but he was determined to find out.

Burying the blade of the axe into the large stump, he reached for his shirt.

As he strode toward the main house, he tried to ignore the fact that he could have found out what he wanted to know simply by asking his brother.

He tried to convince himself that it wasn't the lure of seeing Emma again that drew him to the house.

Pausing at the door, he watched her through the screen, wondering once again what the hell it was about her that tied him up in knots.

He couldn't take his eyes from her as she worked in the kitchen, her movements smooth and efficient from long practice.

He wondered what she'd think if she knew he got hard just watching her transfer the fried chicken and salads they'd discovered earlier to the table.

Hell, he got hard watching her do anything.

She seemed distracted as she piled cold chicken onto a platter, her low curses telling him that whatever had angered Remington had angered her as well. "Asshole. Jerk. Prick."

Not used to being a peacemaker, he knocked on the door, wanting to get a shower so they could go to the auction where Charlene would be waiting.

If anyone could make them forget about Emma, it would be Charlene.

To his horror, Emma spun with a gasp, the platter slipping from her hands and crashing to the floor.

He bit back a groan when he realized she wasn't wearing a bra.

"Don't move!" Yanking the screen door open, he rushed toward her, sweeping her high against his chest.

"Damn it, Emma!" The feel of her body against his was like a punch to his senses.

"You and Remington say that a lot."

Gritting his teeth at the feel of her firm breasts and beaded nipples pressed against his chest, he snapped at her, his immediate arousal twisting his insides.

"That's because you frustrate the hell out of both of us!" Turning, he set her on the island, glancing at the pale, pink scrap of lace next to her. "Don't you dare move."

He gestured toward her dainty feet, growing angrier by the second. "Why the hell do you insist on going around barefoot? You almost stepped on one of the big shards of glass. If I wasn't here, you would have ripped your feet to shreds!"

The thought of her delicate feet cut and bleeding from the jagged glass fueled his anger. "You gonna have to learn to be more careful, Emma! I mean it. Hell. I have to watch you every minute."

The shock and hurt in her eyes made him feel like a heel.

The reminder that his temper stood between him and having a woman like Emma in his life sent another surge of anger through him, but Emma ignored the warning signs and met his anger with her own.

"You asshole! If you hadn't startled me, I wouldn't have dropped the damned thing."

Fascinated by the sparkle of gold glittering in her eyes, Hunter turned away with a grunt. "Just stay there while I clean this up." He opened the closet where he knew a broom and dustpan were stored.

"My chicken's all over the floor!"

"Fuck your chicken!"

"Listen—"

Spinning, he hit the island with the broom handle. "No! You listen. You stay right where you are until I deal with this glass."

Crossing her arms over her chest, Emma had the audacity to smile at him.

"Has anyone ever told you that you're bossy? And arrogant?"

"All the time. I also have a temper." Turning, he swept up the glass. "Something I've warned you about often. What's your point?"

When she didn't answer, he turned to find her ogling his ass.

She smiled, apparently not the least bit embarrassed to be caught staring. "Do you really think your temper scares me?"

"It should."

"It doesn't. Not at all. Are you done? I want to get down."

After dumping the broken glass and chicken into the garbage can, he put the broom and dustpan on the back steps to hose off later.

Coming back inside, he sent her a warning look. "Stay put until I wash my hands."

Waiting until he could look in her eyes, he washed and dried his hands before approaching her again. Closing his hands on her waist, he eased her down.

"What did you do to piss Remington off?"

Smiling, she sidestepped him and moved to the refrigerator, bringing out another plate of chicken.

"What makes you so sure that I did anything?"

Hunter frowned, wondering at her attempt to avoid answering his question. "Because he came over here to wash the lawnmower and came back to the house mad as hell—just minutes after you got home."

"And you think it was my fault?"

Watching her retrieve another plate of cold chicken from the refrigerator, he leaned back against the counter. "You seem to have a knack for it." He carried the macaroni and potato salads from the counter to the island, wondering who she'd invited to dinner. "So what happened between you two?"

Emma glanced in his direction and went to the cabinet. "Why don't you ask him?"

Jealousy darkened his mood. "Because I'm asking you."

Looking over her shoulder, she gave him a saucy grin that made his hands itch to paddle her well-rounded ass.

"Well, he *did* get a little upset when I crashed into your new lawnmower."

"What?" Stunned, he gaped at her. "Are you all right?"

"Obviously."

The itch on his palm grew steadily. "You're a menace to yourself and everyone around you!"

Emma smiled sadly, making him regret his outburst. "Your brother had a similar opinion."

He seemed to hurt her no matter how he tried to avoid it.

To give himself a few minutes too cool down, he turned away and strode to the front of the house and out the front door to have a good look at his now mangled lawnmower.

Standing there, he stared from the lawnmower to her car and back again.

He moved to her car, squatting down to see that the front bumper had a small dent and some of the paint had been scratched.

He'd have to call Ryder and Dillon to fix it.

Straightening, he eyed his lawnmower again.

He'd have to go buy a new one.

He was just glad Emma hadn't been hurt.

He strode back into the house and to the kitchen, his mouth watering at the feast laid out on the island.

"I think I've died and gone to heaven."

Grinning, she poured sweet tea into two glasses. "Help yourself. I've got some lima beans on the back burner."

Hunter went to the cupboard for two plates, the warm feeling of moving around the kitchen with Emma unlike what he'd experienced as a child.

Silence and tension had once ruled the house he stood in, everyone afraid of saying or doing something that would rile his father's temper.

He and Remington would never subject a child to that.

Emma turned, eyeing him curiously. "Something wrong?"

Hiding his thoughts, Hunter allowed a small smile. "I saw the lawnmower."

"I'm sorry. I got distracted." She glanced at him again as she placed the plate full of chicken on the island. "You mad at me, too?"

"No."

Leaning against the island, Hunter watched her, intrigued at her unwillingness to tell him what had gone on between her and his brother.

He knew that, although Remington might have gotten a little upset about the lawnmower, it wouldn't have made him as angry as he looked when he'd flown past him, and it certainly wouldn't have driven him to want to go to the club.

"Your car needs some work."

"I'll take care of it."

"No. I'll handle it." Smiling his thanks when she handed him a glass of sweet tea, he straightened. "You really are a menace."

Especially to his peace of mind.

"So you've said." Setting the bowl of beans on the table, she looked away. "I already told Remington that my insurance would cover it."

He picked up the bra from the edge of the island, dangling the pink lace from his finger. "What else happened between you and Remington?"

Her lips twitched as she held out the plate of chicken and snatched the bra from his hand. "I took my top off and tried to seduce him. Chicken?"

Narrowing his eyes at the amusement in hers, he accepted the plate. "You asking if I want some of this or if I'm afraid of you?"

Emma shrugged, her eyes dancing. "Now, why would a big, strong man like you be afraid of me?"

Grateful that sitting at the island hid his erection from her, Hunter served her a piece of chicken. "Women are the most dangerous creatures on earth."

After serving himself, he set the plate of chicken aside. "You wanna tell me why you decided to seduce Remington?"

Lifting her chin, she smiled—a challenge if he'd ever seen one. "Because I want him. I want you, too. I didn't expect to fall in love with both of you, but I did."

In the process of lifting a chicken leg to his mouth, Hunter paused, lowering it again. "Excuse me?"

Emma turned a delightful shade of pink. "I figured he'd already told you."

Adopting a stern expression to hide the turmoil raging inside him, Hunter wiped his hands on a napkin, never taking his eyes from hers.

"He didn't."

"Oh." Emma's smile made his cock twitch. "I was sexy as hell, too."

He couldn't resist the challenge in her eyes, the need to prove that he was more than capable of handling intimacy with her overwhelming.

Just a taste.

He promised himself that just a taste would be enough to satisfy his craving for her.

Just a little show of dominance would be enough to teach her a lesson about tempting him.

Pushing his plate aside, he sat back, crossing his arms over his chest.

"Show me."

Shifting in her seat, a dead giveaway to her nervousness, she raised a brow. "Show you what?"

"How you tried to seduce Rem. Lose the shirt."

Her eyes narrowed in suspicion. "Why?"

Hunter shrugged. "I'd like to see why it made him so mad."

Emma shot to her feet, her eyes glittering with excitement.

"It made him mad because he wants me but doesn't have the courage to take me."

Rising to his feet, Hunter slowly moved toward her, steering her toward the counter. "He's only trying to protect you. You don't understand the violence in our blood."

Emma's eyes went wide when she realized she'd been backed against the counter—the wall on one side and Hunter's body on the other preventing an escape.

Still, she lifted her chin, her bravado a challenge he couldn't ignore. "You're both delusional. You're not violent, and I'm sure as hell not afraid of either one of you."

To tease himself, Hunter ran the back of his finger over her cheek, his cock swelling at the flare of need in her eyes.

"You should be."

"So you've both said."

Sliding his finger over her jaw line, he raised a brow. "Aren't you going to try to seduce *me*?"

Staring into his eyes, Emma shook her head and smiled. "No."

Hunter slid his hands to her waist, gently massaging.

"Why not?"

Her breathing hitched, making his cock throb, but she lifted her chin, giving him another of the sassy smiles he loved. "Because you'll do the same thing he did. You'll get mad and storm out. There's no point."

Bending close enough to feel her breath on his lips, Hunter bit back a groan.

"We want you. Make no mistake about that. You get to me. To us."

He slid his hands higher, stopping just under her breasts.

"I want you—so much it would scare the hell out of you. I want nothing more than to strip you naked and explore every inch of you."

He slid his hands to her waist again and under the hem of her shirt, forcing himself to keep them there.

"But my feelings for you aren't gentle. They're violent and so primitive that I would probably terrify you. If you were mine, I'd make you wild with lust, and I wouldn't be satisfied until you submitted."

His hands clenched on her waist, the softness of her skin irresistible.

"I wouldn't be satisfied until I had it all. I'd want—need—you to belong to me in every way a woman could belong to a man."

Emma shivered, leaning closer. "Tell me."

His hands went to her bottom. "I'd paddle your ass if you disobeyed me or put yourself in danger." He squeezed her full bottom, his cock swelling at the firm fullness.

"Hunter."

Her breathless plea drew more of his dominant needs out of hiding.

He pulled her away from the counter, turning her to face the island. Leaning over her, he forced her to bend over, pressing his cock against her lower back.

Smiling at her shiver, he touched his lips to her ear. "Once your bottom was warm, I'd spread your thighs and keep them spread. You'd be soaked by then, and I'd want to explore."

"Oh God."

"I'd tease you mercilessly."

He could imagine it clearly.

Emma wiggled against him, her breathing ragged. "You w-would?"

"Oh, yeah. I'd make you so mindless with pleasure that you'd do anything for release. You'd do anything I wanted you to do. Even beg."

Emma's breath caught. "Confident, aren't you?"

"Lift your shirt for me."

His cock hardened even more when she did it without hesitation.

Reaching around her, he closed his fingers over her nipples. "I'd teach you all about erotic pain."

Pinching her nipples, he scraped his teeth over her neck, reveling in her sharp cries of pleasure. "It adds an edge that's addictive. It's an edge that I'll teach you to crave."

He released her nipples, pleased at her soft cry, a response to the blood flowing back into them. To heighten the sensation, he pressed her down until her nipples came into contact with the cool granite.

"Pain for pleasure. Pain for discipline."

Another shiver went through her.

"Discipline?"

"Of course."

To please both of them, he nuzzled the soft skin of her neck, right beneath her ear. "You don't think I'd let you get away with that attitude of yours, do you?"

For the most part, he would, mainly because he enjoyed her spirit so much, but he'd use it as an excuse to get his hands on her and draw her into a web of erotic pain and pleasure.

Scraping his teeth over her neck again, he lifted her slightly and rolled her nipples between his thumbs and forefingers, applying just enough pressure to bring her to her toes.

Using his thigh to lift her higher onto the surface of the island, he pressed his cock against her ass, almost coming in his jeans at the contact.

A surge of lust and possessiveness hit him hard—so hard that he came close to throwing caution to the wind and claiming her for his own in the most basic way possible.

"Hunter! Please."

Reality crept in, saving him from making the biggest mistake in his life.

With a curse, he lowered her to the floor and took a step back. "Don't tempt either one of us again. We want you too damned much to be the gentle lovers you need."

He couldn't resist. He needed just one taste.

Spinning her to face him, he yanked her against him and kissed her, pouring all of his need for her into a kiss meant to punish.

To brand her as his own.

Panicked at the thought, he released her, backing away.

"We're no good for you. We could hurt you so easily."

Shaking her head, her lips swollen and red from his kiss, Emma reached for him.

"You won't."

Hunter had never wanted anything as much in his life. Struggling for control, he took another step back.

"I'm not willing to take that chance."

"I am."

"Too bad. Stay away from us."

Turning, he strode for the back door.

Rem was right.

A night at the club was what they both needed.

They'd find and fuck a woman who would make both of them forget all about Emma.

Chapter Sixteen

Sitting at the bar in the men's club, Hunter glanced at his brother, uneasy at Remington's disinterest in the scantily clad woman sitting between them, a disinterest that mirrored his own.

He'd hoped that the woman they'd dominated on and off for two years would arouse them.

His hopes had been in vain.

He had a sneaky suspicion that he and Remington were well and truly screwed.

Charlene had gone to special pains with her appearance, her long blonde hair caught up in a high ponytail the way he liked it.

The way Emma wore hers.

Striking in the tight red dress that had strategically placed ties that held it together, Charlene leaned into him, pursing her red lips. "Hunter, Remy, I need you so bad. Look. We've sat here so long that someone took our spot."

Hunter wanted to want her.

He *needed* to want her.

But the mental image of Emma, dressed in the red dress she'd worn to the grocery store, kept popping into his head, replacing Charlene's.

With rows of ties, Charlene's dress had been designed for a submissive.

He could have stripped it from her in seconds and revealed a body that had given him countless hours of pleasure.

Instead, he could think only about the way Emma's ass swayed in the flirty red dress and the challenge in her eyes when he'd touched her earlier.

Her cries of pleasure still echoed in his mind, the memory strong enough to block out the loud music playing in the club.

Ordering another drink, he glanced at Remington, grimacing when he saw that his brother continued to throw back whiskeys faster than usual.

Emma was getting to both of them.

He knew whiskey wasn't the answer, but he hoped it would dull his need for her, at least for tonight.

He wanted to fall into bed and pass out, without dreams of his sweet and entirely too provocative tenant.

Just one night of sleep and he'd be more in control.

Charlene ran a hand over his thigh, but even with his whiskey-soaked brain, he moved fast enough to catch her hand before it could reach its destination. "Hunnnterrr? I need you. I need you and Remy to take me." Pouting, her red lips shiny in the faint light, she stood and rubbed her ass against his thigh, looking up at him over her shoulder. "I've been bad. Really bad. Don't you want to spank me?" She arched, offering her breasts to Remington.

Remington grimaced and shook his head. "No, Charlene. Find someone else."

"Someone else?" Charlene's shrill voice grated on Hunter's nerves. "Not a chance in hell. You're mine."

Remington's brow went up, his features hard and cold. "There were never any promises between us, Charlene, and you know it."

Charlene appeared to back down, apparently shaken by Remington's coldness. Bowing her head, she looked up at him through her lashes, a small smile playing at her lips. "I'm sorry, Master. Please forgive me. I deserve your punishment."

Hunter tossed back his whiskey, welcoming the burn. "Not in the mood to punish anyone tonight."

The only ass he wanted to see was Emma's.

He realized he was just as angry at Emma as he was at Charlene.

The life they'd convinced themselves they *had* to live seemed to be crumbling under their feet.

And he blamed Emma for it.

She'd shaken his world, forcing him to look at things that he'd rather not inspect too closely.

Lifting his hand to signal for another drink, he raised a brow when the new bartender, Bill Savage, held out his hand.

Bill was a large, bald man, who appeared to be somewhere in his mid-thirties. Standing six feet, eight inches tall, the quiet bartender with bulging muscles and tattooed biceps rarely spoke, but a dark look from him spoke volumes.

"What?"

"Keys."

Not in the mood to walk home, Hunter glared at him. "No. Two more whiskeys."

Fueling his temper, Bill waited him out, the bartender not giving in an inch.

Irritating Hunter further, Charlene turned to him and pressed against his side, running a hand down his chest. "We're not done. I'll do anything. You know I can make you feel good. I don't want another Master. I want you and Remy."

Hunter winced at the shrill demand in Charlene's voice, and dropped his keys into Bill's hand with a sigh. "Make them doubles."

Bill gave Hunter and Remington a warning glare. "I don't want any trouble."

Hunter glared back. "No trouble."

Beside him, Charlene gripped his arm. "Hunter, I'll do whatever you want me to. You can't just ignore me. I've given you a lot of pleasure."

"And we've given you a lot of pleasure in return." Irritated that Charlene's whining kept interfering with his thoughts of Emma, he turned to her. "You did what we wanted you to do because it suited your purpose."

After downing his whiskey, he stood abruptly, throwing several bills on the bar before turning away. "A lot of men want you, Charlene, so you won't be lonely."

Remington stood with him. "Just do them a favor and let them know that you're looking for a long-term Master before you get involved with them."

Charlene pouted and started to follow them. "I don't want anyone long term except you two. I thought that once you saw that I wasn't scared of you like the other women, you would see that we belong together. I love you."

"You don't love us!" Hunter whirled on her, furious for allowing himself to get into this position, a position of his own making.

He thought of Emma and her claim to love him. "If you loved us, you wouldn't be in such a hurry to fuck someone else when we weren't here."

Emma didn't even try to make them jealous.

Charlene gasped. "You knew about that?"

Remington inclined his head. "Of course. We know everything that goes on in here when we're not around. There have been other men, of course, some not in this club but in others."

Charlene shrugged. "I have needs, and you've been coming here less and less. I thought maybe I wasn't giving you what you needed, so I approached other Doms to teach me more."

Hunter gritted his teeth, thinking of Emma.

If he'd learned that she'd gone to another man for pleasure, he would have been devastated.

Hunter set his empty glass on the counter with a thud, anxious to see Emma again. "Good-bye, Charlene."

Coming to the club had seemed like a good idea earlier, but no matter how much he drank, or how many women were available to him, he couldn't stop thinking about Emma.

Glancing at his brother, he slid from the stool. "I need to see Emma."

Remington nodded. "I don't like how I left her. I won't sleep tonight until I talk to her."

Before they could reach the door, Blade Royal stepped out of the shadows.

"Everything okay?"

Hunter gritted his teeth. "Everything's fine."

Knowing that nothing could distract Blade like talk of his family, Hunter smiled. "How's the baby? How's Kelly?"

"They're wonderful. Thank you for asking. You about to get a family of your own?"

Remington snorted. "Not likely."

Blade smiled slowly. "I've heard Emma's giving you a run for your money."

Clenching his jaw, Hunter scowled. "I wish everyone would mind their own fucking business."

"In this town?" Chuckling, Blade glanced around, his sharp eyes taking in everything. "Because we're all such a tight-knit community, I know that Emma has company. So if you're rushing off because you feel bad that you left her alone, there's no need."

Hunter's stomach clenched.

He didn't have a lot of experience with it, but he recognized jealousy when he felt it.

"Who the hell's there?"

Blade grinned. "Ace, Hope, Beau, and Charity. Apparently, Hope called and Emma said she had a lot of fried chicken that was going to go to waste."

Remington glanced at Hunter and scowled. "I would have eaten it cold when we went to check on her."

Not wanting to walk into the main house and be the subject of more scrutiny, Hunter decided that he'd give it another hour before going home.

He wanted to talk to Emma alone.

Folding his arms over his chest, Blade blocked the doorway, the dim lighting sharpening the already hard features, emphasizing Blade's Native American heritage and giving him a dark, formidable appearance. "You're not planning to drive to the bar, are you?"

Irritated, but appreciating his friend's concern, Hunter sighed. "No. Your new bartender already took my keys. We're walking there." Frowning, he glared at Blade. "How the hell did you know where we're going?"

Blade shook his head and smiled, something he did more often since he'd married Kelly. "Because I'm not stupid. Something obviously happened between you—"

Hunter stiffened. "How the hell do you know that?"

Lifting a brow, Blade eyed both of them. "Because you showed up here. If you weren't so hardheaded, you'd see what everyone around you sees."

Remington scraped a hand through his hair. "There's nothing to see."

"Uh-huh." Clearly not believing him, Blade stepped aside. "You're fools if you let her get away."

As Hunter started through the doorway, he paused next to Blade. "And you're a fool if you believe Remington and I would be good for any woman."

Narrowing his gaze, Blade looked from Hunter to Remington and back again. "You know, I've seen both of you run to help anyone who needed it—regardless of the danger. I've seen both of you take on the biggest, meanest drunks—here and at the bar."

He smiled slowly. "Don't tell me you're afraid of going home and facing one little woman."

Hunter shoved his friend out of the way. "You're damned right I am!"

Nobody scared him as much as Emma did.

Nobody ever had such power over him.

Nobody else had the ability to break him.

Chapter Seventeen

Beau sat back with a smile, wrapping an arm around his wife and settling it on the back of her chair. He pulled her closer, toying with the ends of her hair.

"Ace told me that you're a good cook, but I thought he was embellishing just a little." He slid his hand over his flat stomach, kissing the top of Charity's head when she leaned into him. "I was wrong. Damn, that was good. Hunter and Remington don't know what they're missing."

Emma shrugged. "They were both in a hurry to get out of here."

Ace's eyes narrowed. "What's wrong? Something else is bothering you, isn't it? Is there anything I can do to help?"

Amused that he saw so much, and touched at his concern, Emma forced a smile. "A woman called right before Hope did. She said that Hunter and Remington went to the club to meet with her."

Hope slapped a hand on the table, jumping up from her chair. "Damn it! I'll bet that was Charlene! That damned woman is a viper. For some reason, she thinks Hunter and Remington belong to her!"

Forcing another smile, Emma started gathering the dishes. "Maybe they do. They sure ran to her in a hurry. If those assholes want sex with her more than they want a relationship with a woman who loves them, they can have it."

When all four stared at her, she realized what she'd admitted.

Avoiding their gazes, she shrugged and stacked the dishes beside the sink before heading back to the table for more. "Yeah. I know. I fell in love with them. Stupid, I know. I didn't mean to do it. They warned me and warned me, but I thought I could change them."

Irritated that tears stung her eyes and her stomach tied up in knots, she waved a hand, so angry she wanted to throw something.

"How many women have thought they could change a man? We can't change them."

Charity gathered dishes and made her way toward the sink, pausing next to her.

"That's different. You're not trying to change them. You're trying to show them what's already inside them. They're the ones fooling themselves."

Hope looked toward Ace, stiffening when his cell phone rang. "Why do men have to be so damned stubborn?"

Beau gave his wife an intimate look. "Women can be just as stubborn."

Ace listened to whoever had called him and rose to his full height, his jaw clenched. "I'll be right there."

He disconnected with a low curse and reached for his hat. "Beau, take Hope home for me."

Hope gripped his arm. "What is it?"

Ace bent to kiss his wife's hair, lifting his gaze to Emma's. "Hunter and Remington are at it again."

Beau rose. "Oh hell. I'll come with you."

Emma lifted her chin. "No. I want to go."

Hope shook her head. "You won't be allowed in the club."

Ace straightened, holding Emma's gaze. "They're not at the club. They showed up at the bar a while ago and were already half-drunk when they got there. I've gotta go before they tear up the place."

Emma rushed after him, pausing in the living room to slip her shoes. "I'll go with you."

"No."

"They're mad at me." Gripping Ace's sleeve, she tugged, hurrying to keep up with his long strides.

"Please, Ace. I have to show them that I'm not afraid of them—even when they're at their worst. I *have* to do this!"

Shaking his head, Ace opened the front door and glanced back at her. "No."

Emma waited until the door closed behind him and cursed, looking back at Hope.

Aware of Beau and Charity in the next room, she kept her voice low. "I'm going."

"Of course you are." Hope glanced toward the kitchen as she shoved Emma's purse at her and pushed her toward the door. "Go! Hurry before Beau figures out what you're doing. We'll clean up here and then clear out. Give 'em hell, honey!"

* * * *

Emma raced to the bar, slamming on the brake just inches from the brick wall. She had her door open before she'd even shut off the engine, cursing when her purse got tangled with her seat belt.

With a low growl, she yanked it free and slammed the car door closed. Anxious to get inside, she hurried around the corner and into the bar, wincing at the sound of breaking glass and a loud crashing sound.

Turning toward the action, she gasped, stunned to see Remington punch a man in the stomach, and with a sense of disbelief, she watched the recipient of Remington's punch fly through the air and hit the wall.

Hard.

John, his expression hard and cold, grabbed Remington to keep him from going after the man he'd just punched.

Another man lay cursing on the floor, struggling to get up from the top of the broken table under him, the obvious result of the crash she'd heard seconds earlier.

Hunter stood over him, his fists clenched at his sides, glaring at Ace, who jumped between them.

The fury tightening Hunter's features momentarily alarmed her, especially when he spun in her direction.

"Get out!"

Silence fell over the bar, the tension making it difficult to breathe.

Ace and John both looked in her direction while Clay and Rio moved to stand between her and the other men, keeping Jesse close as she hurried to Emma's side.

Emma ignored everyone, keeping her gaze focused on Hunter.

"Kiss my ass, tough guy."

Hunter's eyes narrowed, his jaw clenched. "I thought we talked about you tempting me."

Forcing a smile, Emma shook her head.

"Don't worry. I'm not here to tempt you. You're safe."

With Jesse at her side, she went to the bar where Michael stood, his hands braced against the edge of the bar.

"Can I have a beer, please?"

Not even attempting to hide a smile, Michael inclined his head. "Sure thing, darlin'. Jesse?"

"Sure."

"Why the hell would you bring her here?" Hunter's growl held a hint of embarrassment.

Curious, Emma turned on the bar stool to see that he was scowling at Ace.

Ace helped the man lying on the broken table to his feet. "I didn't bring her. As a matter of fact, I told her to stay at the house with Beau, Charity, and my meddling wife." Ace's cold tone sent a shiver down Emma's spine.

Remington cursed and scraped a hand through his hair. "Go home, Em."

"No."

Pleased that her appearance seemed to unsettle then, Emma turned back to the bar and lifted her gaze to Michael's.

"They do this often?"

Michael sighed and placed mugs of beer in front of her and Jesse. "Often enough."

Feeling several gazes on her back, she took a sip of beer and set her mug down again. "They gonna get arrested?" She reached for the nearby bowl of pretzels and pulled it closer.

Michael shook his head, wiping the perfectly clean bar while Ace and John helped Hunter and Remington's victims to their feet. "Nah. Ace'll just take them home. They always pay for the damage. We'll get new tables and chairs. Glasses." Pausing, he looked over her shoulder. "Looks like a new mirror this time, too."

Turning slightly, she shook her head, ignoring Hunter's and Remington's dark looks. "What a mess. When Ace takes them home, I'll help you clean up."

"Go home, Emma." Hunter's deep voice came from somewhere behind her. "We'll clean up our own damned mess."

Emma nodded. "You do that while I sit here and enjoy my beer."

Turning back to the bar, she smiled up at Michael. "The bar's closed tomorrow, isn't it?"

"Sure is."

From the corner of her eye, she watched John, Hunter, and Remington head to the back, deep in low conversation.

She hated that her hand shook when she reached for her beer again. "What started it this time?"

Michael grinned. "You."

"Me?" Glancing at Hunter and Remington as they came back into the bar, both carrying brooms, Emma set her mug down again. "What the hell did I do?"

"Nothing." Michael shook his head. "Those two men your men pounded on saw you walking out of Jesse's store the other day. They wanted to approach you, but they know the way this town works."

Jesse snorted. "It's a good thing. I hate the thought of anyone bothering her."

Emma smiled. "Don't worry. I can take care of myself." Turning back to Michael, she reached for another pretzel. "So they saw me? What's that got to do with what happened here?"

Michael braced his hands against the bar and leaned closer, keeping his voice low. "They were having a conversation at the bar and asked about you. Hunter and Remington were standing over there, at the other end of the bar. They were both already in a bad mood when they got here."

Smiling, he straightened. "When they asked if you belonged to anyone, I told them that you didn't. I was hoping Hunter or Remington would say something, but they just looked even madder."

Jesse groaned, dropping her head in her hands. "Don't tell me. Those two geniuses started talking about Emma."

"Yep." Michael smiled. "Listing all of her gorgeous attributes and talking about the kinds of things they'd liked to do to her."

Jesse took a sip of her beer. "I can imagine Hunter's and Remington's reaction to that."

"Yep. That's pretty much when all hell broke loose."

Emma turned to see that Clay, Rio, and John helped Hunter and Remington clean up the mess, filling the large garbage can they'd brought from the back. "Several people left. I hope this doesn't ruin your night."

Michael shrugged. "We weren't that busy anyway. It's auction night at the club."

"Auction night?" Emma turned to Jesse. "What's that?"

Hunter appeared behind her. "None of your business. What the hell are you doing here?"

Turning to look over her shoulder, Emma met his angry glare with a grin.

"I heard about the entertainment in town. Thought I'd check it out. You finished, or was there someone else you wanted to hit before you leave?"

Hunter's eyes narrowed again. "Paddling your ass sounds real appealing. What the hell were you thinking, walking into the middle of a bar fight?"

Shrugging, Emma reached for her beer again. "I knew you and Rem were here. Nothing was going to happen to me with the two of you here."

Hunter waited until she'd taken a sip of her beer before taking the mug from her and taking a healthy swig. Slamming the mug back down on the counter, he got in her face. "Don't do it again."

Picking up the mug again, Emma purposely placed her lips where his had been and took another small sip. Licking the foam from her lip and hiding a smile when his gaze followed the movement, she set it down again.

"Go away. I'm talking to my friends."

"So talk."

Clay came up behind Jesse. "The band's getting ready to start again. Come and dance with me, baby."

Jesse gave Emma a questioning look, a look Emma met with a smile.

"Thanks for sitting with me, but I'm okay. Go dance with your husband."

Grinning, Jesse slid from the stool, right into Clay's waiting arms. "He's just using it as an excuse to get his hands on me."

Leaning back, Clay looked down at his wife. "Something wrong with that?"

Grinning, Jesse lifted her hands to his wide shoulders. "Not a damned thing. I'd be heartbroken if you ever stopped."

"That's something you're never gonna have to worry about, baby."

Smiling at how happy they were together, and wishing for the same kind of happiness, Emma turned back to Michael, ignoring Remington as he slid onto the school Jesse had just vacated.

"Michael, I've been thinking about what we talked about the other night, and I think I have some ideas."

John approached, bringing her another mug of beer.

"Yeah. I'd like to hear what you came up with."

"I'd rather show you. The bar's closed tomorrow, isn't it?"

Michael nodded. "Yeah. Why?"

Emma grinned. "Why don't you come to the house tomorrow for dinner?"

Remington spun to face her. "What the hell are you doing?"

"Having guests for dinner." Smiling up at Michael and John, she ignored Hunter, who slid onto the stool on her other side.

Michael grinned. "Love to. We'll bring the wine."

Shaking her head, Emma grinned. "Beer goes better."

"Now I'm intrigued." John nodded. "Beer it is."

Hunter gripped her arm. "You're supposed to cook for us! It's part of our arrangement."

Emma reached for her beer. "So? You never want to eat at the house anyway. If you feel like eating with us, you're more than welcome—but only if you're going to behave yourself." She sipped her beer, eyeing Michael and John over the rim of her glass.

John hid the smile dancing in his eyes, but Michael didn't bother, grinning like an idiot.

Remington grumbled under his breath. "If you were mine, I'd turn you over my knee."

Emma shrugged. "And if you were mine, you'd be home in bed with me instead of fucking subs and starting bar fights. Looks like we're both shit out of luck, doesn't it?"

Stunned, Hunter stared at Emma, unable to believe Emma sat there—right in front of him—and had made a date with John and Michael.

His temper, jealousy, and the alcohol he'd consumed took control of his mouth.

"Since you're going to have dates for dinner, I assume that you're not going to have a problem with Remington and I bringing our own."

The flash of hurt in her eyes made him want to take the words back, but she smiled and slid from the stool, reaching into her purse. "No problem."

Her smile widened when she turned to Michael, a smile that made Hunter want to slam his fist into his friend's face. "Dinner's at five. How much do I owe you?"

John shook his head. "Your money's no good here. We'll see you tomorrow night."

Hunter watched her walk out the door, fighting not to rush after her.

Remington slid to Emma's stool and waited until Michael and John moved away. "What the hell were you thinking? Who the hell are we going to invite to dinner?" His eyes widened. "Oh, no. You don't intend to ask Charlene, do you?"

"Who the hell else can I ask?" Hunter reached for Emma's mug and downed the rest of her beer. "If Emma meets her, she'll see that we don't care about Charlene."

He scrubbed a hand over his face, watching Ace approach out of the corner of his eye. "It pissed me off when she invited John and Michael to dinner, and I didn't think before I spoke. I'm sure as hell not gonna sit there watching her with them like a damned fifth wheel."

Remington shook his head. "I've got a bad feeling about this."

"Yeah. So do I." Hunter had regretted his words as soon as they left his mouth, but it was too late to do anything about it.

The phrase *Hell hath no fury* ran through his mind, but he quickly brushed it away.

It was one dinner.

What could go wrong?

* * * *

Hours later, he stood over her, watching her sleep, the light from the hallway illuminating her small form in the darkness.

Frowning when he saw that she'd kicked off the covers again and had curled into a ball to keep herself warm in the cold room, he reached out to pull the covers over her again while Remington did the same from the other side of the bed.

Covering her shoulder, Hunter couldn't resist stroking the curl that brushed against his finger.

Without glancing at his brother, he laid the curl on top of the blanket and straightened.

"I love her."

"I know. So do I."

"We can't allow it."

Remington sighed. "I don't think we can stop it."

An emptiness settled over Hunter, the hole inside him that Emma had begun to fill once again barren and cold.

"I can't help how I feel about her, but I can control what I do about it. Once she sees us having dinner with Charlene, she'll give up on us and it'll get easier."

Remington gave him a hard look. "I think you're wrong. It's a mistake, and it's gonna hurt her."

Hunter knew that, but he'd already weighed the risks.

"It's a hell of a lot better than the alternative." He stopped abruptly when Emma murmured in her sleep and rolled over, stretching a leg out and dislodging the covers again.

After settling the blanket back over her, Hunter sighed. "We've never allowed ourselves to get close to any woman before. We'd only fuck it up, and she'd end up hating us anyway."

Chapter Eighteen

Emma walked in through the back door just in time to hear a knock from the front.

Wiping her hands on the towel she'd flung over her shoulder, Emma rushed to the front door, smiling to see John and Michael standing on her front porch.

Relieved that they'd gotten there before Hunter and Remington arrived with their date, Emma hurriedly pushed the screen door open.

"Hi!"

With a keg of beer perched on his shoulder, Michael grinned and stepped inside. "Hi, yourself. Something smells incredible."

Standing back, she gestured him inside. "It's the ribs."

Pausing next to her, he leaned down and sniffed. "Nope. It's you. Where do you want this?"

"Put it where you think best." She smiled at John as he came inside. "Your friend's a flirt."

"Tell me something I don't know." John paused next to her, brushing a kiss over her hair. "But you do smell wonderful. Thanks for inviting us."

"My pleasure. I just hope that you like my idea."

John smiled. "Ribs, huh? I'm sure we're gonna love them, especially if you can teach us how to do something like that. Thanks for taking the time to come up with something for us."

"Don't thank me until you've tried them."

John gestured toward her white shorts and chambray shirt, which she'd tied below her breasts. "That button is gonna drive Hunter and Remington crazy. You know that, don't you?"

She'd worn a shirt that Hunter had inadvertently left behind, and only buttoned one button. Wearing one of her new push-up bras, she hoped to get Hunter's and Remington's attention.

"I have competition tonight." Emma forced a smile. "I have a feeling it's Charlene. If I'm going to lose them to her, at least I'm going to go out fighting."

With a hand at her back, John led her to the kitchen. "If they're stupid enough to pick her over you, they don't deserve you. That woman's a snake and will do whatever it takes to get what she wants, and she doesn't care who she has to hurt or embarrass to do it. No matter what she says, she's not faithful to Hunter and Remington by any means. She's offered herself to most of the men in Desire, even some of the married ones."

Michael looked up from where he set up the keg. "We're very open-minded in this town, but cheating is something none of us has any tolerance for. Charlene has been around Desire long enough to know that. She's a troublemaker and gets nasty when she doesn't get her way. Watch your back with that one."

Emma went to the cupboard to retrieve glasses, handing them to John, who'd followed her. "I've dealt with people like that, but I'm not stooping to her level. She's *their* guest. I'm more interested in what you think of the ribs. You don't need a kitchen, just a refrigerator and a big grill. I can't wait for you to taste them."

John glanced at Michael. "Neither the diner nor the hotel serves ribs, so we wouldn't be stepping on anyone's toes."

Encouraged, Emma smiled. "How about wings?"

Emma stiffened at the sound of feminine laughter coming from the backyard. "Sounds like they're here."

John patted her arm. "Don't worry. We've got your back."

Emma barely breathed when the back door opened and a beautiful woman, followed closely by Hunter and Remington, walked into her kitchen.

With long, blonde hair that hung down almost to her waist, the woman turned to hang on to Hunter's arm. "Oh. I thought we were eating alone."

"I never said that." Hunter sent a glare in John and Michael's direction before his gaze settled on her.

"Emma, this is our friend, Charlene. Charlene, Emma. You already know John and Michael."

Charlene, dressed in a white, skintight dress and red heels, laid a possessive hand on Hunter's chest, her red nails a sharp contrast to his white T-shirt. "Yes, I know John and Michael *very* well."

John sat back, barely glancing at her. "No. You don't."

Charlene's lips thinned, and she turned to Emma. "It's so nice to meet the woman taking care of Hunter and Remy for me."

Emma wanted to cry.

Her fingers itched to stroke Hunter's chest the way Charlene did, the memory of being held so firmly against him as he carried her almost more than she could bear.

Despite Charlene's sugar-sweet tone, her eyes shot daggers in Emma's direction. She turned, posing provocatively. "It's always good to see you two."

Although John and Michael both nodded politely, their lack of interest seemed to irritate Charlene, earning both men a stiff smile.

Their eyes narrowed, and both men offered Emma a smile of reassurance, making her realize that she appeared as heartbroken as she felt.

Even Hunter and Remington looked uneasy.

Remington stopped short, his gaze heating Emma's skin as it raked over her from head to toe and back again, pausing on both journeys to settle on the button between her breasts.

"Emma doesn't work for us, Charlene. She's renting this house from us, so she cooks for us."

"Not really." Pride had Emma forcing a smile.

She wouldn't give Hunter and Remington the satisfaction of seeing just how much they'd hurt her. "They eat in town. Michael and John were kind enough to bring a keg of beer. Help yourselves."

Michael came back from the cabinet with several glasses, which he placed on the island next to the keg before he started pouring.

Charlene laughed, a sound that grated on Emma's nerves. "I understand. I'm not a very good cook either. We passed the grill on the way in. I smelled meat. I don't eat meat." She ran a hand down her body as if to draw the men's attention to it. "Not if I want to keep this figure."

Michael approached with a beer for both women, sliding a hand around Emma's waist to settle on the bare skin between her top and shorts. "Emma's figure's perfect, and she eats hearty. I hate when a woman picks at her food."

Accepting the glass of beer, Emma smiled her thanks before turning back to Charlene. "I made a spinach quiche as well because I wasn't sure who Hunter and Remington were bringing to dinner."

"Darling?" She looked up at Hunter, fluttering her lashes. "You didn't tell her about me?"

Leaning heavily against Hunter, Charlene handed him her beer with a grimace. "So you and Remy don't live here?"

Hunter's eyes never left Emma's. "No. We live in the guest house. Is that my shirt?"

Pleased that he'd noticed, and aware that Charlene stiffened beside him, Emma shrugged.

"Yes. I think so. When I came home from the hospital, it was in the bag with my dirty laundry. It must have gotten mixed up with my things when you showered in there. It's very comfortable, and I could tie it out of the way to use the grill. I'll wash it and get it back to you."

He kept eyeing the single button she'd buttoned. "Don't bother. It looks better on you."

Michael slid a hand to her waist. "That's what I told her."

Charlene slapped Hunter's arm.

"You haven't said a word about my dress!"

Hunter glanced at her. "What? Oh, yeah. Your dress is fine."

Emma hid a smile, her confidence boosted by the fact that Hunter and Remington seemed more interested in Emma's cleavage, and the one button she'd buttoned, than in Charlene's plunging neckline.

Picking up the tray from the counter, she turned to Michael and John. "Do you want to come out and help me with the ribs?"

Remington stepped forward and reached for the platter, frowning when John took it from her. "I can help."

Emma waved a hand. "No, thank you. I want John and Michael to see them before I take them off of the grill. Get something to drink for Charlene."

Charlene made a face. "Sorry, honey. I don't drink *beer*."

Hiding another smile at Hunter's look of distaste, Emma nodded. "There's some sweet tea in the refrigerator. I just made it this morning. There's also some diet cola in there if you'd like."

Once outside, John went straight to the gas grill and lifted the lid. "Damn. These smell incredible. What can I do to help?"

Glancing back toward the screen door, Emma leaned closer. "My hands are shaking so much I'm afraid I'll drop them. Can you get them off the grill for me?"

"Absolutely."

Michael sighed. "And corn on the cob? I've died and gone to heaven."

Pleased, Emma beamed. "And coleslaw, baked beans, and biscuits. All homemade of course."

John's stomach rumbled. "Holy hell."

Once back inside, Emma got the baked beans and biscuits out of the oven. "Michael, would you please get the coleslaw out of the fridge?"

Remington rushed to the refrigerator, but Michael beat him to it. "I'll take it, Michael."

Hiding another smile, and enjoying the way Charlene's eyes narrowed with jealousy, Emma took the beans to the table and set them on the trivet she'd set there earlier. "Rem, would you please get the deviled eggs out of the refrigerator? The spinach quiche is on the counter cooling."

"Sure, honey." Sending a smug look in Michael's direction, he opened the refrigerator door again. "I can't believe you went to so much trouble."

Hunter seated Charlene and appeared at her side, leaving Charlene to scowl at him. "What can I do?"

Pointing to one of the cabinets, she smiled. "Can you get my basket for the biscuits?"

John came through the back door just then with the large platter piled high with ribs, which he set on the table next to the platter of corn on the cob.

Wrapping an arm around her waist, John grinned. "Emma, this isn't dinner. This is a feast. You'd better not even think about leaving Desire. I'll buy you a house in town and get you the biggest kitchen you ever saw."

Hunter made a sound in his throat that sounded suspiciously like a growl. "This house is just fine for her. If she needs anything else, all she has to do is tell us."

Charlene's frown deepened. "I thought she was leaving Desire after she finished her cookbook."

Michael pulled out a chair for Emma and made a production of seating her. "Not if I can help it. She fits in perfectly. Hell, everyone in town loves her."

John took the seat to her right, and Michael narrowly beat out Remington's effort to take the seat to her left.

Michael picked up the tongs and served ribs to Emma while John served her from the other side. Glancing at Remington, he leaned closer to Emma to help himself to the corn. "Why don't you go over there and sit next to your date?"

While Charlene picked at her quiche, the others dug in to the rest of the food.

John bit into one of her biscuits and groaned. "Oh God. This is heaven." He turned to Emma. "Does Gracie know about your biscuits?"

Grinning, Emma set a rib bone aside and licked her fingers. "Not yet, but she will."

Charlene picked at her quiche and smiled, revealing even white teeth—with pieces of spinach between them.

"Well, I'm sure it's not that hard to make biscuits—or any of this. Anyone with a cookbook full of recipes can cook."

Hunter frowned. "Emma is one of the people who *writes* those cookbooks."

Charlene smiled again, revealing spinach-speckled teeth again. "Well good for you."

As the enemy, Emma didn't want to be the one to tell Charlene about the green streaks on her teeth and was grateful when Remington did it for her.

"You've got spinach in your teeth."

With a look of horror, Charlene grabbed her purse from the back of her chair and pulled out a mirror.

"Damn." Using a long nail, she picked the spinach out of her teeth and closed the mirror again with a snap. Sliding a hand over Remington's arm, she leaned closer to him, her smile faltering when he leaned forward to take another bite of the rib he held.

"I don't cook. My talents are in other areas."

When neither Hunter nor Remington commented, Charlene smiled coldly at Emma, who was in the process of slathering her corn with butter.

"If you keep eating that way, you're going to lose that figure."

Michael laughed and rose to refill Emma's glass. "Don't worry about watching your figure, Emma. I'll watch it for you."

Emma smiled her thanks, pretending not to notice Hunter's and Remington's almost identical glares in Michael's direction or the elbow to the ribs Charlene gave each of them.

Hunter turned to frown at Charlene. "What? Oh, yeah. Your figure's just fine."

To Emma's surprise, John leaned close and kissed her cheek. "This is the best meal I've ever had. These ribs will be perfect for the bar. Will you come with us to Tulsa tomorrow morning and help us pick out a grill and show us all the stuff we'll need?"

"Absolutely! I'd love to go to Tulsa. I need a new platter. I dropped my other one a few days ago."

Michael reached for another biscuit. "You can help us pick out what we'll serve the ribs in and I'll buy you all the platters you want."

Remington tossed his rib bone onto his plate so hard that it bounced off.

Charlene squealed and jumped up. "Oh! Look what you did! You spattered barbeque sauce all over me." She wiped at the spots, smearing them. "Do you know how much this dress cost me?"

Hunter's eyes turned cold, and after wiping the remaining sauce from his hands, he stood, pulled out his wallet, and tossed several bills in her direction. "That should cover it."

He picked up his glass and made his way back to the keg. "Probably not the right thing to wear to a casual dinner."

Charlene moved away from the table and went to the sink, wetting her napkin under the faucet.

"Just because *she* dresses like a country bumpkin doesn't mean that I have to!"

"Hey!" Michael, John, and Remington all barked out at once.

Hunter, walking back to the table, paused to give Charlene a look that sent a chill up Emma's spine.

"Careful. Get your purse. Since you don't seem to be having a good time, I'll take you home."

Remington rose to his feet, looking both furious and embarrassed as he glanced at Emma. "I'm sorry. I guess this wasn't such a good idea."

John sat back with a scowl, settling an arm protectively over the back of Emma's chair. "You think?"

"Good idea. We'll go back to my place and have some fun." Charlene flung her purse over her shoulder and headed for the door. "Really, this isn't the kind of thing we do."

Emma stood and watched them go, aware of the long, searching looks from Hunter and Remington.

Lifting her gaze, she swallowed the lump in her throat when she saw the regret and apology in their eyes.

Forcing another smile, she waved a hand. "Don't you think you'd better go catch up with your girlfriend."

The flash of anger in Hunter's eyes made her feel somewhat better.

"She's not my fucking girlfriend."

Wincing when the door slammed behind them, Emma blew out a breath and dropped back to her seat again.

"They don't seem to get along all that well with Charlene. Hunter and Remington seem to value sex more than caring. They must want to be with her because they can keep an emotional distance. If that's the case, I don't stand a chance with them."

"That's where you're wrong." John reached for his beer. "They saw tonight the mistake they were making. They'll drop her off, and neither one of them will ever want to see her again."

Emma forced a smile. "I wish I could believe that."

"You can. Now that she's gone, you can relax and eat. You've hardly touched a bite." John smiled encouragingly. "These ribs are going to be a big hit."

Michael served himself more coleslaw. "And getting you out of here first thing tomorrow morning will give Hunter and Remington more time to miss you and realize that you're perfect for them."

Emma sighed. "I don't know."

"I do." John handed her a biscuit. "I can't wait to tell Gracie about these biscuits."

* * * *

Hunter was in a rotten mood.

He and Remington had been chopping wood since they returned from breakfast, but it hadn't relieved the tension inside him the way he'd hoped.

He hadn't slept worth a damn and knew his mood wouldn't improve until he apologized to Emma.

He couldn't forget the way her bottom lip had trembled, the hurt in her eyes stabbing him in the heart.

He loved her, and he'd hurt her.

Inviting Charlene to dinner had been an act of desperation, but it had served only to prove to him how much better his life would be with Emma in it.

Jealousy had made him even more irritable, and he'd taken it out on her. None of it had been her fault.

She'd done nothing more than let them know that she loved them.

She'd been nothing but sweet and didn't have a pretentious bone in her body.

And he'd done nothing but hurt her and push her away.

He had to see her.

Rushing across the yard, he took the back steps in one leap and yanked the screen door open.

He knocked several times, but she didn't answer, making him wonder if she was ignoring him.

He deserved it, but he wouldn't let her get away with it.

Knowing that she left the back door open during the day, he went inside, calling her name, but she didn't answer.

The house felt empty, and after checking the living room and her bedroom, he went back downstairs and through the kitchen to the small hallway that led to the garage.

He opened the door to see her car still inside, which meant that John and Michael had picked her up.

With a sigh, he wiped the sweat from his forehead.

Looking at his watch, he realized that she'd probably have lunch with his friends, and they might be gone for hours.

With that realization came another.

It had been a long time since breakfast.

Not wanting to go to the diner sweaty and covered with wood chips, he started toward his house with the intention of taking a shower.

Remington looked up from chopping wood. "Is she home yet?"

"No." Hunter picked up his T-shirt, using it to wipe some of the wood chips from his sweaty chest. "I'm gonna go get some lunch. I'll bring something back for you."

Remington nodded. "Fine." Tossing another log aside, he wiped his forehead. "We fucked up last night. Inviting Charlene was a huge mistake."

"Do you think I don't know that? It was my idea, and I'm trying to find her to apologize. Just stop nagging me about it."

His anger hadn't dimmed in the time it took him to shower and get to the diner.

His mood worsened when he walked into the diner and saw that several of his friends were there, all wearing similar expressions of disappointment.

Feeling even worse, he went to the counter, pride making the decision not to ask Gracie if she knew Emma's whereabouts.

As Gracie approached, he saw a twinkle in her eye that set his teeth on edge. "Hi, Hunter. Where's Remington?"

"Home." When she lifted a brow at his gruff tone, he added a half-smile, hoping it would appease her. Raising his voice to be heard over the din, he shrugged. "Chopping wood. Can I get two of your cheeseburger platters with everything to go?"

"Sure."

Trying to appear casual, Hunter scanned the diner, looking for Michael and John, grinding his teeth when he didn't see either one of them.

He tried not to imagine the two of them in bed with her, but once the image formed in his mind, it wouldn't go away.

He deserved it after what had happened the night before.

Thankful that the noise level prevented conversation from anyone other than those who sat close to him at the counter, he stared straight ahead, glad that the two strangers on either side of him paid their checks and left.

Hunter turned at the sound of the bell over the door chiming.

King Taylor and Royce Harley, part owners of the men's club, walked in with their wife, Brenna, who chatted excitedly about something.

Both men nodded and smiled in his direction as they seated their wife, listening attentively to whatever she said, amusement dancing in their eyes.

Hunter turned away from the obviously happy threesome, his stomach knotting.

The increasing number of happy marriages in town made him even more conscious of what he lacked in his own life, what could very well be right at his fingertips.

Feeling sorry for himself just pissed him off more.

To make matters worse, Jake and Hoyt came in next with Clay and Rio Erickson.

Nat and Jesse would be working together at the store, giving Blade's wife, Kelly, more time to spend with their new baby.

The thought of never having children made the loneliness even worse.

The mental image of Emma, heavy with his and Remington's child, rose in his mind again, an image that haunted him ever since she'd gotten that damned prescription.

He couldn't imagine anything more beautiful than seeing her pregnant with their child.

Knowing it could never be was like a kick to his gut.

Why the hell did she have to come into my life?

The knot in his stomach grew as he listened to the men place their order for lunch to go.

Each of them looked happy, even Hoyt, who'd been grim-faced when he'd arrived in town several months earlier.

Lovesick fools.

He'd become one of them, the need to see Emma so intense it had become a living, breathing thing.

Biting back a groan when Law and Zach Tyler walked through the door with their new bride, Courtney, Hunter turned away from the sight they made and looked straight ahead again.

Just back from their honeymoon, the three of them looked tanned and relaxed—and very much in love.

Courtney's giggle reminded him too much of Emma's for comfort.

Fisting his hands on the counter in front of him, Hunter fought to block it out, stiffening when Hoyt made his way to the counter.

Lowering himself to the empty seat on Hunter's right, Hoyt took a sip of the coffee he'd ordered. "She's at the bar."

Surprised, Hunter turned to look at Hoyt. "Is she?" Shrugging, he turned away. "She's entitled to do whatever she wants."

"Thought you might be interested. If not, my mistake. If she's the one, though, I'd claim her fast. I let my woman get away and lived to regret it."

Curious, Hunter toyed with the napkin holder. "You got her back, though."

"Yeah, thanks to Jake. He's the one that she looks toward for comfort. He's her rock. Don't get me wrong, she loves me, but I missed years I can never get back. There are memories between those two that I can never be a part of. Don't make the same mistake. I should have married her years ago. I was young and stupid. You can't use youth as an excuse. Just stubbornness."

The knots in Hunter's stomach tightened. "I don't plan to ever marry. I'm not good for her."

Blowing out a breath, Hoyt shook his head. "I've met men who were violent against women. Nobody in this town thinks you are, and I understand that most of them have known you your entire adult life."

Hunter's mood and Hoyt's concern loosened his tongue. "Rem and I realize that we couldn't do to her what my father did to my mother, but that doesn't mean we know anything about tenderness."

"Yes you do." Hoyt's lips twitched. "You just won't see it.'

"I'm not willing to take the chance of hurting her."

Hoyt shrugged, his eyes giving away nothing. "That's up to you, but there's no sense in being miserable when you can be happier than you'd ever thought you could be."

"That's not in the cards for me."

Hoyt shrugged and sipped his coffee. "Not too long ago, I thought the same thing. You'll never know if you don't take the risk."

Unable to breathe, Hunter rose, throwing several bills on the counter. "Taking a risk could very well cause Emma a lot of pain.. How the hell am I ever going to be able to do that? I've already hurt her. More than once. There's a bitterness and anger inside me that eats me up at times. Who the hell knows what I'm capable of? Tell Gracie I'm not hungry anymore."

Aware of the searching looks from his friends, Hunter stormed from the diner, knowing that, as much as he wanted to avoid Emma, he wouldn't be able to settle until he saw for himself that she was all right—and to apologize for the huge mistake he'd made.

* * * *

Watching John and Michael bite into the ribs they'd spent the best part of the day barbequing, Emma grinned. "Well? What do you think?"

Hot and sweaty after spending hours on the concrete patio behind the bar, she sipped from her water bottle. "I think we made them with just the right amount of heat."

John grinned and licked his fingers. "You make the best ribs I've ever had."

Emma smiled at that and took another bite of her own, giggling when Michael finished his and reached for another. "I didn't make them. You did. I just walked you through it."

Michael finished his second rib and reached for his third. "Best I ever had."

She finished her own rib and tossed the bone into the trash, gesturing toward the new grill they'd bought that morning. "So, do you think it's something you can handle?"

Michael nodded and reached for another rib. "Absolutely. I think we ought to do ribs one night during the week to draw more business, but we should do a preview on Saturday night. I can start them early enough in the day that I don't have to deal with them later. The grill's huge, and I have more than enough room to make what we need. Thanks for helping us out with it, Emma."

John smiled. "I really appreciate this. We can handle the barbeque easily. We wanted to offer food, but we can't spend all night in the kitchen, especially just for bar food. I like your idea about the wings, too. It sounds easy enough."

"I'll be glad to show you how to make them."

Frowning, Michael wiped his hands on the towel he'd tucked into his waistband. "I really wish you'd let us pay for your time."

"Don't be ridiculous. I'm glad to help. Besides, I thought we were friends."

John smiled. "We are. Are the recipes for the ribs and the wings really in your cookbooks?"

Nodding, Emma reached for another rib. "Yes. They are. Do you think your customers will like them?"

John nodded and wiped his hands. "I think they'll love them. We're having fliers made to post all over town. We'll have them Saturday night when we're busy so that our customers can try them."

Straightening, he smiled and put his arm around her, closing his hand on her shoulder when she jolted at the contact. "You *are* coming, aren't you? I'd like you to be there to see how much of a hit these ribs are gonna be."

"I wouldn't miss it." Seeing Hunter out of the corner of her eye, she grinned, suddenly understanding why John had his arm around her. She swallowed heavily and turned to face him. "Hi, Hunter."

Her pulse tripped, her body tightening and warming at the sight of him.

Hunter grunted a greeting, directing a cold glare in John's direction.

When his gaze shifted to her, something flashed in his eyes but disappeared almost immediately. "Heard you were here. I just wanted to make sure you're okay."

"I'm fine. We had a great time this morning." Trembling with need and excitement, she acted on impulse, picking up one of the ribs and starting toward him. "Would you like a rib—oh!"

Tripping over one of Michael's feet, she fell headlong into Hunter, who caught her against him. Mortified that she'd smeared barbeque sauce down the front of his shirt, she hurriedly tried to pull away. "Oh, Hunter. I'm so sorry."

He paid no attention to the stain, his grip on her upper arms holding her steady. "Are you all right?"

Michael and John had both rushed forward and reached for her, stopping abruptly at Hunter's sharp glare.

John touched her shoulder. "You all right, honey?"

"I'm fine." Lifting her face, she stared into Hunter's eyes. "Thank you."

Gripping her wrist, Hunter lifted the hand holding the barbequed rib to his mouth and bit into the juicy meat, his gaze holding hers. "Hmm. Delicious. I didn't get to eat my fill last night."

Still holding her wrist, he took the rib from her, taking her fingers, one by one, into his mouth and cleaning the sauce from them. He slowed, his eyes never leaving hers. "That's even better."

Ribbons of tingling heat raced from her fingers to her nipples, making them bead even tighter.

Aching for his touch, she leaned into him, the familiarity of his arm going around her both exciting and comforting. "I'm, uh, glad you like it."

"I do. I looked all over the house for you."

Emma gulped and tried to pull her hand away. "We went into Tulsa for the grill and had to put it together. We've been barbequing for hours."

Hunter nibbled at her fingertip, glancing over her head to glare at John and Michael. "You've been a busy girl."

Michael's voice came from behind her. "Emma's been helping us with bar food. Those ribs should be a hit."

Hunter's eyes became shuttered as he released her. "They will be. Emma seems to have a knack for making everything better."

Despite the hot day, Emma suddenly felt cold. Turning to include both Michael and John in her smile, she gathered her things. "I'd better go home."

John inclined his head. "I'll take you."

Hunter shook his head. "I'll take her home. I'm headed back there anyway."

Pleased to have the chance to spend some time with Hunter, she smiled her thanks and turned back to John. "Thank you for my platters."

John smiled back, his eyes softening. "A small price to pay. I hope you think of us when you use them."

Touched, Emma leaned forward to kiss his cheek. "I will. I'll see you Saturday night."

John nodded. "I'll pick you up."

Hunter stiffened, his eyes going hard and cold. "I'll bring her."

Emma shook her head, not wanting a repeat of the previous night. "No, thanks. I wouldn't want to inconvenience you or be a third wheel." Waving a hand, she strode to the back door of the bar. "I'll get my packages and wait in the truck."

Hunter watched her go, furious at himself for the distance he'd put between them.

John reached for another rib. "Did you come to see us about something, or were you looking for Emma?"

Struggling to tamp down jealousy, Hunter clenched his jaw. "I fucked up, and I need to make it right."

John's brow went up. "You gonna claim her?"

Hunter sighed, his stomach in knots, and before he knew it, he found himself confiding in them, something he seemed to be doing a lot lately. "The more time I spend with her, the more I fall for her."

Michael glanced at John. "That's great. Isn't it?"

Shaking his head, Hunter smiled humorlessly. "The more I fall for her, the more I'm afraid of hurting her. I keep putting distance between us because, if I don't, I'm gonna fall headlong in love with her."

He wasn't yet ready to admit to anyone but his brother that he already had fallen in love with her.

"Once she's mine, I won't be able to let her go—even if I'm bad for her."

"You're not bad for her, Hunter. If anything, you're *too* protective of women." John reached for another rib. "She needs that. She's used to being alone and having no one to lean on. No one to share things with. Give it a chance, Hunter."

"I care about her too much to take the chance of hurting her."

John smiled. "It sounds like you care about her too much to let her go. You can't go on this way, Hunter."

"I know that, damn it! I've got to go. I need to talk to her."

Michael reached for another rib. "Good idea. While you're at it, why don't you try to explain to her that she's hooked on two assholes who can't see what's right in front of them?"

* * * *

Hunter glanced at Emma as he slid into the driver's seat.

"I made a big mistake."

Holding her purse and packages on her lap, Emma stared out the front window, her sunglasses making it impossible to see her eyes.

"Did you?"

"Yeah." He started the engine and cranked the air-conditioning to high. "Charlene and I never date. We've never met anyone except the club. I only invited her to dinner because I was jealous."

"You have no reason to be jealous. I already told you that. John and Michael are friends. I like them quite a bit, and they asked for my help."

Disgusted with himself, Hunter started toward home. "I know. I told you I made a mistake. I wasn't thinking. I just reacted."

Emma snorted. "Impossible. You never just react. You think things to death."

Furious that she wouldn't look at him, Hunter reached over and grabbed her arm.

"I'm trying to apologize here."

Emma shrugged. "So apologize."

He wanted to shake her. He wanted to rip her sunglasses off so he could see her eyes.

He hated the monotone voice she used, a voice completely lacking in emotion.

Taking a deep breath, he released her arm, shaken that he'd gotten physical.

"I'm sorry."

Emma glanced at him, and even though he couldn't see her eyes, he could see that her smile was forced.

"I accept your apology."

Hunter gritted his teeth, reaching over to tug her glasses away. "Look at me, damn it!"

Turning her head, Emma faced him, her eyes brimming with tears.

"What?"

Shaken, he turned to pull onto their street. "Please don't cry. I can't stand it."

Grabbing her glasses back from him, she slid them on again, lifting her chin.

"I'm not crying." Her bottom lip wobbled, giving her away.

Hunter kept glancing at her, and not wanting to upset her further, inclined his head. "Okay. My mistake."

He pulled into the driveway and hit the brake, catching her arm before she could open the door.

"Is it okay if Rem and I come to dinner?"

Shaking her head, Emma opened the door and tried to pull her arm free. "Sorry. I won't be here. There's some lunch meat if you want a sandwich, and the leftover chicken and dumplings is in the freezer."

Pulling her closer, Hunter turned in his seat and slid an arm around her waist, relieved at her sharp intake of breath. Releasing his hold on her arm, he removed her glasses again and bent close, staring into her eyes.

"You still want me, don't you?"

Emma gulped, the hitch in her breath one of the most exciting sounds he'd ever heard.

"It doesn't matter. Does it?"

Unable to resist, he brushed his lips over hers, sliding his hand higher to caress the underside of her breast. "It matters to me."

Her breathing quickened. "Why?"

"Because it does." He worked his thumb over her nipple, delighted to find it beaded and tight.

His cock jumped at her gasp, and unable to resist, he did it again.

And again.

Smiling when she slumped against him, he cupped her breast.

"I love the way you respond to my touch. Christ, you excite me."

With a low moan, she straightened and pushed him away.

"No!" Shaking, she pushed at his chest. "I'm not going to let you do this to me anymore. Just stay away from me."

Gripping a fistful of hair, he yanked her close again, so close that he felt her warm breath against his lips. "I can't do that. I care too much about you, damn it! You make me crazy. I want you so fucking much, but I know I can't have you. I can't even fucking sleep anymore."

"Don't."

Startled when her voice broke, he released her. "Emma?"

Shaking her head, she grabbed her packages that had fallen to the floor and scrambled out of the truck.

When she turned to him again, tears shimmered in her eyes.

"Don't come see me anymore. Don't care about me. It hurts too much. I can't stand being around you and knowing that you'll never belong to me."

Frustrated that he couldn't be what she needed and furious at himself for hurting her, Hunter reached for her, more shaken when she avoided him than he wanted to admit. "Emma!"

"I'll ask around and find another place to live."

The bottom fell out of his world. "No. Don't."

Her sad smile ripped his heart to shreds. "It's for the best. Once I get Gracie's recipes, I'll be leaving Desire anyway. I'll have what I came for."

Hunter jumped out of the truck, finding he had to swallow the lump in his throat before speaking. "Please don't."

His insides had tightened so badly, it hurt.

He couldn't imagine no longer having her in his life.

"I have to. Good-bye, Hunter."

He watched her go up the steps and into the house, the finality of her words making it difficult to breathe.

Turning, he braced his hands on the hood of the truck, his head dropping at the weight of the years of emptiness ahead of him.

If she walked away, he'd never survive it.

Remington appeared beside him. "Hunter? What's wrong?" Gripping his shoulder, Remington leaned down to see his face. "Are you okay?"

"No." Straightening, Hunter took a steadying breath, hoping to loosen the tightness in his chest. "Emma's leaving."

It felt as if someone was ripping his heart out.

"What? You went to get lunch and come back with Emma just to tell me she's leaving? What the fuck happened?"

"I've got to talk to her."

Stiffening at the sound of the garage door going up, Hunter stared at Emma as she pulled out and drove away.

"She didn't even look this way."

"Where's she going?"

"I don't know. Said she had plans."

Shaking his head, Hunter sighed. "Go ahead and get something to eat. I'm not hungry."

Remington stared after Emma before turning back. "I'll get something for both of us. While we eat, you can tell me what the hell happened between the two of you."

Hunter clenched his hands at his sides, welcoming the numbness that eased some of the pain inside him. "I won't lose her. I can't."

The pain rose up again. "Why the hell did I have to fall in love with her?"

"We both did, Hunter." Remington patted his back. "We'll figure it out. I don't want to live without her. If she leaves, we'll follow her."

"No." Shaking his head, Hunter straightened and stared at the house, picturing Emma on the front porch with children playing in the yard. "We need to stay with her in Desire. She'll be safe here. Safe from us."

Chapter Nineteen

Remington walked into the diner with his brother, still restless that when they'd gone to see Emma minutes earlier, she'd already gone out.

Carrying a pot of coffee, Gracie hurried past them. "Good morning. Have a seat. I'll be right there."

Remington touched her arm, relieved when she paused. "Have you seen Emma this morning?"

Gracie flashed him a smile. "Yep. She's been here and gone. She wants the recipes for my meatloaf and peach cobbler real bad."

Hunter's lips twitched, but his expression remained bleak. "Are you gonna give them to her?"

Gracie's smile fell, her eyes narrowing. "Nope. She says she's gonna put 'em in her new cookbook."

"That's an honor, isn't it?"

Gracie pulled her arm away. "I figured you'd be on her side. You can take that charm and stick it in your pocket. She's not getting those recipes no matter how much she asks. Do you want breakfast?"

Remington nodded. "Yes. The usual. Do you know where she went?"

"She went off with Ethan and Brandon about a half an hour ago. What's wrong?"

"Nothing." Gritting his teeth, Remington shared a look with Hunter, knowing that neither one of them would settle until they'd made things right with Emma. "Thanks."

They'd just sat in the booth when Gracie appeared with the coffee pot.

Eyeing Hunter, she poured their coffee.

"You still gonna eat, or are you gonna go runnin' after her? I made a couple of burgers yesterday, and when I came out to bring them to you, you were gone."

Hunter leaned back. "We'll catch up with her later."

"Uh-huh." Gracie looked at each of them, her gaze searching. "I'll be right back with your breakfast."

Remington nodded, but his impatience to go find Emma had him tapping his fingers on the table. Staring at the door, he sipped his coffee, straightening when Dillon Tanner and Ryder Hayes walked into the diner. "Damned if it ain't hard to sit here and not go find her."

Hunter sighed. "Yeah, it is." He took another sip of coffee and glanced over his shoulder as Dillon and Tanner approached. "We're gonna fuck this up."

Remington had already come to that conclusion, his stomach tightening with rage at the knowledge that Emma would have figured it out as well. "We've already fucked up. She loves us, and we pushed her away."

Nodding, Hunter stared down into his cup. "I don't like jumping into something that's gonna get us all hurt. I'm willing to give up my lifestyle for her. I don't want to make her uncomfortable." Setting his cup down, he clenched his jaw. "I just hope like hell Brandon and Ethan aren't interested in her. With our luck, they'd finally find a woman they both wanted, and it would be Emma."

"I think it's a mistake to give up our lifestyle without discussing it with Emma." Smiling at the thought of Emma's response to being dominated, Remington leaned back. "She seems to like it just fine. I'd love to explore all that passion locked up inside her."

Turning from the counter, Ryder approached, his grin spelling trouble. "So, your tenant is with Ethan and Brandon. It's rare for a woman to go unclaimed around here. Sounds like she's got quite a few men chasin' after her."

Jealousy reared its ugly head and had Remington clenching his hands into fists. "Who?"

Ryder's grin widened as he leaned back against the wall. "Just about every single man in town wants to meet her. Some of them aren't lucky enough to have found a woman of their own yet."

Folding his arms across his chest accentuated the tattoos peeking out from his short sleeves. "Brandon and Ethan aren't exactly agreeing on the woman they want, and now it looks like they're just dating the kind of woman who annoys the other."

Dillon approached and stood next to Ryder. "And they're both miserable."

Ryder straightened and slapped Remington on the back. "But they both like Emma. Maybe after they both spend some time with her, they'll be in better moods. She's a sweetheart. Food's ready. I've got to get back to my own woman." Chuckling, he turned away with a wave, passing Gracie on his way to the counter.

Dillon watched Ryder walk away, shaking his head. Turning back, he sighed. "He's a changed man since we found Alison. I am, too, for that matter. Having her in our lives has changed everything. If you love Emma, and she loves you, don't let her get away. You'll regret it for the rest of your lives. You'll always wonder." With a nod, Dillon walked away, obviously anxious to get back to his wife.

Gracie appeared with their breakfast, eyeing both Hunter and Remington as she set their plates in front of them. "You've been in bad moods for years. That girl's right for the two of you, and you know it. You're good men, even if you're too stupid to see it."

Before she could turn away, Remington touched her arm. "Gracie, you knew our parents."

Her eyes shimmered with tears. "Your mother, Mary, Isabel, and I were best friends. You know that."

"How well did you know our father?"

Gracie's smile held a sadness that made Remington regret his question. "Neither one of you has ever asked me about your father before."

Hunter shrugged. "I don't think either one of us wanted to know more than we already did. Now, since meeting Emma, we need some answers."

To Remington's surprise, Grace slid into the booth beside him and shared a look with her husband, Garrett, who nodded from the counter and smiled in Remington's direction.

Folding her hands in front of her, Gracie toyed with the three thin wedding bands on her ring finger. "Isabel and I knew Tom Ross, probably more than he wanted us to. He threatened both of us when we tried to interfere. Garrett, Drew, and Finn went over and told him that if he ever talked to me again, they would kick his ass. Wade, Ben, and Conal Preston did the same thing to protect Isabel."

Shocked at that, Remington glanced at his brother. "Our father actually threatened to hurt you?"

"He did. He was an ass. He was cruel. He was evil." Shaking her head, she stared straight ahead as if caught in the memories. "But everyone loved Mary and you two, and we wanted to help." She paused, obviously lost in memories. "Your father didn't scare easily and told them that the next time any of them showed up at his house he would shoot them. Threatened to shoot Isabel and me, too. We begged Mary to leave him. Begged. She wouldn't. She thought she could change him. Always made excuses for him and his drinking. She wasn't allowed to go to the grocery store any more or come to the diner."

Gracie sniffed and wiped her eyes. "When she disappeared, we all thought he was just keeping her locked in the house. We didn't know that he'd killed her and buried her at the base of the mountains. He took away your mother, and then died in prison, leaving the two of you alone. Son of a bitch."

Touched by her tears, Remington rubbed her back. "We weren't alone. We had all of you. I remember how you and Isabel used to sneak into the house while we were at school and fill the cupboards and refrigerator with food."

Hunter's lips twitched. "You spoiled us."

Gracie smiled through her tears. "You were easy to spoil. You both always had such anger inside you. We all understood it, of course, but it broke our hearts. No matter how angry you were, you've always been protective of women. You've always been fiercely loyal to your friends and neighbors, and you're always eager to help someone in trouble."

Rising, she wiped her eyes and took a shuddering breath. "You're nothing like him. Never were. Never could be. He cared about nothing but himself." She faced them both squarely. "He never would have put aside his own needs to protect anyone else the way you two do with Emma. No." Smiling, she wiped her eyes again. "You care too much. You're your mother through and through. Now, go get that girl. You deserve all the happiness you can get. She'll be a lucky girl to get two such caring men."

Hunter smiled faintly. "How come you didn't tell us any of this before?"

"You just weren't ready to listen. You are now. Your momma would be real proud of the men you've become."

She started to walk away and paused, hesitating for several long seconds before turning back.

Remington, surprised to see Gracie's deep blush, glanced at Hunter. Lowering his fork, he frowned. "Is there something else?"

"Yes. Because of our friendship with your mother, Isabel and I have kept tabs on you two through the years. It's a small town." If possible, her blush deepened. "Just be yourself with Emma. Don't hide what you need. Be honest with her. Don't shock her with any surprises."

Remington blinked, feeling his own cheeks turning hot, but Gracie had already turned away. Shaking his head, he met his brother's gaze, struck by the anticipation in his eyes. "She's talking about our need to dominate a woman, isn't she?"

"Sounds like it." Hunter sighed. "We can do without that. I just want *her*. The rest doesn't matter. As soon as we finish our breakfast, we'll go find her. The three of us need to talk."

Sipping his coffee, Remington sat back, Gracie's words playing over and over in his head. "Do you think Gracie's right? I never realized that our father actually threatened other people. He even threatened to shoot women. There's no way we could ever be the monster he was, could we?"

A muscle worked in Hunter's jaw. "No. Neither one of us would ever do something like that, but the pleasure we get from dominating women can't be ignored, Rem. Plain vanilla has never been our style. We've always had to be in control. Ever think there might be a reason for that?"

Remington shrugged. "No. There are plenty of people in Desire who have the same needs. Like you said, though, we can live without it. I just hate the thought of having limitations put on sex with Emma. How many times have we heard that Dominants and submissives in steady relationships are much closer?"

Hunter frowned. "I don't know. I never felt that close with Charlene. With Emma, I want more. Hurry up and eat. I want to go find her."

* * * *

Finding Emma proved to be more difficult than Hunter had anticipated.

Their first stop was the hotel restaurant, where they found both Ethan and Brandon in the kitchen, animatedly talking to their head chef while looking through a book lying on a large steel table.

All three men looked up when Hunter and Remington walked in, Ethan straightening with a smile, looking more relaxed than he had in months.

"Hey! What are you doing here?"

Gritting his teeth, Hunter searched for any sign that they'd become attached to Emma. "Looking for Emma."

Brandon glanced up at him as he turned the page. "She left about a half hour ago." Straightening, he smiled and turned to ladle soup into two bowls. "Taste this."

Accepting the bowl, Hunter allowed a small smile. "Emma make this?"

The creamy potato and bacon soup was the best he'd ever had. "Damn. This is delicious. You gonna put this on your menu?"

Ethan nodded. "You're damned right. She showed us a few more recipes to consider."

The chef moved away, his smile surprising. "I've got to go place an order."

Remington closed the book, eyeing the cover. "This is one of her cookbooks!"

Ethan nodded. "The first one. She looks really pretty in that picture, doesn't she? She said she was scared to death when they took it. That's why she has that haunted look in her eyes. Real nice woman."

Finishing his soup, Remington frowned. "And your chef doesn't have a problem with her adding to your menu?"

Chuckling softly, Brandon ran a finger over the book cover. "Hell, no. She had him in the palm of her hand when she kept sneaking bits of his food and moaning with pleasure with every bite. I think they're friends for life."

Hunter stared at the cover of her book, focusing on the sadness and uncertainty in Emma's eyes.

He had a feeling that it had nothing to do with being nervous about posing for her book cover and had everything to do with being hurt and feeling alone because of the breakup of her marriage.

If he had his way, she'd never feel that way again.

Setting the bowl aside, Hunter narrowed his eyes, not trusting the amusement in theirs. "Where is she?"

"She said she had to stop at the grocery store for a few things." Ethan raised a brow, his smile devious. "She's a hell of a woman, you know."

"I know." Hunter allowed a small smile. "Don't get any ideas. She's ours."

Brandon looked up from the cookbook, his look of stunned amazement almost comical. "Really? You claiming her?"

"Yep." Hunter's stomach had been in knots ever since he'd made the decision to make Emma his, but saying it out loud made it even more real. "We've got a lot to work out."

"Well, you'd better hurry." Ethan's lips twitched. "She's sure getting a lot of interest around here."

Hunter smiled coldly. "If anyone tries to take her from us, we're going to kick their asses."

Brandon threw his head back and laughed. "Yeah, well, I think you're going to have some competition. We explained to Emma how claiming works, and she knows that she has to accept it before it counts."

Remington fisted his hands on the table and leaned toward Ethan and Brandon, his eyes narrowed. "That was real nice of you to fill her in."

Ethan grinned and leaned toward him, his eyes sparkling with mischief. "Our pleasure. We're not gonna make this easy for you. You've been a pain in the ass for too long."

* * * *

Leaning back against the counter, Ethan watched his friends, delighted and slightly stunned to see the light of anticipation and hope in their eyes. "I have no idea why, but Emma seems really taken with the two of you."

That was an understatement.

Her eyes lit up whenever they'd mentioned Hunter or Remington, and there had been a catch in her voice the few times she'd spoken of them.

She was heartbroken, and it thrilled Ethan to see that Hunter and Remington planned to claim her for their own.

Remington grinned. "Because she has good taste."

Ethan couldn't help but poke at his friends, unable to resist the chance to make them jealous. "I forgot to mention that, when she left here, she was with Lucas, Devlin, and Caleb."

Hunter's faint smile fell, a muscle working in his jaw. "What? What the hell is she doing with them?"

Enjoying himself immensely, Ethan stepped aside as another order came in and the sous chefs bustled around them. "They were here having breakfast with Logan, and I happened to mention that Emma was here. They were answering her questions about the men's club when they left."

Hunter and Remington's sudden departure didn't surprise him at all.

Grinning, he watched them rush out, and glanced at his friend. "So, Brandon, what do you think?"

Brandon's smile came easier than it had in a long time. "Meeting Emma, a woman we both liked, makes me think that we can find someone for both of us in the future."

Ethan grinned again. "I was thinking along the same lines. It seems we're both looking for the same thing in a woman after all."

Chapter Twenty

"Are you sure you've got everything you need?" Caleb Ward set two bags of groceries in her backseat while Devlin Monroe carried out another.

"Absolutely." She looked up at Lucas Hart as he opened the car door for her. "I really appreciate this. You didn't have to buy the groceries, though. You're supposed to be my taste testers."

He smiled faintly, his gaze constantly scanning the area. "It's our pleasure. We appreciate the invitation. I've done a lot of things in my life, but I have to admit, I've never been a guinea pig for a taste-testing dinner. I'm intrigued."

Emma paused, frowning up at him. "You make it sound awful."

Ethan and Brandon had introduced her to the three men from Desire Securities at the hotel, and she'd liked them at once.

When they'd invited her to have a drink with them, she'd accepted, and they'd soon begun talking about food.

When Caleb made a remark about craving chili, Emma had immediately invited them for dinner.

To her amusement and delight, they'd readily accepted.

The three men had insisted on going to the grocery store with her and seemed to go out of their way to make her smile.

Shaking his head, Lucas smiled again, still holding the door open for her. "Not at all. I'm looking forward to it. We all are. You said five o'clock. Would you like us to come early and help you?"

"No." Grinning, Emma slid into the driver's seat. "I prefer to be alone in my kitchen when I'm cooking."

"Oh?" He closed the car door behind her and waited until she started the car and rolled down the window. "How do Hunter and Remington react when you kick them out of the kitchen?"

Forcing a smile, Emma shifted the car to reverse, forcing a smile as Devlin and Caleb moved to stand in front of the car. "That isn't an issue. Hunter and Remington have been doing their best to stay away from me."

Straightening, Lucas smiled, his attention on something in the street behind her. "Doesn't appear to be working."

"It's working just fine. See you later." With another forced smile, she glanced in the rearview mirror and turned the radio up, nodding at Devlin as he yelled something at her, which she assumed had to do with seeing her later.

She turned her head to look out the back window and started to slowly back out, her heart in her throat when she saw Hunter staring back at her.

Sitting in the driver's seat of his truck, he'd stopped behind her, blocking her in.

His grin stole her breath, the desire in his look rattling her so much that she jerked, inadvertently hitting the gas pedal.

She slammed on her brakes, but it was too late.

Wincing at the sound of crunching medal, she jerked as her car came to an abrupt halt.

Again.

Mortified, and aware that five men stood around watching the scene, she took a deep breath and slowly looked up into the rearview mirror.

Horrified to see that she'd run into the driver's side door of Hunter and Remington's truck, she hurriedly looked away, unable to look at him.

Wincing, and shaking with nerves, she pulled back into the parking place and threw the car into park.

Lucas yanked her door open, his expression tight with concern. "Are you all right?"

Remington was there in seconds, laying a hand on her thigh as he knelt beside her. "You okay, baby doll?"

It had taken only a few seconds, but her little fender bender had already started to draw a crowd.

Two of Isabel's husbands, Wade and Ben Preston, came running out of the grocery store, joining Lucas, Devlin, and Caleb beside her car.

Shocked at what she'd done, she looked into the rearview mirror again, grimacing when she saw Hunter's failed effort to open the door.

Remington ran his hands over her, setting off a riot of sensations. "Are you all right? Stay still. Let me look at you. Do you hurt anywhere?"

Stunned by the fear in his eyes, she forced a smile.

"I'm fine, Rem." She patted his arm and turned to look at their truck, her face burning when she saw Hunter's approach, his long strides bringing him to her side in seconds. "Sorry about that. I didn't see you."

Remington lifted her chin, his smile indulgent, but the concern still lingered in his eyes. "You didn't see that big-ass truck?"

"She all right?"

Several deep voices asked the question almost simultaneously, but Hunter's stood out, the sharp concern in it like a stab to her stomach.

Still holding her chin, Remington searched her features, the tenderness in his eyes stealing her breath. "She's fine. Shaken, but okay." He moved to the side, allowing Hunter to get closer to her. "See for yourself."

Gathering her against him, Hunter ran his hands over her, leaving a trail of fire behind. "You don't hurt anywhere?"

"No."

"Good." Wrapping one arm around her waist, he sank the fingers of his other hand into her hair and bent, taking her mouth in a searing kiss.

Of their own volition, her hands lifted, her fingers sinking into his thick hair, seeking something to hold on to as the maelstrom of sensation made her dizzy.

Swallowing her moan, Hunter lifted her off her feet, holding her impossibly close, his kiss filled with a possessiveness and hunger that brought tears to her eyes.

Not until he lifted his head did she become aware of the applause around them.

Gripping her shoulders, he held her away from her, his gaze sharp as he searched her features. "You backed right into my truck."

"I said I was sorry!"

To her surprise, Hunter's lips twitched. "Maybe I should just get all my vehicles painted red." His gaze sharpened, raking over her features. "You seem to get all flustered when you're around us. I'm gonna have to see what I can do about that. If you keep having these little accidents, you're gonna get hurt. I can't have that."

Embarrassed and aware of their audience, she slapped at him, pulling out of his grip. "What do you mean, *you* can't have that? What I do is none of your business!"

Hunter raised a brow in that arrogant way that both irritated and aroused her. "I beg to differ."

Remington wrapped his arms around her from behind. "We're claiming you, baby doll. You're ours."

Emma's heart leapt to her throat. "What do you mean?"

She didn't dare hope that they could be in love with her.

Both Hunter and Remington eyed her cautiously.

Hunter's eyes narrowed. "I think you know damned well what we mean. You want us, and we sure as hell want you."

The edge off desperation in his voice gave her hope, but she didn't want bits and pieces of them.

She wanted it all.

Leaning back against Remington, she met Hunter's gaze, depressed at the thought that she would probably give in and take whatever they offered. "Don't you think we need to talk about this?"

Hunter's faint smile gave her hope. "Oh, I'm sure we'll do plenty of talking. In the meantime, you're ours, and if you try to leave Desire, I'll drag you back so fast your head'll swim."

She wanted to believe that they'd finally decided that the three of them belonged together, but she didn't dare.

Too much was at stake.

Remington chuckled, pressing his lips to her hair. "And enjoy the hunt immensely. Now get in the car out of this heat so we can get you home."

Intensely aware that neither man had spoken of love, Emma pushed away from them. "You're both too arrogant. If you think I'm just going to do whatever you tell me to do, you'd better think again. Move that heap out of the way so I can get home before my groceries spoil in this heat!"

Lucas covered his mouth, his cough sounding suspiciously like a laugh. "I called Dillon. He's on his way with the tow truck. Just move your truck out of the way, and we'll wait for him. I wouldn't want Emma's food to spoil."

From the back of her car, Devlin straightened. "Of course, Jared and Caleb could take you and I can ride with Emma to make sure she gets home safely.

Hunter's smile widened. "No, thanks. We'll take Emma's car. Thanks. We'll see you around."

Leaning back against their SUV, Devlin grinned. "Oh, you'll see us soon. Emma invited us to dinner."

Remington turned to her, his eyes narrowed. "Did she?"

Pleased to have the tables turned, Emma grinned. "Yes. They've agreed to give me their honest opinion about my chili, and it'll be so nice to have someone to cook for. I won't have to eat alone." She lifted her gaze to Lucas's. "You're still coming, right?"

Lucas winked at her, his slow smile filled with mischief. "Wouldn't miss it for the world."

* * * *

Emma didn't object when Remington urged her into the backseat of her car, especially when he got in behind her.

Giggling when he stretched her out on the seat and covered her body with his, she squirmed against him.

"Can I help you with something?"

Using his thighs to part her legs, he brushed her lips with his. "You already have someone to cook for. Hunter and I will be your guinea pigs from now on."

"Will you?"

"Damn it!" Remington moved and fell to the floor, sending Emma into a fit of laughter. Sitting up, he worked his way back onto the seat, dragging her onto his lap.

"Your car's too damned small for seduction." Pulling her close, he ran a hand under her shirt to cup her breast, smiling as he stared down at her.

"Is that what this is?" With a moan, she arched into his caress, loving the feel of being in his arms.

Hunter glanced back at them with a grin, appearing much more relaxed than he'd looked earlier. "You should try driving it. I've got the seat pushed all the way back and my knees are still in my chest."

Thrilled to see their smiles after so many weeks of frowning, Emma laid her head and her hand against Remington's chest.

"What brought all this on?"

Hunter glanced back, his expression more serious than she'd expected.

"We came to our senses. No more drinking until we're drunk to make the loneliness go away. Living in Desire, you're safe."

Leaning her back over his arm, Remington nibbled at her bottom lip, stroking her nipple through her bra. "Lace. Is it pink?"

Crying out at the slide of his thumb over her nipple, she rubbed her thighs together against the ache that settled there, struggling to focus on her conversation with Hunter.

"What do you mean? Of course I'm safe."

"Yes, you are." Remington gathered her close. "We're going to be so gentle with you and go so slowly that you'll be begging to come."

Emma stilled, getting an uneasy feeling in the pit of her stomach. "You don't have to be gentle with me all the time. You like to dominate. I've been looking forward to experiencing it."

Remington sipped at her lips, his hand gently massaging her breast.

"You don't have to worry about that." Cupping the back of her head, he unerringly found her nipple, sending jagged shards of lust through her. "We don't need that anymore. We've got *you*."

Emma pushed out of his arms, needing to distance herself in order to think clearly. "Wait. What? I thought that it excited you to dominate a woman."

Hunter pulled into the driveway and threw her car in park. "It did. You excite me more."

Emma shook her head as he turned her car off and got out, shoving her own door open to join him. "You're not doing this because you want to. You're giving up the kind of sex you like because you think you *have* to. I'm not going to let you give up something that's been a part of you for so long because you're trying to protect me."

Hunter leaned in to gather her bags of groceries while Remington did the same from the other side of the car.

Adjusting the bags in his arms to free one of his hands, Hunter reached out to grip her chin, chuckling as he bent and touched his lips to hers. "I'd give up anything to have you. If we weren't expecting company soon, I'd show you."

Pressing his thumb to her bottom lip, he stared into her eyes, holding her gaze for several heart-stopping seconds before abruptly releasing her.

The satisfaction that gleamed in his eyes when he'd forced her mouth open had almost immediately hardened into regret and then his eyes became shuttered, giving nothing away.

Running a hand over her hair, he turned away. "I'd prefer to take my time when I take you, and I don't want you thinking about your damned chili."

"Hunter!" Hurrying to catch up with him, she grabbed his arm and tugged, her panic turning to anger in a heartbeat. "Damn it! We have to talk about this! I'm not going into this relationship half-assed! I want it all, or I don't want any of it!"

She followed them to the kitchen, stunned when Hunter slammed the bags on the counter and spun, gripping her by the shoulders and lifting her to her toes.

His eyes flashed with something hard and ice cold as he bent close, bracing a hand on the island on either side of her.

"If you think you're walking away from us, baby, you'd better think again. You're here where you belong, and that's where you're staying."

Lifting her chin, Emma glanced at Remington as he moved in beside Hunter.

"Don't expect more from me than you're willing to give. If you're going to hold back parts of yourself, then so will I. I'm going to go ahead and make my plans to leave. With all of us holding back, this pretense won't last long anyway."

Remington made a sound in his throat, his eyes flashing. "Pretense? Is that what you think this is? Do you think this is some kind of a game?"

Emma pushed away from them and started putting the groceries away. "I think you're playing a dangerous one. I've talked to people, and I understand a little about dominance and submission."

Remington's brows went up. "Really? Do tell."

Ignoring his sarcasm, Emma laid out the ingredients for the chili. "And I understand that it's kind of like sharing. Either you're into it or not."

Turning, she leaned back against the counter, facing both of them.

"I never thought I was the type of woman who could love two men. Hell, I never thought I could trust enough to love again. But I do. I'm all in. Are you?"

Scraping a hand over his face, Hunter sighed. "You're the most frustrating woman."

"Yeah, but you'll get used to it." Confident that she'd given them something to think about, she pulled out two of her largest pots. "Now get out of my way. I want to start my chili and get a shower before the others get here."

Remington blew out a breath. "This conversation isn't over. We're gonna talk about this."

"You're damned right we are." Emma glanced at both of them over her shoulder. "Taking on both of you means that I'm going to have to put my foot down now and then, or you'll just run me over. I want it all, and once you come to terms that I won't settle for less—at least without trying—then we'll move forward."

Hunter's lips twitched. "You're awfully brave, aren't you? You sure you're not biting off more than you can chew?"

Emma set the pots on the stove and turned with a smile.

"Are you sure you're not the ones biting off more than you can chew? I've got the balls to take on both of you, warts and all. When you can say the same about me, we'll talk. In the meantime, I've got company coming."

* * * *

Fresh from her shower, Emma was still smiling when she walked back into the kitchen an hour later.

Hunter and Remington had watched silently while she'd started both pots of chili, but she'd caught them looking at each other several times, some silent conversation apparently taking place between them.

Amused, she'd pretended not to notice and gone to take a shower.

It appeared that both men had done the same, wearing fresh T-shirts and jeans, their hair still damp.

She crossed to the stove to stir both pots, which she'd left simmering. "Well, hello. Chili won't be ready for a while. Is there something I can do for you, or would you like to help me?"

Remington grinned, his gaze raking over her from head to toe. "Darlin', if I tell you what you can do for me, I'd scare you to death. Did you wear that dress to drive me crazy?"

She'd worn the red dress that they both seemed to like, along with one of the new pink thongs she'd bought in town. "Maybe."

Waving a hand dismissively, Emma scooped some chili onto a spoon to taste it. "Do you really think you could scare me? You obviously have me confused with someone who's easily intimidated. You don't scare me."

Stirring chili with a hand that shook, she looked over her shoulder to find both men watching her.

Hunter smiled.

"What we want to do to you shouldn't scare you. You know that we're both going to be very careful with you. It will make you nervous, though."

Remington smiled. "Just enough to add an edge."

Not about to show them just how nervous she was about embarking on such an erotic journey, she smiled. "We'll see."

Swallowing heavily, she turned back to stirring, inadvertently grabbing the edge of the pot to support it. "Ow! Damn it."

Both men leapt to her side, Remington reaching her first.

Holding her arm, he rushed her to the sink, jerking the large spoon out of her other hand with a curse. "What the hell? Emma, what's wrong with you? Do we really scare you that much?"

"You don't scare me at all. I'm just in a hurry. Lucas, Devlin, and Caleb will be here soon."

Remington held firm when she tried to pull away. "Be still. Keep it under the cold water for a few minutes. Damn, Emma. You're a walking accident."

Frustrated, Emma glared at him. "It's your fault."

With a slow smile, Remington bent to kiss her shoulder. "Yeah. I know. We fluster you. Makes a man feel real good."

"Get over yourself." Turning the water off, she tried to pull out of his grip.

"I'll bet your panties are soaked." The heat of Hunter's body pressed against her back, his hands coming around to settle right below her breasts. "Did you invite them over to make us jealous?"

Emma bit back a moan as another rush of moisture escaped to dampen her panties and had to swallow heavily before answering him. "No. I didn't." Sucking in a breath at the feel of his thumbs moving back and forth over her nipples, she fisted her hands on the edge of the sink. "I told you from the beginning that I need to work on my cookbook. I try out the recipes, and I only have so much room in the freezer for leftovers. Besides, I want opinions. I have several recipes for the same thing, and I want to put the best in my book."

Remington lifted her wet hand and patted it dry, inspecting it critically. "It doesn't look too bad, but we should put something on it."

"I'll get some ointment." Hunter disappeared out the back door.

Emma moved aside and started setting the table, almost dropping the plates when Remington's arm slid around her waist.

Taking the bowls from her, he touched his lips to her forehead.

"I'll set the table. You just do whatever you're doing."

"Thanks." She'd just started making the cornbread when Hunter came back in, carrying a tube. Setting her spoon aside, she reached for the tube, surprised when he shook his head and unscrewed the cap.

"I can do it."

Hunter didn't even slow, gripping her wrist and smearing ointment on the heel of her hand.

"One thing you're going to have to understand is that part of the lifestyle we live—the part that we've never been able to experience before—is taking care of our woman."

He had a stillness about him—a watchfulness—as he began to wrap the lower part of her hand with gauze.

"It's something that Rem and I thought we'd never have." Once he finished, he lifted her hand to his lips and placed a kiss over the burn.

"It's a part of us you'll have to accept."

Smiling to ease the trepidation in his eyes, Emma lifted her face for his kiss.

"I'll accept that. I have a feeling it's going to be a pain in the ass at times, but I'll accept it—as long as you accept that I'm going to tell you that you're a pain in the ass sometimes."

Accepting her invitation, Hunter smiled and touched his lips to hers. "Deal."

Remington opened the drawer and grabbed a handful of spoons.

"As long as we're on the subject of taking care of you, I want you to know that Hunter and I are both safe. We've never taken a woman without a condom and get checked regularly by Dr. Hansen."

Turning away, she went back to the stove and began stirring her chili again, tasting it to make sure she'd added enough spices.

"What about the other night when you went to the club?"

Her stomach clenched at the memory.

Remington slammed the drawer shut. "How did you know about that?"

Glancing back, she forced a smile. "You must be kidding. It's a small town."

Hunter took her spoon away again, throwing it on the counter before gripping her shoulder, turning her to face him.

"We went. Charlene was there. We couldn't touch her."

Remington moved in behind her, his hands on her waist.

"We wanted to, just to forget about you, but we couldn't. It pissed us off, which is why we got drunk. We couldn't stand to be in the club when all we could do was think about you, so we left to go to the bar. You should be happy, brat. We can't touch another woman because the only woman we want is you."

Smiling to hide the hurt that they didn't claim to love her, she leaned back against the counter and pressed a hand to her chest. "Be still, my heart."

Hunter's eyes flashed with heat—her only warning.

Between one heartbeat and the next, he closed the distance between them, gripped her shoulders, and pulled her against him.

She didn't have the chance to do more than suck in a breath before his lips closed over hers, his arms going around her as he deepened his kiss, a kiss far more possessive and sexual than the last one.

Thrilling at the hard lines of his body against hers, she moaned, tangling her tongue with his in an erotic dance that made her dizzy.

Lifting his head slightly, he nibbled at her bottom lip, sliding one hand to the base of her neck to hold her in place while his other hand closed over her breast.

His eyes narrowed at her gasp, becoming sharper when she cried out at the friction against her nipple.

Fisting her hands in his hair, she held on, her head spinning.

She'd never known a kiss could be so sexual.

Straightening, Hunter stared down at her, his hooded gaze glittering with need. Flattening his hand against her chest, he smiled faintly. "If your heart was still, I wouldn't be doing my job as your lover. It's pounding, baby."

Slipping his hand lower and under her sundress, he tore her panties from her and tossed them aside. "I like you flustered." His lips twitched as he gripped her chin and lifted his face to his. "The green in your eyes is more prevalent when you're aroused. It drives me nuts. Let's see if I'm right."

Remington's hands moved higher to close over her waist, holding her in place while Hunter slid a hand between her thighs. Pressing his cock against her back, Remington groaned. "I don't know how in the hell I'm supposed to get through dinner."

Staring into her eyes, Hunter slipped a finger into her pussy. "You're soaking wet, baby."

Gripping his shoulders, she moved against him, crying out at the feel of his finger moving in her pussy. "Is teasing me part of dominating me?"

Hunter picked up her panties and stuck them in his pocket, his expression tight with need. "There'll be lots of teasing. We're lovers now, Emma. You're ours."

Cupping her cheek, he slid his thumb back and forth over her lips. "We'll do whatever it takes to be together."

The doorbell rang, but it did nothing to ease the tension.

Acutely aware that she wore no panties under her dress, Emma caught Hunter's arm as he started to turn away. "What does that mean?"

Remington smiled, averting his gaze. "It means just that. Nothing in our lives is more important than having you."

* * * *

Devlin leaned back, rubbing his stomach. "Damn, that was good chili. Both of them. If you'd invited me for chicken chili, I would have passed, but I liked it as much as the beef chili."

Her face burned, the combination of Hunter's and Remington's attention and her guests' knowing looks all through dinner making it impossible to stop smiling.

"Good. I'm glad. The more I think of it, the more I think I'm going to put both in my next book." Emma hid a smile behind her coffee cup. "Sorry I can't offer you much in the way of leftovers. Both pots are about gone."

Remington patted her thigh under the table. "You didn't eat much."

She'd barely eaten a thing, finding it difficult to concentrate on something as mundane as food with her bare ass on the kitchen chair.

She'd moved all of her papers and cards to the island and went to retrieve her chili recipes and tablet and came back to the table, very aware of Hunter's and Remington's gazes on her ass.

Once she sat back at the table, a hand went to each of her thighs, sending another rush of moisture to coat her inner thighs.

Caleb set his coffee cup aside, his eyes filled with mischief. "Why don't you just marry us? We wouldn't leave you alone for meals and we'd praise you every day."

Giggling, Emma pulled her recipe cards and pen closer to make a few notes. "Gee, Caleb, that's a tempting offer, but if that's all you've got, I'm going to have to say no."

Lucas sipped his coffee, his eyes narrowed. "You get any better offers?"

Leaning forward, Emma tapped her pen on her cheek and considered that, her pussy clenching at Hunter's and Remington's searching looks. "Let's see. Brandon and Ethan are now going to carry my books in the store in their hotel lobby and have offered to let me use their kitchen and sous chef whenever I need them. I get free drinks forever at the bar because Michael and John are grateful for the rib recipe. I still have more work to do there."

Remington leaned back, studying her. "Yeah? Like what?"

"Well, they're going to have stuffed baked potatoes and we're working on wings. They're going to offer mild, medium, and hot."

After making a few notations, Emma picked up her coffee again, shifting restlessly in her seat. "I saw a sign today about the Fourth of July picnic. I saw that there are several contests for different types of food."

Hunter frowned. "We don't often go to that. I suppose you'll want to go."

"Oh, I'm going. What are the categories?"

Lucas sat forward. "Barbeque. Pies. Cakes. There's jams. All kinds of things." His lips twitched. "And chili."

Emma grinned, her competitive spirit doing cartwheels. "How do you know all that?"

Lucas allowed a small smile and took another sip of coffee. "Because Nat always railroads me into being a judge. As long as I don't have a vested interest in the results…"

Emma nodded, sucking in a breath when Remington's fingers slid to her inner thigh. "Good. I'll make sure the bar wins for barbeque. It'll be good for business. The hotel will win for cake. The pastry chef there is a real sweetheart and eager to please."

Beside her, Remington stiffened. "Exactly *how* eager to please."

Emma slapped at his hand, earning a look that promised retribution. "Don't start with me. He's very sweet and has offered to help with some of my pastry recipes and to give me some pointers and shortcuts. Oh! By the way, Brandon and Ethan said that I can use their kitchen for the photos."

"It sounds like everyone's been real helpful."

Ignoring the sarcasm in Hunter's voice, Emma rose from the table, including Lucas, Devlin, and Caleb in her smile. "Everyone has been. Thank you all so much for being my guinea pigs."

"Anytime." Raising a brow, Devlin gave her a slow smile. "So you plan on Michael and John winning for barbeque, and the hotel for cake. Any other predictions?"

Emma grinned, already mentally flipping through her recipes. "Well, it'll be my apple pie against Gracie's. It's pretty even. Of course, although you're too loyal to mention it, my chili's better than hers."

Setting his empty coffee aside, Lucas rose to his feet. "You know I can't be bribed or play favorites. It's all a matter of opinion, and I'm not the only judge. On top of that, they don't tell us who made what we're tasting. They just give us a small portion, and we judge."

"That's what I'm counting on. I don't know how Gracie's jam is, or if she even includes it." Tapping her chin with the pen, she mentally went through her jam recipes and decided she didn't want to go to the trouble.

It was more important to spend her time working on her cookbooks and dealing with Hunter and Remington.

"She does." Hunter rose and joined her at the island, rubbing a hand down her back. "Gracie always wins the biscuit competition, too. Nobody can touch her."

"Biscuits, huh?"

Remington nodded. "Gracie's biscuits are legendary." Bending, he touched his lips to her hair. "Yours are better, of course."

Emma grinned, meeting the looks of surprise on her guests' faces. "That's how I'm going to get Gracie's recipe for her meatloaf and peach cobbler."

Hunter grimaced. "But, honey, you might win the competition, but she can get the recipe out of one of your recipe books. Once that happens, you won't have anything to bargain with."

Shaking her head, Emma grinned up at him "No. She can't. That's one of my secret recipes, and used for bribing purposes only." She winked at him, enjoying his amusement. "Anyone ready for dessert? I made strawberry shortcake."

Remington's eyes narrowed. "I'm sure Lucas, Devlin, and Caleb have things to do."

Devlin rose. "Absolutely. We'll wash the dishes. It's the least we can do after such a great meal." He grinned at Remington. "*Then* we'll have strawberry shortcake."

Lucas studied Emma, glancing at both Hunter and Remington, smiling faintly at their glares. "Why don't you sit down and relax. You've been on your feet for hours. And you haven't told me yet if these two have made you an offer."

Running a hand over her back, Hunter smiled down at her. "We have. She's ours. We have a few things to iron out, but that'll all be settled soon."

Emma stiffened at the slide of Hunter's hot hand under her dress and over her bottom, struggling not to betray anything to the others.

As his hand slid lower, forcing its way between the cheeks of her ass, she fought to keep her breathing even, pressing her thighs together when her pussy clenched and more moisture escaped.

Lucas raised a brow. "Since you're so damned stubborn, you're bound to fuck up. When he does, Emma, you can come stay with us until he apologizes."

Hunter's warm hand settled on her back again, his eyes dancing with amusement. "You know, before you came along, I used to intimidate people."

Rubbing his shoulder, Emma pouted. "You intimidate me. Isn't that good enough for you?"

Carrying dishes to the sink where Devlin waited, Remington paused to drop a quick kiss on her lips. "That's encouraging."

Emma jolted at the sharp stab of need that tightened her stomach, and if not for Remington's sharp reflexes, she would have knocked the dishes out of his hands. "Damn it, Remington!"

Chuckling softly, he kissed her again. "Flustering you is a hell of a lot of fun." He glanced pointedly downward, the knowledge of her predicament gleaming in his eyes.

"Shut up." Emma couldn't hold back a grin and pushed him away, leaning back into Hunter's warm embrace.

With the intention of clearing the table and getting dessert, Emma tried to straighten, but Hunter's arms tightened around her, holding her in place.

"You're fine where you are." Bending, he touched his lips to her ear. "You feel good in my arms. Just let me hold you for a while."

Wondering how any woman could refuse such a request, Emma leaned back against him, pretending that he loved her.

It was a fantasy, one that she allowed herself, if only for a little while.

Perhaps one day it would come true.

Chapter Twenty-One

Emma watched her guests leave, her pulse tripping at the look in Remington's eyes as he closed the door behind him. "You were both very rude to them."

Slipping a hand to her waist, Hunter frowned as he led her back toward the kitchen. "Why? Because we told them it was time to leave? They were only staying to irritate us."

Remington closed in on her other side, taking her hand in his. "Besides, they're used to our rudeness. Now that they're gone, we have you all to ourselves. You made a few demands earlier, and the men in Desire pride themselves on meeting their woman's demands."

The erotic promise in his voice sent ripples of desire through her, but it was the affection in their eyes and in their touch that stunned her.

It made the desire more potent, adding layers that weakened her knees. "I'm not going to let you do what you did before. I'm not going to let you pleasure me and then walk away."

"No more of that." Hunter turned her to face him, backing her against the wall closest to the stairs, his hands closing on her waist. His eyes narrowed as he lowered his head. "I can't live with not knowing either."

Emma stilled, struck by Hunter's gravelly tone. "What are you saying?"

Hunter's hands slid up her sides to her arms and all the way to her wrists, lifting her arms and settling her hands on his shoulders. "I'm saying that I've realized that the need to be in control is even stronger than before. There's more at stake now. Keep your hands where I put them."

The steel in Hunter's tone held an erotic demand that she obeyed without hesitation.

In sharp contrast, the vulnerability in his eyes drew her in, mesmerizing her.

Suspecting that the next few minutes would dramatically change their relationship, she nodded and kept silent.

Tension emanated from him, his hooded gaze holding hers. "I want you, but you have to understand that the fear of hurting you isn't something that's gonna go away overnight."

Nodding, Emma gulped when Hunter's hands reversed their journey, sucking in a breath when they reached the outer curve of her breasts and stopped. "I understand."

Remington moved in beside her, his hands warm on her hips. "Good."

"We have no experience with tender, so you'll have to be patient with us." Hunter's thumbs moved slowly back and forth across her nipples, his caress firm and demanding. "We're too rough. Too controlling."

Remington's hands clenched on her hips. "Too fucking hungry."

Staring into Hunter's eyes, Emma tightened her grip on his shoulders, her entire body trembling with need. "You'd never hurt me. You're the gentlest men I've ever known."

With a deep groan, Remington slid his hands over her belly and back, the frustration in his eyes painful to see. "We're not gentle. We never have been. We don't know how the hell to be gentle." He fisted a hand in her hair, tilting her face to his. "What I want from you has nothing to do with gentle. There's a possessiveness I hadn't counted on that makes the hunger even more intense."

Hunter cupped her chin, his fingers firm on her cheek. "It scares me. I'm scared of what would happen if we lost control."

His eyes narrowed on hers, watching her closely while caressing her nipples again. "It's gonna get scary at times, but if we walk away, I want you to promise that you won't come after us."

Sucking in a breath at the sharp sensation, Emma gripped his shoulders tighter. She'd do anything to prove to them that she trusted them not to hurt her. "Yes. I'm not afraid of you. I know you would never hurt me. I want to give you what you need, but I need to have you, too. I need to have *all* of you."

Remington pulled her back against him, bending to nuzzle her neck. "You're so delicate. We want you so damned much. We could hurt you so easily."

Leaning back against him, Emma lifted her arms to fist her hands in his hair. "You won't. Please, Rem, don't treat me like I'm made of glass. I want all that naughty stuff you do in the club."

Turning her head to look up at him, she tugged his hair. "I want to make you forget every woman you've ever touched."

Hunter's eyes flared, and with a firm hand around her waist, he tugged her closer, sliding his other hand under her dress to run his fingertips over her mound. "Already forgotten. I only know you, but not nearly well enough. I won't be satisfied until I know your body and your responses better than you do."

He bent and lifted her, his eyes on hers as he held her against his chest. "Starting now."

He adjusted his hold until she faced him, his fingers digging into the cheeks of her ass. "Put your legs around me."

Remington turned away. "I'll be right there."

Wrapping her legs around him, Emma slid her hands to his hair and rubbed her slit against his cotton shirt. "Why did you take my panties off?" Moaning at the feel of his body moving against hers as he carried her up the stairs, she touched her lips to his jaw. "Why did you make me go through dinner without wearing panties? Is that part of it?"

"In a way. There's no definite rules, other than everything is consensual. It's up to us. It's whatever we make it." With a firm hand, he pressed her head against his shoulder, the fingers of his other hand delving between her thighs, moving insistently over her folds. "You're drenched, and you have been for hours. Going without panties heightened your awareness, didn't it?"

With another moan, Emma moved against him, trying to get his finger inside her. "Yes. God yes! Just knowing that you could touch me whenever you wanted made me feel so exposed."

Hunter slid his hand higher, gripping her ass cheek. "It's something we all enjoyed, so it'll be something that we'll expect of you often." Climbing the stairs, he touched his lips to her hair. "See how that works?"

Lifting her head, she smiled and pressed her lips to his jaw. "What if I don't like it?"

Hunter paused next to her bed, his eyes darkening. "If there's something you don't like, or that makes you extremely uncomfortable, we won't do it anymore." Setting her on her feet, he ran his fingers through her hair and bent to turn on the lamp on the nightstand. "We'd lead you step by step into another world—a world where nothing matters but the pleasure. You'll feel things you never thought you could feel."

Bending slightly, he gathered the hem of her dress and lifted it to her waist, exposing her from the waist down. "So will we. We're very much looking forward to having a woman of our own, someone we could have all day every day."

Remington's hand slid over her exposed bottom as he leaned over to turn on the bedside lamp. "We never thought we could. We're gonna have to be careful that we don't scare you so badly that you run away."

Not a chance in hell!

Running her hands over his chest, she smiled and rubbed against him. "I've heard some things from the other women, but I'm not sure how this works. What if you ask me to do something and I refuse?" Looking up at him through her lashes, she giggled. "What if I was bad?"

His eyes narrowed, the challenge in them tripping her pulse. "I'll spank your bottom." His lips twitched, his eyes becoming even darker. "Or something else. I wouldn't want to become boring."

Emma sucked in a breath when he parted her folds, a low moan escaping at the friction of his rough finger moving gently over her clit.

Gripping his shoulders, Emma lifted to her toes, her breathing ragged.

"I don't think that's going to be an issue."

Feeling Remington's gaze on her exposed bottom, she started to turn to look at him, but Hunter's hand tightened in her hair.

His eyes narrowed, his head bending to brush his lips over her lips. Her cheek. Her jaw.

"No. Keep your eyes on me. Don't look away."

Trembling at the raw sexual demand in his tone, Emma sucked in a breath and then another. "Okay."

Something came and went in Hunter's eyes, something that looked mysteriously like relief, followed by a hunger so sharp it stole her breath. "Good." He released the hem of her dress, allowing it to fall again.

"Hunter?"

"Yes?" His gaze held hers, and with deft fingers, he unzipped her dress.

Shaking uncontrollably, Emma sucked in breath after breath, pinpricks of need and awareness dancing over every inch of her body.

"What do you want me to do? Please. I need—"

"I know what you need." His confidence and attentiveness told her that this would be no ordinary lovemaking. "Trust me."

Remington sat on the bed behind her, his fingers sliding over the sensitive skin at the back of her knee. "Trust *us.* Trust us to give you pleasure. To protect you. To care for you. Trust us to know what we're doing—and what you're feeling."

Emma cried out, gripping fistfuls of Hunter's shirt when he removed his fingers from her slit. "Oh." Shifting restlessly, Emma tried to press her thighs together, but a denim-clad leg slid between hers and stood in her way.

Hunter raised a brow, silently telling her that he knew what she was doing.

Looking up at him through her lashes, she smiled. "You're very observant, aren't you?"

"When it comes to you, yes I am." Pushing a stray tendril of her hair back from her face, he lifted her chin. "I'll learn your body and your responses, and soon, I'll know how you'll react even before you do. Lift your arms over your head."

Staring into his eyes, she readily obeyed him, his attentiveness adding yet another layer to her experience in lovemaking.

"Very good." Gathering the hem of her dress again, he lifted it over her head, exposing her new pink lace bra.

Assuming that he would remove her dress, she started to pull her arms free of the material, sucking in a breath when he caught her wrists and the hem of her dress above her head in one large hand.

To her shock, he held her wrists and the material of her dress in his strong grip, leaving her face and arms covered and the rest of her body completely exposed.

Every nerve ending hummed with excitement at being unable to see them while being exposed to both of them.

It was a new experience, one that she suspected would be the first of many.

She wanted to see their faces and squirmed to pull the dress free but froze at Hunter's sharp command.

"Be still." A hard, warm hand slid over her ass, a hand she assumed belonged to Hunter. "We want to see you. We're going to do a little exploring, and I want you to stay still."

* * * *

Hunter smiled at her, grateful that she couldn't see him.

He'd deliberately covered her face so that she couldn't see the raw hunger on theirs.

Knowing she was new at this, and that she belonged to them, gave their possession of her an edge and intensity that he hadn't truly been prepared for.

The sparkle of challenge in her eyes and his own hunger for her meant that he had to do whatever it took to get control of the situation—and he had to do it from the very beginning.

Gritting his teeth when she shivered again, he teased both of them by sliding his fingertips down her side.

His cock throbbed when she shivered and moaned again, her passion arousing him more than any woman he'd ever known.

He had to take control of her and himself, and he had to keep it.

Confident that once they gave her more pleasure than she'd ever known she'd be putty in their hands, he reached out to tug a nipple, his cock jumping at her soft cry of pleasure. "Be still while we explore you a little."

Emma leaned into him, fueling his need to earn her submission. "Hunter." Whispering his name on a breath, Emma leaned into him, fueling his need to earn her submission.

"I'm here, baby." His endearment for her slipped out without his consent, something that had never happened to him before.

"I'm shaking everywhere. I can feel you and Remington looking at me."

Inordinately pleased with himself—and her—Hunter smiled, sharing a look with Remington. "Of course we're looking at you. You have a beautiful body, baby. You wouldn't deny us the chance to admire it, would you? After all, you're ours now, aren't you?"

Easy. Don't scare her off.

Shifting restlessly, Emma let out a small whine. "Yes, but I want to touch you!"

Imagining her small, soft hands on his cock, Hunter bit back a groan, struggling to inject a forcefulness into his tone, one strong enough to get her attention, but not enough to scare her. "Not until we allow it. We're in charge, remember? Now, spread those pretty thighs."

Another shiver went through her, her moan like a stroke to his cock. "I need to see your face."

Knowing that he had to stand firm, Hunter glanced at Remington and did something that made him nervous as hell, understanding that it would either ruin everything or take things deeper.

Holding his breath, he lightly slapped her ass, his stomach clenched as he waited for her reaction.

It proved more than he'd bargained for.

Crying out, she rubbed her nipples against him. "Hunter. Please! Oh God. Please. Don't tease me." She stamped her feet, her movements becoming more violent as she tried to free herself of the dress. "I'm aroused already! What the hell are you waiting for?"

Delighted with her, Hunter smiled, grateful that she couldn't see it.

"We know you're aroused, baby, but we're not rushing this."

Injecting steel into his tone, he slid into the role of Dominant with an ease that filled him with relief. "You don't have any say in whether we take you or not. There may be times when we just arouse you and leave you hanging, especially if you've disobeyed us."

He could well imagine her reaction to that and had a feeling that he'd never get away with doing such a thing,

"Damn it."

Closing his fingers over a nipple, he squeezed lightly, watching her closely to judge her response. "Behave. If you're a good girl, you'll get what you want."

"Just tell me what you want me to do. I'll do anything."

Swallowing heavily, Hunter glanced at Remington, who smiled slowly and edged closer. "Good. Then be still and let me do a little exploring."

* * * *

Emma struggled to stay still, listening for Remington and desperate to show both of them that she could be everything they needed.

They were everything she needed and more.

Her bottom still burned from his light slap, the heat that spread through her clit made the throbbing almost unbearable. Frustrated that he kept her from getting the friction she needed, she moved restlessly, stilling at the slide of another hand down her back.

Remington's voice came from directly behind her, the playfulness in his tone unable to disguise the sexual tension. "You're not obeying, darlin'."

Hunter's voice, deep with erotic demand, vibrated against her ear. "I told you to spread those thighs. I don't like repeating myself." Lifting her wrists higher, he held her so that she no longer leaned against him.

A shiver went up her spine, anticipation like champagne bubbling through her veins. Gulping, she spread her legs several inches apart, her breathing ragged.

"Farther apart, baby. More. Very nice."

Standing with her feet about shoulder-width apart, Emma locked her knees, her toes curling. Her heart beat nearly out of her chest—her pussy clenching as she waited for him to thrust a finger into her.

Because she hadn't expected it, she jolted when he closed a thumb and forefinger over her nipple and began to squeeze.

"Be still."

To her shock another hand slid over her ass, kneading gently.

Remington.

She sucked in a breath again, feeling more naked and vulnerable than she'd ever felt in her life.

The slight pain from her nipple had ripples of awareness shooting to her clit, the ache so unbearable she closed her thighs, rubbing them together in an effort to get some relief.

Feeling the tension emanating from both of them, Emma immediately knew she'd made a mistake.

The fingers on her nipple and the hand on her ass slipped away, leaving her bereft.

Hunter's grip changed slightly, and before she knew it, the dress had been tossed away and he'd released her.

Finding herself suddenly free and able to see left her disconcerted and worse, disconnected. She reached for Hunter, pulling her hands back when he crossed his massive arms over his chest.

A dark brow went up, his eyes going flat and cool. "Are we done here?"

"No!" Laying her hands on his forearms, she gulped, fighting the urge to look over her shoulder at Remington. "It aches so badly. Every time you touch me, it's just so intense!"

Deciding that she would be as honest with them as she could, she dropped her forehead to his arms. "I've never felt this kind of pleasure. I don't know how to handle it."

Lifting her head, she wiped away a tear, shaking with emotion and arousal. "I'm sure you're used to women who know what to do or say, but—"

Her throat clogged, keeping her from saying more.

"Quiet." Unfolding his arms, Hunter reached for her, his smile tender. "No other woman ever mattered. There's just you." Cupping both breasts, he bent to brush his lips over hers. "We've never had a woman of our own before—never wanted one badly enough to hope that we could have someone to care for."

From behind her, Remington ran a hand down her back. "And we've never trained a sub. We never trusted ourselves enough to do that either." His fingertips trailed down to her bottom. Following the crease, he bent to touch his lips to her shoulder. "Now we find ourselves in a unique position, one we hadn't expected. We have a woman who we can't let go."

Emma gulped. "Sub?"

Releasing her breast, he slid his hand up to cup her cheek, his other hand sliding lower to her waist. "A submissive. This is what you wanted, isn't it?"

"Yes. I want to belong to you." Her breathing hitched, the feel of their hands sliding over her drawing her deeper into their web of seduction. "I want to be what you want, what you need."

She couldn't imagine living the rest of her life never feeling like this again.

"And we want to be what you need." Hunter smiled and pushed her hair back. "You need lovers who will draw out all that passion inside you. You need lovers that can handle your strength."

Tapping her nipples, Hunter stared down at her, his eyes narrowing at her cry of pleasure. "We can. We're going to draw out even more of that passion, and we're going to show you that you're stronger than you know. You'll be expected to do what you're told. We're going to teach you things about yourself you never suspected."

Emma smiled.

I'm going to teach you things about yourself, too.

Grinning, she lifted her chin. "I can take whatever you dish out." She fluttered her lashes, holding back a giggle when his eyes narrowed in suspicion. "I wonder what I can teach the two of you about yourselves. Are you going to tell me what you want me to do, or am I supposed to guess? I want you to take me."

"You'll know exactly what's expected of you at all times." Bending to touch his lips to hers again, he smiled faintly. "We're patient, but pausing like this is not something we'll be patient with for long. We know you're new at this, so we'll give you a little leeway to ease your nervousness, but you'll soon learn that once we begin, we expect you to do what you're told and take what we give you."

"What if it's something that I don't like?"

Hunter tapped her chin. "You're going to have to trust us to read your response to whatever we do, but we want to push you to accept more and more. If you tell us to stop, we will, but I want you to give things a chance." Smiling again, he closed his fingers over a nipple. "You'll find yourself begging for things that you never thought you would."

"I found some scarves." Remington spoke from somewhere behind her seconds before he covered her eyes with one of her scarves and tied it securely.

"Spread those fucking thighs."

Alarmed at Hunter's cold tone, Emma rushed to obey him, her alarm growing at being unable to see if his eyes held affection or ice.

Hearing the rustle of material and feeling the brush of the covers against the backs of her legs, she realized that Remington had turned back the covers.

Seconds later, she heard the sound if his boots hitting the floor and the rustle of clothing.

The thought of him naked weakened her knees.

"I heard Remington get undressed. If he's naked, I want to see. Why don't you get undressed, Hunter?"

Remington chuckled from somewhere behind her. "Damn, she's gonna need a lot of training. She doesn't have any self-control at all. We're definitely gonna have to go buy some things."

Hunter gathered her wrists and quickly tied them together with an efficiency that had her jealous of every woman who'd contributed to his experience. Seconds later, her bra fell free, and a finger tightened on a nipple—this time with no bra in the way. "You'll learn self-control, Emma, but since you're having trouble controlling yourself now, I'll do it for you."

He picked her up and laid her on the cool sheets with a speed that left her dizzy, immediately raising her hands above her head and tying her wrists to the headboard. "You won't always know what we're going to do—or why we're doing it—but you're going to have to accept it. I told you why you're being restrained. You're being blindfolded because I want to focus your attention. Bend your knees and spread them."

Remington bent low, his voice dark and menacing. "I have a knife in my hand. You're going to feel the back of the blade against your skin while I cut your bra off of you. Don't move. It's gonna be cold. Don't even jerk."

Breathing harshly, Emma fisted her hands in the scarves and braced herself, sucking in a breath when the cool blade of the knife touched her skin.

Remington cut one strap free, and then the other. "Very nice. Now let's see how still you can be."

Another rustle of clothing heightened her arousal, her awareness razor sharp.

Hunter's voice came from somewhere at her feet. "I told you to spread those knees. Wide. I want to see what belongs to me, and I want every part of you available to me at my whim. Do you understand me?"

Emma sucked in a breath and then another, every inch of her body trembling with a combination of nerves and excitement that she never wanted to end. "Yes."

"Then do it."

Emma's trembling grew stronger, and knowing that both men watched her, she spread her legs, digging her heels into the cool sheets. Startled by the vulnerable position she found herself in, she struggled to stay still, jolting when the bed shifted and a hard thigh brushed against her left hip.

Although she hadn't heard him move, Hunter's voice came from her right.

"Let's get those breasts higher." Yanking the pillow lower, he adjusted it behind her upper back, forcing her breasts higher as her head fell back against the mattress.

Exposed and defenseless, Emma pulled at her restraints, an erotic thrill going through her when she realized that they didn't give an inch.

Callused fingers closed over both nipples at once, squeezing with more force than before. "Very pretty. These beautiful breasts and sensitive nipples are going to give me a great deal of pleasure. For now, though, they're going to be the object of your punishment for making me tell you twice to spread those thighs."

"But—"

"Quiet!" Hunter pinched a nipple. "You're not to speak unless you're asked a question or you feel that you can't handle what we're doing to you. If that happens on our first session, we're going to be extremely disappointed."

Emma nodded, determined not to do anything to stop them.

Remington slid a hand down her body. "Remember the knife, darlin'?"

Emma's legs shook, and she had to swallow before she could answer. "Yes."

Oh God. What were they going to do with it?

"You're gonna learn how to be completely still. There will be many times that we want to play with you, and we don't want you to move at all. We'll want you to remain perfectly still."

Emma nodded again, biting her lip and bracing herself for whatever he had in store for her.

With her entire body naked and vulnerable, she knew they would be counting on her trust to get her though this, and she wasn't about to disappoint them.

She hadn't counted on the tinkle of ice coming from right next to her, something Remington must have gotten from the kitchen before coming up.

The fact that he'd planned ahead gave her a sense of security but also filled her with trepidation.

The silence in the room lengthened, but suspecting that they were testing her, she fought to remain still and silent.

Seconds ticked by, or it could have been minutes, and just as she found herself beginning to relax, the flat edge of the ice-cold blade of the knife pressed against her nipple.

Shocked, she cried out and jolted, immediately regretting it.

"I'm sorry. I'm sorry. I—"

Remington lifted the blade. "Quiet. Do we need to gag you?"

When the bed shifted on the other side, she waited expectantly for Hunter's touch, but it didn't come.

"I'm waiting for an answer." Remington's gravelly tone had an edge to it now, all playfulness gone.

"No." Curling her toes against the strength of her arousal, Emma took a steadying breath. "I won't talk anymore. I just wanted to apologize."

Lips closed over her left nipple, sucking lightly before releasing it. "No apologies tonight. You're new at this, something that gives both Hunter and me a great deal of pleasure. We just want to do a little exploring."

Since he hadn't asked her a question, she bit her lip to keep from answering.

"Very good." The cold blade of the knife unexpectedly touched her raised knee. "Now be still."

The blade moved away again, and she heard another tinkle of ice.

Stiffening, she waited, sucking in a breath when something cold and wet touched her belly. Her stomach muscles quivered under the slow slide of the ice over her belly, the extreme cold heightening her awareness and bringing every nerve ending to life.

When the path of the ice moved higher toward her breasts, Emma's breathing became more ragged, her nipples beading so tight it was almost painful.

Soft whimpers escaped, the effort it cost her to remain still overwhelming.

It got even worse when the bed shifted again as Hunter moved to kneel between her thighs, his hair-roughened legs against her feet keeping them parted.

The ice melted as it moved higher between her breasts, rivulets of cold water trailing over the underside of her breasts, perilously close to her nipples.

The bed shifted slightly, and she felt Hunter move over her, a hand braced on either side of her raised arms.

Suddenly, Remington shifted the ice to her left nipple while Hunter took her right nipple into his hot mouth.

The sharp contrast left her reeling, sending sharp stabs of intense awareness to her clit.

Biting her lip to hold back her cries of pleasure, Emma squirmed restlessly, unable to resist trying to press her thighs closed, but Hunter's hard thighs kept them spread.

After scraping his teeth over her nipple, Hunter lifted his head.

"No, love. You're not closing those legs. I'm gonna use my fingers and my mouth on that pussy." Hunter let his fingertips trail down her body. "Tomorrow, you're going to the spa and getting waxed. I don't want anything hiding you from me."

"Oh God."

Emma arched into his touch, crying out again when he lightly slapped her inner thigh.

Sitting back and lifting her thighs over his, Hunter spread her wider. "Be still. I'm gonna explore my new toy a little, and I don't want your wiggling to get in my way."

Her pussy and bottom clenched with need, the tingling awareness in her nipples driving her insane.

Remington removed the ice and sucked a nipple hard, pressing it against the roof of his mouth before releasing it, the heat and sharp pressure so intense she couldn't hold back her cry.

"Rem! I can't stand it. God, I'm gonna come."

Running the flat of his tongue over her nipple, he brushed his thumb over the other. "You can take it. I'll bet that clit's throbbing, isn't it?"

"Yes! Oh God."

The muscles in her thighs and bottom tightened and released, her hips rocking as the hunger intensified.

The warning tingling of an impending orgasm began in her clit, and she whimpered at the effort to hold back.

Hunter slid his hands over her inner thighs until his thumbs pressed against her folds. "Do you think thrusting that pussy is going to get you attention any sooner?"

"Yes. No. I don't know." The scarf over her eyes was damp with tears of frustration. "I can't stop. It aches."

Parting her folds, Hunter pushed her thighs wider. "What aches?"

"Everything!"

"I want to hear the words, Emma. I won't tolerate shyness or embarrassment during sex. What do you want me to touch? I want to hear the words from you."

Wishing she could see his face, she pulled at her restraints, her body screaming with arousal. "Everything! Damn it, Hunter! You're the one experienced in this. You know what I need. You said so. My nipples ache. My clit is throbbing so bad. I'm so close to coming."

"I know, baby." His hands slid over her abdomen and higher to her breasts to stroke his thumbs over her nipples. "I know what you need. But I need something from you."

"What?" Frustrated, she snapped at him. "What else do you need? I'm giving you everything!"

Hunter surprised her by leaning over her and taking her mouth in a deep kiss filled with possession and a tenderness she hadn't expected. Lifting his head, he cupped her jaw, his cock hard against her belly. "No. You're not, but I can't blame you. You're giving me more than I deserve—or expected."

Surprising her further, he slid down her body, touching his lips to her scar. "Just be still. I'll give you what you need."

"I need *you*." The need to have him and Remington in her life grew stronger every day, their masculinity and strength an intoxicating combination.

After a long pause, Hunter stiffened and straightened. "I know what you need better than you do. Be still so I can inspect your pussy."

She heard a groan coming from her left and felt Remington's fingertips on the underside of her breast, carefully avoiding her nipple. Imagining him watching what Hunter did to her, she turned toward him, crying out at the feel of Hunter's firm finger thrusting into her pussy. "Oh God!"

"Nice and wet. Remington and I are going to keep you this way all the time. Wet and needy."

"I'll die!"

"No you won't." Pressing his finger against her inner walls, he used the fingers of his other hand to hold her folds open. "She's clenching hard. Exploring her is going to have to be done in small doses. She gets too aroused."

Emma rocked her hips, her breath coming out in harsh gasps. "Of course I'm aroused. Your finger's inside me!"

"Inside you where?"

Emma had never been one to talk dirty, even in the bedroom, but the strength of her need wiped away all embarrassment. "My pussy. Please. Move faster!" She tried to rock her hips harder, stunned when he slid his finger free. "No! Put it back, damn you!"

A slap on her inner thigh shocked her into immobility, the feel of her folds being parted wider sending the heat from Hunter's slap straight to her clit. "Touch me, damn it!"

Her clit throbbed, aching so badly that she'd do anything for attention there. Trying to twist to rub her clit on Hunter's leg, she groaned when he slapped her other thigh.

"Behave. You're not getting attention there until you do what you're told."

"Please! What do I have to do?" Pumping her hips in the air, she thrashed her head from side to side.

"I already told you. Be still. Rem, hand me a condom."

"I can't stay still. I need to come." Digging her heels into the bedding, she pumped her hips.

Remington chuckled from beside her. "It's gonna be a hell of a lot of fun to tame her."

Insulted, Emma stiffened, panicking when Hunter rose. "Tame me? Tame me?" Turning toward where she knew both of them stood, she kicked her legs, pleased when she managed to connect with a naked leg. "I'll show you tame!"

The bed shifted again as Hunter moved between her thighs. "A hell of a lot of fun, but I'm afraid she's *too* damned tempting." Lifting her thighs to rest on his, he spread her folds again. "Look at how pretty she is. We'll be able to see her better once she's waxed."

Emma cried out at the friction of a firm fingertip stroking her clit, jolting so hard that she knocked his finger free.

She was so close to coming she could taste it. "Please. Please. I need—"

"I know what you need, Emma. You've already been told that you'll get it, but you have to behave."

Hunter's deep voice had lowered even more, the thread of satisfaction in it making her even more determined to please him.

A shiver of delight went through her when the head of his cock pressed against her pussy opening. "Yes!"

She moaned as his cock pressed deeper, the thick head like steel, forcing her inner walls to stretch to accommodate it. "Oh God! So good."

"Yes. It is." Holding her hips, he groaned, and with one smooth stroke, thrust into her, filling her completely. "Come for me."

Her body responded immediately, obeying him without hesitation.

With Hunter's cock held deep inside her, Emma sucked in a breath, her pussy clenching on him in hard spasms.

Every muscle in her body tightened, the slide of his thumb over her clit like liquid fire, sending her over in a hard rush of the most sublime pleasure she'd ever known.

Crying out her release, she gripped the scarf binding her wrists, every inch of her body alive with pinpricks of pleasure.

Just as her orgasm crested, Hunter began to move, fucking her in slow, smooth strokes, dragging out the pleasure until she thought she would die of it.

"You like that, do you?" His voice had taken on a jagged edge that rippled through her, his hands tightening on her hips as he began to thrust faster. "Keep coming. More. Yeah, that's it."

She couldn't seem to stop, her cries accompanying each new wave of pleasure.

Rising to his knees, he released her hip and slid the scarf blindfolding her from her face.

Bracing an elbow on the mattress next to her, he bent to scrape his teeth over her nipple, his strokes slowing as if knowing just when her orgasm began to subside. "Now that we've taken the edge off, I can take some time to explore you."

Chapter Twenty-Two

Remington knelt next to the bed, not wanting to miss a single nuance of Emma's responses.

Listening to her cries of pleasure, he couldn't help but remember the day they'd bought the bed Emma lay in.

They'd been in a particularly pensive mood, the fantasy of sharing a woman of their own guiding their purchase.

Seeing Hunter take Emma in the bed they'd never thought would be used, Remington felt a surge of possessiveness toward her that scared the hell out of him.

With his cock still inside her, Hunter began arousing her all over again.

Clearly enthralled with her, Hunter drew Remington's attention almost as much as Emma did.

He'd seen his brother take many women in the past, but he'd never seen Hunter look at a woman the way he looked at Emma.

Remington shifted restlessly, anticipation of taking her ass making his cock ache.

The anticipation grew as he watched her respond so beautifully to every slide of Hunter's hands on her body.

Every lick.

Every nibble.

"You owe me something."

Hunter's voice sounded as ragged and harsh as if he'd swallowed glass.

The need clouding Emma's eyes made his cock jump, the breathlessness in her voice making him ache to hold her.

Emma whimpered when Hunter withdrew from her, the effort it cost her to remain still when he leaned back and parted her folds showing clearly on her face.

"What d-do I owe you?"

Hunter raised a brow, his eyes flaring with heat at the trepidation in her eyes. "I want to taste you." Parting her folds, he ran the tip of his finger down her slit, pausing to stroke her clit. "If you're going to be mine, I want to know your taste. I want to explore every part of you."

Remington already knew her taste and couldn't wait to taste her again.

Tonight, however, was a night for discovery, their main goal to see if she enjoyed the role of submissive.

She was perfect.

Her passion and response to them was more than they could have ever hoped for while her determination and independence made her a force to be reckoned with.

No other woman had ever shown such stubbornness in getting them to hope for more than they thought they could have.

Stunned at the change Emma had made in their lives, Remington watched them together, the connection between them making his chest tighten.

He could only hope to establish the same connection with her, even knowing that a growing intimacy between them would be dangerous to his control.

"Yes! Oh God! I can't come again, though. I can't." Writhing now, Emma kept lifting her head to stare into Hunter's eyes. "I've never—"

Hunter's lips thinned. "Whatever's happened in the past has no bearing on what happens now. I'm going to use my mouth on you, but instead of me taking, you're going to give."

Reaching up, he untied her hands and sat back on his heels. "Spread your folds and offer yourself to me."

* * * *

As soon as Hunter released her, Emma reached for him, her body still trembling from the remnants of her orgasm and desperate with need for another. "Take me."

Hunter's slow smile filled her with apprehension. "Uh-uh. I need more than that from you. Spread those folds and tell me that everything you're showing me is mine." He ran his fingertips up her inner thighs, sending a surge of heat to her clit.

Unable to resist the challenge in his eyes, Emma slid the pillow higher, propping it against the headboard.

Lying back, she snuck a glance at Remington to find him watching her with narrowed eyes, his eyes glittering with hunger. Intrigued by Hunter's warning look, Emma ran her hands down her belly to her mound.

"What does it mean if I do?"

Glancing at her hands, Hunter smiled faintly. "It means that it's mine. To enjoy. To use. Anytime. Anyplace." His eyes narrowed at her hesitation. "Don't worry. You'll never be shown to anyone else besides Rem. I find that I'm very selfish and possessive of you."

Pleased that her plan seemed to be working and too aroused to deny him, Emma watched his face and obeyed him, knowing how much it would mean to him.

Sliding her fingers lower, she parted her folds, exposing her aching clit. "There. It's yours. So what are you going to do about it?"

Hunter's eyes narrowed but his lips twitched. "That smart mouth is gonna get you in trouble real soon."

Rocking her hips, Emma smiled, her pussy and ass clenching at the thought of being turned over his lap. "Go ahead, darlin'. Impress me."

Something dark and dangerous flashed in his eyes, his hands firm on her thighs as he lifted them higher. "Let's see what I can do to impress you."

Emma barely had a chance to suck in a breath before Hunter delivered a sharp slap to her clit.

"Oh! Oh my God!" Releasing her folds, she hurriedly tried to cover herself, only to have her wrists caught in one hand by Remington.

Her clit burned and throbbed, feeling swollen and heavy.

To her shock, she found herself on the verge of coming again, the need for friction on her clit unbearable.

Held spread wide, she didn't stand a chance of rubbing her thighs together and fought to get her hands free to do it herself.

Remington smiled and tugged at a nipple, intensifying the need. "You really don't think you're gonna get away, do you, baby doll?"

"Stop calling me that!"

"Nope." Remington brushed a callused palm over one breast and then the other. "You're my own little doll to play with whenever I want. I've never had one of my own before so you're gonna be played with often."

Still holding her wrists in one hand above her head, he reached beside him with the other. "Is that clit too hot, baby doll?"

Emma gasped, guessing his intention. "No. Oh God. Don't put that—ahhh!"

The extreme cold against her hot clit had her bucking against Hunter, who tightened his hold high on her thighs, raising her hips higher.

Remington kept his fingers over her slit, holding the ice in place.

"I can hold this against your clit until it melts, or I can remove it. If I remove it, though, it goes somewhere else—and you're going to get another slap on your clit."

She wanted it, the anticipation in his voice and in his eyes spurring her to want more.

"Take it off. I'll take my punishment."

Satisfaction and something more intense flared in their eyes, a relief in her trust combined with an emotion she didn't dare hope for.

She didn't fear them and hoped it showed.

They seemed to know what the other was thinking because, as soon as Hunter lifted her higher, Remington watched her eyes as he slid the small piece of ice lower, holding it against her puckered opening for a second or two before slipping it into her ass.

Stunned at the cold and the sharpened awareness in her ass, Emma kicked, fighting to get free—and hoping they wouldn't let her.

They didn't disappoint her.

Holding her hips high, Hunter slapped her clit again, spreading fire over the swollen bundle of nerves.

Already sensitive from their recent lovemaking, her clit burned, throbbing with every beat of her heart.

"Hunter!"

The realization that she had a lot to learn about their brand of sex hit her just as Hunter's hot mouth closed over her cold clit.

He sucked hard, using his tongue to stroke her clit, overcoming her struggles against such an intense sensation.

"Hunter. Hunter. I can't stand it! Oh God! I'm coming. I'm coming again. It's not possible."

Held in the grip of yet another orgasm, she cried out his name, her cries becoming louder when he replaced his tongue with one of his callused thumbs and thrust deep into her again.

The bed shifted as Remington stretched out beside her. "It looks real possible to me."

She barely heard him, the pleasure all consuming.

Ripples of it shimmered through her, from her clit outward.

Clenching on Hunter's cock, she rode the waves of a release that seemed never-ending. Her nipples tingled and ached, the slow slide of Remington's thumb over first one, and then the other, sharpening the pleasure almost to pain.

She lost herself, the dizzying pleasure taking over, making her weak and shaky.

"I can't move. God. I'm shaking everywhere. Hunter. Oh God."

Hunter groaned and thrust again, holding himself deep inside her. Releasing her hands, he covered her body with his, strong arms going around her and pulling her close. "That's it. I've got you."

Gripping his shoulders, Emma buried her face against his neck, whimpering when her hands slid to the mattress. "Hunter."

Lifting his head, he smiled down at her. "Yes, baby?"

Tears burned her eyes, but she didn't even begin to understand why. "I t-told you."

* * * *

Hunter held her trembling body close, stunned by how hard she shook.

Delighted with her passion, he pulled the covers over her, rubbing her back.

"Told me what, baby?"

Cupping the back of her head, he withdrew and rolled to his side, taking her with him.

Loving the feel of her in his arms, he cuddled her close and shared a look with his brother, silently asking Remington to wait to take her.

She was too vulnerable for what Remington wanted, her strong passion and inexperience leaving her too weak and shaky for more.

Remington nodded, turning and leaving the room, closing the door behind him.

Left alone with Emma, Hunter ran his hands up and down her back, breathing in the scent of her. Surprised to find that holding her gave him as much satisfaction as taking her, he pressed his lips to her hair, running his hands over her in long, firm strokes.

Emma shivered and curled into him so trustingly, the intimacy of the moment leaving him stunned and more than a little uneasy.

"I told you that you wouldn't hurt me. You're such a wonderful man. I wish you could see yourself the way I see you."

"I know myself very well, warts and all." Leaning back in order to see her eyes, Hunter smiled. "I took you." Emma's slow smile, filled with feminine fulfillment and an edge of smugness, eased his misgivings.

"Yeah. You did. You also used a condom."

"We still have a lot to sort out, and Rem and I want you for ourselves for a while."

Looking up at him through her lashes, she ran a fingertip over his chest.

"If you'd told me that I would like something like that, I would have called you a liar."

Sliding higher, she nibbled at his bottom lip.

"I hope you're going to show me more."

"I plan to."

With a hand on her bottom, he pulled her closer, cupping her chin and holding her in place for his kiss. He sipped at her at first, delighted when she threaded her fingers through his hair and pulled him closer.

Swallowing her moans, he deepened his kiss, the Dominant inside him thrilling when she softened against him and opened to give him more.

Taking her wasn't enough.

Giving her pleasure wasn't enough.

Earning her submission wouldn't be enough.

What he wanted from her could either be the best thing that ever happened to them or the worst.

She made him believe.

His stomach clenched, the very real possibility that he may have to walk away from the magnificent creature in his arms bringing a lump to his throat.

Lifting his head, he stared into her clouded eyes, wondering if he'd ever seen anything as beautiful.

For his own sanity, he needed to put some distance between them. Running his fingers through her hair, he studied her softened features and just wanted to be closer.

"You dared me in bed. It seems I have a submissive with an attitude."

A lover.

With a sigh of contentment, Emma stretched, running her hand over his bicep.

"Do you mind?"

"Not a bit. I can handle your attitude." He patted her bottom playfully. "Should I brace for more?"

Closing her eyes, she sighed again and leaned into him. "Maybe later. Right now, I can't seem to stop shaking."

Dropping his head on the pillow with a smile, he tightened an arm around her and pulled her closer, pillowing her head with his chest. "You came hard, baby. Rem didn't even get to have any time with you."

"I'm sorry."

"There's nothing to be sorry for." He kissed her damp forehead, pulling the covers higher so she wouldn't get chilled in the air conditioning. "You'll have time with him when it's right for both of you."

Lifting her head, she glanced toward the door before dropping her head back again as if too weary to hold it up. "I didn't know I was capable of feeling something like that. I knew it would be special, but sex has never been very exciting for me. I thought it was me."

Hating the sadness and self-anger in her voice, Hunter rolled her to her back, leaning over her and forcing her to look at him. "It's not you."

Knowing he was in trouble, and already wanting her again, he used his fingertips to push her hair back from her face and sighed. "You are the most exciting and captivating woman I've ever known—and you scare the hell out of me."

Chapter Twenty-Three

Emma woke with a smile and, despite the coolness of the room, found herself cocooned in a warmth that went all the way to her bones.

She'd slept soundly, the combination of incredible sex and the feel of Hunter's and Remington's warm bodies surrounding her allowing the best night of sleep she'd had in ages.

Her nose was cold, though, so she burrowed against the chest she was pillowed on, giggling at Remington's flinch.

"Damn, Emma." Turning to lie on his side to face her, he rubbed her hair, holding her against his chest. "I thought I had you all warmed up."

Pressing her face against his chest, she sighed, not bothering to open her eyes.

It was hard to believe she'd found the love and happiness she'd thought impossible.

Cuddling against him, she smiled at the feel of his cock against her thigh.

"Everything's warm except my nose. I like to sleep in a cold room, but it's like a refrigerator in here."

Behind her, Hunter ran a hand over her ass and chuckled. "You seem warm enough everywhere else." Rolling to his side, he spooned her, his lips warm on her shoulder and his cock hard and hot against the back of her thigh. "Good morning, baby. I'll go start the coffee. Rem, I won't be long."

The reassurance in his gruff tone had her turning to glare at him, her pulse tripping at seeing him so sleep tumbled. "Why are you telling him that? It better not be because you're afraid he's going to hurt me."

He ran his hand over her ass again before rolling away to sit at the edge of the bed. "I told you that we were gonna have to take this slow, and that we don't quite trust ourselves. You're just gonna have to be patient."

Sitting up, she held the covers over her breasts, aware that Remington stiffened beside her.

"I'm done with this."

Pushing away from Remington, she rose from the bed, striding naked to the bathroom. She paused at the doorway, aware that they divided their attention between her face and her body. Hunter growled. "Where the hell are you going?"

Raising a brow, she eyed each of them. "You don't really expect me to give everything if you're not willing to do the same? Do you?"

Hunter started toward her at the same time Remington rose from the bed.

"Emma, you know we care for you. We're here. With you!"

"Are you?"

Leaning against the door, she shook her head in frustration. "You know, the funny thing is, every man I've met since I came to this town seems willing to commit everything he is to the woman he loves. I guess that tells me all I need to know. I'll be down to fix breakfast in a few minutes." Shaking her head, she smiled humorlessly, knowing the risk she was taking. "Just my luck to fall for the two men I can't have."

Hunter stepped forward. "Emma, we need to talk about this."

She had a weakness for them that would have her giving in again within minutes. She wanted to think, and she needed to give *them* time to think.

"There's nothing to talk about. I've got things to do today, so I'll be leaving right after breakfast."

"Emma!"

"Please, Hunter. Don't. Words are useless. I deserve more than the bits and pieces you're comfortable giving."

She started to close the door, only to open it again. Leaning against the doorway, she smiled. "I'll have sex with you. I know how much you need it in order to prove to yourself that you're not the monster you think you are."

Straightening, she smiled. "But don't expect more from me than sex. Don't expect things from me that you aren't willing to give in return."

* * * *

Hunter clenched his jaw and inwardly winced when Emma disappeared into the bathroom and closed the door behind her.

She's right.

Turning to Remington, he sighed. "She's right. Words are useless. I told you that I'd be back soon because I wanted you to relax with her, but as soon as I saw your face, I realized that you weren't worried at all."

He'd been scared to death at the thought of being alone with her, his own need for her making his dominance unpredictable.

"No. I wasn't." Smiling, Remington gestured toward the closed door. "I could no more hurt her than I could hurt myself. Neither would you, but you're too used to protecting women—hell—you even try to protect me. You protect everyone to try to make up for not protecting Mom. Do you really think you're going to hurt someone as sweet and adorable as Emma— a woman we both love?"

Love.

His chest tightened, butterflies taking flight in his stomach.

He didn't know how to love a woman.

He knew how to protect Emma, but he didn't know how to let down his guard with her.

He'd been on guard for his entire life, and it had become ingrained in him.

Hunter dropped to the edge of the bed, scraping a hand over his face, letting his voice rise slightly when he heard the shower start. "We don't need to dominate to get satisfaction. I can make love like a normal man."

Remington reached for his jeans. "Excuse me? So we're not normal now?"

Hunter knew he was making a mess of the entire situation and hated the feeling of losing control, but the tightness in his gut wouldn't go away and left him anxious.

"You know what I mean. Damn it, Rem. She wants something I don't know that I can give. I hate ultimatums." Irritated at himself, his brother, and Emma, he rose again. "She still doesn't understand what's inside me."

The knot in his stomach tightened. "Last night was incredible, but you and I both know that things are very different when we're angry, or we get lost in passion."

He loved Emma with a strength that stunned him. "Did you see how beautifully she responded last night?" Shaking his head, he pulled on his jeans, wincing when his hard cock made the task more difficult. "When I took her, it was intense—too intense. Christ, it made me dizzy. What I feel for her is too strong to ignore. I've never felt so strongly about any woman. Loving her so deeply, I just don't trust myself."

Remington chuckled and slapped his shoulder. "You're still protecting her, Hunter. You know the truth, but it's probably gonna take a sledgehammer over the head to convince you that it'll work. We have tempers, but neither one of us is gonna take it out on her."

Hunter stared at the closed bathroom door. "She's right about something else. I *can't* relax around her. I can't make love to her without thinking about how badly I could hurt her. I can't make love to her without worrying about scaring her."

Turning his head, he met his brother's gaze, the worry and shock in Remington's eyes making him feel even worse. "How the hell am I supposed to get past that?"

Scrubbing a hand over his face, Remington cursed. "I have no fucking idea, but I no longer believe we have it in ourselves to hurt her—or any woman."

"And if you're wrong?" Hunter grabbed his shirt from the chair and started from the room. "Last night never should have happened. Allowing ourselves to get close to her is just gonna end up hurting all of us."

Pausing at the door, he turned. "I don't blame Emma. She can't do this half-assed, and neither can I. Tell her that I'll eat at the diner."

"How you gonna get there?"

Hunter stopped, dropping his head back. "Shit. I forgot. My truck's in the shop. I'll walk. Maybe I can walk off this frustration."

* * * *

Remington sipped his coffee and watched Emma roll out biscuits. "Are you making those biscuits for me?"

Dressed in a blue cotton skirt that ended right above her knees and a blue and white striped T-shirt, she looked cool and fresh, despite the warmth of the kitchen.

She'd pulled her hair up in some kind of intricate twist that left her neck bare, enticing him to do a little exploring.

"No. I'm making them for Gracie." A faint smile played at her lips. "You sure you want to be here alone with me? Your baser instincts might take over and you may find yourself caught in my web of seduction."

"Can I do anything to help?" Moving to stand behind her, he placed his hands over hers on the rolling pin. Bending, he touched his lips to her neck, smiling at her shiver.

"No. Just sit down, drink your coffee, and stay out of my way."

"No."

Remington slid his hands up her T-shirt, pulling it over her breasts and opening the front clasp of her bra, groaning at the feel of her breasts spilling into his hands.

"Remington! Damn it!" Giggling, she pushed back against him. "I'm making biscuits."

"I see that." Nuzzling her neck, he began to massage her breasts, delighted that her nipples poked against his palms. "Don't let me interrupt you."

Emma smiled and leaned back against him, loving the feel of being in his arms.

"I have to cut them out."

"So do it. Don't pay any attention to me." His fingertips closed over her nipples, sending rivulets of heat to her clit. "Focus on what you're doing."

Emma set the rolling pin aside and reached for the biscuit cutter. "You're making it difficult."

"Am I?"

Emma's hands shook as she began to cut out biscuits.

"Can I ask you something?"

Remington scraped his teeth over her neck. "Anything."

Dropping her head back against his shoulder, she let her eyes flutter closed, tilting her neck to give him better access.

"Do you feel the same way Hunter feels?"

Lifting his head, he kissed the top of hers, his fingertips moving almost absently over her nipples.

"Yes, and no."

Straightening, she cut out another biscuit, smiling to be doing something so mundane while her arousal built. "That's real definite."

Reaching out to run his fingertips down her body, he chuckled softly. "You've got to remember that you've turned our world upside down. I know that I'd never hurt you physically."

His hands went back to her nipples, tugging gently and sending a shock through her that made her drop the biscuit cutter.

"Well, maybe just a little. The thought of putting nipple clamps on you and watching you squirm is real enticing."

Emma's sucked in a breath, her pussy clenching. "Don't say things like that."

"Why not?" He ran his hands under her skirt and over her bare ass. "Hmm. You're wearing one of your new thongs."

Emma shivered when the delicate lace ripped at both sides and her panties fell away.

"Not anymore."

"Just the way I like you. Keep cutting your biscuits while I roll on a condom."

Her pussy clenched again in anticipation when he took a step back.

Picking up the biscuit cutter again, she cut another biscuit, still thinking about Hunter.

"You didn't finish. Do you feel the same way Hunter feels about getting involved with me?"

Remington sighed. "I know I can satisfy you physically, but I'm sure to fuck up in other ways and hurt you." Running a hand over her ass, he lifted her skirt. "I honestly don't know if I'm able to give you what you need emotionally. Never tried it before."

Cupping her jaw, he turned her face to his. "Hunter and I have seen too much to be cavalier about having a relationship. It's too important. Too much can go wrong. We want a family, Emma, but we're scared of repeating our father's mistakes. I won't want any other children to have to go through what we did."

His touch gentled, his eyes filled with memories. "I wouldn't want my wife enduring what our mother did."

Emma turned in his arms and cupped his jaw. "I'll bet your father never gave a thought to any of that."

Remington's hands went to her waist, lifting her to the island. His hands lowered to her bottom, pulling her to the edge and pressing his cock at her pussy entrance.

"Hunter and I think of little else."

Emma sucked in a breath when he thrust deep, wrapping her legs around him. Leaning back, she braced a hand behind her on either side, bracing herself for his thrusts.

She stared into his eyes as he began to move, her breathing ragged as she struggled to accommodate his thick cock.

"I just want you to think about me." Straightening, she slid her hands under his shirt, running her hands over his chest. "God it feels so good."

Remington released her just long enough to grab the hem of his T-shirt and lift it over his head, tossing it aside. "It's gonna feel better."

Gripping her by the waist, he fucked her hard and deep, his expression tight with hunger again.

"You're so fucking perfect for us. So hot. So sexy."

Each stroke drove her relentlessly toward the edge, her pussy clamping incessantly on his cock and making it feel even bigger.

Pressing a hand to her abdomen, Emma leaned back, amazed at how large and hard his cock felt inside her.

Stunned by the hunger in his touch and possessiveness in eyes that narrowed to slits, Emma reached for him. "I *am* perfect for you. God!"

The slide of his thumb over her clit made thought impossible.

Flames of delight licked at her everywhere, her nipples still sensitized from his ministrations. Her clit burned hotter with every stroke of his thumb, tingling with a heat that told her she wouldn't last much longer.

"Yes, you are." Remington knew just where to touch her and just how much pressure she needed.

His cock felt even harder inside her as he began to thrust faster.

Still stroking her clit, he lifted her against him, his eyes laser sharp on hers. "And I'm gonna do whatever it takes to keep you."

"Rem! I'm gonna come!"

He smiled and stroked her clit faster. "Yes. You are."

Before he even finished speaking, Emma went over in a rush of heat that began at her slit and exploded outward.

With a groan, he thrust deep and stilled, slowing his strokes to her clit.

"That's my girl." Remington's voice had deepened and become rougher, the possessiveness even stronger.

The feel of his cock pulsing inside her set off more ripples of pleasure, the slow slide of his thumb over her clit dragging out her orgasm.

Sliding his hands up her back, he pulled her against him. "You're mine now, aren't you?"

She slumped against him, burying her face against his chest and breathing in the warm clean scent of him. "Yes."

Being in his arms felt so right, as if she'd finally found the home she'd never thought to find.

* * * *

Remington held her trembling softness against him, struggling to come to terms with his intense feelings for her.

He'd never come so hard, never felt so close to a woman he'd taken.

Losing her wasn't an option, but convincing Hunter that they could make a family with Emma would take some doing.

Running his hands over her, he waited until she settled, pressing his lips to her hair. "I'm not about to lose you."

He knew, though, that committing to her without his brother would drive a wedge between them that could ruin everything.

Leaning back, he slid a hand into her hair, tilting her head back to look into her eyes.

"I love you, Emma."

Her eyes widened, the flash of emotion and tears shimmering in them like a fist around his heart. "Oh, Remington. I love you, too."

Smiling faintly, he touched his lips to hers, reveling at the way she softened against him.

Lifting his head, he stared into her eyes, amazed that he'd found the love that he'd thought impossible.

"You understand that this won't work unless Hunter's involved, don't you?"

Nodding, Emma smiled, a sad smile that appeared forced. "I know. It would be a mess. Hunter would be mad at both of us. Hell, he'd probably leave."

Remington smiled at the frustration and sadness when she talked about his brother. "You love him, don't you?"

"I already told you that I love both of you." One tear leaked from the corner of her eye, and even though he'd already come, he found himself moving slowly inside her.

Sliding her hands into his hair, she clamped down on his cock. "I never thought I could love two men, but you're right. It wouldn't be the same without both of you."

Cupping her breast, he tilted her back over his arm.

"It looks like you and I are gonna have to work together to convince Hunter that this is possible."

Her smile eased some of the tightness in his chest, but he knew he wouldn't relax until she wore their rings on her finger. "Absolutely. You'd better come up with a plan."

* * * *

Emma couldn't stop smiling as she finished making the biscuits, taking another shower while they were in the oven.

Remington insisted on drying her, which made it take even longer.

"Rem!" Giggling, she shoved at him. "My biscuits are going to burn."

Bending, he closed his mouth over a nipple. "Just wanted to make sure you got all the flour off."

Once downstairs, she raced toward the oven, grateful to see that the biscuits were perfectly browned.

"Thank God. I didn't want to have to start over."

Remington ran his hand over her denim shorts, lightly squeezing her ass.

"Oh, I wouldn't mind a repeat. Since meeting you, I keep a fistful of condoms in my pocket at all times."

"Behave." Secretly delighted, she struggled for a stern expression. "I have plans, and I don't want to be late."

"What plans?"

"It's a secret. A surprise for you and Hunter."

"Now I'm intrigued." He snagged one of the hot biscuits from the tray she took out of the oven, tossing it from one hand to the other. "You really think Gracie's gonna trade her recipe for meatloaf and peach cobbler for your biscuit recipe?"

Emma's smug grin stirred his cock. "Hasn't failed me yet."

Watching her dish up their breakfasts, he waited until the biscuit in his hand had cooled enough to eat.

He took a bite, the slight crispness of the outside giving way to a moist, buttery flakiness that made his taste buds explode. "Jesus, Emma! These are incredible. I was too pissed off the other night to enjoy them, but these are the best I ever had."

Grinning, Emma transferred the hot biscuits into a napkin-lined basket. "I know. Gracie's biscuits are good, but they can't hold a candle to mine."

Reaching for another, Remington smiled back, enjoying the chance to spend time with her. "I want to see her face when she tastes them. I think you just might get your recipes, after all."

Emma glanced up at him with a smile that immediately roused his suspicions. "I will. I'm not the type who gives up easily, especially when it's something that I want badly enough."

Chapter Twenty-Four

Feeling more confident and still loose from Remington's lovemaking, Emma walked into the diner with Remington at her side. Aware of Hunter's eyes following her, she approached the counter where he sat, plopping into the seat next to him. "Hi, Hunter."

His eyes narrowed, and looking over her head, he shared a look with Remington. "What are you doing here?"

Looking straight ahead, she shook her head, smiling when Gracie approached. "Don't worry. I didn't come to see you. I came to see Gracie."

Gracie's brows went up when she saw the basket of still warm biscuits. "What's this?"

The napkins folded over concealed the contents, but there was no mistaking the scent.

Emma held back a smile. "I brought you something."

Remington reached into the basket and handed one of the biscuits to Hunter. "You gotta taste this. They're even better than I remembered."

Hunter watched her as he bit into one, his eyes widening. "Holy shit."

Glancing at Hunter before turning her attention back to Emma, Gracie's eyes narrowed. "You brought me biscuits?"

Wiping his hands, Garrett walked up behind Gracie. "Hi, Emma. What's going on?"

Gracie frowned at Emma, clearly confused as she pulled back the edges of the napkin. "Emma brought us biscuits."

Garrett smiled kindly. "Honey, you know we make our own biscuits."

Not bothering to hide her smile when Hunter and Remington each reached for another, Emma pushed the basket closer. "Not like these, you don't. Call me if you change your mind about those two recipes I want."

With a last glance at Remington, she turned away, feeling Hunter's gaze on her back as she left the diner.

* * * *

Amused and proud, Hunter sipped his coffee, hiding a smile when both Gracie and Garrett watched Emma leave before reaching into the basket.

Biting into one of the fragrant biscuits, Garrett groaned and turned to his wife. "These are the best damned biscuits I've ever tasted."

The bell over the door chimed again, and Hunter whipped around, anticipating Emma. Disappointed to see Ace come through the doorway, he took another sip of coffee and glanced at his brother. "How was she?"

"She's fine." Remington glanced toward where Gracie and Garrett huddled together and spoke in a low voice and lowered himself to the stool Emma had just vacated. "I took her. She's so damned loving. Ornery, too. Did you see that look on her face when she walked out?"

Stiffening, Hunter lowered his cup, turning to face his brother fully. "What kind of look?"

"Like she was up to something. When I made a comment about getting the recipes she wanted in exchange for the recipe for those biscuits, she made a comment about not stopping until she got what she wanted." Remington's lips twitched. "I got the feeling she was talking about something other than those biscuits."

Ace accepted the biscuit Gracie offered him, his eyes going wide when he bit into it. "Damn, Gracie. These are good. New recipe?"

Garrett grabbed another biscuit and turned toward the kitchen. "I want that recipe. Give Emma whatever she wants."

Ace smiled at that, winking at his mother-in-law. "So these are Emma's secret weapon. I have to admit I didn't think they'd be better than yours."

"That girl's gonna drive me crazy." Gracie sniffed and turned away, disappearing into the kitchen.

Ace's lips twitched as he lowered himself onto one of the stools at the counter, setting his hat on the counter next to him. "Ran into your woman outside."

Hearing Emma referred to as his woman warmed something inside Hunter while simultaneously filling him with unease. "Did you?"

Smiling his thanks when Gracie brought him a cup of coffee, Ace glanced in their direction, his eyes dancing with amusement. "Yep. I was outside talking to Hope, who's on her way to the spa, when Emma came out grinning from ear to ear. She also had a look about her. I'd watch out if I were you."

He took a sip of his coffee, smiling when he lowered his cup again. "Married to Hope, I know mischief when I see it. Emma definitely looked smug about something."

Gesturing toward the kitchen, where Gracie and her husbands stood gathered around the basket of biscuits, Ace grinned. "My guess is that it has something to do with those biscuits."

Filled with pride, Hunter allowed a small smile. "She sure as hell can cook."

Remington chuckled. "A woman of many talents."

Ace took another sip of coffee. "Yeah. She's a lot like Hope. I wouldn't underestimate her if I were you." Turning, he smiled. "She went to the spa with Hope."

Hunter stiffened, the mental image of Emma, smooth and waxed, stirring his cock into life. "She did?"

Lifting a brow, Ace eyed both of them. "She said that you told her to."

The memory of what they'd been doing when they had that conversation had Hunter's cock hardening uncomfortably.

Ace's lips twitched. "Now that you have a woman, you need to set up an account there and let them know what you want them to do to her."

Remington whipped his head around to Hunter, clearly surprised and delighted. Turning back to Ace, he rose. "Do you mean that we get to pick what they do to her?"

Ace grinned and rose. "Yep. They understand the way things are done in this town and don't want to take the chance of losing our business. They have a menu with prices. You just go over there and pick out everything, and they'll make sure she gets it. Plan on a nice bill. Hope will probably try to talk Emma into getting what she gets."

Ace reached for his hat, a small smile tugging at his lips. "You're new to this, so I let you in on something. If it's your woman, and you're paying for her treatments, you have the right to inspect her before she gets dressed."

Remington whistled. "No shit."

Hunter's cock jumped. "Damn."

Inclining his head, Ace started to turn. "Enjoy yourselves."

Hunter had already started for the door. "I'm startin' to think there's a lot we have to learn about havin' a woman of our own."

Remington stopped abruptly, gripping his arm. "Don't toy with me, Hunter, and don't toy with Emma."

Hunter shook off his brother's grip. "I'm not." With a sigh, he glanced pointedly at the others and led Remington out the door and to the sidewalk. "Emma doesn't have to know how worried I am about hurting her or not being able to be what she needs."

"What the hell are you saying?"

Running a hand through his hair, Hunter paused as Ace came out, waiting until the sheriff got into his SUV and pulled away. "I want her, Rem, and I'll do whatever it takes to have her, even if I have to omit telling her a few things. I'll convince her that I've had time to think and realized that she was right. I'll lie through my teeth if I have to. She doesn't need to know that I'm still worried about hurting her, and she sure as hell doesn't need to know that I'm afraid I can't give her what she needs emotionally. I shouldn't have told her to begin with."

After a pause, Remington frowned. "I love her, and I'm not afraid of hurting her. If you have doubts, get them all sorted out before you tell Emma you love her. I won't lie to her, Hunter. Even for you."

Chapter Twenty-Five

Dressed in the softest robe she'd ever felt, Emma crossed the surprisingly luxurious lounge to where Hope sat sipping what appeared to be pink champagne.

"This place is incredible!" Dropping into the chair next to her new friend, Emma looked around, surprised to see the small-town spa so crowded.

Music played in the background, low enough to create a soothing atmosphere and allow clients to carry on a conversation but loud enough to allow privacy if someone whispered.

Grinning, Hope handed her a glass of champagne. "It is. I started coming here as soon as Charity and I came home after college. Now that I'm married to Ace, I come here even more often."

She took a sip of champagne and winked. "He insists." Lowering her glass again, she leaned back against the headrest, turning to Emma with a smile. "Hunter and Remington will, too."

After a sip of champagne, Emma sighed and set the glass aside. "We'll see. Hunter didn't want to leave me alone with Remington this morning, and I blew up at him."

Deciding to confide in Hope, Emma curled into the lounge chair and leaned toward her, keeping her voice low. "Hunter slapped my inner thigh and...."

Looking around, she trailed off, too embarrassed to continue.

Hope showed no such embarrassment. "Your clit?"

Nodding, Emma gulped champagne, swallowing heavily. "Yeah. Then he ruined it by feeling bad about it. I could see it in his eyes."

Grimacing, Hope reached for the bottle and refilled their glasses. "That sucks."

After another sip of champagne, Emma nodded. "Yeah. And then this morning, he didn't want to leave me alone with Remington."

Frowning, Hope edged closer. "Why not?"

"He was going down to make coffee and paused to reassure Remington that he wouldn't be long. He was nervous about leaving me alone to have sex with Remington without sitting there watching us to make sure Remington didn't hurt me."

Hope snorted. "Remington isn't going to hurt you." Wagging her brows, Hope giggled. "Except in the most delightful ways."

Eyeing Emma over the rim of her glass, she finished off the rest of her champagne and reached for the bottle again. "We might as well drink up. It helps when the waxing begins." Meeting Emma's gaze as she refilled their glasses, Hope smiled. "Has anyone ever done anything like that to you before? I mean slap you or spank you, anything like that?"

"No." Deliciously light-headed, Emma giggled. "It was amazing. Donny, my ex, was lazy in bed. Wanted to have sex, but wanted me to do all the work."

Hope sighed and smiled dreamily. "When you have a Dom for a lover, that's not an issue. The men in Desire take great pride in pleasing their women. Hell, that's why they all get together at the men's club. To talk about us. They're always looking for more decadent ways to torture us. It's fabulous."

Her mischievous grin made Emma feel a little better. "That's why we opened the women's club. Charity and I organize a lot of demonstrations and speakers to give us ideas. We also get together to give each other advice. You'll never find a support system like the one you have here."

Emma slapped a hand over her mouth when a giggle escaped, her movement clumsy. "I want to join. I want to see what kinds of things you talk about." She finished off her glass of champagne and held her glass out for another refill. "Hunter's worried about what they're going to do when they're mad at me. Maybe I'll just piss them off so he sees the truth."

Frowning when she missed, Hope tried again, pouring the champagne carefully into Emma's glass. "Keep your hand still." Sticking her tongue out, she concentrated as she poured and set the bottle aside. "You can't just piss them off. You have to do it in a way that arouses them, too. You have to challenge them. You have to do something that they just can't let go, a challenge they can't allow themselves to ignore."

"Is that what you do to Ace?"

Dropping her head back, Hope giggled. "Absolutely! Daring him is like waving a red flag in front of a bull. I do things that he can't ignore and has to address." She sighed again. "Ace is so attentive. He doesn't miss a damned thing, and he doesn't let me get away with anything. It's always exciting. Always an adventure. God, I love that man. No man has ever excited me as much as he does. No man has ever been able to handle me the way he does."

Stretching, she sighed again. "And he's always especially forceful when I've been bad or had a trip to the spa." Giggling, she leaned closer again. "They'll call him when I'm done, and he comes over in his uniform and inspects me."

Hope sighed again, a dreamy look in her eyes. "He tells me not to come while he's inspecting me, and I almost always do, so I know I have a punishment waiting when he gets home from work."

Emma gaped, both aroused and jealous. "Really?" Pouting, she took another sip of champagne. "I wish Hunter and Remington would do something like that."

Hope reached out and patted her arm. "In this town, our willingness to tell our fantasies makes them come true. Once I tell Ace that you want Hunter and Remington to do that, he'll tell them."

She gestured toward the key Emma wore around her wrist. "They keep mine and give it to Ace when he gets here. He gives it to me after he makes sure *everything* is just right. When they start bringing you here, they'll do the same with you."

Depressed, Emma forced a smile. "I hope so. I'm not going to give up."

"Atta girl. If you need advice, I may be able to help you with that." Hope giggled again, the effects of the champagne evident. Leaning back again, she curled up in the chair. "I've perfected ways of getting Ace's attention." She stared down at her empty glass and sighed. "I can't get any more speeding tickets, though. Our insurance rates are going through the roof. We need another bottle."

Emma stared into her glass while Hope ordered another bottle of champagne. "I shouldn't drink anymore. How the hell am I gonna drive home?"

"Ace is gonna have to pick me up. He'll take you home."

"Home." Emma sighed. "I love that house. I wish I could live there forever and ever."

She paused when one of the women who worked there brought another bottle of champagne and stopped in front of her. "Are you Emma Smith?"

Emma rose to her feet, slightly alarmed that she staggered. "Yep. You can't be ready for me. You don't even know what I'm having done. Hell, I don't even know what I'm having done." Dropping back into her seat, she turned to Hope. "I thought you said there was some kind of a menu or something."

The other woman held out her hand, eyeing Emma cautiously. "Um, I need to ask you for your key."

Emma blinked, wondering if she'd done something wrong. "Excuse me?"

The other woman smiled. "Your men are out front. They ordered your treatments and insist on inspecting you when you're done. You should have told us when you came in. I'm so sorry for the mix-up."

With a gasp, Emma turned to Hope. "Did I hear that right?"

"Yes!" Hope squealed. "I knew they couldn't resist."

Emma rose again, setting her glass on one of the side tables. "I'll be right back."

"Good luck, honey. Hurry back. I want details."

Emma started for the lobby, waving off the spa employee who hurried after her. "You're not getting my key until I talk to them."

* * * *

Grinning, Remington reached for the door handle, knowing that the next few hours would go far too slowly. "I can't wait to see her face."

"I can't wait to see the rest of her." Hunter seemed more relaxed since he'd made the decision to keep Emma in the dark about his feelings.

He hated keeping that secret from Emma as much as he hated conspiring with her to get Hunter to see that they could be together.

If either one of them ever found out, there'd be hell to pay.

"What the hell do you think you're doing?"

Stopping abruptly at the sound of Emma's voice coming from somewhere behind them, Remington turned, letting the door close again.

Surprised to see her, wearing nothing but a robe and one slipper, Remington rushed to her side only a heartbeat behind Hunter. "What the hell?"

Gripping her arm when she staggered, Remington studied her features. "You're drunk."

"Not yet. Workin' on it. Gonna need a ride home." She tried to push at Hunter, her jerky movements loosening her robe enough to fall from her shoulder and expose the upper curve of her breast and start to part it in the middle. "What's goin' on? Why did you come here? Why did you order my treatments? I'll bet you paid for them, too. Didn't you?"

Holding on to her while Remington pulled the edges of her robe together and retied them, Hunter appeared to fight a smile. "We did. Why didn't you tell us you were coming here?"

"I don't have to tell you anything! I don't belong to you." Swaying slightly, Emma held on to his forearm. "Besides, you told me to get waxed. It was s'pose to be a surprise to make you want me."

Amused that she slurred her words, Remington lifted her chin. "We do want you."

"Bullshit! You don't even know me."

Hunter kept his arm around her waist, steadying her. "We know you well enough. We'll spend the rest of our lives learning everything there is to know about you." Bending to touch his lips to her hair, he met Remington's gaze. "I adore you. We'll see you later. Get your car keys. We'll use your car today since our truck's still in the shop."

Hunter stared lovingly at Emma, but she appeared to be too intoxicated to notice.

"They'll call us when you're done. We're going to inspect you to make sure that everything was done to our satisfaction."

"Ace inspects Hope. She said she even comes sometimes, even when he forb-forbims—forbids it." Gripping Remington's shirt, she pulled him down, her whisper louder than he suspected she'd intended. "Then he punishes her. She loves that. I got excited just thinking about it."

Delighted with her, and amused at Hunter's look of shocked enchantment, Remington adopted a stern expression.

"You don't really think we're gonna let you come in the spa, do you?"

Hunter fixed the belt of her robe again. "We're definitely not gonna allow that." Leaning close, he whispered in her ear. "If you do, I'm gonna spank that pretty bottom."

Emma gasped, grinning from ear to ear. "Promise?"

Hunter's lips twitched, but he managed to keep a stern tone. "Absolutely. You'll be punished for disobeying me."

"Okay. I gotta go. Hope's ordering more champagne."

Remington smiled as she turned away and disappeared through the doorway again, even more amused to see Hunter stare after her. "Ready to go?"

Hunter's eyes narrowed. "Do you think she meant that?"

"Sounded like she did. I guess we'll find out in a couple of hours."

Turning, he made his way to the door again, pleased that things seemed to be moving in the right direction.

* * * *

Vibrating with excitement at the thought of seeing Hunter and Remington again, and relaxed from an amazing massage and pink champagne, Emma followed the spa worker to a private room where Hunter and Remington waited.

Remington smiled and offered a hand, silently urging her to come closer. "How do you feel?"

"Exfoliated, steamed, creamed, waxed, shampooed, conditioned, and a little tipsy." Frowning, she slumped against him. "And hungry. I think I forgot to eat lunch. I fell asleep during my massage."

Hunter's smile reminded her of the way he'd smiled at her when he'd brought her home from the hospital. Tender. Cautious.

But with a hunger and possessiveness that made her heart beat faster.

Remington wrapped both arms around her, gathering her close. "We'll get you something to eat when we leave here. How would you like to go to the hotel restaurant?"

Emma leaned back to look at him, and probably would have fallen if he hadn't supported her. "Can we have one of those booths with the curtains? I'm all soft and smooth, and I plan to seduce you."

Lifting his gaze to meet Hunter's, he smiled at the affection in his brother's eyes. "Of course. I'll call and see if they have a vacancy." Since it was a weeknight, they had a better chance of getting a booth than on a weekend, and Brandon and Ethan usually left one booth free for the residents of Desire.

Remington glanced at Hunter, hiding a smile at the anticipation in his brother's eyes.

Remington would have the chance to show Hunter just how perfect Emma was for them, but they would be in a place where Hunter would feel safe dominating her, knowing that she could scream for help and any number of people would come running.

It was perfect.

Knowing that they had to keep her distracted and off-balance, Remington unbelted her robe and parted the edges, sliding his hand inside.

Her immediate reaction made him hard as a rock in an instant.

Gripping the front of his shirt, she moaned, her knees giving out. "God, it feels so good when you touch me."

Touching the softest skin he'd ever felt, Remington tightened his arm around her, keeping his strokes to her nipple light and slow. "She's even softer than before." Bending, he touched his lips to hers. "We're going to have to bring you here more often."

Hunter closed in on her other side, one hand sliding under her robe to caress her ass while the other slid down her body. Running his fingers over her mound, he smiled down at her. "Very nice. Very soft. How does it feel?"

Emma's eyes closed, her head falling back. "It makes me feel so naked."

"Good." Remington smiled down at her, loving the way she felt in his arms. "Because we're going to keep you this way, and we're going to keep you naked as often as possible."

Hunter lifted her chin, holding her gaze. "I want you to spread those thighs and stay perfectly still. I want to see if they waxed you to my satisfaction."

Emma laid a hand on his chest, her face a fiery red. "They waxed more than I thought they would."

Hunter raised a brow, clearly enjoying himself. "I know exactly what they did, and I'll be checking it. Now, spread your legs and let me inspect you. I'm hungry, and I want to go eat. Don't you dare come. Focus on something else while I check you."

Holding Emma back against him, Remington supported her weight, smiling at the shiver that went through her as she spread her legs.

To please himself, he cupped her breasts, running his thumbs back and forth over her nipples.

His cock throbbed, pressing painfully against his zipper. "Does it feel good to be waxed?"

Emma shivered again, her breath catching when Hunter went to his knees in front of her.

"It feels so strange. I feel so naked. Even the feel of the air blowing over it excites me. I don't know if I can stand it."

Hunter lifted his gaze to hold hers. "If you're gonna belong to us, you're gonna have to. You'll be waxed and smooth at all times. Is that gonna be a problem?"

"No. I'll do whatever you want me to do."

She hadn't thought it possible to feel more exposed than they'd already made her feel, but she'd been wrong.

It felt incredible.

The slow slide of Hunter's fingertip over her mound sent her senses reeling.

"Good." He slid his fingertip over every centimeter of her mound and folds, creating an intense awareness that weakened her knees.

Grateful for Remington's support, she slumped more heavily against him, biting her lip to hold back a moan when Hunter used his thumbs to part her folds, the feel of his fingers against the sensitive flesh much more intense.

Her legs shook, the slide of Hunter's fingers over her folds as he exposed her clit and the relentless strokes of Remington's fingers over her nipples driving her closer and closer to orgasm.

Her stomach muscles clenched, her thighs soaked with her juices.

The tingling awareness grew stronger with every heartbeat, her clit throbbing with the need for Hunter's touch.

"Turn her around."

Emma gasped when Remington spun her in his arms, her heart pounding when he raised her robe to her waist, a hard arm holding both it and her in place.

She cried out when Hunter parted the cheeks of her ass, whimpering with hunger and burying her face against Remington's chest at the feel of Hunter's hot tongue against her puckered opening.

Remington startled her by lifting her hands to his shoulders. "Keep them there."

To her astonishment, he knelt in front of her, his position forcing her to bend slightly at the waist in order to keep her hands on his shoulders.

Using his tongue on her folds, Remington groaned. "So soft. So smooth. They did a hell of a job."

"Here, too." Hunter used his thumbs to part her ass cheeks wider. "I'm not gonna let her wear panties when she's with us. I want access to her pussy and ass at all times."

Remington murmured his approval, parting her folds and running a finger over her clit.

Crying out, she dug her fingers into the hard muscles of Remington's shoulders.

Hunter chose that moment to slide his tongue over her puckered opening again and, to her shock, push it inside her.

She'd never known anything so intimate, never known such raw sexuality.

Tilting his head back, Remington met her gaze before taking a nipple into his mouth, scraping his teeth lightly over it as he continued stroking her clit.

Shaking helplessly, Emma struggled to remain quiet, her breathing ragged at the effort it took to hold back.

After just a few strokes, she knew the battle was lost.

"Please. I'm gonna come."

She didn't know how long her legs would hold her, the attention to her nipple, clit, and forbidden opening too much to take in.

Controlled by their light strokes, Emma felt her knees give out, but their strong hands caught her.

"No." Remington lifted his head. "I'm barely stroking your clit. You can take it."

"No." Her clit burned and began tingling hotly, the feel of Hunter's tongue moving slowly just inside her making holding back impossible. "I can't help it. Oh God!"

The rush of pleasure stunned her, but when Hunter and Remington both stopped touching her at the same time, she cried out in frustration.

"I'm not done. Oh God. Please. Please."

Hunter stood, wrapping a hand around her waist and pulling her back against him. "No more. If you'd waited, you would have gotten the satisfaction that you wanted."

Nuzzling her neck, he ran his hands over her breasts before closing her robe and belting it securely.

"Since you only got a slight rush of relief, I'm sure you're gonna be more than willing to do whatever it takes to get the satisfaction you need over dinner."

Lifting her robe in the back, he slapped her ass. "Go get dressed. And hurry up. No touching yourself. After we've had dinner, I'm going to have *you* for dessert."

Chapter Twenty-Six

Still shaking with the combination of arousal, nerves, and excitement, Emma shifted restlessly in the booth between Hunter and Remington.

Looking around, she took in the heavy, expensive-looking drapes, the soft leather covering the booth, and the intimate lighting.

From the small lamp on the table hung crystals that cast sparkles of light everywhere, giving the place a sophisticated, but unreal feel that she hadn't expected. "It's so *nice* in here."

Hunter's lips twitched. "You sound like you thought it would look like the inside of a cheap motel."

Hoping that the darkened interior hid her burning face, Emma glanced at each of them, finding both men watching her. "Why didn't I get a menu?"

Remington smiled and ran his fingers over her hair. "Because these booths are mainly used by Doms and their subs. Hunter and I are expected to choose for you."

"Really?" Intrigued, Emma leaned closer to him, trembling with excitement and eagerness to learn more.

She knew he planned to prove to Hunter that she was right for them but had no idea what would be involved.

Still, she hadn't expected them to order dinner for her and realized that she had a lot more to learn. "I thought it was only about sex."

"It depends on the people involved." Hunter set his menu aside, watching her searchingly. "It can be anything they want it to be. It can be just a little playfulness in the bedroom all the way to something more extreme."

Remington took her hand. "For example, Hunter and I could keep you naked at home all the time. We could spank or whip you when you disobey." He shrugged. "Or we could just dominate you during sex, and not all the time."

Turning to look at Hunter, Emma laid a hand on his arm. "What do *you* want?"

Hunter's jaw clenched. "For us, it's always, out of necessity, been based on sex alone." Running a finger down her arm, he smiled faintly. "I have to admit that I'm enjoying the other aspects of having a woman of our own. I'm afraid that I would be an awfully demanding Dom."

From what she'd experienced so far, Emma had a feeling it would be overwhelming.

She couldn't wait.

Remington held out his hand. "Give me your panties."

"They're in my purse."

Smiling, Remington patted her thigh. "Good girl. Now I want the bra."

Emma glanced at Hunter to find him sipping his beer and watching her expectantly.

Not about to disappoint them and eager to find the release she needed, Emma worked her bra off from under her shirt and handed it to Remington.

Lifting it to his nose, he watched her, his lips twitching as he stuck it into his pocket.

"Very good. I ordered when I called for the reservation. As soon as the waiter brings our dinners, I want you naked. Slip off your shoes."

Sliding her sandals off, she dug her toes into the thick carpet.

Hunter toyed with the hair at her nape, the heat from his fingers travelling to her nipples. "You're being very good. I wonder how long you'll last."

Lifting her chin, she smiled, her smile widening when his gaze lowered to where her nipples poked at her T-shirt. "How long will you last before I scare you away?"

Sitting up, Hunter released her and reached for the glass of sweet tea that the waiter had placed in front of her when they'd first arrived, holding it up to her lips.

"No wine for you. You've had enough today, and I want you fully aware of what we're doing to you."

When she reached for the glass, he surprised her by moving it out of her reach.

"I'll hold it. Drink."

Watching his eyes, she took a sip and sat back, glancing at Remington to see the approval in his eyes.

Sitting back again, she smiled at Hunter.

"Oh. I'm aware of everything."

Adrenaline had taken over and the last effects of the champagne had faded away, replaced by a dizziness that had nothing to do with alcohol and everything to do with arousal.

"Good." Setting his glass on the table, he reached out and pushed a button, one that Emma hadn't noticed.

"What's that for?"

Hunter leaned back, turning lightly to study her features. "That button tells the waiter that it's okay to come in. the light came on a few seconds ago to tell us our dinner is ready."

"Oh."

He reached for his beer again. "Don't try to make conversation with the waiter. While you're in here, he considers you our property. He won't talk to you or look at you without our permission."

Unable to decipher their odd tenseness, Emma realized that she still had a lot to learn about her lovers.

Remington had ordered steak, baked potato, and salad for each of them, something she'd learned was a favorite meal for both of them.

More curious than insulted that they hadn't asked her what she wanted, she found herself even more intrigued when the waiter eyed each of them while holding her plate.

Remington made a gesture with his hand, indicating that he wanted the plate set in front of him.

As soon as the waiter left, Hunter reached over, gripped the hem of her shirt, and lifted it over her head, tossing her shirt onto the seat on the other side of him. "Kneel on the seat."

Emma's nipples beaded tighter, the steel in his voice and in his hooded gaze a little unsettling. "Hunter?"

"Yes?"

"What if the waiter comes back in?"

"He won't come back in until we push that button again." Frowning, he picked up his beer. "Trust is gonna be very important for us, don't you think?"

Emma bristled. "I trust you! I probably trust you more than you trust yourself."

After taking a sip of his beer, Hunter set it aside again. "Remington and I are very selfish. Your body and the sounds of pleasure you make are for us alone. I'm not comfortable with how possessive I am of you, but if you're going to take us on, you're going to have to deal with that."

Emma couldn't get over the feeling that he was testing her, daring her to push him away.

Not a chance in hell.

Getting to her knees, she faced him, her stomach muscles quivering when his knuckles brushed against her belly as he unfastened her shorts and tugged them to her knees.

"Lie back." Hunter's steely tone held a coldness that made her slightly uneasy, but trusting him, she obeyed him with only a momentary hesitation.

Hunter slipped her shorts down her legs and off, tossing them on top of her shirt on the other side of him with a look that told her that she would get her clothing back only when he gave it to her.

Leaning forward, she lifted her face for his kiss. "I feel so naughty."

Accepting her invitation, Hunter bent to touch his lips to hers, letting them linger before he lifted his head again. "Good. You're going to feel even naughtier."

Emma couldn't help it. She wrapped her hands around his arm and leaned against him. "I must seem so naïve to you. I'm new at this. I'm nervous, but I want to please you."

His smile warmed her all the way through, his hug bringing tears of relief to her eyes. "I know, baby." After dropping a kiss on her forehead, he pushed her hair back from her face, his eyes hooded and unreadable. "You have no idea how much pleasure it gives me to know that you've never submitted to anyone before."

Remington leaned toward her, holding a bite of steak to her lips. "Open."

Meeting his gaze, she opened her mouth, moaning at the burst of flavor as she chewed. "Damn, that's good. Why did you have him give my plate to you? I'm hungry."

Remington ran his hand over the curve of her breast. "Because I'm going to feed you."

Hunter cut into his own steak and offered her a bite. "You're the one who wanted the privacy booth. You get everything that goes with it. Open."

"Opening her mouth, she crossed her legs, the feel of being naked so soon after being waxed leaving her feeling extremely naked and vulnerable.

"Uh-uh. I don't think so." Hunter tapped her thigh. "Spread those legs and put your hands behind your back."

Emma spread her legs, unnerved by the feel of air on her wet slit.

With a sigh, Remington shook his head, set his fork aside, and parted her thighs wide. He ran a fingertip over her freshly waxed mound, the combination of playfulness and coolness in his eyes tripping her pulse.

"Do you think we're gonna get you waxed and then let you try to hide yourself from us?"

From her right, Hunter bent over her, teasing one nipple with his fingertip while trailing the fingers of his other hand down her spine. "Arch your back. I don't want you hunched over like that. I won't give these breasts any attention if they're not thrust out and offered to me."

Emma's stomach muscles tightened, the erotic awareness sudden and sharp.

Arching her back, she moaned at the sharp stab of sexual awareness at offering herself so wantonly.

Hunter's eyes flared, his gaze lowering to the nipple he teased. "Very nice. You're slipping into the role of submissive very beautifully. Rem and I are going to push you a little further each time. Don't worry. We'll stop if we think it's too much, and we won't hurt you."

Resisting the urge to reach for him, she kept her hands behind her back. "Not even a spanking?"

"Later." Remington's fingers tightened on her nipple, bringing her attention back to him. "Your ass is gonna get quite a bit of attention tonight. Now keep those thighs spread while I feed you your dinner."

* * * *

Hunter adjusted his jeans, his cock so hard he feared it might just burst through his zipper.

Hunger for a woman had never been as sharp, nor had it ever had the possessive edge that it did now.

He wanted Emma in ways that alarmed him, the need to tie her to him in every possible way like a drug in his veins.

More addictive every day.

More intoxicating.

Never enough.

Determined to make her forget everything except her own need for release, he kept sliding his fingertips over her body as Remington fed her.

He couldn't resist touching her, her soft, scented body and uninhibited response urging him on.

Her sharp intake of breath when he circled her nipple both excited and amused him.

He kept watching for a sign that he needed to slow down or that she'd begun to get scared, but she seemed to embrace everything with a wonder that gave him a renewed appreciate for the lifestyle that he'd begun to lose interest in.

To his amazement, he found himself more preoccupied with the shocked delight in her eyes than with not hurting her.

And to his own wonder, he realized that his gentle firmness came naturally.

Setting his fork aside, he bent to kiss her shoulder, letting his fingertips trail down the center of her body and to her mound.

Amused at her sensual enjoyment of both his touch and her food, Hunter chuckled. "I like that you let your enjoyment for things show. It makes you such a fascinating and irresistible lover."

And an amazingly satisfying and control-challenging submissive.

She swallowed heavily, her breath catching. "I've never felt like this before. Everything feels so amazing."

"I agree." Hunter bent to touch his tongue to her nipple, smiling at her sharp cry of pleasure.

"Eat your dinner. I'm gonna have you for dessert."

Watching his brother feed her fulfilled something in Hunter.

The need to spoil her, pamper her, and protect her that had seemed so natural when she was ill and during her recovery had become something more intense.

Something he hadn't thought he'd ever have—and now faced with the reality—delighted him on more levels than he could have thought possible.

Staring down into her beautiful features—flushed with passion—he realized the enormity of what he felt and saw the future laid out in front of him.

He and Remington would be responsible for protecting her in ways their father had never protected their mother.

They would earn her submission but, unlike their father had with their mother, would never break her spirit.

They would move into the big house and spend their nights loving her and would give her the sense of security she deserved.

And have the sense of security and love he and Remington had missed all their lives.

Emma was quickly becoming everything to him, and he wasn't about to let her get away.

He pressed a fingertip to her damp clit, thrilling at her sharp cry of pleasure.

Leaning over her, he nipped her bottom lip. "When we're at home, you can make all the sounds you want, but for now, you need to be quiet."

Eager to protect her from the embarrassment she'd feel when she realized that everyone in the restaurant had heard her cries, Hunter smiled in encouragement. "Quiet as a little mouse. You don't want all those people in the restaurant to hear you. Do you?"

"No." Breathing harshly, she rocked her hips in an apparent attempt to get friction against her clit.

Remington held another bite to her lips. "You're gonna have to concentrate, darlin'."

Chewing her food, she shook her head from side to side, writhing on the seat. "How am I supposed to concentrate on anything when—oh God—when Hunter's doing that?"

Hunter straightened and scooped a bite of his baked potato, liberally coated with butter, and held it to her lips, sliding his free hand down her back. "What are you going to do when I get my mouth on you?"

* * * *

Emma opened her mouth, moaning at the taste of the buttery potatoes and his touch. Leaning into his slow caress, she smiled. "Probably scream with pleasure."

The slide of Hunter's fingertips over her body as she ate made it almost impossible to concentrate on conversation.

Hunter stabbed another bite of steak, touching a finger to her clit again and almost sending her over. Removing it again, he left her frustrated. "She's too aroused for our plans. Emma, arch that back. More. Thrust those breasts out and keep those thighs parted."

He ran his fingertips lightly over her thighs before giving his attention to her nipple, sending sharp, jagged need to her pussy and clit.

Remington offered her another bite, running the backs of his fingers over her other breast. "Very nice. Let's see how she does with the clips."

Finding it difficult to eat while her body shook with a different kind of hunger, Emma hurriedly chewed and swallowed, not tasting anything. "What clips?"

Remington shook his head and set his fork aside. "She's too aroused to enjoy her food." He reached into his pocket and pulled out something that shone in the low light, dangling it in front of her.

"These."

The chain he held out had a clip dangling from each end, the clips she suspected would be attached to each nipple.

Her nipples, already sensitized, tingled with anticipation.

Her breath caught, and she found herself staring at the clips, unable to look away. "You're so different today."

Remington touched the clip to her left nipple, teasing her with it and making her nipple bead even more. "Are we? How?"

Emma shivered at the feel of Hunter's fingers trailing down her back. "It's hard to explain."

Her pussy clenched with need, another rush of moisture escaping when Remington opened the clip and positioned it over her nipple.

Hunter tugged at her other nipple, forcing her to smother a cry. "Try."

"More intense." Dropping her head back, she closed her eyes, moaning at the slide of Hunter's finger down her center to her clit. "Raw. Physical. I don't know. You're more primitive tonight."

"You haven't seen anything yet." Remington closed the clip over her nipple, covering her mouth with his to swallow her cry.

The sharp pain stunned her, and she automatically tried to reach for her nipple to ease it.

Remington lifted his head, catching her hand in his, his gaze holding hers. "Easy, baby. Breathe through it. Yes. That's it. Hmm. Isn't that better?"

Hunter ran his hand over her other breast. "You didn't put it on too tight, did you?"

"Of course not. Just tight enough so that it doesn't fall off. She's not ready for more yet."

Hunter turned her face to his, his eyes filled with a heat that stole her breath. "She doesn't ever have to take more. Her nipples are too sensitive. Just that look in her eyes is enough."

A sob escaped, and then another, the sensation so intense that she couldn't think of anything else.

Electric sparks seemed to travel along every nerve ending all the way to her clit, making the bundle of nerves tingle with a heat that had her writhing on the seat for relief.

"Be still." Hunter's voice—as jagged as if he'd swallowed glass—sent quivers of delight and nerves through her.

To her surprise, instead of attaching the other clip to leave the chain dangling between her breasts, he wound it around the nape of her neck and to the other side. "Arch that back."

Hunter made some kind of adjustment before poising the clip directly over her nipple. "Look at me."

Biting her lip to hold back her cries, she whimpered at the need clawing at her, willing to do whatever it took to get the relief she so desperately needed.

"I'm going to attach this, and when I do, you're gonna hold back your cry. Not a sound. If you're a good girl, I'll give you the relief you need."

Nodding, Emma braced herself, but the initial surge of pain stunned her all over again.

Remington leaned in close from her other side. "Breathe. Then it'll feel as good as the first one. That's a girl. Another breath. Deep. Now another."

The pain eased, and the overwhelming pleasure increased, the need for friction on her clit bringing tears to her eyes. "Please. I need to come so bad."

Remington slid a hand to her nape, lightly tugging the chain. "If you don't keep your back arched and those breasts thrust out, it's gonna pull, darlin'."

Craving more, she slumped her shoulders, gasping at the sharp tug to her nipples.

Hunter chuckled, running the backs of his fingers over the underside of her breast. "Maybe we *will* tighten them next time. Our little sub seems to want more."

Remington ran his fingers over her mound.

"You're going to leave here with a butt plug inside your tight ass to stretch you a little until we get home and I fuck you there."

Stunned, Emma could only stare up at him, her breath catching when Hunter's fingers slid down her body again, her stomach muscles quivering as he made his way to her clit. "I've never been taken there."

Gripping her chin, Remington turned her face to his, his gaze sharp. "I know." He smiled faintly, his grip tightening when she started to squirm. "Be still. Keep your eyes on me. Hunter's gonna make you come, and you're going to be quiet."

Hunter tapped her clit. "If you cry out, I'll stop. I don't want anyone else to hear those beautiful cries of pleasure."

Emma pressed her lips together and nodded, not wanting a repeat of what had happened earlier.

The knowledge that they could make her come hard enough to weaken her, or to just take the edge of and leave her desperate for more, gave her a new respect for them and added an edge to sex that she hadn't anticipated.

Sucking in a breath when he touched his finger to her swollen clit, Emma kept looking at Remington, not wanting to do anything to jeopardize her chance to get relief from such an overwhelming arousal.

Hunter pressed just hard enough and moved just fast enough to keep her on the edge, making the need to come unbearable.

Fisting her hands on the seat on either side of her, she gritted her teeth, anger taking over. "Make me come, damn it! Stop teasing me. I can't take it. I can't take it. Please!"

Remington tugged the chain at her nape, the pull on both nipples startling a cry from her.

"Behave." His expression lost all playfulness, becoming serious and thoughtful.

"You really are something, aren't you?" He touched his lips to hers, nipping gently. "I could happily spend the rest of my life training you."

Another slide of Hunter's finger over her clit drew another whimper. "Training me?"

Hunter slid his finger into her pussy, thrusting it into her several times before touching his slick finger over her clit again.

"Don't sound so indignant. Training you is giving you an awful lot of pleasure. Learning to hold back your orgasm is going to make coming very intense—much more intense than you're used to. I'll let you come now to take the edge off, but there'll be no more coming for you until we get home."

Remington's lips hovered over hers, his smile so wicked, she shivered.

"No matter what we do."

"Please can I have a big one?"

Hunter held his finger against her clit, not moving. "A big what, baby? You have to say the words."

Emma shifted restlessly, her breath catching at the friction on her clit, a groan of frustration escaping when he removed his finger.

"Please can I have a big orgasm? Not like the one at the spa. I can't take it." Her lips brushed against Remington's as she spoke, her breathless plea for relief getting both men's full attention.

Remington's eyes flared with heat, and she could feel Hunter's gaze as he ran his fingertips up and down her inner thigh.

Hunter parted her folds again. "Since you asked so nicely, the answer is yes."

The friction on her clit came without warning, his strokes sending her over almost immediately.

Remington covered her mouth with his, swallowing a cry of pleasure she couldn't hold back.

Needing to get her hands on him more than she needed her next breath, Emma lifted her arms and clung to Remington, crying out again when his hand closed over her breast.

Swallowing her cry, he brushed his rough palm over her clamped nipple, the friction adding to the delightful tightening of her body.

With a groan of satisfaction, he deepened his kiss, cutting off her cries as Hunter continued his ministrations.

The wave of ecstasy crested, holding her in its grip for several heart-pounding moments before releasing her into the safety of Remington's arms.

Dizzy and shaking, she welcomed his strength and warmth, focusing on him like a lifeline to combat the intense vulnerability.

From her other side, Hunter released her clit and pressed his lips against her hair. "Easy, baby. You're so damned passionate."

Slipping an arm around her, Remington pulled her onto his lap, nuzzling her temple. "You sure are, darlin'. It's more exciting than you can imagine. Let's get you settled down, honey. You're shaking."

Emma slumped, curling into him. Feeling even more naked nestled against his fully clothed body, she pressed her face against his neck.

"I can't believe it. I thought it was a fluke. When either one of you touch me, I just melt." Her words came out in a breathless rush, her voice quivering.

Her trembling decreased bit by bit, the safe haven of his arms around her settling her.

His low murmurs of reassurance and teasing added to the intimacy, making her smile.

""Good. I like when you melt." His lips pressed against her hair. "You're so damned adorable. You're okay, honey. I've got you."

The hard arms that held her so closely and warm hands that moved over her back and hip made her feel adored.

Cherished.

Special.

He somehow seemed to know the feeling of defenselessness that consumed her, comforting her until she stopped trembling.

Lifting her face, she studied Remington's features, relieved to see affection in his eyes. "Why do you do that? Don't get me wrong. I like it, but…" Emma shrugged, not knowing how to ask if it was just part of what they did as Dominants and it didn't really mean anything.

He reached for her glass of tea and held it to her lips. "Do what, honey?"

She took a sip before answering in an effort to ease her dry mouth. "You know. Hold me afterward."

Irritated that her face burned, she shrugged and reached for the glass, frowning when Remington grabbed it before she could. "No. It's more than that. You take time with me after I come when most men would have just considered their part done."

She lifted her gaze to Hunter's to find him sipping his beer, watching her steadily. "Hunter does it, too."

Holding the glass out of her reach until she lowered her hand again, Remington smiled. "We're not most men."

Once again holding the glass to her lips, he glanced at his brother. "A Dominant takes care of his submissive. That's part of the trust between them."

He waited until she finished drinking and set the glass aside before stabbing another bite of steak. "You're more than that. You're our woman." He slipped the bite between her lips and smiled again, the hesitancy in his smile both endearing and unnerving.

"Caring for you comes in many forms, some you may not like."

Finished with his dinner, Hunter pushed his plate aside. "Protecting you is our primary concern." Lifting his head, he held her gaze with his sharp one. "From everything. And every*one*. You might not like the way we do it, but you have to trust that we'll do what's best for you."

Reading between the lines, Emma understood one thing very clearly.

If they thought they were a threat to her, they'd protect her—even from themselves.

* * * *

Remington felt her stiffen, and knowing Emma's disbelief that either one of them would hurt her—a belief he'd come to agree with—he shot a glare at his brother.

Hunter met his glare with one of his own and reached for her. "Come here. I want my dessert."

Emma shivered, wiggling on his lap. "Hunter, I think we should talk about this."

"I don't. You're soaking wet, and I want it. Now."

Recognizing the hunger in his brother's eyes, Remington eased Emma from his lap and toward him. "Hunter looks real hungry for his dessert, darlin'." Resting her head on his lap, he couldn't resist her beaded nipples, smiling at her soft cries when he simultaneously released both clamps, something he knew would have the blood flowing into them again.

Emma bit her lip, thrashing her head from side to side, her face flushed with passion. "We need to talk about this."

Hunter spread her thighs and hooked them over her shoulders. "No. You promised to trust us to keep you safe. That's what we're doing."

"But—"

"I know one way to shut you up." Hunter lowered his head, sliding his tongue over her mound.

Knowing how sensitive she would be there, Remington smiled and slid his hands to her sides, expecting her jolt. Sliding back to lean over her in case he had to silence her cries, Remington dug into his pocket for the plug and lube he'd need in just a few minutes.

Amused by her sharp gasps, he bent to touch his lips to hers, glancing down to meet Hunter's gaze. "Hunter hasn't even used his tongue on your slit yet. He's just enjoying how smooth your mound and folds are."

Amazed at how quickly they'd aroused her again, and Hunter's expertise with his devious mouth and hands, Emma snarled up at Remington. "It drives me crazy when you tell me what he's thinking when he's doing something to me. Hunter did the—oh God—the same thing."

"Why does it make you crazy, honey?"

* * * *

Emma sucked in a breath, trembling harder with anticipation when Hunter lifted his head slightly and used his thumbs to part her folds. "Because it's so erotic. It's so personal to be held by one man while another touches me."

A moan escaped, the feel of Hunter's warm breath against her clit making it feel even more swollen. Her pussy clenched hard, releasing even more of her juices.

"When you talk about what you're doing or thinking, it's so damned sexy." She gripped his shirt, arching to press her breasts more firmly into his hands.

"You both drive me crazy."

Hunter pressed a kiss to her mound. "Good—because you make me crazy as hell."

Emma gasped at the feel of his hot tongue sliding into her pussy, his grip easily overcoming her uncontrollable need to move.

Fire raced through her when he began to fuck her with his tongue, the need to be quiet forcing her to press her face against Remington's chest. "Oh God. Oh God. I can't take any more."

Remington pulled her close. "You really have no choice, baby doll. Christ, I'm hard as a rock at the thought of fucking that ass when we get home."

Her bottom clenched, tingling with an awareness that left her breathless.

Hunter lifted his head. "I'm gonna have a little fun with it first." Flipping her to her belly, he lifted her to her knees with a speed that had her fighting to hold on to Remington.

Burying her face into Remington's lap, she pressed her mouth against his thigh, the hot slide of Hunter's tongue over her forbidden opening stunning her.

It was so sexual.

So demanding.

So incredibly arousing.

Embarrassed to be enjoying such a carnal act, she tried to pull away from him, thrilling at the strength of his grip holding her in place.

She didn't know what it said about her to be aroused at their dominant natures, but she didn't care.

It just felt so good.

So did the feel of Remington's hard cock pressing against her cheek through his jeans.

Aroused and needy, she lifted her head, struggling to undo Remington's zipper.

She wanted to taste him.

She wanted to give him as much pleasure as he gave her.

Shuddering, she moaned, throwing her head back. The feel of Hunter's tongue moving back and forth over her puckered opening so extreme she had trouble focusing on her task.

"No." Remington pulled her hand away, his voice gravelly. "I already want you too much."

Hunter slid his tongue to the cheek of her ass, biting into it with a groan. "Damn, she's something. Turn her around. I want her mouth on my cock."

Thrilling at Hunter's harsh tone and looking forward to turning him into putty, she smiled as they turned her, her smile falling when she saw what he held out.

His own smile widened, the playful hunger in his eyes so stunning her breath caught.

Lifting the butt plug, he pressed it against her lips. "I'm gonna have my cock in your mouth while I watch Remington work this into your ass."

With a gasp, Emma pulled away enough to see the plug clearly, her bottom clenching. "I thought you said it was small."

Hunter's brow went up. "This *is* small. It's just to wake your ass up for Remington's cock."

"Oh God."

Without a word, Remington repositioned her, draping her over his lap. "Now we're gonna have a little fun. Suck Hunter's cock, darlin'. Make him come."

"No." Hunter undid his jeans and freed his cock, fisting it as he reached for her. "She's different, Rem. I'm not about to come in her mouth."

Emma had other ideas, and although she'd never done it before, she was determined to make Hunter come.

Guided by his hand at the back of her head, she closed her lips over the head of his cock, moaning at the hard thickness forcing her to open her mouth wide.

Encouraged by Hunter's low groans, she focused on giving him pleasure, her concentration broken by the feel of Remington's firm hand sliding over her bottom.

Her toes curled when he parted and lifted her bottom cheeks, the knowledge that he could see her puckered opening clearly intensifying the feeling of vulnerability.

Remington added to the sensation by running his finger over the sensitive flesh he'd exposed, still moist from Hunter's tongue. "Pretty."

The sudden cold made her jolt, shivers of nerves and delight going up and down her spine as Remington's firm finger began to press into her.

She'd never known she could be capable of such primitive arousal or that every part of her body could achieve such a heightened sexual awareness.

Including her mind.

Hunter's hand tightened in her hair. "Suck, Emma. I'm enjoying watching Remington lube you up." Slipping a hand under her, he tugged at one of her nipples. "Concentrate on what you're doing to me. As soon as that plug's inside you, we're going home, and we're both gonna fuck you together."

Remington's finger moved in and out of her ass, pressing against her anal walls with each stroke. "We've got to get you lubed real good for this plug and my cock."

She'd never imagined anything could feel so intimate.

She didn't think they could do anything to her to make her feel so sexual and defenseless.

Each slow stroke of Remington's finger in her ass taught her more about herself and tied her to them in ways she knew she could never escape.

She clenched her bottom in an involuntary effort to close her cheeks, but Remington only chuckled, his fingers firmly holding her open. "You don't really think I'm gonna let you close this ass against me, do you? Do you really think there's anything you could do to keep me out?"

His finger slid free, only to press into her again with more of the cold lube.

"This plug is gonna be nice and snug inside you." The strokes of his finger came faster, the fingers of his other hand still holding her cheeks parted wide, so wide that her opening began to sting. "Very pretty. Yeah, darlin'. Hunter, do you see how she's lifting her hips?"

Hunter's hand moved in her hair, his thumb moving over her cheek. "I see it." Caressing her breast, he chuckled softly as she redoubled her efforts. "She's trying to make me come, too."

Turning her head slightly, he pulled his cock from her mouth until only the head remained inside. "No more sucking. Keep your mouth closed over the head of my cock while Remington works the plug in. I don't want anyone else to hear your cries. Look at me, Emma."

Emma took a shuddering breath, opening her eyes to meet Hunter's hooded gaze just as Remington slid his finger from her bottom.

Hunter smiled, stroking her breast and her cheek. "Do you have any idea how beautiful you look with my cock in your mouth and that combination of nerves and arousal in your eyes? Once that plug starts going into you and you realize how much it's stretching you, your eyes are going to darken and widen, filled with vulnerability. You're the perfect little sub, aren't you?"

The press of the hard plug against her puckered opening felt much different than Remington's warm finger, the reality of having something hard and cold being pushed inside her more startling than she'd expected.

Hunter smiled. "There it is." He continued to run his thumb back and forth over her cheek, his expression thoughtful. "Damn if you don't get to me. Keep your mouth closed over the head of my cock. No crying out."

Remington pushed the plug deeper, and the cold alien feeling of it widening as it pushed inside her curled Emma's toes. "Hang on, honey. It's barely inside you."

"Go slow." Hunter's eyes narrowed. "She's already a little overwhelmed."

Emma lifted her head, sucking in a breath. "Overwhelmed?"

Careful to keep her voice low, she bit back a moan as the plug went deeper, stretching her wider. "He's shoving that thing up my ass! Oh God. I feel so full. It's so hard."

Hunter's dark brow went up, his look of arrogance as exciting as his strokes to her nipple. "Our cocks will be harder." He glanced toward her ass. "Yep. All the way in." Gripping the back of her head, he urged her to his cock again. "I want to feel that mouth again."

Remington pushed the plug deeper, pulling it out slightly before pushing it even deeper.

Each time it went deeper, it awakened an awareness just beyond where the plug reached, making her desperate for more.

Shaken, Emma rocked her hips in time to his slow thrusts in an attempt to take more of the plug inside her.

To be stretched even more.

She groaned around Hunter's cock when the plug slid deeper, the feel of the flat base against her bottom telling her that it was all the way in.

Releasing her cheeks, Remington lifted her from Hunter's cock and settled her on his lap. Running his hands over her, he bent to touch his lips to her, the intense possessiveness in his eyes showing her a side to him that she hadn't seen before.

Reaching up to cup his jaw, she bit back a moan at the shift of the plug. "Remington?"

"You okay, baby?"

"Yes." It came out as a whimper, the feel of the plug filling her, his hands moving over her and his hard, denim-clad thigh beneath her made her ache everywhere.

Nodding once, he didn't speak as he began to dress her again, sharing a look with Hunter.

Hunter rose, grimacing as he forced his cock back into his jeans and fastened them again. "I'll take care of the check and meet you out front."

After he disappeared through the curtain, Emma turned to Remington. "Is something wrong?"

Remington turned her away from him and zipped her dress again. "Not a thing. You're beautiful. Let's go home."

Emma's heart stopped and then started pounding. Smiling, she touched her lips to his.

"I'm afraid I already am. Don't break my heart."

"Not a chance. Darlin', I don't know what I expected when I made up my mind to keep you, but you've floored Hunter and me." Shaking his head when she would have spoken, he touched a finger to his lips.

"You make us want more. You make us believe that we can do this, but we hadn't counted on the possessiveness. We've never been possessive before."

His smile appeared forced. "Our feelings for you are turning out to be more than either one of us bargained for. Give us a little time to adjust to it, okay, babe?"

Wrapping her arms around him, she smiled. "As long as you don't try to push me away."

Helping her to her feet, Remington lifted her shirt and attached both clips again, the pressure and shift of the plug in her ass forcing a whimper from her.

With a hand in her hair, he tilted her head back, staring into her eyes as he tugged the chain before covering her breasts again.

"Baby doll, I don't think that's even possible anymore."

Chapter Twenty-Seven

Shocked at his burning possessiveness toward Emma, Hunter threw off his clothes and reached for her, yanking her against him, his cock jumping at the feel of her nakedness against his.

"You make me want you too damned much."

The feel of her softness against him turned his hunger into a living, breathing thing that threatened his sanity.

Afraid he would hurt her, he forced himself to loosen his grip slightly, but it only gave Emma the room she needed to close her hand around his cock.

"Good. I want you to want me too damned much." She ran her small, soft hand up and down his cock, the hesitancy in her touch a sharp contrast to her daring.

She excited him on so many levels that he couldn't keep up.

Having his emotions involved made everything hotter.

Sweeter.

More intense.

He wouldn't be satisfied until she belonged to them in every way.

Unwrapping her hand from his cock, he took both of her hands against his, holding them against his chest.

Frowning, she fought his hold. "Let go. I want to touch you."

Delighted with her, he bent to touch his lips to hers, touching his finger to the chain between her breasts and sending it swaying.

"Are you forgetting who's in charge here?"

Naked, Remington moved in behind her, and judging by Emma's gasp, pressed against the plug.

"It looks like training our little sub is gonna take a while."

Emma held on to Hunter, her head tilted back in a way he couldn't resist. "Hmm. Forever. It's hard to remember when I'm aroused."

Wrapping one arm around her, Hunter pulled her close, taking her mouth while reaching into the drawer for one of the condoms they'd put in there days earlier.

"We'll remind you."

Once he'd rolled it on, he handed one to Remington and reached for her again.

With an arm around her, he tugged at the chain, his cock jumping at her soft cry.

"You look beautiful wearing this. We're gonna have to buy you some more and some of the weights that attach to it."

He and Remington had already bought jewelry, lingerie, and leather clothing for her, and had enjoyed themselves immensely.

Their plans for a playroom in the basement were already in progress, keeping both him and Remington busy picking out items, something both of them were enjoying as well.

* * * *

Emma rubbed her thighs together, unsurprised that her inner thighs had become coated with her juices.

"You're kidding. Weights?" She cried out when Hunter tugged at the chain again.

"Yep." Lifting her high against him, he lowered himself to the bed and draped her over him. "I think you've had these on long enough, though."

With his hands on her waist, he positioned her over his cock. "I want my cock inside you before we take it off and before Remington works on that ass."

Gripping his forearms, Emma threw her head back and looked up at Remington, his slow smile more than a little intimidating.

Her bottom kept clenching on the plug, the awareness there leaving her incredibly aroused and unsteady.

Sucking in a breath when Hunter started to lower her onto his cock, she reached out to run a hand over Remington's smooth muscular chest, the sight of his cock making her bottom clench again. "I feel like I'm dreaming."

Her head spun, the myriad of sensations making her entire body tingle hotly.

Trembling uncontrollably, she sucked in a breath at the feel of Hunter's cock slowly filling her, the plug in her ass making it even tighter.

Hunter's hands tightened on her waist, his voice gravelly. "Not a dream, babe. It's real. *Real* real."

Each slow stroke took Hunter's cock even deeper, shifting the plug in her bottom and making her feel impossibly full.

Watching her, Hunter groaned. "Rem, take the clips off." He lifted her slightly and lowered her again. "Look at me, baby."

Emma stared into Hunter's eyes, anticipation of the intense sensation to come leaving her breathless.

The bed shifted when Remington moved in behind her. Bending to nuzzle her neck, he cupped her breasts, running his fingers back and forth over her nipples.

"Your nipples are so sensitive. We haven't forgotten that. We haven't forgotten a damned thing about you and never will. We won't be happy until we know it all."

His warm breath against her neck had her leaning into him, lifting her hands to bury them into his thick hair.

Apparently pleased that she'd left herself vulnerable for him, Remington murmured his approval, his lips pressing against her neck. "Very nice. I like the way you offer yourself to me."

Hunter's hands tightened on her hips. "Very natural, too. I love the way she reaches for us when she's feeling vulnerable and how she offers herself so beautifully."

With her eyes closed, Emma cuddled against Remington and smiled. "I've never known men who talk the way you do. I—oh!"

The sudden rush of blood flowing into her nipples when Remington released both clips simultaneously had her writhing against Hunter, taking more of his cock.

Sitting up, Hunter lifted her again slightly. "All the way now. Hold on to me."

Emma gripped his shoulders as he began to lower her again, another whimper escaping at the incredible fullness.

Holding her close, Hunter cupped the back of her head, staring into her eyes. "Easy, love. A little more. That's it. Yeah. Now my cock's all the way inside you. So fucking tight. Don't fucking move."

The demand in his harsh tone sent ripples of delight through her.

Gulping in air, she clung to him, her pussy clamping down on his cock as she struggled to adjust. "Hunter! Oh God. I feel so full. So good. Please. Move."

She rocked her hips, crying out and then groaning with frustration when Hunter cursed and gripped her hips.

Pressing a hand to her abdomen, she sucked in a breath. "Oh God. It's so deep."

Hunter groaned and pulled her down to his chest, the movement withdrawing several inches of his cock from her. "Too much. Hurry up, Rem."

The hand at her back slid down to her bottom, gripping the base of the plug. With a brush of his lips against her shoulder, Remington moved the plug inside her. "Just knowing this is her first time is driving me crazy."

"Easy, baby. Hold on to me."

She obeyed Hunter's growled demand without hesitation, not knowing if it was due to the steel in his tone or the affection.

Sliding a hand into her hair at her nape, he held her against his chest. "No moving until Rem's inside you."

With a hand pressed flat on her back, Remington began to ease the plug from her, pressing a hand to her bottom when she wiggled.

"Easy, Em." He moved the plug in slow circles, his voice low and soothing. "I'm just working the widest part out. There we go. Now I'm gonna lube you a little more. Hold her still, Hunter. She bucked when I put the plug in. I can only imagine what she's gonna do when I start working my cock into her."

Emma sucked in a breath when the plug slid free, struggling to move on Hunter's cock when the need became unbearable.

She felt empty in a way she never had before, the sensation overpowering.

Frustrated and aroused at the strength of Hunter's hold, Emma fought to move against him, ignoring his soothing urges to stay still.

"No, baby. You can't move yet. Stay still for me."

Gripping his shoulders, she pushed against him in an effort to sit up, crying out when Remington's finger, coated with cold lube, slid into her ass again with almost no resistance.

"Oh! Hunter. Rem. Damn." She involuntarily tried to straighten her legs, but Remington's hair-roughened thighs prevented it.

Her clit throbbed and felt ten times its normal size.

Her pussy clenched on Hunter's cock, making her feel even fuller.

The empty sensation in her ass made her desperate to be filled there again, a hunger that even her nervousness couldn't overcome.

Remington's chuckle faded away, the sound of foil ripping ominous.

"I'll go nice and slow. Jesus, she's tight."

Watching her steadily, Hunter kept a firm hand on her back and one on the back of her neck, pulling her down to his chest again. "Be still. You can do this. We won't hurt you. It's gonna be a little overwhelming, but we've got you."

"Hunter, hold me." Her breath caught and became even more ragged when Remington pushed the head of his cock against her puckered opening.

"I've got you, baby." His lips pressed against her forehead. "I'm never letting go."

Remington ran his hand over her back as if knowing how vulnerable she felt.

"Got her, Hunter?"

Hunter's arm tightened around her, his lips warm in her hair. "I've definitely got her. Look at me, Em."

Her breath hitched, coming out in ragged gasps at the relentless press of Remington's cock against her puckered opening.

Arching her back, she lifted her head slightly to meet Hunter's gaze, struck by the tenderness in his eyes. "It's so hot. It's burning. Oh God. What if it doesn't fit?"

Cupping her cheek, Hunter pulled her down for a kiss, sipping at her lips as he spoke in a soothing tone. "You'll be able to take him. You can take both of us."

Sliding his hand into her hair, he nibbled at her bottom lip. "You're perfect for both of us."

Emma stiffened, her toes curling as Remington pushed the head of his cock past the tight ring of muscle and into her, the fullness and burning sensation alarming her.

"Oh! Oh God. Hunter! He's inside me."

"Yes. I am." Remington rubbed her bottom before spreading her cheeks wide. "And I'm going deeper. Just a little more and Hunter and I are gonna start moving. Hold on to Hunter, babe."

Shivers raced up and down her spine as Remington slid deeper, the lube easing his way.

"Oh God!"

She couldn't stop clamping down on his cock, the unfamiliar feel of her bottom hole being held wide open nothing short of stunning.

Clenching on both cocks, Emma let the voices of her lovers wash over her as they began to move.

Hunter lowered his hands to her hips, allowing her to raise herself slightly. "Christ, I've never felt anything this good before."

Stunned at the feel of their dual penetration, Emma sucked in a breath when he lifted her slightly from his cock while Remington thrust a little deeper.

Fisting her hands on his chest, she stared into Hunter's eyes as he lowered her again, struck by his watchfulness.

Another rush of moisture escaped to coat his cock, her pussy clenching as he thrust into her again.

"I c-can't believe I-I'm taking both of you. You're both inside me."

The friction against the inner walls of her pussy and ass sent her climbing the rungs of arousal but in a much slower way than when they stroked her clit.

It was if her mind struggled to keep up with the sensations bombarding her, leaving her stunned and dizzy and gripping Hunter like a lifeline.

Remington cupped her breasts and thrust into her again, setting up a rhythm with Hunter that melted away the last of her nervousness and filled her with a kind of hunger that went beyond the physical.

Her mind went blank. Nothing but pleasure and love for the men who took her existed.

"Oh God."

Remington groaned and thrust again, sliding a hand over her belly. "So fucking tight. So damned passionate. You're ours now, Emma. Fucking ours. Christ, Hunter."

Hunter moved faster, the sounds coming from him harsh and filled with hunger. "Yes. Ours."

Their thrusts came faster, their need for her evident in every stroke.

Every caress.

Tingling waves of sensation washed over her, the warning ripples going on and on.

Emma's whimpers and soft cries of pleasure seemed to spur them on.

Hunter thrust his hips upward. "Emma, you're ours now. *Ours.* Do you hear me?"

"Yes!"

Remington scraped his teeth over her shoulder, his thrusts coming faster. "You're never getting away from us now, darlin'."

They moved together as if they'd been doing it for years, Emma's pussy and ass stretching to accommodate their cocks, which seemed to grow harder and thicker with every stroke.

Surrounded by heat and masculinity, Emma had never felt so vulnerable—or safe.

Sliding her hands higher on Hunter's chest, she let sensation take over, crying out as she clamped down on them.

The first hot wave of tingling heat left her breathless, holding her in its grip with a strength that stunned her.

Another wave layered over the first, and with cry after harsh cry, she clung to Hunter, her hands fisting on his chest as Remington cursed and surged deep, followed only seconds later by Hunter.

Another wave crested, followed by ripples of sublime pleasure.

Throwing her head back with another weak cry, she let the ripples wash over her, her hips pumping of their own volition.

Her nipples tingled hotly, her clit burning and so sensitive that she whimpered each time they brushed against Hunter's skin.

She couldn't stop clamping down on their cocks, drawing groans and soft curses from both of them.

She felt it everywhere, the total loss of control scaring her.

She couldn't feel herself holding on to Hunter.

She couldn't move.

She couldn't even open her eyes.

Through it all, she felt Hunter's and Remington's sharp attention.

Felt their affection.

The pleasure gradually dimmed, leaving her body so sensitized that she gasped at the slightest touch.

She couldn't think, every inch of her body trembling with the remnants of a pleasure that was all consuming.

Raw.

Hot.

So primitive that she no longer felt like herself.

To her horror, a sob escaped.

And another.

Aware of the shock and reassuring crooning from both men, she started to cry in earnest, scared because she didn't know why.

* * * *

When Hunter gathered her closer, Remington eased his cock from her, running his hands up and down her back.

"Christ, I love her." Remington bent to press his lips to her bottom, lifting his head to meet Hunter's eyes over her shoulder.

Unsurprised at the emotion and tenderness in his brother's eyes, Remington eased to their side, running his hand up and down her back and his lips over her shoulder while Hunter crooned to her.

"You're all right, baby. I've got you. You came hard, honey. So beautiful." Hunter smiled and pushed her hair back, wiping her tears with a tenderness that moved Remington.

Emma sucked in a shaky breath. "I don't know what's wrong with me. Why the hell am I crying?"

Cupping her cheek, Hunter smiled, brushing his lips against her jaw. "Because you trusted us enough to let go. Completely. You came hard—very hard. You knew that we would take care of you. That means everything to us."

Emma whimpered again. "It was too much. I never felt like that before." Lifting her head, she glanced at Remington, smiling when he bent close to kiss her.

Ruffling her hair, Remington rose. "I'll go get cleaned up and start a bath for her. Thank God we put that big tub in. Bring her in when you're ready so I can cuddle with her."

To his amusement, Emma yawned. "I don't wanna move. I'll take a shower later."

Hunter sat up, taking her with him. "No. You'll feel better after your bath. It'll relax you, and the warm water will soothe your bottom."

Emma blushed delightfully. "You two are so damned intimate."

Remington thought about some of the gifts they'd already bought her and their plans for the playroom.

He thought about the ring they'd ordered for her and the years ahead of them.

He suspected she referred to physical intimacy, the realization of the emotional intimacy probably not hitting her yet.

Smiling, he started toward the bathroom, anxious to hold her. "Baby doll, you have no idea."

Chapter Twenty-Eight

Emma studied her reflection in the mirror above her dresser, pleased with her appearance.

Wearing the red dress both men seemed to love and a new pink thong and matching bra, she knew she looked her best.

A small clear crystal pendant hung from a thin gold chain to rest between her breasts, something she hoped would draw Hunter's and Remington's attention.

She'd pulled her long hair into a tight ponytail to keep it out of her way and keep her cooler while she danced.

Hearing the back door open and close, she smiled to herself, her pulse leaping in anticipation. She took a deep breath and slipped on a pair of low-heeled sandals that would be comfortable for dancing. Grabbing her smaller purse, she left the bedroom and went down the stairs.

Unsurprised to find both Hunter and Remington standing in her kitchen, Emma went to the refrigerator for a glass of the sweet tea she kept there, smiling to herself to see that both men had already helped themselves to some, their empty glasses side by side on the island.

"Thanks for taking me tonight. I didn't want to disappoint Michael and John. I didn't know if you'd get back in time."

Remington smiled. "Of course. We wouldn't want you to miss your big night."

She closed the refrigerator and sipped her tea, her throat going dry at the intensity of their gazes.

She hadn't seen either one of them since waking up between them that morning, both men saying that had errands to run in town.

Hunter had showered recently, his hair still damp and slicked back. "Yes, but we'd like to talk to you before we go."

Remington, who'd also recently showered, moved closer, so close that she could smell the soap he'd used and feel the heat from his body. He took the glass from her hand, making a show of turning it to drink from the place her lips had touched. "You're ours now. You admitted it last night."

Emma sucked in a breath when he traced the chain she wore to the pendant dangling from it. "Yes. I love you. Both of you."

Her lips tingled under his stare, the awareness in her nipples sharpening at the slide of his fingers only inches away.

Remington lowered the glass, brushing it back and forth over her nipple. "I love you. I won't let you go."

Swallowing heavily, she glanced at Hunter.

Something else in his eyes made her heart beat faster, a shimmer of emotion that she couldn't allow herself to believe.

Setting the glass on the counter, Remington tugged lightly at the chain, applying just enough pressure to urge her closer as he bent toward her. "We want you to be ours forever."

His breath, warm on her lips, carried the scent of mint, his low, intimate whisper drawing her even closer.

Emma licked her lips to relieve the tingling sensation, leaning close enough to warm her cold nipple against his chest. "Yes."

Hunter stepped forward, taking her hand in his. "We want you to marry us."

Emma forgot to breathe.

She looked from Hunter to Remington and back again, not sure she'd heard him right.

"What?"

Hunter's lips twitched as he slid a gold ring on her finger, a ring with two square-cut diamonds side by side.

"Will you marry us?"

A sob escaped, making it difficult to speak.

Her heart felt as if it might explode, love for both of them nearly choking her.

"Is it really possible?"

Her breath caught at the feel of Remington's hands closing on her waist. "Please tell me it's possible."

Remington smiled faintly, his hands clenching on her waist. "It's possible. Because Hunter's older, you'll legally be married to him, but we're in Desire where the rules are different than the outside world. You'll be married in every other way that counts to both of us."

With a cry, she leapt at him, reaching for Hunter. "Yes. Yes. Yes!"

She wrapped her legs around Remington, holding on to him and to Hunter, tears blurring her vision.

"Are you sure?"

Hunter cupped the back of her head and bent to touch his lips to hers, his eyes hooded. "We're positive."

Hunter hadn't told her he loved her.

Glancing at Remington, she tried to smile at his look of encouragement, remembering his advice to be patient.

Staring into her eyes, he stroked his thumb back and forth over her nipple, his eyes narrowing at her shocked cry of pleasure.

"You're so damned beautiful."

Hunter slid his hand around to cup her other breast, his touch firmer and just as arousing. Nuzzling her hair, he closed his thumb and forefinger over her nipple, squeezing lightly, a groan escaping at her breathless cry.

"You excite me like no other woman ever has. You're the only woman in the world who could ever make me take such a risk, the only woman who could make me live in this house again."

Smiling, Emma ran a hand down his chest, stunned to find herself engaged to two such magnificent men.

Two men.

Taking her from Remington's arms, Hunter lifted her to the island and wrapped a hand around her ponytail, tilting her head back and staring into her eyes. Circling her nipple with a callused fingertip, he clenched his jaw, the hunger in his eyes so strong it stole her breath.

"You make me want you too damned much."

"You could never want me too much."

Laying a hand on his shoulder, she stared at her ring.

"My ring's beautiful."

Remington rubbed her back. "So are you. Jake said that it was a good style for you because it won't get caught on anything while you're cooking. We ordered your wedding rings while we were there."

"I can't believe it."

Hunter nipped her bottom lip, his breathing harsh. "Believe it."

It felt so strange to be touching Remington while looking into Hunter's eyes, the awareness of both of their hands on her like an erotic fantasy.

Still sliding a hand over Remington's chest, she reached up and gripped the ends of Hunter's hair. "Nothing in my life has ever felt so right."

Hunter smiled faintly, dropping a hard kiss on her lips. "It's a damned good thing because I love you and you're not getting away from me."

Emma jerked away to see his face. "You do?"

Hunter frowned. "'Fraid so. It's not comfortable, and the more I care about you, the more I worry about hurting you."

"You won't."

He lifted her against him, wrapping his arms around her as if she was the most precious thing on earth.

"If I ever did, it would kill me."

Happier than she'd ever been in her life, she nuzzled against him.

"If anything, you're both too damned protective. I've been taking care of myself for a long time."

Remington ran a hand over her hair.

"Now you have us to take care of you."

Emma grinned and reached for him, running her hand over his chest.

"Something tells me this is going to get real interesting."

Smiling, she held on to Hunter's shoulders and jumped down from the counter.

"I'd better call Michael and John and tell them I won't be there."

Remington shook his head. "No. I want you to have a good time tonight, and I want you to meet some people you haven't met yet."

Hunter chuckled, a beautiful sound that tightened the fist around her heart.

"We'll announce our engagement. That way the entire town will know by morning, and we probably won't have to buy a drink all night."

Running a finger down Remington's chest, she looked up at him through her lashes.

"Since the two of you are going to be moving in here, what would I have to do to talk the two of you into letting me turn the guest house into a large kitchen?"

Hunter threw his head back and laughed, a sound that brought tears to her eyes.

With a hand around her waist, he led her toward the front door.

"I'm sure we'll think of something."

Remington took her left hand in his and kissed her ring. "We'll get started on it right after the wedding."

Emma stopped in her tracks, looking at each of them.

"I didn't mean for *you* to do it."

Shaking his head, Remington pulled her toward the door. "All you have to do is tell us what you want. We'll take care of it, and if we need help, we'll get it."

"But—"

Opening the door, Remington guided her though it. "You're in Desire now, and that's how it's done."

Chapter Twenty-Nine

Emma laughed and shook her head, waving a hand as she turned back to the bar. "I need a rest."

She took the empty seat between Hunter and Remington, pleased to see them both looking so relaxed.

Leaning back against the bar, they seemed content to watch her dance and talk to the others, something that seemed to surprise everyone.

Devlin Monroe grinned. "And we've all been taking it easy on you because of your recent surgery." He slid a glance at Hunter and Remington. "And because we're still not sure how these two are gonna react. Congratulations again on your engagement. Any date for the wedding?"

Hunter smiled and reached for his beer. "Next Saturday."

"What?" Emma jumped from the barstool. "I can't be ready to get married in a week."

Remington smiled and wrapped an arm around her. "I'm afraid we're not much for waiting. Especially Hunter. We're real organized around here. We'll get everything organized. All you have to do is pick out a pretty dress."

Hunter grabbed her hand. "You're pretty popular. You must be thirsty after all that dancing. Why don't you have another one of your drinks?"

John chuckled. "And her ribs are just as popular. I'll get your drink. I've got a blender full of them. Hell, even they're popular tonight."

She smiled her thanks at John when he handed her another one of the non-alcoholic drinks he'd created for her. "I'm only popular because men vastly outnumber women in this town."

She had to raise her voice to be heard over the music. "Even the ones who are married seem to still need another partner on the dance floor. Clay doesn't seem to want to let go of Jesse, and Rio sure wants to dance tonight."

"So do I. I'm next." Caleb dropped into the seat on the other side of Hunter. Smiling, he nodded his thanks when John handed him another beer. "I've got to work off all those ribs. Damn, honey. You sure can cook."

Flattered at the response to Rib Night, Emma shrugged and got back onto the bar stool. "John and Michael cooked them. I'm just glad everyone likes them. Quite a turnout, huh? Is it usually this busy on Friday nights?"

Devlin leaned close. "It's a busy place, but tonight, it's packed. Not only is everyone anxious to be here for the first Rib Night but I think everyone wanted to see the three of you together."

Emma shook her head, her stomach tightening when Charlene walked through the door, wearing a skintight black leather dress that barely held her curves.

"Hell."

Hunter and Remington both stiffened beside her.

Hunter leaned close, his lips brushing her ear. "Don't let her ruin your night. She's nothing to us, and you better damned well know it."

Remington stood and moved to stand in front of her. With his hands around her waist, he lifted her from the bar stool and set her on her feet before grabbing her hand. "Come on. Let's dance. This is a nice slow one so I can hold you close. Caleb's not gettin' this one."

Emma allowed him to take her in his arms and began to dance with him, aware that Charlene moved to the bar and sat on *her* stool. "She's pissing me off." Leaning back, she looked up at his handsome features.

"There's no reason to be jealous. We love *you*."

Even in the warmth and security of Remington's arms, a chill went up Emma's spine.

"I know." Emma glanced over her shoulder to see Charlene leaning toward Hunter, her hand resting on his forearm, her eyes shooting daggers at Emma.

"I don't trust her. I don't think she's ready to give either one of you up."

Turning her in a way that blocked her view of Hunter and Charlene, Remington lifted her left hand to his lips.

"We never belonged to her. We belong to you."

Grinning, she lifted both hands to his nape, playing with the ends of his hair. "I like the sound of that."

Jesse and Clay danced closer, and with a smile, Jesse touched Emma's arm. "It's good to see you together. They look hungry. Lucky girl."

Clay blinked and leaned back to stare down at his wife. "You think I'm not hungry for you, baby?"

Jesse grinned up at him, leaning close and sliding her hands up his chest to his shoulders. "If you and Rio were any hungrier, I'd never get out of the house."

Clay's slow smile had Jesse leaning closer. "Baby, you're lucky we let you out of the bedroom."

Jesse's eyes went wide before they almost closed, her cheeks flushing a deep pink. "Oh, Clay." Her breath came out in a rush, the desire shimmering in her eyes making Emma feel like a voyeur. "You always say or do something to make me fall in love with you all over again."

"Good." Clay ran a hand over her hair. "Because if you ever fall out of love with me, baby, I wouldn't even want to live."

"Oh, Clay!"

Remington smiled as they danced away, running a hand over her back the way he had earlier. "I know how he feels."

Incredibly touched and still a little stunned that Hunter and Remington loved her, Emma blinked back tears. "Oh God. I love you. Please don't make me cry in front of everyone." She glanced toward the bar, where Hunter pushed Charlene's hand from his thigh, his expression hard and cold.

Furious, Emma stopped abruptly. "I've had enough of that woman!"

It had taken a lot for Hunter and Remington to realize that they could have love in their lives, and the newness of their relationship kept Emma on edge.

Pulling out of Remington's arms, she marched across the small dance floor to Hunter and jumped onto his lap to straddle him, secure in the knowledge that he would catch her.

She wanted to smile at his look of surprise but plastered her lips to his instead.

Kissing him with all the passion inside her, she pressed her breasts against his chest, inwardly smiling when his hands closed over her hips.

Running her hands through his hair, she forgot about their audience and poured everything she had into her kiss.

Hunter quickly took control of their kiss, clenching his hands on her hips and pulling her closer.

His hands moved higher, sliding up her sides to settle just under her breasts, the affection in his touch thrilling her. Lifting his head, he smiled down at her, his eyes dancing and full of promise.

"Well, that was fun. You finished dancing with Remington?"

Aware of Charlene's fury and the heat of Remington's body against her back, Emma smiled, pleased to see Hunter looking more relaxed again.

"For now."

Charlene ran a hand over her hair. "We were having a private conversation."

Hunter ran his hands down Emma's ponytail, tugging playfully. "No. We weren't."

Remington leaned past Emma to retrieve her drink and his, glaring at Charlene. "You're in Emma's seat."

Hunter smiled and touched his lips to hers. "Emma's fine where she is. I was just telling Charlene about our engagement."

"Yeah?" She held her left hand up, the low light in the bar making the twin diamonds glitter. "What do you think of my ring? Isn't it gorgeous?"

Charlene glared at her, glancing at both Hunter and Remington. "Yeah. Lovely."

Emma smiled when Charlene rose with a huff and stormed away. Wrapping her arms around Hunter's neck, she leaned close.

"I can think of somewhere better to be than on your lap."

"Oh?" Hunter's eyes narrowed, his slow smile filled with sexual promise. "How about over my knee?"

Emma smiled, running her fingertips down her chest. "Do it and I'll kick you in the balls the first chance I get."

From behind her, Remington slapped her ass, making it sting and setting off a barrage of erotic explosions throughout her slit. "I'll take my chances. Feisty little thing, aren't you?"

Emma shrugged, digging her fingertips into hard muscle. "She took my stool, but that's because she's trying to take my man. I'm possessive. You're mine. Worked too hard to let you get away."

Setting a fresh fruit drink on the bar for her, Michael laughed, smiling in approval. Slapping Hunter on the shoulder, he winked at her.

"That'll put you in your place, won't it, Hunter?"

His eyes narrowed. "Putting her over my lap is sounding more appealing by the minute."

Emma leaned forward, pressing her lips to Hunter's jaw.

"You don't scare me." Sitting back, she wiggled on his lap, her breath catching when the bulge at her slit hardened even more.

"I can handle you."

Remington bent to nuzzle her neck. "Something tells me that you're going to handle us just fine."

Leaning back against him, Emma wrapped an arm around his neck, staring into Hunter's eyes.

"I can, and the sooner you trust me to accept every part of you, the sooner you'll see that."

When both men stilled, Emma smiled and met their gazes. "You didn't think I believed you'd turned around completely, did you? Even Hunter admitted that he still worried about hurting me, but you love me so you don't want me to get away."

Sliding from Hunter's lap, she reached for her fruit drink to ease her dry throat, gesturing toward the couples on the dance floor.

"I want what they have. I want the closeness. I want a family. I want all of both of you."

Hunter sighed. "I know, baby. We're getting there."

Taking her hand in his, he lifted it to his lips. "We're just trying to protect you."

"I'm familiar with some of Desire's eccentricities." Smiling, she raised a brow. "Don't *all* the men in Desire have a responsibility to watch out for *all* the women?"

Caleb Ward dropped onto the stool next to her, meeting Remington's glare with a grin.

"They sure do." Accepting a beer from John, he turned to wink at her. "Especially once they've been claimed by our friends."

"You *do* realize how chauvinistic that is?"

"Yep." Caleb sipped his beer and reached for the pretzels. "But that's the way it is, and we're not about to change things. Women need to be protected, and the men here need to do the protecting. Women are safer in our town than they are anywhere else."

Smiling at the pride in his voice, Emma nodded. "And do you consider Hunter and Remington your friends?"

Caleb pretended to consider that, his eyes full of mischief.

"At times. They can be a pain in the ass, especially when I have to help break up a bar fight."

"There won't be any more of them." Emma sent a warning look toward Hunter and Remington, a look met with smiles of amusement.

Remington let his gaze rake over her, leaving a trail of erotic awareness in its wake.

"We'll just have to find something else to expend our energy on."

"You do that." Turning back to Caleb, she smiled. "So do I fall under that umbrella of protection?"

Caleb inclined his head, his smile falling. "Absolutely."

"Thank you." Leaning back against Hunter, she smiled when his arm came around her waist.

"So, Caleb, do you think Hunter and Remington are dangerous?"

"Absolutely, but not to you." With a faint smile, he eyed both men. "But if someone hurt or threatened you, I'd stand back because all hell's gonna break loose."

Chapter Thirty

Sitting at the table, Emma sorted through recipes, separating them into piles of rejections, possibilities, and those that would definitely go into her new cookbook.

"You got those recipes from Gracie in there?"

With a smile, Emma turned to look at Hunter, who stood leaning back against the counter, watching her as he sipped his coffee.

"I sure do." Wrinkling her nose at him, she turned back to her cards. "You didn't think I'd get those recipes, did you?"

"I'm starting to think you can do pretty much anything you set your mind to."

Turning to grin at him again, she paused to watch Remington walk back into the room.

Shoving his phone back into his pocket, Remington went to the coffee pot to pour himself another cup. "That was Ryder. The truck is done. You want another cup of coffee, babe?"

"No. Thank you. I have to leave in a few minutes."

Hunter finished his coffee and rinsed his cup.

"Emma's going shopping for a dress with Jesse and Hope. If the truck's ready, we'll walk down and pick it up before we go meet with Cole Madison about the plans for the guest house."

Turning back to Emma, he raised a brow. "We'll meet back here around dinnertime and run out to the new steakhouse. Okay with you?"

"Fine." Putting her cards away, Emma rose, moving to stand between Hunter's splayed thighs as he lowered himself to one of the stools. "I hope I find something."

Bending to touch his lips to hers, Hunter smiled. "You will. If you need more time, give one of us a call and eat in Tulsa with Jesse and Hope. We'll go to the steak house another time."

Remington finished his coffee, set his cup aside, and closed in behind her. "Have a nice day, baby. Do you need any money?"

"No." Emma bristled. "Don't start that."

Scraping his teeth down her neck, Remington slapped her ass.

"Our job is to take care of you. Don't buck us, or you'll get turned over one of our laps so fast your head'll swim."

Giggling, Emma leaned back against him, the heat from his sharp slap thrilling her. "Promises. Promises."

Hunter's brow went up. "You're playing a dangerous game."

Leaning forward, she laid a hand on Hunter's fly, smiling when his cock jumped beneath her palm. "Life—like food—needs a little spice. Don't you agree?"

"Hmm." Hunter's eyes narrowed. "Looks like we need to go into this subject a little deeper."

Remington rubbed her ass. "A lot deeper." Wrapping an arm around her waist, he turned her to kiss her hard. "We'll see you later. Don't go crazy looking for a dress. I don't give a damn if you show up in jeans and T-shirt."

Hunter rose, sliding a hand over her hair. "Or that red dress. See you later, baby."

* * * *

Charlene listened from right outside the back door, gritting her teeth at how natural and relaxed the three of them seemed together.

Hunter and Remington would get bored with that soon.

They lived for sex. Raw. Gritty. Intense.

They might pretend they wanted a family, but Charlene knew better.

She knew what they wanted.

She knew what they needed.

She'd been giving them pleasure for years, and she certainly wasn't about to let an outsider come to town and take what belonged to her.

She no longer heard any voices, cursing when the air conditioner kicked on and made it even harder to hear.

She knew she didn't have much time and that this might be her only chance to make everything right again.

Moving quietly, she peered around the corner of the house, just in time to see Hunter and Remington walk down the driveway and turn in the direction of the body shop.

It was now or never.

Racing around to the front of the house, she stood just outside the garage doors, staying low to make sure no one on the street had seen her.

She'd parked her car on Main Street and had even shopped in several stores so that if anything came back to her, she could convince them that she'd been in town shopping all morning.

She'd even bought lunch to go from the diner so that she could say that she went to sit and eat it in the park.

She'd thought of everything.

Slipping the retractable baton from her back pocket, she waited breathlessly for the garage door to open.

When it did, she moved fast, rushing in through it before it had even opened halfway.

The look of shock on Emma's face had barely turned to anger when Charlene hit her in the head with the club.

Momentarily stunned that she'd actually done it, Charlene kicked Emma to make sure she was really unconscious, spinning when the garage door went silent again.

Stepping cautiously over Emma's prone form, she tucked the baton back into her pocket and reached in the car, pushing the remote to close the garage again.

Without looking at Emma, she took the keys Emma had dropped when she fell and started the car, pulling her scarf over her nose while she rummaged through Emma's large purse for her cell phone.

Because she'd been eavesdropping, she knew what she had to do to get more time.

Mentally patting herself on the back for her attention to detail, she looked up both Jesse's and Hope's numbers—numbers neither woman had ever given to her—and sent them each a text message.

Holding the scarf over her face, she looked around to make sure she'd thought of everything.

The fumes would be getting too strong to stay any longer, and she had to get out of here and back to town to be seen.

Pleased with herself, she ran up the steps and opened the door to the house, rushing through to the kitchen where she'd spent her last hours with Hunter and Remington.

Promising herself she'd be back again with them soon, she made her way out the back door, her heart pounding furiously.

Not until she made her way back to Main Street again did she breathe easy.

She'd done it.

It would look like she'd slipped on the floor and hit her head on the concrete.

Emma would be dead soon, and things would go back to the way they should be.

Hunter and Remington would be hers again.

Right where they belonged.

Chapter Thirty-One

Hunter looked at his phone, frowning when he saw that the call was from Hope.

"Hunter. What's up?"

"That's what I'd like to know. Why the hell did you ask to take Emma shopping when you know damned well we're having a bridal shower for her?"

Hunter's stomach clenched, ripples of fear racing through him.

Something was very wrong.

"Hope, Rem and I left the house about a half hour ago, and Emma was getting ready to leave to meet you at the club."

"Hunter, I don't like this. I just got a text from her and so did Jesse. 'Sorry, Hunter and Remy want me to go with them. Talk to you later.'"

"Remy?" The knots in Hunter's stomach got tighter.

Only one person in the world called Remington *Remy*.

Hope sucked in a breath. "I'm scared, Hunter. I've tried to call her several times, but she doesn't answer. Not her cell and not the house."

Hunter held a hand up at Remington's questioning look. "Call Ace. Charlene's behind this. We're going to the house now."

Disconnecting, he raced for the truck, Remington right beside him. "Something's wrong. Emma didn't show up, and Jesse and Hope got a text saying she was going out with us. Hunter and *Remy*."

The horror in Remington's eyes mirrored his own.

"She wouldn't." Remington jumped into the passenger seat beside him, barely managing to close the truck door before Hunter tore out of the parking lot of the body shop. "You don't really think Charlene would do something to hurt Emma?"

Hunter pressed his foot to the floor, the few blocks to their house seeming to take forever.

"When it comes to Emma, I don't trust anyone."

Wiping the sweat from his eyes, Hunter turned into the driveway and slammed on the brakes.

* * * *

Remington was already out of the truck and racing for the front door when Hunter threw the truck in park.

Finding the door locked, Remington frowned and pulled out his key, opening the door and rushing in. "Emma?"

With Hunter at his heels, he ran into the kitchen, stopping abruptly to find it empty.

"Her purse is gone." Hunter ran to the back door and looked outside. "She's not out here. Let's see if her car is gone."

Remington froze. "Do you hear that? It sounds like her car's running in the garage."

He raced down the hallway to the garage, frantic to find her. "Jesus! The garage door was closed."

Remington yanked the door open and leapt over the stairs, his heart stopping at the sight of Emma lying motionless on the garage floor.

"Dear God." He raced to her side, praying that she was still alive.

He had to get her out of here.

He picked her up as gently as he could while Hunter, cursing steadily in a voice that shook, hit the remote to open the garage door and turned off her engine.

Remington ran outside with her and laid her in the shade, his heart pounding out of his chest as he checked her pulse.

Hunter was already on the phone, calling for an ambulance and for whoever was on duty.

Kneeling next to her, Remington breathed a sigh of relief, tears burning his eyes.

"She's alive."

Hunter disconnected and knelt on the other side of her. "You've got blood on your shirt."

Turning her as gently as they could, they found blood on the back of her head.

Cradling her against him, Remington began to rock her. "How long was she breathing in carbon monoxide? Oh God, Hunter. Emma, wake up, baby. Wake up. Please."

Hunter's eyes were terrible to see, the terror in them leaving Remington even more shaken.

Lifting his head at the sound of tires squealing, Remington continued to rock Emma as Linc pulled into the driveway and came to a screeching halt.

Jumping out of his car, the deputy rushed forward, carrying a small oxygen tank, his expression grim.

"Let's get this on her. The paramedics will be here soon."

Hunter's jaw clenched. "We've got to get our own firemen and paramedics."

While Remington held Emma, Hunter fitted the mask over Emma's face while Linc adjusted the oxygen flow.

Sitting back on his heels, Linc nodded. "Ace is working on it. It costs money."

Remington stared down at Emma's pale features. "We're in. Why the hell isn't she waking up?"

He'd never been so scared.

Linc eyed each of them. "What the hell happened?"

Remington glanced at Hunter. "That's what we'd like to know."

Holding the mask over her face, he continued to rock her, praying for her to open her eyes.

He'd never been so scared in his life.

Hunter held her hand, playing with her fingers. "Baby, please wake up. Christ, I didn't know how much I love her until now."

"Neither did I." Remington held his breath when her eyelids fluttered. "Em! Open those eyes, Em. That's a girl. Open them."

Her low moan had to be the sweetest sound he'd ever heard.

"Yes! That's it. That's my baby. I love you, damn it! You're not getting away from me."

Hunter lifted her hand to his lips. "You're okay now. We've got you. Don't move." Allowing her to pull her hand from his, Hunter caught it again when she started to reach for the back of her head.

"No, baby. Don't touch it. I know it hurts. An ambulance is coming. You're gonna be fine. We won't let anything happen to you."

She closed her eyes again, tears escaping to trickle into her hair. Her lips moved, but no sound emerged.

"Don't try to talk." Remington glanced at Hunter. "Nothing matters now except getting you to the hospital."

Linc, who'd stepped away without Remington even realizing it, came back to kneel next to Hunter, his expression grim.

"Ace just arrested Charlene. She had a retractable baton in her purse." He stared down at Emma. "It had blood on it. They're sending it to the lab. It's your blood, isn't it, Emma? Charlene did this to you, didn't she?"

Emma nodded once and grimaced.

Remington cursed. "Don't move. Just stay still." Pulling her closer, he buried his face against her neck.

"The ambulance is here. We'll be with you all the way." He lifted his head, giving her a smile of reassurance.

"I know."

Hunter's eyes glimmered with tears. "Always. I love you more than my own life, Emma. I let you down." Lifting her hand to his lips again, he clenched his jaw. "We didn't do such a good job of protecting you. That's something that'll never happen again. I promise. If I have to wrap you in cotton and stuff you in my pocket, I will."

* * * *

"Be careful with her!"

Despite the pain in her head, Emma couldn't help but smile at Remington's sharp demand.

"Sir, I—"

"I'm riding in with her. Rem, follow us in the truck."

"Sir, you can't—"

Hunter actually growled. "You try to separate us, and you'll regret it." Still holding her hand, he got into the ambulance beside her, glaring at the paramedic.

Linc stood at the door, shaking his head and smiling faintly. "Let him ride in with her. If you try to kick him out, you're in for a heap of trouble. She's been through enough, and it'll calm both of them."

On the way to the hospital, Hunter shifted restlessly like a caged animal. "When the hell are you gonna give her something for the pain. Look at her eyes. Can't you see she's hurting?"

"Sir, I can't give her anything for the pain. She has a head injury. The doctors need to see her first. She probably has a concussion."

"A concussion. Son of a bitch!" He raised his voice to yell at the driver. "Can't you drive any faster? What the hell is the siren for?"

Emma grimaced, tightening her hold on his hand while sliding the oxygen mask lower.

"Hunter. It's okay."

"Shh." Leaning over her, he glared at the paramedic and beat the other man to the mask. "Keep this on. I know everything's okay."

Smiling, he lifted her hand and touched his lips to her palm. "You're the one who made me fall in love with you. The thought of losing you scares the hell out of me. Seeing you lying on the floor of the garage, and not knowing if you were alive or not—"

His voice broke, and to her amazement, tears glimmered in his eyes.

"I can't lose you, baby. You're my life." He straightened, a muscle working in his jaw. "It's our fault that this happened. We didn't see just how jealous and evil she is. She's gonna pay. I promise."

"Please, Hunter. Let the police handle it."

Shaking his head, Hunter clenched his jaw again.

"Don't even think about telling me how to protect you. That's my job, and I didn't do it very well. That won't happen again."

Knowing he was thinking about how he hadn't been there for his mother, Emma squeezed his hand again.

"This wasn't your fault."

"It was. Just relax. We're almost there."

* * * *

Two days later, Emma leaned against Remington on the ride home from the hospital. "Are you going to tell me what happened this morning, or am I going to have to ask Hope?"

Taking her hand in his, Hunter lifted it to his lips. "We went to see Charlene before she was transferred to the jail in Oklahoma City."

"And?"

Remington shared a look with Hunter. "I've never in my life wanted to hurt a woman. I mean *really* hurt a woman."

He turned to look out the windshield again. "She came close. I could have reached her though the bars." His voice became thoughtful. "It would have been so easy to grab her by the throat."

Something in their expressions confused her. "Please tell me you didn't do anything."

Despite the concern darkening his eyes, Hunter smiled, gently squeezing her hand.

"Of course we didn't do anything. Turns out we can beat the shit out of a man but can't hurt a woman."

Understanding what he was telling her, Emma swallowed a sob.

Sitting up, Emma leaned into him, resting her chin on his upper arm, the relief that the two of them finally realized that they wouldn't hurt her bringing tears to her eyes. "Imagine that."

As they drove down Main Street, Hunter stopped for a red light and threw the truck in park. Turning, he took her in his arms, carefully avoiding the back of her head where she'd been hit. "Yeah. Imagine that."

With his face just inches from hers, he stared down at him, the love shining in his eyes stealing her breath.

"You're really all ours now. I love you, woman, more than I thought I could ever love anyone."

Remington ran a hand down her back. "After the scare we just had, though, we're gonna be more diligent with you."

Reaching back, Emma smiled when Remington immediately took her hand in his. "As long as I know you love me, and that you're not going to hold back on me anymore, I can put up with your protectiveness."

Brushing his lips over hers, Hunter smiled. "Love doesn't quite describe what I feel for you."

The sound of a blaring horn and laughter had Emma sitting up to look over Hunter's shoulder, her face burning when she saw Ace standing next to the window, trying—but failing—to hide a smile.

"Oh God."

She pressed her face against Hunter's shoulder, embarrassed despite both men's chuckles.

Remington pulled her back against him. "Honey, Ace knows it's you."

Crossing his arms over his massive chest, Ace regarded Hunter steadily. "So we're going from bar fights to blocking traffic?"

Emma's breath caught at Hunter's wide smile, and she found herself falling even more deeply in love with him. "We're sorry, Ace."

Hunter turned to her, running a hand over her thigh. "Speak for yourself." He turned back to Ace. "My fiancée needed a kiss. I wasn't about to wait until we got home."

Ace ran his tongue over his teeth. "Understood. Try not to make a habit of it."

"No promises."

With a wave, Hunter started down the street again, he and Remington waving to Hoyt and Nat, who stood on the sidewalk laughing.

Hope stood several yards away, pumping a fist in the air as they passed.

With a groan, Emma shook her head. "This'll be the talk of the town for days."

Remington eased her onto his lap. "Probably longer. Everyone in town has been telling us that there was a woman out there for us."

"And you didn't believe them." Emma pressed a hand to his chest. "I don't even want to think about what would have happened if I hadn't chosen another town to visit."

"Neither do I." Hunter took her hand in his. "It didn't work out that way so I don't want to think about it. Once we get home, I want you to go to bed and rest. Rem can stay with you while I go get dinner."

"Hunter, I—"

Remington dropped a hard kiss on her lips. "No arguing."

Emma sighed and looked up at Remington through her lashes. "I guess I could have dinner in bed, especially if it's followed by a nice foot rub."

Remington threw his head back and laughed. "I'm sure you think you're manipulating me, but that's okay. You have no idea how much I can do to you with a foot rub."

* * * *

Hours later, Emma fought to catch her breath, her entire body trembling from the aftereffects of a mind-numbing orgasm.

Stretched out on her bed, wearing the nightgown she'd bought to seduce them, she looked down to see both Hunter and Remington reclining next to her thighs.

Both men were still fully dressed, refusing to make love to her until after she's recovered.

Running their fingertips over her, they alternately played with the ribbons they'd untied, their small smiles filled with satisfaction.

Remington lifted her left foot, running his fingers over a particularly sensitive spot. "So how was your foot rub?"

Gulping, Emma tried to glare at them but failed miserably. "You were rubbing more than my feet."

Remington grinned. "We started at your feet. If you didn't want attention anywhere else, you wouldn't have worn that lingerie."

Rolling from the bed, Hunter stared down at her. "You're ours. It's up to us to take care of you—and your needs. We're not taking you again until our wedding night."

"I can't believe you finished organizing everything from the hospital."

Pressing a kiss against her belly, Remington rose and went to her dresser. "We weren't about to leave you. Let's get you into one of your comfortable nightgowns. You're starting to get a headache again."

Shocked, Emma frowned. "How did you know that?"

Shaking his head, Remington came back to the bed and began to strip her out of her sexy nightgown, exchanging it for a soft, cotton one. "Because you're ours. One day you'll understand what that means to us."

Emma watched them put away the stuff they'd brought from the hospital, wondering if she'd ever know the depths of the amazing men she loved.

Smiling at the knowledge that she had a lifetime to learn everything about them, she settled back and closed her eyes, secure in the knowledge that they would be joining her soon.

When she woke again, the room was dark. Hunter's shoulder pillowed her head, and Remington spooned her from behind.

Remington stirred. "You okay?"

"I'm wonderful."

Hunter's lips touched her hair. "Headache gone?"

"Yep." Smiling, she pressed her face against his chest. "You know, it's going to take a while to get used to having husbands who are so attentive."

Remington nuzzled her neck. "Don't worry. You've got all the time in the world to get used to it."

Epilogue

Emma ran her fingers over the rings on her left hand, leaning back against Hunter.

"It looks like a dream."

Candles and glittering lights from above made the ballroom of the hotel appear as if thousands of fireflies had taken flight.

Flowers on every surface scented the air, adding to the magical atmosphere.

Hunter's arms tightened around her as he bent to nuzzle her neck. "So do you."

Tears blurred her vision. "I can't believe we're really married."

"Believe it." Turning her in his arms, Hunter held her close, his fingers closing on her chin to life her face to his. "You're ours now, legally and every other way."

Emma smiled at Remington's approach. "We're a family."

"We are." Hunter's eyes narrowed. "I'm sorry about your mother."

Nodding, Emma forced a smile.

She'd been in a strange mood ever since they'd had Ace check on her mother, only to learn that her mother had died several years ago from a drug overdose.

Bending, Hunter brushed his lips over hers. "You have a family now."

Remington moved in behind her. "Probably more family than you realize."

Looking around, Emma saw that several of her new friends waved, smiled, and lifted their glasses.

"Everyone's been so nice. I can't believe they even threw a bridal shower for me."

"They like you." Remington turned her to face him. "Dance with me."

Remington danced like a dream, holding her close with a hand at her back. "Did I tell you how beautiful you look?"

Smiling, Emma lifted her face for his kiss. "Yes, but I never get tired of hearing it." She'd bought the dress only yesterday, knowing that the pink lace was perfect the moment she saw it.

Sliding a hand over his chest, she sucked in a breath. "You and Hunter take my breath away in your tuxedos.

"Wait until we get you naked tonight." Grinning, Remington glanced down at her breasts. "Please tell me you're wearing pink lace under that."

The hunger in his eyes sparked her own. "Some. I'm afraid it's not very much."

"Dear God." Remington closed his eyes, his cock pressing against her belly. "How long before we can leave?"

Hunter came up beside them. "We're not leaving early. Let Emma enjoy her day." His gaze raked over her. "Yeah, I heard about the pink lace under that dress, but I can control myself for a few hours."

Smiling up at him, Emma leaned into Remington, unable to resist the urge to tease them. "Did I mention that I have a pink lace garter belt and stockings under this, too?"

Hunter's eyes narrowed. "You enjoy living dangerously, don't you?"

Giggling, Emma moved in Remington's arms. "Of course. I have husbands who seem to be perfectly capable of handling it."

"We can certainly handle you." Taking her from Remington, Hunter turned with her in his arms, positioning her so that Remington was now at her back.

"I know." Running her hand over Hunter's chest, she raised her voice slightly to make sure Remington heard her. "I can't believe you're willing to travel with me to find new recipes."

Hunter frowned. "You didn't actually think we'd let you go without us, did you? We can go wherever you want, and when you get what you need, we'll come back home. You can write your books here."

"I told you that it would work." Grinning, Emma leaned back to eye both of them. "Now when are you going to tell me what's going on in the basement?"

Chucking, Remington hugged her. "We'll tell you now. It's a wedding present to all of us." Leaning close, he whispered in her ear. "A playroom."

She missed a step, but Remington caught her. "What do you mean? Like for children?"

"No." Taking her hand, Hunter led her from the dance floor and out to the terrace, Remington following close behind. "It's very much for adults. It'll remain locked until one or both of us takes you down there."

Alone on the terrace, they made their way to the edge, where only torches provided light.

Lowering himself to one of the concrete benches, Hunter settled her on his lap. Taking her left hand in his, he ran his thumb over the two gold bands and the engagement ring nestled between them.

"It's a room designed for pleasure. It's something Rem and I have never been able to have." Lifting her hand to his lips, he kissed the rings he and Remington had placed there only hours earlier.

She leaned into him, smiling when Remington sat beside Hunter and lifted her feet onto his lap. "And now you can?"

Remington smiled and slid his hand up her leg. "And now we can. You've shown us that we can play when we want to without fear. It's very…liberating."

"Once we finish the playroom, we can do all the things to you that our need for dominance demands. I can't wait to strap you to the table and play with those nipples until you beg for release. To clip them. Tug them."

Remington's eyes narrowed. "Strap her on her belly and explore that delightful ass. We can fill her with plugs. Vibrators. Fuck her long and deep."

Hunter's jaw clenched. "I have a lot of plans for that ass, and that sweet pussy. Fuck her until she's ready to come and withdraw before she gets there. Watch her squirm and listen to her beg for release. I'm very much looking forward to attaching one of those portable vibrators to her clit and attaching her wrists to a hook on the ceiling."

Emma shivered, the mental image of having such things done to her making her pussy clench.

"God. I'm close to coming just hearing about it."

Running his hand over her knee, Remington leaned forward, his eyes hooded. "There's a hunger in us that neither of us ever fully understood until we met you, a need for the kind of intimacy that we've never been able to have before. A physical intimacy with a woman who we can hold in our arms at night and an emotional intimacy with a woman we're dominating. Making love with you is more than just sex. You're ours. To love. To protect. To pleasure. Ours." He smiled, shaking his head. "It's a hell of a heady feeling and one I didn't quite plan on."

The music and voices drifted out to them, but since they were hidden from view, Hunter cupped her breast. "We've got a lifetime of pleasure ahead of us."

Arching into Hunter's caress, Emma cupped his jaw, gripping Remington's hand. "And love."

Hunter's eyes glittered with emotion. "And definitely love."

Remington pressed a hand to her abdomen. "And definitely a family."

Thunder rumbled in the distance, and a streak of lightning illuminated the night sky.

Hunter rose with her in his arms. "A thunderstorm. It must be an omen, baby. We met because of a thunderstorm. Now it appears we'll have a thunderstorm on our wedding night."

Emma laughed and wrapped her arms around his neck. "We can make a storm of our own—our own recipe."

Remington took her hand in his and moved closer, lowering his voice to an erotic whisper. "Two parts male, one part delicious female. Strip. Caress. Whip as necessary."

Pressing against her side, he let his gaze rake over her. "Apply heat."

"Stroke to create juices." Hunter lowered her to her feet, an arm around her waist steadying her. "Sounds delicious. Maybe we should write our own cookbook."

Pressing her thighs together did nothing to alleviate the ache that had settled there. Leaning into Remington, she fisted her hands on his chest.

Smiling at the need in his eyes and a possessiveness that always sent a thrill through her, Emma brushed her breasts against his chest. "I can hardly wait to try your recipes. Let's go home."

Hunter ran a hand over her hair, the hunger in his eyes weakening her knees.

"No. Enjoy the reception. After all you've been through, you deserve it." Dropping a kiss on her lips, he smiled. "We've got a lifetime ahead of us. I want to savor every minute of it."

He slid his hands up her sides, letting them rest just under her breasts. "Just like I plan to savor you."

Remington grinned, his eyes suspiciously moist. "Amen. For once, we've got a lot to look forward to."

Emma blinked back tears, smiling as several of their friends came forward. "Yeah. We do, don't we?"

She'd finally found a place to call home and the kind of love she'd never thought possible.

She'd come to Desire for recipes for her book, and instead, had found the recipe for love.

The greatest recipe of all.

THE END

WWW.LEAHBROOKE.NET

ABOUT THE AUTHOR

Leah Brooke spends most of her time with her family, spoiling her furbabies, and always writing her next story.

For all titles by Leah Brooke, please visit
www.bookstrand.com/leah-brooke

Siren Publishing, Inc.
www.SirenPublishing.com

Lightning Source UK Ltd.
Milton Keynes UK
UKOW01f0759160617
303414UK00012B/302/P

9 781682 956526